DAUGHTER OF
ABRAHAM

DAUGHTER OF ABRAHAM

A Genomic Apocalypse/

Book II

KD McMahon

This is a work of fiction. Names, characters, places and incidents either are the product of the author's imagination or are used fictitiously, and any resemblance to any actual persons, living or dead, events, or locales is entirely coincidental.

This book was printed in the United States of America.

To order additional copies of this book, contact:
Xlibris Corporation
1-888-795-4274
www.Xlibris.com
Orders@Xlibris.com
15338

CONTENTS

Part III: Half a Time

Whoever falls on the stone will be broken; but on whomever it falls,
it will grind him to powder.

~Matthew 21:44

DEDICATION

To my parents, Leo and Caroline.
My father was a storyteller.
My mother listened patiently.
My wife and I are keeping the tradition alive.

ACKNOWLEDGMENT

I am in the debt of so many people who have supported me through their editorial assistance and encouragement. Many thanks to Beth and Greg Gath. They competed against each other to see who could find the most grammatical and spelling mistakes. They had so much fun I decided to leave a few mistakes for they to discover. Gwenda Lynn gave me much helpful advice regarding military equipment and special operations. Archpriest Michael Moran, Pastor of the Byzantine Catholic Cathedral of Saint Mary's, made sure that my theology did not stray too far from the path of Christian orthodoxy.

No matter how many times I read my manuscript, mistakes manage to slip through. It takes more careful eyes than mine to spot to spot mistakes. See what I mean! I am indebted to my sister, Alicia, and brother, Leo, for proof reading my galleys. I am even more grateful for their ceaseless encouragement, especially during those times when I questioned why I was even undertaking such a project.

I am especially grateful to Anne Petach. My humble story hardly warranted her valuable time. Anne is incredibly well read, and I have benefitted immeasurably from her literary insights. It is because of her mentoring, that I dare to say that I am now not only a storyteller, but an author.

AUTHOR'S FOREWORD

It hardly seems the time to write a story about cooperation between Jews, Christians, and Muslims. Yet, perhaps it is timely to remind those of us who claim Abraham as our father, that we all worship the same God. Our understanding of God and what it means to be His sons and daughters is different, and this has all too frequently led to shameful, if not blasphemous behavior. While it may not be possible to reconcile our understanding of Him who is beyond understanding, at the least we must never forget that we also share the same nemesis. And it may be that before we can recognize each other as truly brethren, we may first have to acknowledge that the enemy of my enemy can be a friend and ally.

Although it is generally agreed that the West has entered a post-religious era, a vague notion of a divine benevolence is still held by a majority. However, the idea that there exists a malevolent personality bent on thwarting Providence and His plan for humanity is no longer generally accepted. Yet, believers acknowledge the powerful influence that Satan has in human affairs. This idea of a cosmic struggle between Good and Evil and human participation in it must be embraced (at least for the duration of this storytelling), otherwise, little of what lies ahead of the reader will seem reasonable.

FROM THE INTRODUCTION TO:

The Journal of Maria Theresa O'Conner

edited by: Madison Ryan

When Maria asked me to edit her journal, I could hardly believe it. After all, I had stolen her journal earlier and had tried to use it to discredit her. God does indeed work in mysterious ways! Maria was, in fact, reluctant to keep a journal. She didn't believe that her life was extraordinary—"not worth writing about," she had told Cardinal McIntyre. I recently asked the Cardinal why he had asked her to keep a journal those last few months of her life. "Did you have a premonition of what would happen?" I asked him. "No, I leave such things to Brother Nikitas," he replied with a twinkle in his eyes.

It was Brother Nikitas who revealed to Maria her destiny—God had called her to be a *yurodivyi*. It is not easy to explain what this means, particularly to a Westerner. A *yurodivyi* is a phenomenon of the Christian East that eludes an easy definition. Is a *yurodivyi* a saint? Yes, they exhibit the "heroic virtues" of a saint yet this title does not capture the essence and mission of the *yurodivyi*. Recognizing that the Western mind demands a definitive explanation, I asked Orthodox Bishop,

George Kavasilas for help. He smiled. I knew immediately what his smile meant, "You experienced a *yurodivyi*. That is enough."

"I know, but . . . ." I protested.

He nodded, stood, and went over to the bookcase. His fingers walked across the spines of innumerable books as if they were probing the wisdom of ages, seeking an answer not just to my question, but *the* question. His fingers stopped, then continued, but then went back. He pulled out a little, red book, more like a pamphlet. He thumbed through it, stopped, read a minute, and then nodded.

"*Creative Suffering*, by Iulia de Beausobre," Bishop Kavasilas said. "A little jewel," he added and then handed the book to me while directing my attention to a particular passage:

> *The aim of the yurodivyi is to participate in evil through suffering. He makes of this his life's work because, to the Russian, good and evil are, here on earth, inextricably bound up together. This is, to us, the great mystery of life on earth. Where evil is at its most intense, there too must be the greatest good. To us this is not even a hypothesis. It is axiomatic . . . .*
>
> *Evil must not be shunned, but first participated in and understood through participation, and then through understanding transfigured . . . .*

PROLOGUE

"You cannot go in there," said the voice from behind him. Colin turned around but kept his hand on the doorknob. A middle-aged woman in a nurse's uniform was leaning against a counter; she peered over several computer terminals, which she had been monitoring when Colin approached the door to the Harvesting Center repository.

"You cannot go in there," she repeated. "You need authorization."

Colin released the doorknob and walked over to the nurses' station. He looked at the woman's identity badge while removing his wallet from his trouser pocket.

"Nurse Beckford," he said, reading the woman's name, "I believe you will find this to be sufficient authorization." He showed her the identification card in his wallet.

"Oh excuse me, Secretary O'Conner," the nurse said, turning pale. "I'm sorry I didn't recognize you. Certainly you may go in. No one informed me that the Secretary of the Office of Justice and Tolerance would be visiting us today. Had I known . . ."

"That's okay," replied Colin, putting his wallet back into his back pocket.

The woman removed a medallion she was wearing underneath her nurse's uniform. She held it out for him to see. Her hand was trembling. He recognized the Star of David and the tree emblem.

"I want . . . you to know . . . how happy . . . I am . . . to be . . . ." she stammered.

"Yes?" asked Colin.

"A Jew . . . I mean, a Tree of Life Jew," she added hastily.

"Oh," replied Colin. He placed his hand on her trembling hand and smiled reassuringly. "I'm sure you are. Don't worry Miss Beckford, we have not heard anything to the contrary. Now, if you don't mind . . . ."

"Yes, go right ahead," the nurse said eagerly. "And if there is anything I can do?"

"Yes. There is something you can do. You won't mention to anyone that I was here today, will you?"

"No, no. Certainly not."

Colin nodded and smiled, then walked back to the door. He turned the doorknob and pushed the door open. There was a difference in air pressure between the two rooms. He could feel the warm, moist air as it hissed out from the room he was about to enter. It reeked of fresh flesh and blood as one might smell in a butcher shop. He stepped into a small foyer that served as a sterile airlock between the outside and the Repository. He waited for the green light to signal that, he could enter the next room. When it did, he hesitated, then taking a deep breath he pushed open the door that led to the Repository. As he entered the room he could hardly believe his eyes. It was a vast warehouse with row after row of hospital beds. Each bed was covered with a clear plastic tent. Numerous tubes entered and exited each tent carrying fluids to and from the hapless patients inside. Colin began to walk down one of the many aisles that were formed by the rows of beds. The tents were covered with a layer of condensation making it difficult to see inside. He wasn't sure he wanted to see inside. But, what he could see, the mutilated forms of men, women, and even children made him nauseous. Then suddenly he felt a hand on his shoulder.

"Can I help you?"

Startled, Colin jumped and turned.

"Oh, Mr. Secretary," said the medical technician surprised to see

O'Conner. "What a privilege it is to meet you," he continued extending his hand.

Colin looked down at the extended hand that was covered by a surgical glove stained with blood. Embarrassed, the technician withdrew his hand.

Colin removed a picture from his shirt pocket and handed it to the technician. "I'm looking for this man."

The technician placed the picture on the handheld computer he was carrying. He scanned a bar code off the picture with a pen.

"Ah yes; he's here," replied the technician. "This way."

The technician led Colin through the labyrinth of hospital beds while peering at his computer screen. He maneuvered between the beds and their occupants noting them only through his peripheral vision. It was evident from the technician's cavalier attitude that he viewed these hapless individuals with no more regard than if they were wrecked cars heaped in a junk yard; valuable only for their parts.

"He's a recent arrival," the technician said, while tapping the screen to reveal more information about the patient. "There are still plenty of harvestable organs and tissues. Were you looking for something in particular?"

"No," replied Colin.

The technician looked at Colin curiously. He had assumed that the Secretary needed harvestable organs. Why else would he be here? The technician led him to a bed.

"Here we are," said the technician. "Donor 4027."

"Thank you," said Colin.

The technician waited.

"I'd like to be alone," said Colin.

The technician nodded and walked away. He turned around once and then went about the business of cataloguing the current inventory.

The tent had a heavy layer of condensation covering the inside. Colin drew closer to it and stooped to get a better view of the individual inside. The naked body of a black man lay upon the bed. His thoracic and abdominal cavities were open and some of his organs, while still connected, lay partially outside his body. Pieces of flesh had been removed from the arms and legs. An empty eye-socket stared vacuously up at the ceiling. The body looked more like a cadaver in the midst of dissection than a living human being. Indeed, the man could be mistaken for dead if it were not for his heart, which was exposed and visibly beating. This was far worse than Colin had expected.

"Jesus!" he exclaimed. He steadied himself against the bed feeling that he might faint.

The patient in the bed stirred. Colin was shocked that he wasn't heavily sedated. As the man turned to face him, Colin could see in the man's remaining eye that he was fully cognizant. His initial response was to turn away from the horrible sight and run. Instead, he drew a deep breath, reached under the tent, grasped the man's hand and held it. The man turned Colin's hand over and looked at his palm. It oozed plasma and blood from a dark-red circular mark. It almost appeared as if Colin's hand had just been branded by white-hot metal. The man smiled at Colin as a tear welled-up and then dripped down his face.

Now, Colin understood what the Reverend had meant. He could say nothing. He could do nothing, except yield to love. He felt as if a weight of guilt was beginning to lift off him. But, he knew that this was only the beginning: the beginning of a redemption which would require a yielding to love more painful than the blood plague; more painful than the brand on his palm. He would suffer the selfless love of others as they ravaged and redeemed his soul.

PART I

Time

God is love.

~ First John 4:16

The Holy Grail of cosmological science is the Theory of Everything. It is the aspiration of scientists to discover that single axiom upon which the Universe came into existence and continues to be. All physical laws and phenomena, ranging from the motion of planets to the attraction of subatomic particles would, thus be deducible from this most fundamental of all axioms. No doubt, it would come as a great disappointment for these scientists to learn that this axiom has already been revealed. It is expressed with potent simplicity by John the Evangelist in the fourth chapter of his first epistle—*God is love.*

God is love is the ontological singularity from which all things have their being and to which all things are drawn. During the eternity before Creation, the Father begot the Son in love and the love shared is the Holy Spirit. Then *in the beginning, Love* created, in love, the cosmos. Man, made in the image of God, is destined to be conformed to the likeness of *Love.* To this end, the Father, who so loved the world, sent His only begotten Son. The Son in loving obedience to the Father emptied Himself and took on the likeness of man so that we might take on the likeness of Him Who is *Love.*

~Saint Maria Theresa O'Conner (Journal)

07/00 NEWERA[1]

A New Name

To him who conquers . . . I will give him a white stone, with a new name written on the stone which no one knows except him who receives it.

~Revelation 2:17

T hen it's decided," said Father Suarez. "But now what do we do when the Federales come looking?"

"We can drag the remains of the helicopter and bury them in the forest," replied Alferez. "We will tell them that we know nothing of this business."

"No," said Mateas. "Too many people saw the helicopter in Palenque. While we might be able to convince the Mayans to speak nothing of the Federales helicopter, I would not count on ladinos[2] for their silence."

"So what are you suggesting?" asked Father Suarez.

"I say we deliver pieces of the helicopter and body parts to officials in San Cristobal. Then we tell them that they can expect the same the next time they send one of their damn helicopters into our territory."

"But that could lead to reprisals," protested Father Suarez, "and besides, they still might come looking for the child."

"Not if we included one of her body parts," said Mateas.

"What!" exclaimed Father Suarez.

"My son is right," said Rosario calmly. "It is the only way. The dragon will continue to pursue her. He will spare nothing and no one to devour the child. He must believe that she is dead."

"I agree with Rosario," spoke Alferez. The other elders nodded in agreement. "It is the only way to protect the child and our families."

"Perhaps we can just give them some of her hair," offered Father Suarez, hopefully.

Mateas shook his head. "Whoever was after this child was damned determined to get her—I don't think they will be convinced by that. Perhaps a fin . . . ."

"Her left arm," interrupted Rosario.

"What!" exclaimed Mateas, and Father Suarez simultaneously.

"No," said Father Suarez. "That's . . . that's too much. It's barbaric to maim her like that!"

"It is better to enter the Kingdom maimed . . ." began Rosario.

"You've done enough Bible quoting for one day," protested Mateas who was embarrassed by his mother's devotion to her Mayan-Catholic beliefs.

Alferez turned to Rosario. "Is this the *only* way?"

"It is," replied Rosario. "The dragon will not be satisfied with anything less. If you do not do this, he will return and devour her and our people."

"I will not permit it!" protested Father Suarez.

"You are not in charge of this village," Alferez politely reminded the priest. "We all must be willing to sacrifice our blood for the peace and security of the people."

"I will not allow Sister Margarita to perform the operation," insisted Father Suarez.

"Then I will do it myself," said Julio, one of the elders. "I have butchered many animals. A child cannot be much different from a goat."

Alferez knew that Julio was not serious; it was simply a clever ploy to convince Father to relent. It worked.

"Very well," said Father Suarez, shaking his head. "I will speak with Sister Margarita. But, I cannot guarantee that she will do it."

"Tell her," said Julio, "that Julio is sharpening his knife."

Father Suarez's eyes narrowed, and he scowled at the elder. There were some among his Mayan flock that did not care for the priest or his Mission. To them he was just another ladino who was trying to make them give up their Mayan ways. Julio was one of these. He was always trying to undermine Father Suarez's influence in the community. For the most part he was not successful because Suarez had secured, with considerable effort, Rosario's support.

"And what of Aguilar?" asked Alferez.

"He's too much of a risk. I say we kill him," said Mateas.

"No, absolutely not!" exclaimed Father Suarez. "I will see to it that he is not a threat. If need be, we can keep him locked up in the Mission."

Mateas and the elders reluctantly agreed. They could deal with him later if he gave them any trouble. Anyway, it was late and there was no time to waste. It was possible that the Federales had already begun to search for their missing helicopter and men. As the elders left the meeting to begin the grisly task ahead, Rosario called to Father Suarez.

"Father, if I might speak with you for a moment."

"Yes?" replied Father Suarez, apprehensive about what other comments or requests she might make.

"I need more time to prepare the child."

"I don't understand," replied the priest.

"The conclusion of the 13-*baktun* cycle, the end of Mayan time, is approaching. The child will not be ready."

"And what do you expect me to do about that? Didn't your ancestors make this calendar over three thousand years ago?"

"Yes that is right. They observed the heavens and learned the cycle of the stars. From this they foretold the great events of Mayan history. We are now approaching the time when the Tree of Life, what you call the Milky Way, crosses the ecliptic. When it does, the door to the realm of the Earthlord will open, and great evil will be loosed upon the earth."

"I still don't know what you want me to do. Surely, you don't expect me to stop the stars in their tracks through the universe!"

"Why not! How little faith you have in the authority Christos has given you. Did he not say that what you loose on earth will be loosed in heaven? Bind the door closed until we are ready."

Father Suarez shook his head. "How can I pray for something I do not even believe in?"

"It is not a hard thing that I am asking. Humor an old woman."

"All right, I will pray as you asked, and God can do what He wills with my prayers. And I will pray for the child. She will need our prayers."

Father Suarez turned to leave and join the rest of the men when he turned around and spoke again to Rosario.

"We can't keep calling her *the child*. What shall we name her?"

Ch'ucha,[3] replied Rosario.

"Little frog?!" exclaimed Father Suarez. "I think a saint's name would be more appropriate."

"Frogs, saints, they are all the same," responded Rosario.

Father Suarez shook his head. He was well aware of the syncretic tendencies of his Mayan flock with respect to Catholicism and their mythology. Mayans were particularly fascinated with frogs. The entire community was engulfed with frogs during the spring when they reproduced in Malthusian numbers. Mayans associated frogs with Easter and the Resurrection; they had significant religious meaning for them.

"And what about a surname?" asked Father Suarez. "Shouldn't we give her another name; perhaps *Ch'ucha' de Miguel Archangelo?*"

"No," replied Rosario recognizing Father's clever attempt to persuade her by using the name of her patron. "God will reveal to *Ch'ucha'* the name He has chosen for her from the foundation of time."

Frederick III

*Then I saw another beast come up out of the earth . . . It wielded
all the authority of the first beast . . . and made the earth and its
inhabitants worship the first beast, whose mortal wound had been
healed.*

~Revelation 13: 11,12

"This business of canonizing your late wife is getting out of
hand," said Obermann. "McIntyre is in charge of this
business, isn't he?"

"Yes," replied Colin. "He is what is known as the Vice-Postulator.
He and Madison Ryan are collecting the information that they intend
to give to the Congregation for the Causes of Saints. The Vatican and
the Orthodox are putting her on the fast track for beatification."

"Beatification?" queried Obermann.

"Before she can be declared a saint, she must be declared 'blessed.'
Right now, she is known as a Servant of God."

"Servant of God! What nonsense! Anyway, doesn't all this take a
miracle or something?"

"Yes," answered Colin. "They are claiming that her death was a miracle."

"What a bunch of crap!" exclaimed Obermann. "I told you this would happen. We need to stop this before it gets out of control. I want you to arrest McIntyre and Ryan."

"But the Attorney General . . . ."

"The hell with the Attorney General!"

"But there's insufficient evidence . . . ."

Obermann looked at Colin with disdain. He was disappointed that he still hadn't perceived the nature of power. He was about to give him a lecture when his phone rang.

"Yes?" said Obermann.

"Dr. Richardson is here. She says that she has the result of the DNA tests."

"Send her in."

Dr. Richardson, head of Chimæra research and development, entered Obermann's office. She was surprised to see Colin O'Conner. She was unsure how Colin would take the results she was about to share with her boss.

"Well?" said Obermann.

Richardson nodded and turned to Colin. "I'm sorry." She then turned to Obermann. "There is no doubt. The remains are that of Mrs. O'Conner's baby."

Colin closed his eyes, lowered his head and rubbed his brow with his fingertips. He had prepared himself for these results, but he was still shaken to hear that the child that he had never seen, that he would never see, was dead. He was stricken by guilt at the news of the death of his daughter, even though just weeks ago he had tried to have her aborted.

"And the others?" asked Obermann.

"The leg we received was identified as belonging to an Officer Aguilar who had accompanied Mr. Zokoroff on the mission to rescue the O'Conner child," said Richardson.

"And Zokoroff?"

"We did not have much to work with, but I'm sorry to say, that we were able to identify that he too was among those killed."

Obermann nodded and thanked Richardson who then left his office. She wanted to place her hand on Colin's shoulder, but she didn't. She was unsure what Obermann might think of her acknowledgment of Colin's grief.

"Zokoroff was a good man," mused Obermann aloud. "He will be hard to replace." But, maybe it was better this way, he thought. The child was dead and no longer a threat. And everyone directly involved in the mission was dead too. There would be less chance of this being traced back to him. Everyone could just go on thinking that the baby was missing. They would forget about her just as they would forget about her mother.

"O'Conner," said Obermann forcefully.

Colin looked up composing himself. It would not be good to disappoint Obermann by an excessive display of emotion.

"I'm sorry about your kid. But, I want to keep this whole business under wraps. If people find out that she was killed in our rescue attempt they'll blame us for it. I did everything I could to bring her home to you. You must forget about her now and move on with your life. Speaking of which, here's how you deal with McIntyre. You have that Congregation priest on death row?"

"Right," replied Colin. "He confessed to the crime. The dumb bastard even bragged about it in court. But, we could never get him to implicate McIntyre."

"Talk with him. Tell him that if he doesn't implicate McIntyre we'll inject him with Chimæra."

"But he's on death row. What good is Chimæra going to do if they execute him?"

"I never said it was for good," replied Obermann with a sinister smile.

How naive Colin was, thought Obermann. But, Obermann knew that the priest would understand. Perhaps, Obermann thought, it would be more satisfying if the damned priest refused to implicate McIntyre.

What the hell! I'll have him injected anyway. His soul trapped in his rotting corpse was just punishment for the bastard who murdered me and my wife.

A few days later, Dr. Richardson called Hans Obermann asking him to come to the clinic as quickly as possible. When he arrived, she brought him to the secret room where Fletcher's corpse lay naked connected to numerous tubes and monitors. It continued to serve as an incubator for the gestation of Obermann's son. Her abdomen was swollen as with a normal pregnancy, and her breasts were enlarged as they were preparing for lactation. The rest of her body was shriveled and ashen, parasitized by the developing fetus which allowed only those systems that were required to maintain the pregnancy to receive adequate nutrients and oxygen. It was a ghastly sight for Dr. Richardson who especially tried to avoid looking at Fletcher's empty eye sockets. Obermann, however, was unmoved.

"There is a lot of fetal movement," said Dr. Richardson. "I believe the baby is ready to be born."

"Have there been any contractions or effacement of the cervix?" asked Obermann.

"No, that's what has me and the obstetrician concerned. I talked with him on the phone. He'll be here soon. I think we will need to do a Caesarean."

"Let's do it then. I want to see my son!"

"I'll begin to prepare . . . ." began Richardson when she noticed a large mass appearing under Fletcher's abdomen. It looked like a hand pushing from the inside. Both Richardson and Obermann watched as the activity intensified. Then a fist broke through the abdomen. Richardson shrieked. Obermann smiled and began to approach Fletcher's body.

"Come, my son, you can do it!" he said.

Richardson stood back in horror as she saw two hands appear, grasp opposite sides of the wound that the fist had made, and then rend the desiccated flesh like tissue making a large gaping wound. The child pushed and crawled its way out, covered with blood and amniotic fluid. It sat up, looked around, saw its mother's breast and crawled over to them dragging the umbilicus behind him. He grabbed a nipple with his hand, bent down, and began to nurse.

Obermann got a warm damp towel and wiped the baby as it suckled.

"You are my beloved son," he said. He then bent down and kissed the back of the child's head. He looked up at Richardson. Blood and amniotic fluid dripped from his lips.

"Isn't little Frederick handsome?"

Majnun

And surely, We have created many of the jinns and mankind for Hell. They have hearts wherewith they understand not, they have eyes wherewith they see not, and they have ears wherewith they hear not (the truth). They are like cattle, nay even more astray; those! They are the heedless ones.

- The Holy Qur'an-Al-A'raaf 7:179

The burnished crescent moon hung low upon the western horizon suspended like a necklace between the twin *ma'thineh*⁴ of Masjid Bilall mosque. The call to evening prayers echoed from the towers and pierced every corner of the city of Al Karmah. The devoted poured into Masjid Bilall like water from the great hydroelectric dam of Al Yesaf. But, another type of energy was being produced at Masjid Bilall. Prince Abdullah Mohammed Saïd felt the power as he laid down his prayer rug with the vast throng. His father, King Saïd, feared this power. He had ordered his son to stay away from the mosque and the elderly, charismatic Sheik al-Ahbar. But Prince Abdullah was not a child anymore. Now, at seventeen, he felt the *Call*; he would not, could not, disobey that Call. He bent low as he knelt upon the prayer rug. His prayers joined the vast multitude filling every corner of the mosque.

He tried to focus his attention wholly on his prayers, but his thoughts invariably drifted to his mother, the Queen. She was a good mother and faithful wife, he thought. Even from his youth he had recognized his mother's devotion to the True Path. As he grew into manhood, he could discern the subtle wisdom of the Queen as she deftly mitigated the King's harshness. It was she that had kept Sheik al-Ahbar from exile, or worse, his father's appalling prisons. But, she was ill now; struck down by the scourge of ovarian cancer in the blossom of her reign. She was dying, and her husband was heartsick and bitter that *Allah* should deal with him so cruelly. Abdullah prayed for a holy death for his mother and mercy for his father.

"The Hour has drawn near and the moon is split!"⁵

Abdullah tingled as he heard the old sheik begin his instruction. He recognized the first verse from chapter fifty-four of the Holy Qur'an. He also recognized the apocalyptic implications of the verse and the term, *the Hour*. Although he was still young, many had begun to recognize Abdullah's gift of knowledge and wisdom. Sheik al-Ahbar had long discerned the young prince's earnestness and talents; Abdullah was his brightest and most devoted disciple.

His father also recognized Abdullah's passion for the "Way of the Prophet." He had tolerated it to an extent, but the sheik's rhetoric was becoming increasingly hostile towards the regime. The King had forbidden his son to attend prayers at the mosque. It took some effort, but Abdullah had been able to elude Palace security on more than one occasion.

Abdullah had thought he was terribly clever sneaking out of the Palace complex and making his way to the mosque unnoticed. One time, however, he could have sworn that Amir al-Sharif, the Captain in charge of Security, had seen him slip over the wall. The Captain had turned away as if he hadn't seen him. Perhaps he didn't see me, thought Abdullah. Or could it be that the Captain was sympathetic to my desire to pursue the True Path. But why?

Captain al-Sharif, had been groomed by his father, for the important position he now held. Apparently, the Captain and Abdullah's mother, the Queen, had known each other since childhood. When his father died suddenly, al-Sharif took over his command. The Captain was a serious man, polite to be sure, but not especially friendly. Abdullah had once asked his mother why Captain al-Sharif was always so grave. His mother did not answer. Instead, Queen Miriam looked down and said nothing. Abdullah was not sure why his question had made her uncomfortable. He thought it best not to ask any more questions about the handsome Captain al-Sharif.

Abdullah was more concerned that his older stepbrother, Malik, might catch him and tell their father. Malik was the only surviving child of the King's first marriage and the heir to the throne. Considerably older than Abdullah, Malik resembled his father both in appearance and temperament. Malik had nothing but contempt for his stepmother and her son. He resented Abdullah; not because their father favored him, he did not, but because Abdullah never sought his favor. Indeed, Abdullah never sought the power, prestige, or wealth that Malik prized above all else. Malik hated him for it. Abdullah knew it and didn't care. Malik despised him all the more for not caring.

A couple of years earlier, their father had appointed Malik as second in command under General Masud, the head of the military. Malik soon implicated Masud in a plot against the King. Abdullah had suspected that the charges against Masud were contrived. It was not unusual for members of the government, who were thought to have secured too much personal power, to be accused of treason. This was just one of the ways that the King maintained his authority over the kingdom. Masud fled the country and Malik assumed his authority. Malik then assumed control of the Secret Police. Aside from the King, Malik had become the most feared man in the Kingdom.

"The *Hour* is coming, no doubt about it,"[6] said the old sheik continuing to quote from the *Qur'an*.

Abdullah shook himself from his reverie.

"From the West the *jahiliyyah*[7] returns. It is the Chimæra; and indeed that is what it is. It is the unholy union of clay and smokeless flame, of man and *jinn*. It will be powerful and deceive many from the ways of the Prophet. It will promise immortality, but we know that it lies, for the Holy Qur'an says that 'every soul shall taste death.'[8] It is *Allah*, the beneficent and merciful, who fixes the term of a man.[9] *Allah*, may His name be blessed, is not mocked. He shall raise up the *Mahdi* and say to him, 'take away from you the uncleanness of the *Shayâtin*,[10] the *jinn* that whispers deceit into the heart of man that leads him away from the True Path. Cast terror into the hearts of those who disbelieve . . . strike off their heads and strike off every fingertip of them.'"[11]

The *Mahdi!* Abdullah thought excitedly. The restorer of true religion, the redresser of injustice—can it be true? Might the *Mahdi* be amongst us?

The doors of the mosque burst in. The King's security forces stormed the mosque, seized the elderly sheik and began to drag him out of the house of prayer. Shouts and cries erupted. The mass of worshipers surged towards the soldiers. Abdullah tried to peer above the heads of those that pressed around him. He could hear his father's name being cursed and felt the sting of tear gas in his eyes. The worshipers covered their faces with their *kaffiyehs*[12] as they ran to the exits. Abdullah felt strong hands grab and pull him toward one of the exits. Several of his father's soldiers had seized him.

"Damn you! I am Prince Abdullah! Let go of me!"

The soldiers ignored his protests and dragged him out of Masjid Bilall. He could see people fleeing the mosque. Soldiers were firing shots in the air to disperse the crowd. Abdullah was pushed inside a Mercedes limousine that was waiting for him.

"Greetings brother."

"Malik!" exclaimed Abdullah, recognizing his brother. Abdullah sat across from his brother.

His brother's morbidly obese body nearly filled the back seat of the vehicle. The uniform that barely fit around Malik's ponderous body was covered with medals won in military campaigns by his heroic predecessor, General Masud. Next to Malik sat a pale, effeminate boy who was just a few years younger than Abdullah. Malik stroked the boy's thigh and smiled knowing that his behavior would disgust Abdullah.

"By what authority do you . . . ."

The car door slammed shut.

"Security headquarters," barked Malik at the driver.

The Mercedes sped off towards the ordered destination.

"Calm yourself, brother," replied Malik. "I am my own authority, but if you do not think that is sufficient, my arrest of Sheik al-Ahbar was ordered by the King."

"Release me this instant!" ordered Abdullah.

"Our father is not pleased that you continue to disobey him," said Malik, ignoring his brother's demand. "Will not prayers be heard just as well in the mosque at the Palace compound?"

"No," said Abdullah, "I do not believe they will. But, I need not answer your questions. Where have they taken Sheik al-Ahbar?"

"To Security Headquarters where I will be interrogating him later. But now for the reason I have been sent to retrieve you. Our father has some exciting news. He wishes to share his joy with you this evening."

Abdullah said nothing.

"Are you not interested?" asked Malik.

Abdullah folded his arms across his chest, turned away and looked out the window, ignoring his brother. This behavior incensed Malik who rightly interpreted Abdullah's actions as minimizing his importance.

"It's about *your* mother," Malik continued in an irritated tone.

Abdullah turned and faced Malik. Malik could see that he now had his brother's attention.

"What?" asked Abdullah, concerned. "Did she . . . ."

"Die?" finished Malik. Rather than answer immediately, Malik studied Abdullah, enjoying the dismay that he had caused him.

"How very much you look like your mother," said Malik, purposely ignoring Abdullah's question. "In fact, you don't look like father at all. I have often wondered if . . ."

Abdullah's eyes narrowed. He was livid, not because Malik had offended him, but that he dared impugn the dignity of his mother. He felt the knife that he always wore at his side, the *saiyf wa khanjar* the ceremonial knife that his mother had given him when he had come of age. Abdullah gripped the handle of the knife and grit his teeth. Malik smiled, aware of his brother's thoughts and action. Abdullah released the knife.

"Is my mother dead?" asked Abdullah, finally getting control of his anger.

The Mercedes stopped in front of Security Headquarters. Malik stepped out of the car seemingly ignoring his brother's question. He held out his hand to the boy who took it and slid out of the car. Malik was about to close the door when he turned around,

"Forgive me brother, I have an interrogation to conduct. As for your mother," Malik smiled maliciously, "I suspect you would prefer her dead." Malik ordered the driver to take Abdullah to the palace and then slammed the door.

The Mercedes entered the palace compound. They drove past the residences and went to the infirmary. The Queen had been moved there so that she could receive more intensive therapy. She was prepared for her death; the King was not. In desperation, the King had brought in physicians from Europe and America. Abdullah's mother quietly suffered the injections, the radiation, the nausea, the pain. But, it was all to no avail. The physicians agreed that she had only a few days, perhaps a week to live.

As the Mercedes stopped in front of the infirmary, a servant stepped forward to open the prince's door but Abdullah had already stepped out of the car and run up the stairs to the entrance. His head was filled with a whirlwind of emotions. He was angry at the arrest of the sheik and the brutality of his father's security forces. But, what was this exciting news that was the cause of great joy? Was his mother miraculously better?

He could see his father on the second floor landing outside his mother's room. King Saïd was a very large man both in height and girth. Even his features were grotesquely large. It had not always been so. He was never a handsome man, but as the years passed his physiognomy began to mirror the malignant influence that power had wreaked upon his soul. Abdullah's companions used to wonder among themselves how it was possible that the prince even could have been conceived. They grimaced at the thought of the beautiful Queen Miriam submitting to such a foul entity as her husband, the King. But of course their marriage was politically, not romantically, inspired. Even so, the Queen was a faithful, if not loving, spouse. Her gentle influence had saved the lives of more than a few of the King's political foes. Abdullah's companions agreed that he was his mother's son in both appearance and temperament. Certainly, he shared his mother's compassion for the people.

One time, after his father had dealt brutally with the political opposition, the Queen took Abdullah aside. She opened the *Qur'an*, pointed to a verse, and then handed the holy book to him. "Read, my son."

> *"O you who believe! be maintainers of justice, bearers of witness for Allah's sake, though it may be against your own selves or your parents or near relatives; if he be rich or poor, Allah is nearer to them both in compassion; therefore do not follow your low desires, lest you deviate; and if you swerve or turn aside, then surely Allah is aware of what you do."*[13]

"Do you understand the Prophet's meaning?" asked Queen Miriam.

"No, mother, I do not," replied the young prince.

"It means, my dear prince, that *Allah* requires justice for *all*."

"Not just for the *ummah?*[14] But father said . . . ."

Queen Miriam placed a finger on his lips. "When you are king, remember my words. The *Sharia*[15] must extend equal justice to the People of the Book. Now do you understand the Prophet's meaning?"

Abdullah thought for a moment. He considered his father's reign and the kingdoms of other Muslim monarchs throughout history in the light of his mother's wisdom. He finally replied, "Then the true *jihad* occurs within the heart."

Queen Miriam was astonished at her young son's response. She smiled, kissed his forehead and embraced him. She whispered into his ear, "You will be a good King, my young prince. You will serve all the people of *Allah* with justice and compassion."

As Abdullah now bounded up the stairs, he saw his father talking to a woman in a white lab coat. He did not recognize her as one of the physicians that had been attending his mother over the past several months. As soon as his father saw Abdullah, he opened his arms and embraced him. Then he pushed his son back.

"You have disobeyed me again," said the King sternly.

Abdullah was about to protest but his father continued. "But I forgive you as your mother always insists that I do. Besides, my joy is too great to be angry with you!"

"What is it, father? Is mother . . . ," Abdullah did not finish his sentence. He was almost too afraid to state what seemed to be impossible—beyond all hope.

"Yes!" exclaimed his father. "Your mother will be healed. Even better than healed!"

"How can than this be?" cried Abdullah.

"For months," began his father, "we have tried everything. But as you know, your mother only became more ill. I had all but given up hope when I received a call from America just a couple of days ago."

Abdullah's stomach knotted as he anticipated that his father was about to reveal something ominous and blasphemous.

"The American President, Jack Pearson, offered to cure your mother!"

"How?" said Abdullah, trembling with anticipation.

"That's not important. What's important is that your mother has just finished receiving the treatment and the doctor here is confident that she will be cured."

Abdullah turned to the woman in the lab coat. "What did you do to my mother?" he demanded angrily.

"I gave her an injection of Chimæric stem cells," replied the doctor.

"No!" shouted Abdullah. He grabbed the doctor. "Reverse it. Take it away!"

"I can't," replied the startled doctor.

The king grabbed his son.

"Enough!" the king said forcefully. "Get a hold of yourself. You are the Prince. Act like one!"

"Don't you know what you've done?!"

"I know damn well what I've done. What *Allah* refused to do, I have done. I have cured your mother, the Queen of our Kingdom. You should be grateful."

"No," replied Abdullah as tears streamed from his eyes. "You have made her *majnun*.[16] You have damned her to the eternal fires!"

"Shut up!" shouted the King as he slapped Abdullah across the face. "You are speaking nonsense. I myself have taken the treatment. Do I appear any different to you? You will take it too."

"No I will not!" exclaimed Abdullah. "You have become the unbeliever, the *kafir bi na'mat Allah*.[17] "

The King grabbed his son forcibly by the arm. "This is not you speaking. This is that damned Sheik al-Ahbar. I should have had him arrested long ago! General Saïd is interrogating him now. He will either recant or suffer the consequences."

"He will not recant!"

"Then he will die!"

Abdullah pulled away from his father and ran down the stairs. The King could hear him utter as he ran away, "Our Lord . . . cause us to die in submission."[18]

Abdullah ran out of the palace compound. He ran and ran; he ran without any thought as to where he was going. He eventually found himself in an alley not far from the mosque where he had been not more than an hour ago. He stopped, fell against a wall, slid down and sat with his head in his hands. He trembled in the dark. His father's security forces were still patrolling the streets. He could hear the scampering of people fleeing, the dull thud of beatings followed by muffled cries and groans. He loathed his father. The King had blasphemed the True Path, had unleashed tyranny upon his kingdom, and cursed his family. Abdullah wished that he were a simple peasant of Al-Karmah and not the Prince. His head sank between his knees.

Where am I going? What am I doing? he thought. I cannot go back; father will make me *Shayâtin*! Then it occurred to him that Sheik al-Ahbar would know. Sheik al-Ahbar—he is my true father! He knew what he had to do. He had to rescue the sheik or die trying. It was a holy cause.

He stood up, wiped the tears from his face, and brushed himself off. He looked around, got his bearings, and ran off in the direction of the Security compound. He would occasionally stop, dart behind a building or parked vehicle so as not to be spotted by his father's security forces. He finally arrived at his destination and stood in front of the ominous Security Headquarters building. It was a grim building made of concrete, punctuated with a few, small windows. He knew that once he stepped inside the foreboding structure his life would change forever. Chances were he would not leave the building alive. If, however, he did survive, he would be a fugitive, exiled from his own Kingdom, and hunted by his own father. He entered the facility without the faintest idea of how he could liberate the Sheik, but confident in the mercy of *Allah*.

He was surprised to find the Security Headquarters quiet. He had anticipated that it would be bustling with activity. But, apparently most of the security personnel were out patrolling the city. It was a measure of their arrogant confidence, that they felt little need to guard their own headquarters. He recognized the young officer at the security desk who was surrounded by monitors.

The Queen knew of the hatred Malik harbored for her son and feared for Abdullah's safety. She entrusted the protection of her son to Captain al-Sharif. The Captain knew that the best way to protect Abdullah would be to teach the young Prince how to protect himself. An accomplished fencer, Captain al-Sharif taught Abdullah the use of the sword and knife. He then sent the young Prince to the military academy for instruction on the use of various types of firearms. It was during this training that Abdullah had met Jafar Faruq.

Jafar just couldn't take anything seriously and he certainly had no time for religion and politics. Faruq dreamed of being a musician. He was accomplished with the *oud*, a lute-like instrument popular in Arabia. Yet, his father had a different career in mind for Jafar and so he sent him to the military academy where he hoped his son would acquire some much needed discipline.

Abdullah had attempted to engage the young man in a discussion on the *Qur'an*. Jafar had listened politely, smiled, grabbed his *oud*, and then had began to strum a melody.

"My dear Prince," Jafar had said smiling, "now that you have filled my mind with things that I do not understand, I shall sing to you of delicious things the likes of which have not crossed your lips."

Jafar had then proceeded to sing a ribald song, which celebrated the glories of voluptuous women. Abdullah had blushed and admonished his companion for his lack of seriousness. But, he found that he could not remain annoyed with Jafar for long—he was just too likable.

Abdullah was surprised and dismayed to see that Jafar had been assigned to his father's security forces. The lieutenant stood up and saluted the Prince. Abdullah placed his hand on his shoulder.

"Where is Sheik al-Ahbar?"

"He is being interrogated," replied Jafar.

"I have a message from my father, the King, to deliver to his interrogators."

"I will deliver it for you," said Jafar. "An interrogation room is no place for the Prince."

"No," replied Abdullah. "I must deliver it myself."

"Very well. I will take you."

"No, no," stammered Abdullah. "It is better that you not leave your post. Just tell me where I should go."

"Around the corner and to your right you will find the stairs. Take them down to the third level. The guard will direct you from there."

Abdullah nodded, thanked the young lieutenant, and headed down the dimly lit staircase. He wondered how many unfortunate souls had traversed these same stairs never to return. He reached the third level and was greeted by the guard with a salute. Abdullah saw the young man who was Malik's lover seated in a chair across from the guard's station. Abdullah instinctively snarled his lip displaying his disgust towards the youth. The youth fired back with a haughty twist of his shoulders and face feigning indifference towards the Prince.

"Lieutenant Faruq called and informed me that you need to speak with the interrogator of the prisoner in cell 32," said the guard.

"If you can show me the way . . ."

"I am sorry your highness, but I must go with you. Security protocols. You understand."

"Yes, certainly."

The guard got up from behind his desk and led Abdullah down a long, dreary hallway flanked by numerous steel doors. Abdullah could hear groans and curses from behind the doors. He was disgusted at the thought that innocent people were being imprisoned and tortured with the consent of his father. He felt a sickness that, with each passing step, turned into rage.

"Here," said the guard finally stopping. He knocked on the door. A small window inside the door opened from the inside, and a set of eyes peered out questioningly.

"The Prince is here to deliver a message," said the guard.

"Let him in," replied the voice from behind the door.

The guard unlocked the door and opened it. Abdullah stepped into the cold steel and stone room that looked as bereft of hope as it was of furniture. A single large drain hole was the only object that broke the gray continuity between floor and walls. It was through this orifice that the remnants of interrogations were hosed down. Abdullah gagged as he entered the room. Blood, urine, and excrement smeared the floor. In the corner of the room, twisted and broken, lay Sheik al-Ahbar. A tall muscular man stood off to the side. Next to him, leaning against the wall, was a large scimitar; the type used to decapitate those sentenced for execution. Malik stood next to the door wiping his bloodied hands on a towel.

"We have been expecting you, brother," said Malik smiling wickedly.

"You bastard!" exclaimed Abdullah. He began to move towards the sheik, but he was stopped by his brother's firm grip upon his arm.

"Father called and said that you might be joining us. He thought that you might find this instructive. He wanted me to convey to you that neither sheik nor prince is immune from the King's justice."

The muscular man went over to the sheik and dragged him over to the center of the room. He pulled and pushed him until he was bent over in a kneeling position, his head pointed towards Abdullah and

Malik. The executioner stood at attention next to the sheik waiting for General Saïd to give the order. Malik nodded.

"Damn you!" Abdullah shouted.

The executioner reached back, grabbed the scimitar and raised it above his head. Abdullah tried to pull himself away from the Malik's firm grip, but could not. Then he remembered the *saiyf wa khanjar.* He quickly grabbed it with his free hand, pulled it from its sheath, and drove it into his brother's belly. Malik squealed and released him.

Abdullah lunged towards the executioner as he was bringing the scimitar down towards the sheik's neck. Abdullah slipped in the blood and excrement that covered the floor. Sliding between the executioner and his prey he saw the glint of the sword as it sped towards its target. Abdullah raised his dagger and caught the scimitar by the knife's hand-guard. The sword continued in its momentum as Abdullah strained to keep it from reaching the sheik. The sword jerked to a stop. Abdullah grabbed the executioner's arms and pulled himself up while simultaneously drawing the executioner down. As they met midway, Abdullah drove his dagger under the jaw of the executioner. It was an instantaneous and fatal blow. He withdrew the dagger as the lifeless executioner crumpled to the floor.

Abdullah immediately turned his attention to the sheik. He knelt by the dying holy man who lay on the floor. Blood was oozing from the back of his neck. Abdullah had not been completely successful in stopping the executioner's blade. The sheik was not dead, but was mouthing faint, nearly imperceptible words. Abdullah placed his arms around the sheik.

"I am sorry. I have failed you."

"No," the sheik whispered. "Listen. You must flee."

"No," insisted Abdullah, "It is better to die in submission . . ."

"You must live," the sheik interrupted. "The blood of the Prophet flows through your veins." Then mustering what strength remained he said with a loud and authoritative voice, "You are the *Mahdi!*"

Mahdi!? thought Abdullah. The sheik pointed to the sword that was stained by his own blood. "You are the *Sahib al-sayf*.[19] Together, with the other children of Abraham, you are destined to establish the Empire of Truth."

Abdullah was perplexed by the sheik's prophecy. But, now was not the time to ponder his words. He reached over and picked up the sword. He felt an inexplicable power course through his body. A voice spoke inside him; it was as though the sword itself were speaking to him. *I will be your weapon in the malahim*[20] *Together we shall impose a double punishment to those who turn away from the path of Allah and desire to make it crooked.*[21] Abdullah turned back to the sheik. He was dead.

Meanwhile, Malik had stumbled down the hall and called out to the guard. The guard ran down the hall and grabbed the General as he fell to his knees. He was not seriously hurt; the ponderous layers of fat had protected his vital organs from Abdullah's blade.

"The Prince . . . ," Malik gasped. "He stabbed me!"

"What?!"

"That's right. He's mad! He's a traitor! Go in there and shoot the bastard!"

"Your brother? It will be my head!" exclaimed the guard.

"No," replied Malik. "He tried to kill me and he intends to kill the King. You'll be saving the King's life. Now go . . . that's an order."

The guard ran to the cell in which the Prince and sheik were still imprisoned; the door had closed and locked when Malik had stumbled out. The guard stood in front of the door hesitantly. From the end of the corridor Malik waved him on. The guard pulled out his pistol, released the safety and held it ready. He removed his key, stuck it in the lock and turned the bolt. As soon as he had done this, the door burst open. Malik saw a flash. The guard's arm and the pistol fell to the ground. He heard the guard howl, but then he saw another flash. The howling abruptly stopped. Malik turned away and began to frantically crawl further down the hall towards the guard's station. He reached the guard's desk and picked up the telephone receiver. Just as he heard the dial tone, he heard a swish and the phone went dead. Malik fell to the ground holding the receiver, which was no longer connected to the phone. Abdullah stood over him with the curved scimitar blade pointed at his head. Malik trembled as warm blood dripped from the blade onto his bare neck.

"Tell the King that I will return with *jihad*. As the Ark of the Covenant was with the children of Israel so shall the Sword of the Prophet, the *dhul-fiqar*,[22] be with us who will rid our Kingdom of the *Shayâtin*," said Abdullah nicking his brother's chin with the point of the sword.

Abdullah began to leave the room when he heard something behind him. He turned back and saw Malik's lover trembling under the guard's desk. He shook his head with contempt and ran back up the stairs. He passed several security officers who were surprised to see the young Prince. One even asked whether he needed help seeing that he was splattered with blood. Abdullah said nothing as he ran past them. As he reached the front desk, he was startled to see Captain al-Sharif standing next to Lieutenant Faruq behind the front desk. They had witnessed everything that had just occurred in the dungeons below from the monitors at Faruq's post. Faruq raised his pistol and aimed it at the Prince. Abdullah froze and said nothing. Each stood facing the other while time itself seemed to stop. Finally, Captain al-Sharif placed his hand on Faruq's pistol and pushed it down. Faruq looked questioningly at the Captain.

"Go," said the Captain, reaching into his pocket. He pulled out a set of keys and tossed them to the Prince.

"Why should a captain of the King let his enemy escape?" asked Abdullah.

"My loyalty is more to the Queen than your father. I have sworn to your mother that I would protect you. I am powerless to protect you from the vengeance of your father and brother. I see no other alternative than for you to flee."

"Is it true what the Sheik said? Are you the *Mahdi*?" asked Jafar.

"Come," said Abdullah. "We can find out together."

"I will," he said reaching underneath his desk. He pulled out his *oud* and smiled, "and I will sing songs of our adventures. Do *Mahdis* have adventures?"

Abdullah shook his head and would have laughed had the events of the day not been so tragic.

"My truck is outside," said Captain al-Sharif. "Leave quickly."

"Thank you," said Abdullah still amazed that the Captain would help him escape.

"Where shall we go?" asked Jafar.

"To the Jordanian wilderness," replied Abdullah, throwing his arm around his new ally. They hurried towards the exit. As they were about to step out, Abdullah turned around. He looked questioningly at Captain al-Sharif.

"May *Allah* be with you," the Captain said quietly as he watched the two young men drive off into the darkness.

12/00 NEWERA

Three and a Half Years

But the woman was given the two wings of the great eagle, so that
she could fly to her place in the desert, where, far from the serpent, she
was taken care of for a year, two years, and a half-year.
~Revelation 12:14

Madison Ryan and Detective Milton Lewis sat in William
Cardinal McIntyre's former office to which the Cardinal
would no longer be returning. He was serving a life sentence for
conspiring in the murders of the National Security Advisor, General
Walker Pierce and Mr. and Mrs. Hans Obermann. Ryan and Lewis
now waited for the return of his replacement as Postulator, Greek
Orthodox Bishop, George Kavasilas.

Ryan thought about the fact that Maria O'Conner might have
sat in this very chair just a few months ago. She considered how
her life had changed since she had written that first scandalous
article about Maria. Maria had been right. Although Ryan meant
harm, God meant it for good. She glanced over at Detective Lewis.
He was retired now. He had served the city of DC well for over

twenty years and had been forced into retirement because he had continued to investigate the O'Conner case in spite of warnings to cease and desist. He had been changed by Maria, even though he had never actually met her. Yes, the hand of God was on him too. In fact, all who had contact with Maria O'Conner had had their lives deeply changed. More would. Detective Lewis and she would see to that. They were determined to make sure that the Church canonized her.

"Good morning everyone," said Bishop Kavasilas as he entered the office. "Coffee?"

"I'll have a cup," replied Detective Lewis.

"I'm fine," said Ryan.

"A couple of cups of coffee please, Sister Francis," called out Bishop Kavasilas into the adjoining office.

"Who was your slave in your previous life?" asked an elderly woman's voice from the other room.

Bishop Kavasilas sat down in the chair and relaxed.

"Thank God, that in the midst of all this chaos there are some things one can still rely on," said Kavasilas.

"You mean Sister Francis' cantankerousness?" asked Ryan smiling.

Sister Francis walked in with two cups of coffee.

"My ears are burning," said Sister Francis.

"We could never tell with that habit. When are you going to get modern?" teased the bishop.

"The day you cut that ridiculous long beard of yours!" fired back Sister Francis who, as she walked out of the room, winked at Ryan. "And when you quit eating fried chicken," they could hear her say from the other room.

Kavasilas smiled. "Always the last word. Who says a celibate can't sympathize with those who are married!"

Detective Lewis laughed as one who understood.

"Now," said Kavasilas, "What do you have for me? Did you find the file?"

"No, not yet," replied Lewis. "But Jimmy said he put the file where no one would think of looking, so I'm hoping Hans Obermann and his government puppets haven't found it; or better yet, don't even know about it."

Kavasilas turned to Madison. "Have you finished the short biography I asked you to write? I would like to have something when I go to Rome later this week. There are many all over the world, especially among the Russian Orthodox, who are supporting our call for Maria's beatification; but we'll need documentation."

"Yes, your Excellency," she replied.

He smiled. "Please call me George; at least when we're in my office."

"I don't think I can do that," said Ryan.

"All right then, go on," Kavasilas said amused at her disobedience.

Ryan pulled out a parcel, placed it on the bishop's desk and removed two notebooks. One notebook contained the biography of Maria O'Conner that the bishop had asked her to write. The other notebook was Maria's journal which she had just completed editing.

"Excellent," said Bishop Kavasilas. "How did you manage to get it done so quickly?"

"Prison can be a great place to write—very few distractions," she replied.

"And how is that going?" asked Kavasilas. "Is there a chance that you might have to go back?"

"We are always at the whim of our government, now more than ever. I was paroled as part of Obermann's *Day of Amnesty and Reconciliation.* I was told that I had better behave myself," Ryan said humorously.

Kavasilas nodded. "Being involved in the beatification effort of Obermann's chief nemesis probably doesn't qualify as behaving," he said with a laugh.

"I suspect not," said Ryan. "But here's the big news that we wanted to share with you. Last night, I was contacted by Geraldine Thompson. She is the mother of Lisa Thompson, the girl who was cured of her leukemia. Do you remember her?"

"Sounds familiar," said Kavasilas. "Maybe you could refresh my memory."

"Lisa Thompson was eight when she contracted a particularly aggressive form of leukemia. She was only given a few months to live. She was selected by Chimæra for clinical trials of their new stem-cell therapy. It worked. Later, little Lisa was paraded before the American people as a Chimæra success story . . . ."

"Now I remember," said Kavasilas.

"Right. Physically she was healed, but what was never reported, and what her mother revealed to me over the phone last night, was that Lisa began to have terrible nightmares. These nightmares started shortly after her therapy. They grew in frequency and intensity. Then she began to have them even during the day while she was awake . . . like visions."

"What were the dreams and visions like?" asked Kavasilas.

"They were always the same. Lisa saw herself in a box, which from her description her mother took to be a coffin. She would try to run away but she couldn't. And each time she had the dream or vision, she would watch her body decaying a little more. She even described the stench of her rotting flesh!"

"How horrible!" said Kavasilas.

"Yes," continued Ryan. "Needless to say, the stress of this situation was nearly tearing the family apart. They went to psychologists. They didn't help. They tried drugs and that didn't help either. Then Mrs. Thompson read the article I wrote on Maria O'Conner, the one for THE AMERICAN WEEKLY. She became convinced that it was the Chimæric therapy that was the cause of Lisa's nightmares and visions."

"The *garments of skin*," said Kavasilas.

"Exactly. So she contacted the people at Chimæra and asked them if they could reverse the treatment. They insisted that the treatment had nothing to do with Lisa's mental problems. They refused, and informed her that they couldn't reverse the treatment even if they wanted to. That's when Mrs. Thompson decided to pray to Maria O'Conner and ask for her intercession."

"And when was that?" asked Kavasilas.

"The day before yesterday. That night, before Lisa went to bed, they prayed to Maria. Lisa lay in her bed and her mother knelt next to her. They had the picture of Maria that was on the cover of THE

WEEKLY. They prayed until Lisa finally fell asleep, too exhausted to stay awake any longer. Mrs. Thompson fell asleep in her daughter's room. She was surprised to wake up and see the sun shining. Usually, no one in the house slept more than a half-hour at a time; they would be awakened by Lisa's screaming. But, Lisa had slept through the night, or at least that's what Mrs. Thompson thought at first. She got up and checked on her daughter. She said that Lisa had the sweetest smile on her face. The smile she used to have before the treatment. She was dead. It took her most of the day to find my phone number. She called to tell me of the miracle and how grateful she was to Maria O'Conner."

"So Mrs. Thompson is attributing the miraculous death of her daughter to Maria O'Conner. Right?" asked Kavasilas.

"Yes," answered Ryan. "I believe this is the miracle we need to push Maria's beatification forward."

"And the child?" asked Kavasilas turning to Lewis. "Has there been any word on the child?"

"No, nothing," replied Lewis. "Nothing on the Russian woman either. It's as though they both dropped off the face of the earth."

"Well, I've brought some news back from Constantinople that you both might find interesting," said Bishop Kavasilas.

"Really?!" exclaimed Ryan.

"Yes," replied Kavasilas. "After the Council, I had an opportunity to talk briefly with Father Nikitas. I asked him whether Goricsan's government had heard any word regarding Major Nizhniya. I figured that might also shed some light on the whereabouts of Theresa. Unfortunately, all he offered was another one of his cryptic remarks."

"What did he say?" interrupted Ryan.

"He quoted Revelation, '*the woman was given the two wings of the great eagle, so that she could fly to her place in the desert, where, far from the serpent, she was taken care of for a year, two years, and a half-year.*'[23]

"What do you suppose he meant by that?" asked Ryan.

"I asked him the same thing. He replied that we had only a short time to prepare."

Ch'ucha'

*May our sons in their youth be like plants full grown, our daughters
like corner pillars cut for the structure of a palace.*

~Psalm 144:12

Santiago silently watched Mateas from a distance. Mateas leaned
against a tree and seemed to be equally absorbed in watching
something which Santiago could not observe from his vantage point. It
didn't matter. He knew what absorbed Mateas' attention. He walked
over towards his friend, being sure to step on a few twigs so as to
announce his arrival. He saw no point in embarrassing his friend.

"Ah, my friend, what has captured your attention so?" said Santiago
with a smile.

"*Ch'ucha'*," said Mateas.

"Your mother was right about the child," said Santiago. "She is
special."

"Yes," said Mateas. "And just about the time you think you've seen
everything . . . . Watch Ludmelia throw the ball to *Ch'ucha'*."

Santiago shook his head incredulously. "It is hard to believe she is only seven months old. Look at her. She looks like she's two years old. She speaks very well, too. Look at that! It is amazing how she can catch that ball with one hand; although with the way her other arm is growing back, it won't be long until she's catching it with both hands."

"No, Santiago. I do not believe you are seeing what I was talking about."

Santiago strained to see what Mateas was referring to. He saw a pretty little girl laughing as she ran with her chestnut hair bouncing behind her. She was dark-skinned like her Mayan playmates, but she had Caucasian features. Her clear, blue eyes danced as she threw her arms up gleefully after pitching the ball back to her "Mama." Between pitches she would twirl joyously causing her little *huipil* to float above her waist. In many ways she behaved like any other Mayan child of the community surrounding Mission de las Casas. But she was different, very different.

*   *   *

It was as evident to Father Suarez as it was to everyone in the small Mayan community that *Ch'ucha'* was an extraordinary child. The regrowth of her arm and the remarkable rate of her development was seen as miraculous by some, witchcraft by others. Rosario was convinced that *Ch'ucha'* was the child prophesied since Christian and Mayan antiquity. Father Suarez protested that Rosario was confusing prophecies regarding Christ.

"Of course," Rosario had said, "*Ch'ucha'* is not *the Child. Christos* is *the Child.* But throughout the history of His Kingdom, God has brought forth His anointed ones who do battle against the Dragon. It is her destiny to battle the Dragon and his beasts at the fulfillment of Time."

But such mystical explanations were not sufficient for Father Suarez. Contrary to Rosario's wishes, he made several inquires. He had learned that his friend, Francisco Serrano, and his female companion, Gabriela Garcia, had been wanted for the abduction of a child. This was no ordinary child, either. She was the daughter of Maria O'Conner. Even in the depths of the Lacandon, the Mayans had heard of Chimæra and Maria's struggle against it. If the Church were to declare Maria a saint, the Mayan people might make a little statue of her and dress her in a special *huipil* on her feast day. However, Chimæra was not something that interested the Mayans that much. It was all white-man foolishness to them.

When Father Suarez shared his discovery with Rosario he was surprised by the rebuke he received from her.

"So, what have you learned from your inquiries? That she is special? We knew that!"

"But now we know who her mother was and this might help to explain why she is so different. *Ch'ucha'* might have been exposed to Chimæric stem-cells while her mother was carrying her."

"Perhaps," replied Rosario. "But it is more important to know that she is what she is because God has willed it so. He will reveal the meaning of this to her in His own time. You must not speak of this to anyone."

"It may help the Russian woman remember," argued Father Suarez.

"She is beginning to remember already. Just the other day, she remembered that her name is Ludmelia. God is working with her too. Trust Him. He will reveal His plan in His own time."

*　　*　　*

"Watch carefully how Ludmelia is throwing the ball to *Ch'ucha'*," said Mateas.

Santiago watched as Ludmelia pitched the ball. It was too high! She would never be able to catch it. The ball was about to sail over her head, when at the last moment it curved downward into her hand.

"How did she do that?" asked Santiago. "She could be a pitcher for the New York Giants!"

"San Francisco Giants," corrected Mateas.

"Oh," replied Santiago shrugging, "I have never seen a curve ball like that!"

"I do not think she is doing it," replied Mateas. "I think that

Ch'ucha' is causing the ball to change its path."

Santiago watched again. This time, Ludmelia pitched the ball to the left of *Ch'ucha'*. At the last moment the ball curved into *Ch'ucha's* waiting right hand. Santiago's jaw dropped.

"How?" Santiago stammered.

"I'll be damned if I know," exclaimed Mateas. "But she is special. It sure makes sense now why those bastards, whoever they were, wanted her."

Santiago nodded. "They seemed to have taken the bait, haven't they?"

"Perhaps. There has not been a Federales incursion since they arrived. Rosario and Ludmelia still insist that we must remain vigilant."

"Ah yes, Ludmelia. So that is her name?"

"Yes," replied Mateas. "She remembered her name just a few days ago. She still does not remember very much, but my mother seems to think she will as the need arises, particularly in preparing *the Child*, whatever that means."

"She is very protective of *Ch'ucha'*, like a little mother. Perhaps your attention was not wholly on little *Ch'ucha*?" inquired Santiago, smiling.

"My mother says that she is not the mother of the child, remember?" replied Mateas, trying to avoid the intent of Santiago's question.

"All right, then, her godmother, guardian, or whatever you wish to call her."

"Her name is Ludmelia. She doesn't remember her family name. At least not yet," continued Mateas.

"You know what I mean," said Santiago. "I have seen how you have looked at her."

"Ha! And you haven't?! What man in this village hasn't looked at her! I bet Father Suarez says an Act of Contrition every time she walks by!"

"Okay, my friend," said Santiago, smiling and draping his arm around Mateas' shoulder, "I did not mean to make you angry."

Mateas laughed. "No, you are right, Santiago. All these years I have been fighting the Federales I have not thought about women.

Now this one drops into the middle of the Lacandon like a warrior angel, and I cannot think of anything else. I am a fool!"

"You are being too hard on yourself. Have you told her?"

"No!" said Mateas, in shock, as though such an idea was an impossibility.

"It is just as well that she wears the uniform of a Zapatista."

"What do you mean?" asked Mateas who now looked at his friend suspiciously.

"Well, can you imagine her wearing a soft sheer blouse . . . perhaps it is not laced all the way . . ."

"Stop it!" said Mateas as he pushed Santiago away. Santiago laughed gleefully.

"Enough of your jibes! There, see what you've done. They spotted us." Mateas pounded his finger on Santiago's chest as he continued to laugh. "Now, silence! Here they come."

"So," said Nizhniya. "Are you spying on us?"

"No, not at all," answered Santiago. He was surprised at how quickly Nizhniya had picked up Spanish. "Mateas was just telling me how much he was admiring your . . ."

Mateas gave Santiago a gentle nudge to the ribs.

". . . ability to throw a ball."

"Yes, I am sure he was," replied Nizhniya with a frown. "Perhaps your time could be better spent implementing the new security protocols I suggested to you the other day."

"New security protocols, huh?" said Santiago to Mateas. "She not only dresses like a Zapatista," he said, whispering in his ear, "she thinks like one too."

"Everything has been quiet. Mission de las Casas is no less secure now than it was several months ago," replied Mateas.

"Let me remind you, Colonel Valdez, that several months ago a Federales helicopter penetrated your airspace . . . ."

"We brought it down," replied Mateas.

"Only because I slowed them down enough to where you finally had time to respond. And I might add that if they return they will do so with more than a single helicopter."

"Your new protocols call for equipment that we either do not have, cannot afford, or have no way of procuring. That is not to say that I do not like your ideas. They are much better than what I usually get around here," Mateas said, nodding towards Santiago.

"*Muchas gracias*," said Santiago sarcastically.

"*De nada*," Mateas replied. Then turning to Nizhniya he continued, "But you are right. We must remain alert. Before, there was no reason for the Federales to focus on this area. That may be different now. We should prepare for another incursion should they eventually see through our ruse."

The company began to walk towards the Mission. *Ch'ucha'* held Nizhniya's hand and was skipping beside her. From time to time she would glance over her right shoulder, smile and laugh. Santiago wondered what little *Ch'ucha'* saw that no one else could.

Nizhniya, on the other hand, drank in the sights and smells of the Lacandon. She thought that she had never experienced such serenity, or if she had, it must have been long ago. She watched as smoke rose above the tree line as women were preparing the evening meal for their families. The smell of *ocote*, the kindling used to start the cooking fires, was thick, and encompassed the area with the aroma of domestic tranquility. She and *Ch'ucha'* would have dinner with Rosario and Mateas this evening.

Nizhniya was aware of Mateas' interest in her. She liked Mateas. She thought him handsome and intelligent, a man who had dedicated his life to his people. She admired that. But he was like a big brother. She suspected though that Mateas was not interested in being her brother. She thought that perhaps she should spend less time with him and Rosario. That would be difficult. She knew, although she did not understand why she knew, that she must work with him to protect *Ch'ucha'*. Besides, *Ch'ucha'* loved spending time with Rosario who had become, her godmother, her Rina. Rosario had become a mother to Nizhniya as well, helping her to adjust to her new life in Chiapas. It was also with Rosario's help that Nizhniya was beginning to remember fragments of her past.

Nizhniya feared the memories that still hid in her amnesia. She entry**

intuitively knew that as these memories came to light her peace would be shattered; that with these memories came pain and anger. She was not angry now and knew that she was experiencing a respite, which she had not known for many years.

As the group walked past the Mission, Santiago made the Sign of the Cross out of respect for the Blessed Sacrament held in reserve in the Tabernacle. Nizhniya instinctively did likewise seeing her companion do so. Father Suarez, who was trimming some bushes outside the Mission, greeted them.

"How is everyone this evening?"

"Fine, Father," replied Santiago. "And you?"

"Well, if I could keep these darned caterpillars from eating my geraniums I'd be happier. Ah, by the way," Father Suarez said now turning his attention to Nizhniya, "you are definitely Orthodox."

"What?" replied Nizhniya.

"Orthodox, Russian Orthodox I would think," answered Father Suarez. "We all suspected that you were, but I don't know why I never noticed before. Perhaps because you did it the same time as Santiago."

"Did what?" asked Nizhniya perplexed.

"Made the Sign of the Cross. The Orthodox do it differently than we do in the West. They go to their right shoulder first, then to their left. We do it the other way. You did it the Orthodox way."

Nizhniya thought for a moment. She closed her eyes. A montage of images began to emerge from the depths of her consciousness. She saw a little blonde-haired girl kneeling before an icon of the Blessed Theotokos, a Byzantine Cross atop an onion-shaped domed church, silhouetted against a darkening sky, a large gentle man with a full beard. He was a priest, and he wore a large silver crucifix. He reached his arms out to her. She felt drawn to him and the restoration of memory that he held within his arms. Then she saw the same cross, his cross. It leaped out at her as it fell from underneath a man's shirt. She shuddered and cried out, "*Sukin syn!*" as she pulled her consciousness away from the frightening memory.

"Are you all right?" asked Mateas as he kept her from falling. She covered her face with her hands as if trying to block the images that flooded her mind.

"I'm not sure," she finally said. "A memory. I think. I'm not sure."

"Would you like to sit for a while?" Father Suarez asked.

"No. No. I'll be fine. I just feel a little dizzy."

"Come, let me take you to my mother's. She will help. At least she will try to fatten you up," said Mateas, attempting to cheer her up.

Nizhniya forced a smile and nodded.

Santiago slapped Mateas on the back and bid him a good evening. "We'll see you later, Father."

Father Suarez bent down and kissed *Ch'ucha'* on the forehead.

"Adios, Padre," said *Ch'ucha'*. *"Dobriy vecher!"*

Father Suarez looked questioningly at Nizhniya.

"Good evening . . . in Russian," she replied.

Abomination

*The children of sinners are abominable children, and they frequent
the haunts of the ungodly.*

~Sirach 41:5

"Here, let me help you with that!"

Colin turned away from the mirror and threw down
his arms in disgust. "I never could tie one of these damn things," he
replied. "But then again, I have never had much opportunity to wear
one."

"Well, all that has changed now," said Cynthia. "Tuxedoes and
formal attire are requisite to navigate in these circles."

Colin nodded, but wasn't sure if he was as comfortable with these
"circles" as he once thought he would be.

"Don't move," instructed Cynthia as she adjusted the knot in Colin's
bow tie. "So I finally get to meet the remarkable Hans Obermann. So,
what do I call him, the Enlightened One?"

"I think 'Mr. Obermann' will do fine," replied Colin, acknowledging
Cynthia's sarcasm.

"Perfect!" said Cynthia, standing back and examining her handiwork. "And you're not so bad yourself."

Colin reached over, pulled Cynthia to him and gave her a kiss. "Not so," he said as he reached behind her and grabbed her buttocks, "I'm really quite bad."

"No time for that," she said, pushing Colin away. "We have to get Diego ready too. It's really very generous of Obermann to let you bring Diego along."

Cynthia walked over to the sofa where Diego was sprawled out watching cartoons. She took one of his shoes, opened it up wide, and placed it on his foot. "You know, I really don't like these Velcro straps on shoes. How is he going to learn to tie shoe laces with these things?"

"Ah, huh," replied Colin. "Obermann made it a point to invite Diego. He thought that he and Frederick would have fun together."

"I thought Obermann's son was only a few months old. How does he expect Diego to be a playmate to a baby?" asked Cynthia as she completed putting the other shoe on Diego.

"Frederick is pure Chimæric so his rate of development has been nothing less than astounding," replied Colin. "Try not to act too surprised when you see him."

"He's not weird looking or something, is he?" she whispered to Colin.

He shook his head. Colin removed Diego's coat from the hall closet, bent down, and helped Diego on with it.

"Will Mr. Pirate be there?" asked Diego.

Colin was surprised that Diego had even remembered Alexi Zokoroff. "No, son. I'm afraid you will not be seeing Mr. Pirate again."

"Oh," replied Diego. "Is he dead like mommy?"

"Yes, son. He is."

"Then I will say a prayer for him too," Diego said.

"I don't think that will help him much," said Colin. "Do you, Cynthia?"

It was clear to Cynthia that Maria had deeply embedded her faith in Diego. Colin had been trying to enlist her assistance uprooting this faith. At first she had agreed because she believed that Maria was a religious fanatic and that Diego needed to be "deprogrammed." Nevertheless, in the brief time she had spent with Diego, she had observed nothing but genuine sweetness and innocence. She knew that this must have come from his mother, but she didn't understand how; it was inconsistent with what she had heard about Maria. In any event, she was reluctant to interfere with what her predecessor had instilled in Diego.

"Actually, I don't agree," she said, placing her hand under Diego's chin and turning his head so that he looked up at her. "I think you should just keep on praying," she continued, smiling at him. "Maybe He'll answer your prayers. I think God might be pretty well fed up with the rest of us."

As they drove through the imposing gates of the Obermann Estate, they could see the large two-story mansion some fifty yards from the entrance.

"Some place!" said Cynthia.

"Yeah. Wait 'til you see the inside!"

"Elegant, I would imagine," replied Cynthia.

"Well . . . you'll see," answered Colin.

Cynthia wondered what Colin meant by that last remark, but she decided not to pursue it now. They were almost at the house, and she wanted to ask him another question. "So, do you think there might be a chance for me to speak with him? All this talk about his having the 'perception of angels'—I'd like to check it out for myself. Journalistic curiosity, you know," she said as she pulled out a small notebook that she always kept with her to jot down notes and thoughts.

"Why don't you ask him yourself?"

"Maybe I will," replied Cynthia.

Colin stopped the car near the entrance where an attendant stood waiting. The attendant opened Cynthia's door and helped her out.

"Good evening Ms. James," he said.

"Thanks," she replied.

Colin stepped out of the car and helped Diego out of his car seat. The attendant then drove the car away and parked it in the garage. As they walked up the stairs to the entrance of the house, they were again greeted by house staff who opened the door for them. Cynthia was unprepared for what awaited her as she entered the house. She had expected simple elegance in keeping with Obermann's Teutonic heritage. What she experienced was an assault on the senses. The spacious entry was cluttered with paintings. Many were masterpieces that she recognized. But they were not displayed so as to draw one's focused attention and elicit a sense of appreciation for the artists' brilliance. Instead, they were all crammed haphazardly together. Cynthia couldn't keep her eyes from jumping from one painting to another. It was the visual equivalent of a smorgasbord. Why would he do such a thing? she wondered. Surely a man of his reported brilliance had more taste than this! As they followed the servant down a long hallway, she peered into other rooms that seemed equally cluttered by artifacts, many of great value. In every case, no object, modern masterpiece or priceless antiquity, was displayed in such a way as to make one appreciate it. Everything appeared to be strewn about so as to keep the senses busy rather than to produce the attitude of quiet reflection necessary to apprehend beauty. Finally, they were led into an intimate room. Hundreds of books lined the wall. The room was dimly lit by the glow of embers in the fireplace and several lamps whose mica shades emanated an amber glow. A man and a woman sat close together on a burgundy leather sofa. She recognized the woman as the Reverend Muriel Hampton.

Cynthia felt herself relax. At least this room was not a visual cacophony. Her attention was drawn to a brass, cylindrical vessel which stood on a tall wooden stand. The domed-top of the cylinder was adorned with a cross. The door of the cylinder was ornately decorated with a chalice from which rays emanated; angels bowed in reverence. At the base of the door was a keyhole, but the key was not in it. Cynthia recognized Hans Obermann. He casually stood next to it with his right elbow resting on top of its dome. Obermann's posture seemed irreverent to Cynthia. She was not religious; even so, it was obvious that this vessel had been an object of veneration to some group of Christians in the past. One need not be a believer to show respect towards objects that are held in honor by those who do believe. The entire house seemed to suggest an arrogant contempt towards humanity's attempts to capture the transcendent.

Cynthia was uneasily drawn to the vessel. She had an almost uncontrollable desire to open it, to see what was inside it, to rescue what was inside it from . . .

"Mr. Colin O'Conner, Ms. Cynthia James, and Master Diego," announced the servant.

Obermann, a handsome man who appeared to be in his early forties, moved away from the vessel and towards the party of three that had just entered the room. He walked deliberately towards Ms. James with his hand extended. Cynthia was struck by the man's gentle yet, confident demeanor. She reached out and grabbed his hand.

"I am delighted to meet you," said Hans Obermann.

"It's an honor to meet you, sir," replied Cynthia.

"Please, call me Hans. Besides, I feel as if we already know each other. Watching you on television every morning makes me feel like you're almost part of the family."

Cynthia had heard people say that before. When Obermann said it, however, she felt as though he were watching her entire life displayed on a TV screen; it was as if her privacy had been invaded by a voyeur peering through the window blinds. She wondered if she was experiencing Obermann's now legendary "perception of angels." If so, she didn't like it.

Obermann turned his attention to Diego. He reached out and shook Diego's hand. "Freddie will be delighted to see you. He has been looking forward to this evening. I believe he wanted you to see his new pets."

"Pets?!" said Diego excitedly.

"Yes, hamsters. Soft and cuddly," replied Obermann. Then turning to the servant he said, "Why don't you take Master Diego to Frederick's room so they can play. I believe that the chef has prepared pizza for them. They will dine in the Entertainment Room." Diego took the servant's hand, smiled and waved to his daddy, and left the room.

"Introductions all around," ordered Obermann pleasantly.

A middle-aged man stood up from the sofa with some effort. He wore a brown tweed sport coat with leather elbow patches. His collar indicated that he was a cleric and around his neck hung a silver medallion with a tree and a cross on it.

"Bishop Worthington," he said, bowing slightly.

"Nice to meet you, Bishop," replied Cynthia.

Colin smiled. He had met the Bishop and his companion on several occasions. Cynthia and Colin moved over to the woman who remained seated.

"And of course, Dr. Muriel Hampton. I interviewed you several months ago. It's a pleasure to see you again," said Cynthia.

"The pleasure is mine," Hampton responded. "I must tell you it is rare to meet someone in your industry who grasps the significance of the New Era as well as you have."

"And that is why I insisted that Colin bring you along," interrupted Obermann.

At that moment another servant entered the room and announced that dinner was served. The company began to leave the library when to her own surprise Cynthia asked, "The ah . . . brass cylindrical religious object that you were leaning against when we entered . . ."

"The tabernacle," replied Obermann. "A gift from our good bishop here. It was no longer needed in one of the churches that had been recently renovated to Tree of Life specifications. Worthington salvaged it and thought I'd like to have it."

"What's in it?" pressed Cynthia.

Colin frowned. He felt that it was inappropriate for her to be so inquisitive.

Obermann stopped. He walked back to the tabernacle and put his arm around it and smiled.

"You have a journalist's intuition," said Obermann. "You sense that something important is inside. Something that may give you insight into the man who owns it."

A shiver went down Cynthia's spine. She tried not to tremble. She gripped Colin's hand firmly.

"You are right, Ms. James. There is something inside the tabernacle.

But it is not important in itself. It is only important because it gives me pleasure. But, I cannot show you. At least not yet."

Cynthia felt disappointment and relief. She began to feel that something ominous and terrible resided within it and that Obermann had grossly desecrated the artisan's intent for the tabernacle.

Obermann walked away from the tabernacle and stepped between Cynthia and Colin placing his arms around both of their shoulders in an uneasy familiarity. "You see," he continued, directing his response towards Cynthia, "it would be like explaining sex to Diego. He would not understand it; he would think it crude and grotesque. But when he's older and his little testes flood his mind and body with hormones, and he is driven with incomprehensible desire, then he will understand. Then he will see the beauty of penetrating the dark secret that lies within."

Cynthia was shocked at Obermann's comment. She perceived his lustful thoughts, and even felt it from his hand on her shoulder. She pulled away slightly. Obermann smiled and released his grip on her. He walked over to Worthington and Hampton, grabbed them in a similar fashion and directed everyone towards the dining room. Cynthia looked over at Colin. He seemed oblivious to what had just transpired between her and Obermann. She leaned over and whispered into Colin's ear.

"I don't like him."

"Ssh, you will," whispered Colin.

The dining room was tastefully, even sparingly, decorated in stark contrast to the rest of the house. Little place cards indicated where each of the guests would sit. Cynthia found herself next to Colin and uncomfortably close to Obermann. They were all seated around a medium-sized table that made for easy and intimate conversation.

"Perhaps, Reverend," said Obermann to Hampton, "you could lead us in a blessing."

Cynthia looked over at Colin. She was not a religious person. Situations like this made her uncomfortable; she never quite knew what she was supposed to do. Colin just smiled as if to say, "Just ad-lib."

"I would be delighted," Hampton replied. She raised her hands palms up to the heavens in a posture of invocation. "We look inside ourselves and each other for the strength and sustenance we need this day and everyday. We bless the food that is served us in this meal of communion, that it gestate, the eternal seed of the Tree of Life within us so that we may bring forth fruit of personal and societal actualization. Amen."

Cynthia uncomfortably added her "amen" to the chorus of "amens" that followed Hampton's prayer. Worthington gushed like a foolish schoolboy over the profundity of the Reverend's remarks. They gave each other a modest kiss on the lips. Cynthia inadvertently raised an eyebrow in surprise. How preposterous they appeared, she thought.

"I would like to propose a toast," offered Worthington. "I would like to offer my congratulations to you," he lifted his glass towards Obermann, "and to your staff on the successful opening of the first Chimæra Distribution Center."

Everyone lifted and clicked their glasses.

"Yes, congratulations!" offered Hampton. "And, the Day of Amnesty and Reconciliation, in honor of its opening, brilliantly demonstrated the magnanimousness of the New Era."

"Thank you!" said Obermann modestly.

Cynthia placed her glass very deliberately on the table and said nothing. She had overheard a phone conversation that Colin had had with Obermann. From what she had gathered, they were concerned that Madison Ryan would have her second-degree murder charge overturned on appeal. Rather than risk the weakening the Office of Justice and Tolerance that might result from losing the case, Obermann had devised a plan to release Ryan under the pretext of mercy, hence the Day of Amnesty and Reconciliation. There had been nothing magnanimous about Ryan's release at all.

Several courses were served amid polite conversation. But Cynthia knew that there must be more to this dinner party than just an opportunity to spend an evening together and to congratulate one another. She did not have long to wait before Obermann made its purpose clear.

"As you know," began Obermann, "many people, including yourselves, have all been working diligently to establish Chimæra and the New Era. I especially wanted to take the opportunity this evening to thank Bishop Worthington and Reverend Hampton for their tireless efforts to spread Tree of Life fellowships. Working closely with Colin and the Office of Justice and Tolerance, we have seen numerous congregations free themselves from the tyranny of hierarchical systems and establish authentic self-actualizing Tree of Life associations."

Oh brother, thought Cynthia, does he really believe this stuff?

Obermann continued, "But we must not rest on our laurels. Old habits are hard to break and those in power are not easily convinced of the necessity of letting their people go. They are constantly trying to thwart our efforts to liberate congregations from oppression and bring them into the freedom of the New Era. That was evident during our recent Grand Opening ceremony for the first Chimæra Distribution Center in Washington, D.C. several months ago. I think we were all surprised and disappointed by the number of protesters present. Clearly we must double our efforts. We must be committed, no matter what the cost, to establishing freedom and self-actualization for every person."

Cynthia watched as the clerics nodded their heads sympathetically. Colin listened attentively to Obermann as a lieutenant might a commanding officer. Cynthia was by nature a skeptic. Her encounter with Obermann in the library made it even more unlikely that she would embrace the New Era readily. Obermann had detected this during his brief glance into her soul.

"The unification of the Roman Catholic Church and the Orthodox Churches of the East were at first thought to be a setback for the New Era. But, we believe that this will ultimately unravel, as they have allied themselves with a totalitarian regime. The beast they are trying to ride will turn around and devour them."

"Like Babylon, the harlot who has fornicated with the kings of the earth," interrupted Worthington excitedly.

"Yes, exactly," replied Obermann. "And we need to use these scriptures to our advantage to help lead captives out of these oppressive paradigms."

"Depart from her, my people, so as not to take part in her sins and receive a share in her plagues,[24]" said Hampton, quoting Revelation.

"There are many levels at which this must be fought. Recently, we were successful in dismantling an alliance between Russia and the oil rich Muslim country of Arabia, which is now committed to the New Era. We anticipate that the other Islamic members of OPEC will follow King Saïd's lead. Then Russia will be economically isolated; collapse will be inevitable. But this will take time, and there are still many in the West, and particularly here in the United States, who are misguided and sympathetic to the Church and its attempt to establish a new empire. We must do everything in our power to defeat this new Evil Empire."

"Fallen, fallen is Babylon the great that made all the nations drink the wine of her licentious passion,"[25] said Worthington as if he were a prophet.

Cynthia was surprised by the vitriolic rhetoric. She had not taken Obermann and these Tree of Life people all that seriously. She had thought that they were just offering a spruced-up version of an eighties New Age self-enlightenment regimen—kind of an 'I'm Okay You're Okay' with biotechnology. But this was much more serious than that. It was evident that you were not 'okay' if you did not agree with them.

"In this regard," Obermann continued, "we must not underestimate the inestimable harm that Maria O'Conner has done to our cause."

Colin looked down at the mention of his deceased wife. Obermann placed his hand on Colin's shoulder. "I just want everyone to know that Colin did everything he could to rescue her from her self-deception." Obermann nodded to a servant, who left the dining room. "Now we must do everything we can to make sure her deception does not spread like a virus." The servant returned with a tray on which lay five books. He proceeded to place one in front of each member of the dinner party.

"Our contacts in the Vatican intercepted a first draft of Maria O'Conner's Journal and Biography. Miss Ryan has been a busy bee since she was released from prison. It would seem that she did not learn her lesson. I have made copies of the manuscripts for each of you. I want you to read the Journal and be prepared to respond to it. I believe that once the public sees it for what it really is, a thinly veiled piece of hate literature, then we will be able to take appropriate legal action."

"Hate literature?" inquired Colin. Colin knew of the Journal. Parts of it had even been released in the *Washington Enquirer* prior to Madison Ryan's "conversion." Colin knew that his wife was deceived, perhaps even mentally ill. But hate literature? Maria was passionate. But hate? She wasn't capable of it!

"I have flagged and highlighted for you those sections in her Journal that I believe are the most offensive. You might thumb through those sections now. I know you will agree with me."

"Listen to this," said Hampton, *'How many children have been placed on the altar of Choice so that the Self can say, 'I am the god of my own body and destiny; I will have no gods before me.'* That's outrageous to associate abortion rights with human sacrifice! The Courts have already ruled that intolerant speech against a woman's right to choose is not constitutionally protected! But it gets worse . . . *'But we shall hew them down as Samuel did to Agag . . . .*

"That sounds like the rhetoric of the Congregation of Saint Pierre," said Worthington.

"Exactly," said Obermann. "We all suspected that she was sympathetic to their cause and this suggests that she was part of a larger conspiracy that included Cardinal McIntyre, as Colin demonstrated in court."

"But there was no evidence that Maria was in any way a part of your assassination," replied Colin. "Furthermore, that doesn't sound like Maria at all."

Cynthia saw Obermann's eyes narrow, nostrils flare, and chin twitch. She was afraid of what Obermann might do. The "Enlightened One" did not seem all that benevolent to her. He looked over at her and saw her studying him intensely. He took a deep breath, relaxed, and then smiled.

"Well, sometimes we think we know someone, even someone we are close to," said Obermann in a relaxed tone. "But do we really know them? Can we really trust them? Should we not be prepared to take action against those who might turn against us?" Cynthia trembled imperceptibly as he seemingly directed this last comment to her. "Come, Colin. Let's go into the library. We can talk and have a smoke and give our *friends* an opportunity to look over the Journal."

"But I don't smoke . . . ."

"Well, you should," said Obermann. "Did you know Dr. Richardson has shown that smoking has no deleterious effects on Chimærics? Just another sensual pleasure that we no longer have to feel guilty about enjoying."

"In that case, I'd like to join you!" said Worthington.

"No!" said Obermann firmly. Then catching himself he said more gently. "Perhaps a little later. I'm saving a Cuban especially for you Bishop."

"Excellent," said Worthington. "I've never had a Cuban," he said to Hampton with almost childlike glee.

Cynthia watched as Colin and Obermann left the dining room. She looked down at the Journal and opened it up to the first entry. *So what awaits us at the journey's end? Our Beloved; for in baptism we were betrothed to Him.* She remembered seeing pictures of her own baptism when she was an infant. She had been baptized a Lutheran, but had rarely gone to church as a child; never again after she moved away from home. "Betrothed to God," she thought. "How come no one ever told me that?" She felt an inexplicable excitement. She wanted to read more.

"Have a seat," said Obermann pointing to one of the burgundy leather chairs next to the fire. Colin sat in the chair feeling like a child about to be lectured by his father. Obermann took a wooden box off the mantelpiece, opened it, and held it in front of Colin. "Imperials, have one."

"But I don't smoke," repeated Colin.

Obermann placed the box back on the mantelpiece and removed two cigars. He reached into his jacket pocket, removed a small scissor-like device and snipped off the ends of the cigars. He handed Colin one of the cigars.

"That's a hundred dollar cigar there, don't waste it." Obermann then proceeded to take a taper and put it into the fireplace. He removed the flaming wick and lit his cigar. He handed the taper to Colin. "Draw the flame into the cigar." Colin obediently complied. He immediately started coughing. "Don't inhale," Obermann laughed shaking his head. "Draw the aromatic smoke into your mouth. Taste it. Suckle it." Colin watched as Obermann closed his eyes and sucked deeply on the cigar. He appeared rapt by an almost erotic ecstasy. Obermann opened his eyes and looked down on Colin.

"Let me make something clear for you," began Obermann. "I thought you already understood. Humanity is sick, so sick it no longer even knows that it's sick. And what is the cause of this sickness? Hate and intolerance. It is built into our very genome; natural selection has accentuated the ruthless selfishness in each one of us. It will take strong medicine to heal humanity—a powerful genome-changing, mind-changing medicine that will not tolerate intolerance and hate. People like Hampton and Worthington are sugar coating; they make the medicine a little more palatable. But it's people like you and me that have to do the hard work of administering the medicine, particularly to people who don't know what's best for them. People like your wife. I underestimated her once. I won't make that mistake again, even though she is dead! That is why I will not take this business of your wife's Journal lightly."

"I know she didn't write some of that stuff. I never knew her to hate anyone," Colin interrupted.

Obermann stared at Colin for a moment. He then nodded. "You're right. We took a little editorial license with the manuscript. But you are also wrong. She did hate. She hated me, and everything that Chimæra and the New Era stands for. But the average reader doesn't have the intelligence to recognize the hate that is apparent to me in the Journal. So we have had to make it more obvious. The Journal that will appear shortly on the bookshelves will be a great surprise to Madison Ryan, its editor, and Cardinal McIntyre who lent his name for the *Imprimatur*."

"Surely you don't think you'll be able to get away with this?" inquired Colin incredulously.

"Of course we will," replied Obermann confidently.

"They'll deny that it's authentic. They'll say it's been tampered with."

"It doesn't matter what they say. The Office of Justice and Tolerance, under *your* direction, now has all the evidence it needs to prosecute, and then convict, anyone and everyone associated with the Journal of being guilty of hate speech, especially Miss Ryan."

"That's still not going to sit well with the American people. Most people still believe in the freedom of expression," said Colin. "I don't think it would be wise to go for anything more than a misdemeanor offense."

"That's fine. The objective here is to intimidate and get people to recognize Maria for what she really was—a hater."

No, she wasn't, thought Colin.

"Stop it!" demanded Obermann. "She's dead goddamn it! But she haunts your memories and divides your loyalties. I see her in your mind languishing in that Gethsemane of self-recrimination. Kiss her on the cheek. Yes. That's right. Good. Now . . . turn those memories of her over to me. Excellent. They are mine now. See, that wasn't so hard. Now you are free to serve the New Era."

Colin sat trembling in his seat. Obermann bent over and picked up the cigar that Colin had dropped on the floor. He placed it in an ashtray. He walked over to the bar and poured two glasses of brandy. He handed one of them to Colin. "Drink!"

Colin took the glass in both hands and sipped the amber liquid. It burned his throat. He looked up at Obermann. He had crossed the Rubicon; burnt the bridge in his mind that might have led to restoration. His loyalty belonged now wholly to Obermann, and he hated him for it.

Cynthia had completed several entries of the Journal. She heard Worthington and Hampton's exasperated comments about the Journal; she ignored them. She found many of the entries simple and commonplace as one might expect from someone who saw their primary responsibility as a homemaker. There were other entries that were inspired and challenging. Then there were entries that seemed incongruous; inconsistent with the rest of the text. She did not know what to make of these. As she quietly read to herself, sipping a glass of wine, the door opened and a servant entered holding Diego's hand. He was whimpering. When Diego saw Cynthia he ran over to her. She held her arms out to him and embraced him. "I'm scared," he whispered. She looked at him closely and could see that he was terrified.

"Excuse me," Cynthia said to the servant. "Is there a bathroom I could use so that I can wash Diego's face?"

"Yes," said the servant. He took them to the nearest bathroom. Cynthia closed the door behind them, turned on the water, not just so that she could wash Diego's dried tears, but because she instinctively felt that there might be someone listening. The running water would make it more difficult for them to be overheard.

"What scared you, honey?"

"Frederick. He's mean."

"Why do you say that?"

"We were playing with his pet hamsters. He was showing me how they can run in a wheel that turns and turns." Diego stopped and began sucking air as if he were about to cry again.

"Well that sounds fun, not scary."

"He said, 'Watch how I can make him run faster.' Then he looked at the hamster funny and then he ran faster and faster and faster. He was hurting the hamster. I could tell. Blood was coming out of the hamster's mouth. I told him to stop, but he wouldn't. Finally it stopped. It fell over, and it didn't move any more."

Just then the door opened up behind them. They both jumped with a start. It was Frederick. Cynthia held onto Diego tightly. She was terrified but tried to remain calm. The child was beautiful with blond hair, blue eyes. He appeared to be just a little younger than Diego. This fact was enough to unnerve her, but having just listened to Diego's story she shook with fear. She felt powerless before the toddler. She wanted to pick Diego up and run out of the bathroom, and run out of the house, but he stood in her way. Frederick drew his right hand from behind his back and held out a hamster.

"You see, Diego; Fluffy's okay. Go ahead. Pet him."

Cynthia and Diego stared at the hamster that fidgeted in Frederick's hand. Diego tentatively reached his hand out to touch the hamster. Just as he was about to touch the hamster, it turned its head, bared its little, but razor-sharp incisors and hissed at him. Diego pulled his hand away while Cynthia pulled him back into her protective embrace.

"You will come back and play with me again, won't you, Diego?"

Diego buried himself into Cynthia's arms and said nothing. Finally, Cynthia found the courage to speak. "I'm sorry. Diego's tired. It's well past his bedtime. We should be going. I'm sure it must be bedtime for you too." Cynthia picked up Diego and began to move towards the door to leave the bathroom. Frederick didn't move.

"I don't sleep," he said, and then he turned and ran away.

Cynthia and Diego returned to the dining room. Obermann and Colin had rejoined the dinner party. Obermann was standing and talking to Worthington and Hampton.

"We expect that they will be releasing the Journal in a few weeks. When it comes out, I would like you to speak out forcefully against it. Complaints will be filed with the Office of Justice and Tolerance, and then Colin can initiate legal action."

"Excuse me," Cynthia interrupted; she was holding Diego by the hand. "Diego needs to go to bed. I think we should leave now."

Colin turned to Obermann with an expression that seemed to be asking permission to leave.

"As you can see, we have plenty of room here. He could spend the night," replied Obermann.

Diego pulled Cynthia's hand and began to whimper. "No!" she said. Obermann looked at her curiously, apparently wondering why she seemed to be so vigorously opposed to the offer. "No," she repeated more calmly. "I promised Diego that I would . . . take him to work with me tomorrow."

"I don't remember that," said Colin.

"Oh, I thought I told you," answered Cynthia.

Then she could hear Obermann speaking words that no one else could hear—words spoken directly into her consciousness.

Diego is like a son to you; a son that you could have had, a son that you cannot have now. I can heal the mistake made years ago. I can make all things new again. All you need to do is yield to me and let go of the pain.

Cynthia stood mesmerized. He knew her secret—a secret that no one else would condemn her for. But intuitively she knew differently. She had always known different. The fact that what she did was "legal" made her choice no less anguishing, nor the malpractice that occurred during that choice no less debilitating. She felt herself sinking again in to that dark quicksand of guilt and despair. She could see in her mind Obermann's salvific arm reaching out to save her. She began to reach out to grasp it.

"Mommy," said Diego, tugging on her arm. Cynthia looked down at him. He had never called her mommy before.

"Mommy, I want to go home!" Diego implored.

"Yes," Cynthia said. "Let's go home."

As Obermann bid them a good night he felt like a predator whose prey had just slipped out of his grasp. If it hadn't been for that infernal whining! he thought. There is too much of that *woman* in the child!

PART II

Times

Then God said: "Let us make man in our image, after our likeness.
~ Genesis 1:26

The ultimate reality and mystery of man is that he is made in the image of God. This primordial wellspring is the source and cause of all that is uniquely human. From here springs forth self-evident Rights, the appreciation of Beauty, the pursuit of Truth, the demand for Justice, and the Courage to live a life of Charity. The image is a gift given to all and not acquired either through the natural course of physical development or by human effort. The image is a promise to be realized through our cooperation with His grace until we grow into the measure of the stature of the fulness of Christ.

Yet, there are nay sayers among us. They tell us that beauty is in the eye of the beholder, that truth is relative or at best unknowable, and that justice is utilitarian. They tell us that love is merely an evolutionary vestige selected long ago by nature to give our species a competitive edge and that rights as fundamental as life itself are not inherent, but are granted by the state or by the individual who is free to decide when an unborn child is a person or when the aged or the infirm are worthy of life. Are these not those who have traded the birthright of the divine image for the single meal of an illusionary autonomy?

~Saint Maria Theresa O'Conner (Journal)

Miracles

As to miracles . . . if you change from inhumanity to almsgiving, you have stretched forth the hand that was withered. If you withdraw from theaters and go to the church, you have cured the lame foot. If you draw back your eyes from beauty not your own, you have opened them when they were blind. . . . These are the greatest miracles, these are the wonderful signs.

~St. John Chrysostom, Homily on Matthew Chapter 7 and 32

"I knew this would happen," mumbled Artem Sagalovich under his breath as he shivered in the car. This is even worse than I expected, he thought. Sending me out to this god-forsaken desert of ice! What was I to do? They gave me a few hours to get a helicopter. I'm sure the government can figure out something to do with a million dollars worth of O-rings.

Sagalovich wiped the windshield of his car with his glove to remove the steam that had condensed as a result of his complaining. He wondered when the plane would land so he could pick up the "dignitary" from Moscow, whoever he was. It couldn't be anyone important. No one of significance would be sent on such a perilous mission this far into Siberia in the middle of a blizzard. It's just too damn dangerous, he thought. Damn near whiteout conditions. But, these Siberian pilots were another breed altogether. They'd take off in a blizzard, made no difference to them. "So what if you die," a pilot had said to him as he flew him out the other day to some ridiculously remote icefield, "even hell would be better than this," he said with a chuckle. Sagalovich didn't find any humor in that. He just thought about the warmth of his former post in Guatemala. And the women! In Siberia he couldn't even distinguish the women from the men, not even after they removed the multiple layers of sweaters and jackets!

"I will die here," he sighed. "Maybe I'll die tonight frozen in this car!"

He wondered why he had been sent to Volenyski. It was not much more than a ghost town now. Just a few years ago it had been a bustling metropolis, that is, to the extent that anything could bustle in below zero temperatures. The hope of the Russian oil industry lay in ruins now as evidenced by the dilapidated buildings, roads, and the dwindling numbers of people who remained in the city. It was only a matter of time before the entire city was reclaimed by Siberia's vast frozen wilderness.

He thought he saw lights in the distance. He squinted, attempting to see if it might be the airplane he was waiting for. He could just barely make out the running lights of the plane as it began to descend towards the airport. It was a medium-sized jet, but then the airport was not large enough to handle the larger and safer American-made Boeings, the preferred transport of Moscow bureaucracy. It was obvious that the small plane was struggling against the wind and snow. "What type of fool would fly in these conditions! My God!" Sagalovich exclaimed as the plane came it to view. "It's one of our deathtrap planes!"

The plane touched down and successfully came to a halt. Stairs were rolled up to the cabin door. After a few minutes the door opened. Sagalovich stepped out of the car and was struck by the biting cold, a brutal minus 40° Celsius with the windchill. He cursed himself and the

O-rings. He struggled as he walked towards the plane to meet whoever this fool bureaucrat was that he had to pick up at this god-forsaken time, in this god-forsaken weather, in this god-forsaken country. He saw the pilot of the airplane standing next to the cabin door talking to a rather tall man in a military issue winter jacket. They were laughing. Sagalovich imagined they were celebrating their safe arrival. "As soon as they step off the plane they'll wish they were dead!"

The taller man in the military jacket stepped off the plane and began to descend the stairs. He spotted Sagalovich.

"Sagalovich!" the man shouted, attempting to be heard over the engine noise and the wind.

"*Chort poheri,* [26] the fool knows my name," Sagalovich mumbled under his breath. Anonymity was much safer when working in the government; experience had taught him that lesson on more than one unfortunate occasion.

"Yes," he shouted back. "Who is it that I have the pleasure of welcoming to beautiful Siberia?"

The man gripped the rail of the stairs firmly so that the wind wouldn't knock him over in his descent. He reached the bottom and gave Sagalovich a wide and amicable smile.

"Constantin Goricsan. May I suggest we get in your car before we freeze to death!"

"*Govno,* Shit, the Czar!" muttered Sagalovich too stunned to recognize the impropriety of his greeting. He just stared slack-jawed at Goricsan. For a moment, just this very brief moment, he forgot that he was freezing.

Goricsan grabbed him by the arm and pulled him in the direction of the car.

"Is this your car?" Goricsan shouted. Sagalovich nodded. Then recognizing his lack of decorum he started to move to the passenger side to open the door for Goricsan. Goricsan pushed him back towards the driver's side. "I know how to open a door," said Goricsan. "Just get us somewhere warm!"

Sagalovich started the car, turned on the heater and headed towards the airport exit. "I . . . I . . . had no idea that I was picking up you . . .

a . . . your Czarness!" Oh Christ! I can't believe I just said that, thought Sagalovich.

Goricsan laughed heartily. "Of course you didn't," Goricsan finally responded. "I didn't want you to. I didn't want anyone to know. There are only a handful of people who know where I am. I'll be leaving tomorrow afternoon. I do not want you to discuss my visit here with anyone."

"Of course not! My lips are sealed."

"Like a good O-ring!" said Goricsan with a chuckle. He watched Sagalovich's shoulders slouch and his face drop when he mentioned the O-rings. He patted him on the shoulder. "That's okay. We'll figure out what to do with them. But, I do have some questions about that whole affair in Guatemala that I'd like to ask you, but not tonight. Sometime tomorrow. Anyway, where are you taking me?"

"Well, I guess if you don't want anyone to know that you're here I have no choice but to take you to my apartment."

"That's fine."

"It's a pathetic hole!"

"Is it warm?"

"Not enough!"

"Do you have a sofa and an extra blanket?"

"Yes, but you must have my bed!"

"No, a sofa and a blanket will be fine. I am so tired I could sleep on rocks. Enough though, I must sleep. I did not close my eyes once on that flight here." Goricsan leaned his head back on the seat and said with a yawn, "Only a fool would fly in a storm like that."

Sagalovich said nothing but raised an eyebrow upon hearing Goricsan echo his own assessment of his behavior. But, he knew that Goricsan was no fool. There must be a very good reason for this risky adventure.

Sagalovich set the alarm to go off at five. He figured that would give him plenty of time to shower. He would wake the Czar an hour later; that would give the water heater enough time to yield another shower. The damn thing was a Soviet era piece of crap. The alarm went off and Sagalovich almost immediately turned it off. He didn't want it to wake up Goricsan. He twisted his body out of bed and rubbed his eyes. The light was on in the kitchen. Sagalovich patted the nightstand with his hand until he located his glasses. He put them on and stood up. His joints strained and cracked. He was sure that Siberia had added ten years to his body in just the past few months. He felt like a very old thirty-two. He looked over at the sofa. Goricsan was not there. He must have gotten up already. Sagalovich slowly worked his way to the kitchen while rubbing his lower back. Goricsan was sitting at the table reading from a leather bound book and sipping coffee.

"Good morning," said Goricsan. "I took the liberty of making coffee, help yourself."

"Thank you," Sagalovich replied as he walked over to the cupboard and removed a mug. He poured the anemically brown, non-aromatic fluid from the pot. He felt genuine sorrow at having to drink this beverage that had no right to be called coffee. Just a few months ago he had been drinking rich Guatemalan Antigua grown not more than fifty kilometers from his former residence. He sipped the coffee and grimaced.

"I apologize for the coffee," said Sagalovich.

Goricsan looked down at his cup, "It *is* pretty bad." He took a sip and then swallowed hard. "How long do you think it will take to get to the General's house?"

"An hour, depending on the roads. I'll shower and get dressed so that we can get started."

Goricsan nodded as Sagalovich left the room. He went back to reading from the book of prayers that Father Nikitas had given him. He took another sip of coffee and grimaced. He shook his head in dismay as he considered the plight of the average Russian. His dismay was confirmed upon hearing Sagalovich's muffled howl as icy water sprayed from the shower.

Sagalovich's car bounced and skidded along the icy road that led to the General's house.

"So what was the General's response when you delivered the message?"

"Well, now that I know whose message it was that I was delivering I don't know whether I should tell you," replied Sagalovich.

"It's okay. The General has a notorious reputation for being an irascible old coot."

"That I am sure of. But are you sure . . ."

"Tell me all about it," insisted Goricsan.

"Well then, after a most perilous journey, I arrived at the General's house, if you could call it a house. It is more like a shack. He lives there alone. From what I hear he has very few visitors. Those who try to visit him or check to see if he is even still alive, he chases away. Though I cannot say why anyone would care! It was, therefore, with considerable trepidation that I knocked on his door. The door opened and this wild, disheveled, partially naked man appeared. *'Shtob ty sdokh!'*[27] he said and then slammed the door. I knocked on the door again, and shouted to him that I had an important correspondence from Moscow that I had to deliver to him, he responded, *'Shtob ty sgorel!'*[28] He would not open his door. Finally, I slipped the letter under his door. I waited and listened. I heard him pick up the letter and open it. After a moment he shouted out again, *'Gori ty sinim plamenem!'*[29] The rest I believe you know. I contacted the people who sent me the communication in Moscow and told them that I was not successful in delivering the message."

"And that is why I am here," replied Goricsan who had been struggling not to laugh during Sagalovich's telling of his adventure with the General.

"Would you mind if I ask why such a cantankerous old man is so important that the Czar himself should come all this way to meet with him? And, if I may be so bold, I would like to know how I have been so *fortunate* to have been drawn into such important affairs?"

Goricsan laughed noting the tiniest hint of sarcasm in Sagalovich's question. "I would have thought that you might have figured out why I wanted you in on this."

"I am absolutely without a clue!"

"Huh. Well, I had you deliver the letter to Grigorii Zhirinovskii . . ."

"Grigorii Zhirinovskii?!" exclaimed Sagalovich.

"Yes," replied Goricsan. "The General. You did not know that he was the General?"

"No. I thought he was in prison!"

"He was for a while. He was released a couple of years ago."

"Zhirinovskii ruined my career. I put together a multimillion-dollar deal with the Venezuelan Oil Consortium to help modernize the Russian oil industry. And what did Grigorii Zhirinovskii do? He wasted half of it and the other half he embezzled. After that I couldn't do anything in finance. Things were so bad for me at the Venezuelan embassy I finally requested a transfer to Guatemala. There, I was just a low level staffer. No multimillion-dollar scandals. Just filing papers, running errands . . . warm weather and good coffee! Now, Zhirinovskii has wrecked my life again!"

"Calm down, Artem!" rebuked Goricsan. "Do not blame Zhirinovskii. He is called 'the General' for good reason. He ran the Siberian oil fields like a military campaign. It was under his management that Russian oil production reached over twelve million barrels a day, more than any other country in the world. It was not Zhirinovskii that squandered the money; it was the damn bureaucrats from Moscow who interfered with his operations. And it was not Zhirinovskii who embezzled money; it was Levin and his cronies. They framed the General. Perhaps now you can understand why Zhirinovskii was not so happy to receive my letter. He doesn't want to be taken as a *Papa Carlo*[30] again."

"I see," said Sagalovich repentantly, "I had no idea."

"What's important now is that we get these oil fields up and running again. The General is the man who can do it. And you're going to help."

"I don't know what a paper pusher like me can do," said Sagalovich as they approached the General's house

"I have confidence in you. Besides, you can think of it as your way of helping to pay off a million dollars worth of O-rings!"

Goricsan saw that Sagalovich had been right. The "house" was nothing more than a shack. As the car came to a sliding halt, they saw Zhirinovskii step out of the house. He was dressed only in his underpants and boots. Sagalovich wondered why he didn't freeze on the spot. He picked up three logs from a pile on the side of his house. He started back towards the house scratching his rear. He saw his visitors but chose to ignore them.

Goricsan stepped out of the car. "Grigorii Zhirinovskii, I wish to speak with you!"

The General did not look back but shouted, *"vashu mat!"*[51]

"Mat-peremat!"[52] "Your mother twice over!" retorted Goricsan with a sly grin.

"Mat' vashu tak!"[53] parried the General, with an obscene gesture.

"Mat' vashu rastudy!"[54] riposted Goricsan.

The General stopped, laughed and waved Goricsan and Sagalovich to come in. As they entered they were surprised to find the hovel surprisingly well kept; spartan for sure, but clean, with just the bare essentials for existence. The General threw a log on the fire.

"Why have you two *govnyuks*[35] come to see me?" asked the General.

"Excuse me!" rebuked Sagalovich. "Do you know who this is?"

Goricsan raised his hand to Sagalovich. He did not want to be treated differently. The General moved uncomfortably close to Goricsan's face.

"Huh. Constantin Goricsan," the General said. He then turned away and pushed the log in the fire with a poker in one hand while he scratched his rear with the other. "The Czar of all Russia!" he continued.

Sagalovich looked over at Goricsan expecting him to offer a stiff reprimand for the General's insolence. Goricsan just looked serious as though he were considering what he would do next. After the General was finished with the fire, he sat down in an old dilapidated chair and looked at the two visitors.

"I need your help," said Goricsan.

The General raised his left eyebrow. "It does not surprise me," he replied. "I may live out here in the middle of nowhere, but that does not mean I know nothing. I have my shortwave. I know what is going on in the world." He tapped a small shoebox-sized radio that had a makeshift antenna made of a couple of clothes hangers and aluminum foil. "What I hear doesn't inspire me to want to rejoin the rest of humanity. And what is this nonsense about people living hundreds of years?!"

"It may be true. I have forbidden it here in Russia. The Patriarch has declared it a great evil."

"I would call it a great stupidity. Let them live here and they will wish they were dead yesterday! But that is not what brings you here. You believe that I can help you resurrect the once-great Russian oil industry."

"Yes," replied Goricsan. "If anyone can, it is you."

"Maybe. But why would I want to?"

Goricsan stared at the General for a moment, then said, "Because it is better to die for the motherland than to live like an old woman."

"Ha!" the General laughed so hard that his ponderous belly jostled like gelatin. He looked to Sagalovich like a dissolute Father Christmas. "Sit down. I will listen. But I will not make you promises," said the General.

Goricsan and Sagalovich sat down on two stools across from the General.

"Seven years ago you laid out a plan to modernize Russia's oil industry. If you had been allowed to implement your plans, Russia would be producing more oil than OPEC. We would be an economic world power . . . ."

"These things I know. But, how do I know things will be different now? And besides, there is no longer the money to finance such a project. No one will loan Russia the billions that would be needed for the project. Not even your allies in the Middle East. You see, I hear many things on my radio. Arabia has repudiated the Alliance. The Alliance will crumble unless one of its members is a major oil producer; it must have leverage if it is to have any influence on the world oil market."

"Russia will be that major oil producer. The Alliance will hold. It must hold," replied Goricsan.

"You are asking for a *chudo*.[36] And miracles are expensive."

Goricsan reached into his pocket and removed a checkbook. He tossed it onto the General's lap. The General inspected the logo on the check. It bore the two-headed eagle and a shield. Next to this symbol was the name Empire Oil.

"A modest name," said the General.

Goricsan smiled at the General's sarcasm. "Tomorrow there will be a hundred million in that account. I believe that will be enough to get you started."

"You will trust me with this much money?"

"Notice, there are two lines on the checks. Sagalovich signs the bottom line."

Sagalovich was stunned. Why does the Czar have such confidence in me? he thought. In one sense he was gratified, but then on the other hand, it meant that he would continue to be in this dreadful place considerably longer than he had hoped.

"You know this is just the beginning. We will need much more than this."

"I am working on that. And when you start increasing production and we begin to pay off our creditors I plan to send Sagalovich back to Venezuela to show them that we can be trusted. I hope to attract foreign investors again, provided we can be assured of maintaining our autonomy."

"So now what?" asked the General.

"The Board of Directors of the former Siberian Oil Cooperative, which is now Empire Oil, will be expecting you. Sagalovich will keep me informed. If the Board does not cooperate . . . well, they will be looking for other employment."

"And what are your expectations?" asked the General.

"Double your production in a year," replied Goricsan.

The General shook his head. "No. That I *can* do. You asked for a *chudo,*" he said pointing reverently to an icon of the Blessed Theotokos that rested on a corner shelf, "ask for something I cannot do. That will be a miracle!"

"All right then. Double your production in six months!"

"Ha!" the General replied. "That is impossible!" He stood up and slapped Goricsan on the back. "Now you are beginning to act like a Czar!"

"I am glad to see the weather clearing," said Sagalovich as he drove Goricsan back to the airport.

"Yes," said Goricsan. "Perhaps I'll make it back to Moscow in one piece after all," he said with a chuckle.

"You really are asking for a miracle. If not from the General then at least from me."

"You underestimate yourself, Artem. I recognize talent and potential when I see it. That was even clever, how you secured the helicopter for Major Nizhniya."

"Yes, I wonder what became of her. I was told not to investigate her disappearance or to discuss the affair with anyone."

"Tell me what you know," asked Goricsan.

"I was told to say nothing to anyone, but I suppose that doesn't apply to you."

"That order came from me. Or perhaps I should say from someone who is over me."

"Who can be over the Czar?! Is there a czarina that I have not heard about?" Sagalovich joked. He was startled by his boldness with the czar. There was something about Goricsan that put him at such ease that he felt as if he were talking to a friend and an equal. Sagalovich looked over at Goricsan when he did not respond. His eyes were closed. He appeared deep in thought; troubled.

"I am sorry. I forgot myself. I was being too familiar and spoke . . . ."

"No, Artem. What you said was fine. I need you to be honest. But, now tell me . . . tell me about when you saw her last."

"It was after we had loaded her motorcycle on board the helicopter. She was armed with an AKS-92 and her pistol. She gave me a thumbs up as the helicopter lifted off. The pilot said he dropped her off on a dirt road just inside the border of Chiapas, in the Lacandon forest."

"And you never heard anything after that?"

"The only thing we heard was that the Zapatistas brought down a

Mexican army helicopter not far from where the Major was dropped off. Other than that, no, we have heard nothing. But again, we were told not to investigate."

"That was because it was feared that an investigation might draw unwanted attention to the Major's mission. Russia has many foes now. It is an ill wind that blows from the West. Major Nizhniya flew into the heart of this evil hurricane. And unfortunately, I can do nothing except wait."

"Another *chudo?*" asked Sagalovich as he pulled the car into the airport. He noted the pained expression on Goricsan's face. He wondered if the Czar's concern was not only for the success of the "mission," but perhaps also extended to the beautiful Major Nizhniya.

"Yes," replied Goricsan. "We will need many miracles before all of this is over."

*   *   *

Grigorii Zhirinovskii, the General, returned to town. That in itself, thought Sagalovich, was something of a miracle. Unfortunately, he secured an apartment next to his own. It was one thing to have to work with the old coot, having him for a neighbor was nearly impossible! Sagalovich asked whether perhaps they could spend just a small amount of the funds they were allocated to upgrade their lodgings.

"*Nyet!*" replied the General. He offered no further explanation. Sagalovich did not ask again.

It was, therefore, with great surprise and delight that Sagalovich returned from the oil field and found workmen installing a new water heater in his apartment. Sagalovich lovingly stroked the water heater. It was made in Germany! He would be able to stand in a hot shower for twenty minutes!

"Where did this come from?" inquired Sagalovich.

The workmen shrugged. "There was another box that came with it," one of them said pointing over to the table.

Sagalovich opened the box. He found several one-pound bags of Guatemalan Antigua and a note.

Thanks for the hospitality,
~ Constantin Goricsan, Czar of all Russia

Sagalovich smiled. He opened one of the bags and drew the rich aroma of the grounds into his nostrils. "Ahahh!" He held the coffee close to his chest. Maybe if he used it sparingly it would last him several months. The workmen watched the reverence with which Sagalovich held the bag of coffee grounds. No! He had a better idea.

"How would you like a real cup of coffee?" asked Sagalovich surprised by his uncharacteristic generosity. Maybe this *is* an era of miracles he mused to himself.

Jonathan

> *Then David chanted this elegy for Saul and his son Jonathan, . . .*
> *He sang: "Alas! the glory of Israel, Saul, slain upon your heights; how can*
> *the warriors have fallen! Tell it not in Gath, herald it not in the streets*
> *of Ashkelon, Lest the Philistine maidens rejoice . . . . Mountains of*
> *Gilboa, may there be neither dew nor rain upon you, nor upsurgings of*
> *the deeps! Upon you lie begrimed the warriors' shields, the shield of Saul,*
> *no longer anointed with oil. From the blood of the slain, from the*
> *bodies of the valiant, the bow of Jonathan did not turn back, or the*
> *sword of Saul return unstained. Saul and Jonathan, beloved and*
> *cherished, separated neither in life nor in death, swifter than eagles,*
> *stronger than lions!*
>
> *~2Samuel 1:17-23*

There were the usual frayed nerves in the city of Bethlehem: the merchants whose livelihoods depended on the tourist trade during the Christmas season, the security personnel who were responsible for trying to hold together the fragments of a truce, and the multitude of Christian pilgrims who were trusting that God would protect them as they visited the birthplace of Christ. The obligatory threats had been made, some credible, others not. And there were subsequent promises by the government in Tel Aviv of retaliation and the suspension of negotiations if Hamas perpetrated another act of terrorism against Israelis or pilgrims. It seemed to some that it was just another round in the game of cat and mouse that was being played out in the disputed regions of Palestine.

Captain David Eliav of Israeli Special Forces knew better. A credible threat had been made, and it was not by a mouse, but by one of the leaders of Hamas, Ali Hossein. Eliav and three other commandos sat in a rundown apartment in the center of the city waiting for word that Ali had entered the apartment complex. When he entered the apartment they would make their move: capture him if possible, kill him if necessary.

Ali Hossein was a veteran terrorist. He had begun his career two decades earlier as a participant in the *Intifada* in Gaza. It was not long before he discovered that his skill lay more with the throwing of words than Molotov cocktails. He had the *gift*, and with it he inflamed the hearts of fervent young Muslims with visions of an Islamic Empire. Forged by the union of Arab nations, the Islamic Empire would be governed by the *Sharia'* and purged of the corruption of the West and the inevitable infection that resulted by coexisting with the Peoples of the Book.

Hossein never wanted for martyrs ready to lay their lives down in suicide missions against the Zionists and their Western allies. He and his cohorts had exacted a horrific toll of human suffering in Israel, Europe, and North America. In spite of the best efforts of the Israeli Intelligence and its American counterparts, he remained ever elusive.

Then the unexpected occurred. America had developed a new technology that promised to dramatically extend the human life span. Muslims were united in their opposition to the new technology. Hossein was horrified when this unity led to an alliance with infidels. The Great Alliance united Islam with its historical adversary, the Byzantines, or rather, the heir to the Byzantine Empire, Russia. Czar Goricsan had insisted that *Tanzimat*[37] be upheld. *Dhimmi*[38] were to have the same rights and status as *ummah* in the Muslim nations of the Great Alliance. Hossein saw this as a blasphemous assault on the integrity of Islam and Sharia law. He now dedicated himself to the destruction of the Alliance. To this end, he began targeting Christian sites, particularly Orthodox churches and monasteries, in the hope of driving a wedge between the Russians and their Muslim allies.

Israeli intelligence had ascertained that Hossein was planning a Christmas day assault on one or more Christian holy sites in Israel. Examination of recent overseas bank transactions had indicated sizable deposits into the accounts of Hossein and his associates over the past several months. Hossein had apparently acquired a new and very wealthy sponsor. Circumstantial evidence had surfaced that implicated that money had been flowing into Hossein's accounts from several Tree of Life foundations. Eliav thought it was ironic that a devout Muslim would use the resources of the "enemy" to disrupt the unity of his own people. Then again, he had to admit the irony of his own situation. If he and his commandos were successful in taking out Hossein, it could result in the strengthening of an alliance of Israel's adversaries.

Eliav relaxed reading the newspaper. This was his ritual before every operation. His comrades, Sergeants Daniel Ferdman and Sharon Meisner, and Corporal Joel Shansky fidgeted impatiently. They had pretty much exhausted all the familiar topics. In desperation, Daniel looked over at Eliav who was sitting with his legs up on the table. He saw that one of the stories on the front page discussed the ongoing debate in the Knesset regarding the introduction of Chimæra biotechnology in Israel. Orthodox Jews were vehemently opposed to allowing Chimæra into the country. A Muslim cleric had declared a *fatwa* of death against any Chimæric that entered the Holy City of Jerusalem. Orthodox Jews and Muslims found themselves awkwardly in agreement on this issue. But, many in the country were concerned that a ban on Chimæra would weaken Israel's relations with the West, especially the United States. It was unclear how the Prime Minister and the government would act. Many observers believed that the politicians would simply take a wait-and-see attitude. That would allow time for emotions to settle. In the meantime, the government could monitor the growing impact that Chimæra had in Europe and America. Besides, biotechnology was the least of Israel's problems. It still had to deal with the age-old problems of religious and ethnic violence.

"What do you think about this Chimæra business?" Ferdman asked Captain Eliav.

Eliav lowered his paper momentarily to look at Ferdman. Eliav shrugged. "It makes no difference to me. I leave that up to the politicians." Eliav returned to his newspaper.

"But from what I've read," said Shansky, "it not only extends the life span, but it makes you healthier and maybe even smarter."

"I don't care about that," interjected Meisner, "but if it would increase my bust size I'd be game."

"Yeah, maybe that would be a good idea!" laughed Ferdman.

"You left yourself open for that one," said Shansky.

"Well, maybe Chimæra could fix that accident that occurred during your brith."

"Touché!" exclaimed Shansky.

"That's enough, children," said Eliav lowering his newspaper. "You guys act like you're still in junior high. You too, Meisner."

"Maybe you shouldn't be so selfish," admonished Meisner who routinely tried to get under the Captain's stoic veneer. "Your wife might like you to get an injection of Chimæric stem cells. I've heard that men become sex gods and can do it several times a night!"

"He is already," joked Shansky. "At least that's what Ruth tells me."

"How 'bout we keep my wife out of this," admonished Eliav.

All three of the commandos laughed. Finally, Ferdman asked, "Seriously, Captain, why wouldn't you have the treatment. Perhaps it would make you a better soldier?"

Shansky kicked Ferdman. "Don't ask him to be serious. Now we'll get a long lecture."

"I love the respect I get around here," replied Eliav, folding the newspaper and setting it down on the table. Of course, he knew that his comrades respected him. They were devoted to him and would die for him if need be. He didn't mind their harmless ribbing. This was part of the ritual too. They needed to blow off the tension that built up before executing a mission.

"I don't think it would make me a better soldier," began Eliav.

"Oh God! Here we go!" exclaimed Shansky.

"A soldier has to always be aware of his mortality," continued Eliav, ignoring Shansky's comment. "Chimæra might give me a false sense of security or power. That could be dangerous, even fatal. On the other hand, if I believed that I could live perhaps several hundred years, like some people claim, maybe I would be less likely to risk my life. As it is, what do I have, another forty years perhaps? That's not too much to risk, not compared to four hundred! I am not a religious man so I am not expecting to reap some eternal reward or punishment. But, a man dies as he lives. I want to die for Israel."

The three grew silent. They didn't feel like kidding around anymore. Each knew that Eliav might get his wish in the next few minutes. They were not wishing for death, but they knew damn well that it might be lurking down the hallway. They all respected Eliav's Zionist fervor; perhaps Shansky understood it better than the others. He too had lost family in the Holocaust. A Jewish homeland was the only guarantee that such an atrocity would never happen again. They all understood this.

The phone rang. Meisner picked up the receiver. "The chicken has come home to roost," she said.

Without saying a word they began to strap on their body armor. They checked their weapons and then put on their helmets. Captain Eliav assessed the readiness of each of his commandos with a glance. Ferdman and Shansky nodded; Meisner gave Eliav a nervous smile. Eliav placed his hand on her shoulder reassuringly. He lowered his visor. If all went as planned the operation would be over in a few seconds: three seconds to run down to the apartment that Hossein had just entered, one to two seconds to secure the living room. Ferdman would secure the kitchen area, Eliav the bed and bathroom. Hossein would be either in custody or dead within the next fifteen seconds.

Eliav nodded. Ferdman opened the door. Eliav looked down the hall. It was empty. He ran down the hall with the trio close behind him.

He stood in front of the apartment door flanked on his left by Shansky and Meisner and on his right by Ferdman. The trio had their weapons ready, pointing towards the door. Eliav gave the door a ferocious kick; it fell in without resistance. Ferdman and Shansky ran into the room, followed by Meisner and Eliav. The room was sparsely furnished, a table to the left, a sofa about two yards in front of them facing a TV set. A boy of about eight to ten years of age jumped off the sofa startled. He held a video game controller in one hand; a large purple dinosaur danced on the television awaiting instruction from the young boy.

"Don't move!" shouted Meisner to the boy in Arabic. The boy froze. Shansky remained with Meisner and guarded the entrance to the apartment. Ferdman ran into the kitchen while Eliav proceeded to the bedroom. Eliav quickly assessed that there was no one in either the bedroom or the bathroom. He heard in his earphone from Ferdman that there was no one in the kitchen either. This was unexpected. Surveillance indicated that Hossein had entered the apartment. He intuitively knew that there was something wrong. It was a trap. He turned back towards the living room.

"Shoot the boy!" Eliav shouted into his microphone.

"What?" replied Meisner, startled by the order.

Eliav was about to shout the command again when he heard a young voice shout out, *"Allahu Akbar!"*[59] Eliav entered the doorway just in time to see the boy push a red button on the video game controller. Eliav immediately felt his body being lifted off the ground and then being slammed against the bedroom wall. He heard and felt his bones breaking and organs rupturing. Then he no longer felt anything. His body crumpled to the floor. He could not move. He was no longer aware of his surroundings. He had failed in his mission. Somehow it didn't matter anymore. It was no longer his battle, his responsibility. He felt lightened, relieved of the burden of life. He knew a peace he had never known. I am dying for Israel. It is good.

Then he knew the presence of another. Like a mother, not just his, but the mother of us all. It was as though she placed her hand on his cheek, kissed his forehead and whispered in his ear, "Live."

Fellowship

Therefore, since we are surrounded by so great a cloud of witnesses,
let us rid ourselves of every burden and sin that clings to us and persevere in
running the race that lies before us while keeping our eyes fixed on Jesus,
the leader and perfecter of faith. For the sake of the joy that lay before him
he endured the cross, despising its shame, and has taken his seat at the right
of the throne of God. Consider how he endured such opposition from
sinners, in order that you may not grow weary and lose heart.
~Hebrews 12:1-3

What a fellowship, what a joy divine
Leaning on the everlasting arms.
I have joy complete with my Lord so near
Leaning on the everlasting arms.
Leaning... Leaning... Safe and secure from all alarm.
Leaning... Leaning... Leaning on the everlasting arms!

Milton Lewis found himself awkwardly wedged between
Madison Ryan, who clapped to the rhythm of the song,

and his wife, the indomitable Nellie Lewis, who waved her arms back and forth above her head. Ryan knew that religion was still something new for Lewis. It was relatively new for her too. Ryan winked at Lewis' wife; Nellie smiled in return. Milton hadn't been to church since their daughter's wedding fifteen years earlier. It didn't surprise Nellie that he was there. She had said many prayers for him; she expected them to be answered eventually. Her Milton hadn't accepted Jesus yet. He would though. She was a determined woman.

> *What have I to fear, what have I to dread*
> *Leaning on the everlasting arms*
> *With my Lord so near in this pilgrim's way*
> *Leaning on the everlasting arms . . .*

Nellie made sure that her arms waved over her husband's head; that way some of the Holy Spirit might just slop on over to him. She knew that God was at work in her husband's life. But, this whole business with Chimæra and the Catholics and Orthodox had come as a bit of a surprise. She didn't know that much about Catholics; she knew even less about the Orthodox. She hadn't even been sure that they were saved, that is, until she had gotten to know Miss Ryan. It was evident to her that Madison loved the Lord and that she had committed her life to Him. Nellie had also read Maria O'Conner's Journal. She didn't understand all of it, especially the *yurodivyi* business, but it was evident to her that Maria had a special relationship with Jesus. So Nellie had reconciled herself to the fact that God worked in mysterious ways. She trusted that the Good Shepherd would continue the good work He had begun in Milton. Nellie Lewis wasn't about to let Him rest until He finished it!

The Reverend Cornelius Beaugard McGinnis, a Spirit-filled, power-of-God healing, devil-chasin' preacher, strode up to the pulpit and raised his arms as a signal for all to come to attention. Everyone took their seats in eager anticipation of what would likely prove to be another great move of God at Parousia Chapel. Nellie had seen a good many miracles performed by the Reverend McGinnis. It was just a few months ago she saw Eloise Haney's little cripple niece healed. Her left leg grew a good two inches right in front of her eyes! And then there was Alstair Washington. He had been an alcoholic for as long as Nellie could remember. He was not a church-goer. In fact, he bragged that he had never stepped into a church in his entire life. About five years ago, after a prolonged binge that landed him in the hospital, his wife Zoe, dragged her husband's sorry behind into Parousia Chapel.

"Alstair, now you go get your self a blessin,'" she told him during the altar call. When he didn't move, she grabbed him by the collar and dragged him to the front of the church. Nellie was dumbstruck. Zoe was a quiet and patient woman. But her patience had all run out. Jesus was going to use the good Reverend McGinnis to heal her man.

"There's a good man under all that alcohol," said Mrs. Washington to the Reverend. "I need you to deliver my husband from the demon drink!"

Alstair Washington, still recovering from his binge, teetered back and forth like a top nearing the end of its spin. The Reverend McGinnis started towards Alstair. "Demon Drink, you has better run whiles you has a chance. By the power of Jeezus' name . . ." As soon as the Reverend had placed his big black hand on Mr. Washington's head he fell flat like an apple from a tree!

As Nellie took her seat, she looked back and spotted Zoe and Alstair a few pews behind her. Zoe smiled and nodded reassuringly at her. Nellie understood. If God could deliver Alstair from alcoholism, He could certainly deliver Milton from skepticism and his unbelieving ways.

"Brothers and sisters," the Reverend McGinnis began. "We's seen many an outpouring of the Holy Spirit in this place."

"Amen! Hallelujah!"

"And we's set the devil to flight many a time!"

"That's right! Yesum!"

"But the devil . . . he's been getting much more clever these days . . . ."

"Uh huh," said the congregation, a little more subdued.

"He's a liar and a trickster. He's an angel of light. But don't be deceived. He's still prowling around like the same old wily lion he's always been. And he's lookin' to devour. And he's lookin' to devour you!"

"Amen! Save us Jesus!"

"That's right! I need to hear that again!"

"Save us Jesus!"

"One more time!"

"Save us JESUS!"

"Oh how the enemy hates the name of Jesus! Let me hear you say our blessed Lord's name again!"

"JESUS!"

"Amen! There ain't no other name under heaven or earth by which man can be saved! Shall I say it again!"

"YES!"

"There ain't no other name under heaven or earth or in that so called Penumbra Realm by which man can be saved!"

The congregation grew quiet. There were rumors that the Reverend was going to talk about Chimæra, the New Era and the Tree of Life this evening. There was a considerable debate among the congregation as to just how "Christian" all these new things were. Just a few days ago the Reverend McGinnis and the elders of Parousia Chapel had had their obligatory meeting with the Tree of Life representatives. Nellie had heard from Elder Foster that if Parousia Chapel didn't affiliate with the Tree of Life they could lose their tax-exempt status.

"They even said they'd have the zoning changed and we wouldn't be able to have our church anymore if we didn't cooperate," reported Elder Foster.

Nobody knew what to do. They all hoped that Reverend McGinnis would have a "word from God" for them.

"Perhaps you think there is another name?" asked Reverend McGinnis, noting the silence. "Perhaps you think maybe the Tree of Life can save you? Maybe Chimæra or Hans Obermann?"

"No sir," shouted Alstair Washington. "I know that there ain't no other name 'cept Jesus that could have saved me!"

"Amen!" exclaimed Zoe.

"That's right!" echoed Nellie.

Milton Lewis looked around at the congregation. He noted a few heads nodding in agreement. He heard a few "yeses" and "amens" and "that's right, Alstair." But much of the congregation remained quiet and motionless. It was evident to Lewis that the Reverend still had some serious convincing to do. After all, the decision that the elders made might very well determine whether there would continue to be a Parousia Chapel. That's why the Reverend had asked Nellie to see whether she could convince Milton to come along.

"I don't much care one way or another 'bout Parousia Chapel," the Reverend had said to Lewis a few days earlier. "I built it. I'd just as soon burn it down myself than turn it over to the beast of the Apocalypse."

Lewis had raised his eyebrow with that comment. All the time he had spent with Ryan, McIntyre and now Bishop Kavasilas, no one had ever called Obermann the "beast." The Reverend McGinnis didn't make any bones about it. "Oh, he's the beast all right," the Reverend continued, noting Lewis' skeptical expression. "Look what it says here," he said, opening his Bible to the book of Revelation.

> *And I saw one of his heads as it were wounded to death; and his deadly wound was healed; and all the world wondered after the beast.*
> *And they worshipped the dragon which gave power unto the beast saying, Who is like unto the beast? Who is able to make war with him?*[40]

Lewis had had to admit there did seem to be an eerie connection between the scripture and Obermann. After all, he had been shot in the head. And according to all the reports he had been "wounded to death" and the "deadly wound" had been healed.

"But what do you expect me to do?" Lewis had inquired.

"You know Madison Ryan, right?"

"Yes," Lewis had replied. "I've helped her and Cardinal McIntyre with the Maria O'Conner case. Well, that is, until he was arrested for conspiring in the assassination, or attempted assassination . . . whatever . . . of Obermann."

"So tell me more about Miss Ryan," Reverend McGinnis had said.

"Much of her time is spent trying to elude the authorities. They want to question her about hate crimes against Chimærics or some such nonsense."

"You know, you can learn a lot about a person from the type of friends they have," Reverend McGinnis had observed. "The fact that Ryan has you as a friend means she's good people. But, sometimes you can learn even more about a person from the enemies they have. Now I figure that if anybody has that beast Obermann as an enemy then we're on the same side. And I also have to figure that if Obermann hated that Maria O'Conner woman and wants to get his devil hands on Ryan then that pretty much tells me where the front line is."

"Front line of what?" Lewis had asked.

"Why, the war against the beast!" the Reverend had said as he turned to his Bible again and read from the same chapter,

> *And it was given unto him to make war with the saints, and to overcome them: and power was given him over all kindreds, and tongues, and nations.*[41]

"The problem is, those Catholics and Orthodox seemed to have figured this out ahead of us," continued Reverend McGinnis.

"You've lost me," Lewis had said. "I thought all you guys were on the same team."

"Well, pretty much. But you know how it is with a family. You argue 'bout stuff—stuff you'd never argue 'bout with a stranger. Pretty soon, the only thing you remember 'bout the other fella is the stuff you argue 'bout. That's the way it is with us. But those other guys are right this time. And because we're so darned used to arguin' with them many of us on this side of the Reformation just might figure they're wrong about this too. And that scares me. You see I don't give a hoot about Parousia Chapel. No sir, I'm talkin' about the conflagration of the ages, you know, Armageddon. I just wanta make sure that my Bible-believin', God-fearin' brethren are fightin' on the right side. Maybe Miss Ryan can help me make that point."

Lewis had told the Reverend he would talk to Ryan. He had figured he could get her to come to the prayer meeting. Lewis had opened the door of the Reverend's office and was making his exit; at the time he could not believe that he hadn't been asked *the* question.

"So," the Reverend had said, "you're sticking your neck out for the saints."

Lewis had frozen in his tracks facing the door. Oh no, he had thought. Here it comes!

"Does this mean," the Reverend had continued, "that you're ready to accept Jesus as your personal Lord and Savior?"

Lewis had slowly turned around hoping that by the time he faced the good Reverend he'd know what to say. It was true that some pretty amazing and inexplicable things had happened over the past several months—things that you had to figure that some power beyond human understanding was responsible for. And the Reverend's assessment was as good as any he had heard. But, the Reverend was asking for something he just wasn't ready to commit to, at least not yet.

"Well, Reverend," Lewis had finally said, "I suppose that's inevitable. My wife has been pestering God about my salvation since before we were even married. I suspect that God will save me if for no other reason than He's not going to want Nellie mad at Him for all eternity!"

Now, Reverend McGinnis surveyed his congregation and shook his head. He looked behind him at the elders sitting on the platform. They stared back at him. A few of them, including Elder Foster, frowned. The Reverend opened his Bible to I Kings 18:21 and began to read in his most thunderous and prophetic voice,

> *And Elijah came unto all the people, and said, How long halt ye between two opinions? If the Lord be God, follow him: but if Ba'al, then follow him. And the people answered him not a word.*

The Reverend paused, not only for effect, but also to illustrate the parallel between the congregation of Parousia Chapel and Elijah's audience. Alstair Washington stood up and proclaimed, "I don't know about all you folks, but I's just got one thing to say and that the Lord Jesus is God and me and my wife are goin' to follow Him." There were a few more "yeses" and "amens" until the Reverend raised his arms to silence everyone.

"I appreciate that," said Reverend McGinnis. "I know you mean it. But, I want to make it very clear. When I'm talkin' about Ba'al, I'm not talkin' about some old extinct pagan god that done lived three thousand years ago. I'm talkin' about false gods right here and now; they wants you to bow down and worship them. You know who I'm talkin' bout. I'm goin' to tell ya anyway whether you want to hear it or not. Hans Obermann and that Chimæric son of his are the two beasts of the Book of Revelation!"

"Now hold on!" said Elder Foster, jumping out of his seat. "How do you know that Obermann's the beast?! Besides, it's up to the elders to decide what we should do about the Tree of Life and Chimæra!"

"Yes, you're right Elder Foster," said Reverend McGinnis. "But before you do, I want you and all the people to know where I stand."

"Yeah, we'd like to know," retorted Elder Foster. "Particularly since I see you brought that Catholic woman here." Foster pointed menacingly at Madison Ryan. "How do we know it's not you who have sided with the antichrist. After all, many of us have been taught that the antichrist would come from Rome!"

Lewis leaned over to Ryan. "I'm sorry I got you into to this mess!"

Ryan shrugged. "If I learned anything from Maria, it was that we all must bear our crosses."

"Well, now that you mentioned our guest," replied Reverend McGinnis who now turned his attention to Miss Ryan, "I did ask Miss Madison Ryan if she would come here this evening and talk to us tonight about what she knows about Mr. Obermann and Chimæra. Miss Ryan," he said extending his arm out towards her.

Madison Ryan stood up and with trepidation walked up to the pulpit. The Reverend McGinnis stepped down from the pulpit and extended his hand to her. She shook his hand firmly and forced a smile. She stepped up to the pulpit, somewhat reluctantly, looking behind her to make sure the Reverend McGinnis was still there. He nodded and smiled. She nervously looked down at Lewis who gave her a thumbs-up.

"I feel like a Christian being thrown to the Christians," began Ryan. Most of the congregation laughed; some of the elders frowned. "These are difficult times for Christians; indeed, for all people of faith. It seems like we are being offered heaven on earth. Chimæra is offering us a very, very long and healthy life. Obermann and the Tree of Life appear to be offering enlightenment and peace. And what does my Church have to offer? The same thing that all authentic Christian communities must offer—the Cross and death. A dear friend of mine showed me this. I know you have all heard of her. Perhaps you don't know exactly what to think of her. The Church is considering beatifying Maria Theresa O'Conner. This is one step closer to declaring her a saint, which I believe she is. She chose the cross even at the risk of her own salvation. And in so doing, she completed what was lacking in the afflictions of Christ on *your* behalf and on behalf of all those who will someday seek release from the bondage of Chimæra.[42] I can tell you how Satan raged. I was there and felt the force of his fury. He still pursues me, but that is all right. Didn't our Lord say, 'Blessed are you when they insult you and persecute you and utter every kind of evil against you because of me?'[43] I hope that you will join my fellow Catholic and Orthodox brethren at the foot of His Cross. I cannot promise you 'heaven on earth,' only the assurance that your reward will be great in heaven."

The Reverend McGinnis stood at the pulpit next to Madison Ryan and placed his arm around her shoulder. Then quoting from the book of Joshua, proclaimed to his congregation, "If it does not please you to serve the Lord, decide today whom you will serve, the gods your fathers served beyond the River or the gods of the Amorites in whose country you are dwelling. As for me and my household, we will serve the Lord."[44]

Alstair and Zoe Washington stood up. "We're with you Reverend, and you too, Miss Ryan."

As Nellie Lewis stood up she grabbed Milton's arm and pulled him up along with her. "You can count on us, Reverend!" Nellie gave Ryan a wink.

People began to stand up throughout the chapel.

"Reverend, you have my vote!"

"I'm with you all the way, Reverend!"

"Me too!"

"My family will stand with you, Reverend!"

"I never thought I'd be standing arm in arm with a Catholic," said an elderly gentleman leaning against his walker. "But I know something about war having been in a couple myself. And it looks to me like we got one helluva war here. Seems to me it's time to lay aside our differences and, together, maybe we can give that ol' devil the biggest whippin' he's ever gotten."

"Hallelujah!"

"Amen!"

"You tell 'um, Colonel!"

The Reverend McGinnis turned and faced the elders. One by one they began to stand to indicate their support of the Reverend. Finally, Elder Foster stood up. Reverend McGinnis smiled and nodded; not the smile of one who is victorious, but the smile of one who humbly appreciated the deference shown by another.

At that moment the doors at the back of the sanctuary burst open. Everyone turned around to see what the commotion was all about. About a dozen or so police officers entered the sanctuary. There were also several men dressed in suits. One of the plain-clothed officers approached the pulpit.

"Miss Madison Ryan," the man said, "I am placing you under arrest. You are wanted for questioning regarding your complicity in the publication of hate literature and the advocacy of hate crimes against Chimærics. Anything that you say may be used as evidence against you."

Lewis strode up to the man and spun him around. "Reilly, what the hell are you doing?"

Several officers grabbed Lewis, but Reilly raised his arm motioning them to leave Lewis alone.

"I'm sorry, Lewis," said Reilly. "It's my daughter Carol. Her diabetes was getting really bad. The Chimæra folks said they could help her. My wife made . . . ."

"Don't blame Betty, you traitor!" exclaimed Lewis.

By this time some of the congregation began shouting at the police. The old war veteran made his way over to of one of the plain-clothes officers, picked up his walker, placed it on the toe of the officer's shoe and leaned on it. The officer howled. "Take that, you godless fascist!" he said. Things were rapidly getting out of hand.

"Its okay," said Ryan, as she stepped down from the pulpit. "I'll go with you," she said to Reilly. Then turning to the Reverend she said, "I've been arrested before. Perhaps another verse of *What a Fellowship* would be in order."

Reverend McGinnis gave her a hug. "We're with you," he whispered in her ear. "The army of the Lamb just got a little bigger today." He then released her to Officer Reilly who led her out. As Ryan stepped out of the sanctuary she could hear Reverend McGinnis' thunderous voice sing out,

Leaning . . . Leaning . . . Safe and secure from all alarm.
Leaning . . . Leaning . . . . Leaning on the everlasting arms!

03/02 NEWERA

Former Adversaries

Persia is only a matter of one or two thrusts and no Persia will ever be after that. But the Byzantines with horns are people of sea and rock; whenever a horn goes, another replaces it. Alas, they are your associates to the end of time.

– attributed to the Prophet Mohammed

Jafar Faruq strummed his *oud* while he sat around the campfire with his companions. A hundred or so other campfires dotted the numerous rocky niches at the base of the mountains. The Prince's following had grown quickly as many had come to believe that he was the *Mahdi*, the restorer of the True Path. Jafar watched his Prince and friend, Abdullah, as he paced back and forth outside his tent reading a communiqué from some unnamed Jordanian bureaucrat. Jafar shifted himself on the rocky outcropping trying to find a more comfortable position and wished that Abdullah had not refused the more comfortable accommodations offered at the nearby villages.

"No," Abdullah had said. "The desert wilderness will become our school. From her we will learn camaraderie and cunning."

It was also here that the Prince and his followers would also learn the art of war from General Masud. When the General had heard that the Prince was assembling an army to overthrow his father and brother he came out of exile. As to whether Abdullah was the *Mahdi*, Masud neither knew nor cared; he had his own score to settle. He would help the Prince assemble and train his army, and together they would liberate Arabia from the tyranny of the King Saïd and his treacherous son, Malik.

"I will train your army for *jihad*," Masud had said to Abdullah.

"I have no army," Abdullah had said.

"Promise the people justice and give them hope for a better life and they will come," Masud had replied.

And they had: from Arabia, Jordan, Egypt, Palestine, Pakistan, Afghanistan, and even as far away as Europe and North America. Even some of the followers of Ali Hossein had joined the ranks of the Prince.

"*Sahib*, what does the communiqué say?" inquired General Masud who was seated across from Jafar.

"It would seem that we are beginning to wear out our welcome in Jordan," said the Prince, folding up the note.

"What are we to do?" asked Jafar, leaning his *oud* up against a rock.

"Where are we to go?" asked another.

Abdullah paced back and forth before the fire saying nothing. This did not surprise General Masud. As news spread of the *Mahdi's* presence, more and more men had joined their camp. The government in Jordan had tolerated his presence. They had even supported it. Perhaps if the young Prince could succeed in wresting Arabia from his father, he would extend his gratitude towards the impoverished country that had offered him sanctuary.

"It would seem that my father, the King, has threatened to invade the Kingdom of Jordan if the government does not expel us or turn me over to him."

"The government of Jordan is sympathetic to our cause," said Jafar.

"This is true," replied Abdullah, "but their army is incapable of turning back an invasion from Arabia."

"We number over five hundred!" replied another, "And *Allah* will be with us. You are his anointed! You are *Mahdi*!"

The Prince smiled at the young man who was not much younger than him. "*Jihad* will come. When it does, I would prefer to deliver *Allah* victory rather than martyrs." Abdullah looked down at General Masud who was now staring into the fire. "General?"

General Masud looked up at the Prince. "Our numbers grow daily with men who would lay their lives down for you, as our young friend here," Masud said, gesturing towards the man who had just spoken with the Prince. "The regime in Jordan is sympathetic to you, so are the other neighboring kingdoms who are struggling to hold together the Alliance. The dream of a united Arab people was dashed by your father's disaffection. They would unite behind you if they believed you had a reasonable chance in restoring Arabia to the Alliance."

"Perhaps we should join forces with Ali Hossein," said Jafar.

"Hossein is a terrorist and a coward," replied Abdullah. "He who attacks women and children from the shadows is not worthy to be called Muslim. A soldier of *Allah*," Abdullah said, raising two fingers and placing them under his eyes, "looks into the eyes of his enemy. Then the enemy knows and fears, for they see that we love death as much as we love life."

Abdullah turned and walked back towards the fire. He folded his hands behind his back and stared into the flames.

"No," Abdullah continued, "Hossein is as much our enemy as the Chimæric King. He would pervert the *Sharia* and turn Islam into a regime of oppression. I am committed to the principles of the Great Alliance and *Tanzimat*. If it is *Allah's* will that I become king, then the People of the Book will be treated with the dignity they deserve."

"It is well, for they too, are the Sons of Abraham . . . ," said a stranger approaching the fire.

Abdullah's companions jumped up and turned around to see the stranger who had entered the Prince's camp unnoticed. Several men drew pistols and knives as the hooded stranger approached.

". . . and your brothers," the stranger continued as he drew back the hood from his head.

Abdullah squinted to make out the stranger's face. He was startled to hear again the words spoken to him by his mentor, Sheik al-Ahbar. In the flickering light of the campfire he could see that the stranger was a man in his late twenties, perhaps early thirties. He had short-cropped hair and a long beard. His wide, keen eyes were illuminated with an internal intensity rather than by a reflection of the campfire. Abdullah's companions moved to seize him, but the Prince raised his hand.

"At first," Abdullah began, "I thought you might be *jinn* having eluded our sentries so well. But, I see that you wear a cross . . . perhaps an angel delivered you to my tent?"

"Exactly so," replied the stranger.

"There, you see," Abdullah said to his companions, "seizing him would have been to no avail." Then turning to the stranger he asked, "So tell me, Christian, how is it that an angel has delivered you to my camp? How could it be that your God would want to help a Muslim prince?"

"*For our God and your God is one and the same* . . . started the monk.

Abdullah smiled and completed the verse from the *Qur'an*, ". . . *and it is unto him that we surrender ourselves.*"[45]

"It is cold, draw near to the fire," offered Abdullah, motioning to the monk with his arm, "unless you are spirit and have no need of warmth."

"I can assure you I am flesh and blood. The desert night is cold, and I would be pleased to be warmed by your fire."

The stranger approached the fire and rubbed his cold hands together.

"Stranger, you have me at a disadvantage. You know me, but I do not know you?"

"Forgive me," replied the stranger. "I am Father Nikitas. I am the emissary of Czar Constatin Goricsan."

The men in the camp began to murmur to one another. An emissary from the Czar! What can this mean?

"This is intriguing," said Abdullah. "The Czar of Russia sends a Christian monk into the Jordanian wilderness to find an exiled Prince of Arabia. Perhaps the purposes of God are not so inscrutable. Perhaps they are the same as the purposes of the Czar?"

"Like the Prince, we are but God's unworthy servants," replied Nikitas.

"So tell me, emissary of Czar Goricsan, what purpose have you divined?"

"The reestablishment of the Alliance."

"So it is about oil?"

"It is about Chimæra."

Abdullah stared at Nikitas. Could it be true that these Christians recognize the evil of Chimæra, the immense evil that his father had introduced into his beloved mother and had also welcomed into the kingdom? This is why he had resolved to bring *jihad* to Arabia, to rid the kingdom of the *Shayâtin* and to restore the True Path.

"And how does this affect Russia?" asked Abdullah. "Why do you care that Chimæra has infected my kingdom?"

"Because from your country it is poised to infect the entire Muslim world," replied Nikitas.

"Again, I ask, why is that a concern to you? Have we not been adversaries from the beginning?"

"There is but one adversary. Have you not heard the *qari`a*?[46] Have you not felt the *zilzila*?[47] The *ghashiya*[48] is at the gate. It will take all the sons of Abraham to keep him from breaking through."

"You are not the first I have heard speak of the Sons of Abraham. Isaac and Ishmael I know,"[49] challenged Abdullah, "How do you, Christian, claim Abraham as your father?"

"We are Sons of Abraham by faith, grafted on to the trunk of Abraham by Jesus Christ. Together we will make a mighty tree; mighty enough to withstand the *sakha*."[50]

"I am surprised and honored by your knowledge of the Qur'an and the Hadith. But let me ask you this, Monk. Under whose banner shall we engage the *masih al-dajjal*[51] in the *malahim*[52] —the Cross, the Star of David, or the Star and Crescent?" asked Abdullah.

"All three," replied Nikitas. "But before the *infitar*[53] they will be united under her banner."

Her banner?" inquired Abdullah.

"The Daughter of Abraham," replied Nikitas.

"I have had one riddle solved, only to have it replaced by another," Abdullah said with slight irritation.

"You must forgive an old general," interrupted Masud who also found the monk's riddles annoying, "whose understanding is limited to this earthly realm. I appreciate the sentiments of the Czar. But, it will take more than sentiments and his emissary's riddles to overthrow King Saïd. He has a formidable army, and we are but five hundred."

"The general is right," replied Abdullah. "Is the Czar offering more than words?"

Nikitas removed a small box from under his cloak and opened it. It held a small military-issue communicator. He handed it to Abdullah. Abdullah held it incredulously.

"What am I to do with this? Call my father and talk him to death? Perhaps I can perplex him with riddles!" Abdullah's companions laughed. He turned around and faced the monk. The monk was looking at him sternly.

"With this," replied Nikitas, ignoring the laughter of Abdullah's companions, "you will be able to speak directly with Goricsan, and together you can coordinate your jihad."

Abdullah turned questioningly to General Masud.

"State of the art," replied Masud. "Satellite transmittance with encryption I would suspect."

Nikitas nodded. "I cannot explain all the details of what Czar Goricsan has in mind, but I will tell you what I know of his plan. Is it not true that about a third of your father's air force consists of Russian made aircraft?"

"That is true," replied Masud.

"When the time is right," continued Nikitas, "Russian MiGs, helicopter gunships, and troop transports will be secretly stationed in Jordan and in Iraq. They will carry all the markings and the electronic signatures of the Arabic Air force, but they will be Russian, and flown by Russian pilots. While this is being prepared, you will speak with the people of Arabia," Nikitas pointed to the communicator that Abdullah held. "Russian satellites will transmit your message into Arabia and to the people who eagerly await your return and will join with you in jihad."

"Even if we were to successfully penetrate Arabian air defenses with your disguised Russian aircraft and transport my meager five hundred, I do not see how this would be sufficient to overthrow my father."

"If I am not mistaken," replied Masud, "I believe what Goricsan has in mind is that the Arabian armed forces will misinterpret our incursion as an internal coup attempt. They will be momentarily confused . . . who is loyal, who is not, who is most likely to succeed?"

"And if the Prince is able to strengthen his support with the people, which from our intelligence he seems to have already won, I believe that the military may side with the Prince."

Abdullah paced before the fire looking at the communicator that Nikitas had handed him. The plan was risky, needed some development, but had potential. Besides, it might be his only choice.

"And if we are successful, what do I owe Goricsan for his assistance?" inquired Abdullah.

"Arabia's commitment to the Alliance."

"Very well, Monk, I will contact your Czar," said Abdullah, raising the communication device that Nikitas had given him. "And we shall see whether Allah, may His name be praised, is truly with us."

"There is one more thing," said Nikitas. "A gift from my Church to you, or rather, for one you love." Nikitas removed from around his neck a cord to which was attached a stainless steel cylinder. An icon of Michael the Archangel was etched on the outside of the cylinder. He handed it to Abdullah. Abdullah stared at the cylinder; he saw that the top could be removed. He looked at Nikitas, who nodded. Abdullah unscrewed and then lifted off the cap. Projecting out of the felt-lined cylinder was the tip of a glass ampule. He carefully slid the ampule out. The ampule contained a red, viscous fluid . . . blood! He looked up again at Nikitas questioningly.

"It is possible to be liberated from Chimæra if the one who has been infected with it has received it unwillingly or is repentant. But only through death."

"More riddles, Monk?" asked Abdullah, as he placed the ampule back into the cylinder. He then took the cord, and lifted it over his head. The cylinder hung on Abdullah's chest glowing an orange-red as it reflected the light of the campfire.

"Not riddles, Prince, a mystery," replied Nikitas. "There are two ways to combat sin: force and humble love. Before the malahim is over we shall have employed both. But, the latter is far more powerful than the former. What resides within the ampule is the fruit of 'loving humility.' It is a terrible force; through it the world has been conquered. But, you must fast and pray; then God will show you how you must use this gift."

Then, having completed his mission, Father Nikitas covered his head with his cloak, walked towards the darkness and disappeared.

Abdullah's companions jumped up again.

"Where did he go?"

"He vanished like smoke!"

"I knew he was jinn!"

Abdullah just stared into the darkness and grasped the stainless steel cylinder around his neck. He lifted the cylinder and dropped it under his garments. He turned to General Masud, "We will call Goricsan in the morning."

Rescued

Rescue me from death, God, my saving God, that my tongue may praise your healing power. Lord, open my lips; my mouth will proclaim your praise. For you do not desire sacrifice; a burnt offering you would not accept. My sacrifice, God, is a broken spirit; God, do not spurn a broken, humbled heart.

~Psalm 51:17-19

J ust listen to what he has to say," Ruth pleaded.

David Eliav ignored his wife. He picked up the remote control from the coffee table and turned up the television set.

Ruth left the room more out of frustration than anger. She returned to the dishes that had been washed earlier and were now dry. She started to put them away, but then stopped. She looked out the kitchen window. Esther, their seven-year-old daughter, was pulling weeds from the garden. David used to do most of the gardening. That was before the terrible explosion. Now Esther was taking care of the garden until her father was well enough to return to his favorite hobby. But, the doctors were not sure that he would completely recover from his injuries.

What made matters worse was her husband's depression and halfhearted effort during his therapy. He had never said as much, but Ruth knew that this was his way of punishing himself for the death of his comrades.

Ruth was not about to allow her husband to become incapacitated by guilt and depression. She understood how difficult it was for him to accept the death of his friends. It was not his fault. And it was certainly not his fault that he had survived. In fact, the doctors had called it a miracle. Now he needed another miracle. That is why she had spoken with her father.

Douglas Shaeffer, Ruth's father, was a powerful and influential member of the Knesset and one of the leaders of the Labor Party. He had considered running for Prime Minister but had deferred to his senior in the party, Joachim Binur. Binur had neither the vision nor the diplomatic skills to hold the fractious government together; as a result, Likud grew daily in strength and influence. It was only a matter of time before a vote of "no confidence" would be delivered to the government of Binur. This is when Shaeffer planned to make his move, unless by then Binur had so crippled the Labor Party as to make his run for Prime Minister unfeasible. His son-in-law might just be able to help him tip the balance in Labor's favor.

He based his hopes on the heroic exploits of the mysterious "Jonathan." The rescue of Israeli hostages in Cairo and the capture of Sheik al-Maghrizi were just two of the better-known exploits of the mysterious Commander "Jonathan" whose identity had been a carefully guarded state secret. Then when the explosion in Bethlehem nearly killed him, it was revealed that "Jonathan" was Captain David Eliav of Israeli Special Forces. Everyone wanted to know more about the enigmatic Eliav: How was he recovering? What were his plans? Did he have political aspirations? Shaeffer knew that political power was within his son-in-law's reach, if he were willing to reach for it. Unfortunately, at least as far Shaeffer was concerned, Eliav showed no interest in politics. Apparently, he showed little interest in anything now. That's why his daughter Ruth had spoken with him.

"Dad, I really don't care if he becomes involved in politics. I'm just concerned about him. He's been so depressed. He needs . . ." Ruth had searched for the right words, ". . . he needs something to fight for."

"He has you and Esther," Shaeffer had replied. "That should be enough."

You're right, Dad," Ruth had agreed. "I think I know that even better than you. But, were mom and I enough for you?"

"That's not fair," Shaeffer had replied.

"It's true though. And I married a man just like my father. But it's okay. I love him just as he is. But that's the problem. He hasn't been himself since he was hurt."

"That's understandable."

"Of course. And I tried to give him the space he's needed. But, now he just sits around and watches television. He's depressed. And his therapists say that he's not making the progress he could be making."

Shaeffer had nodded sympathetically. "You know I've talked with him before about a career in politics. He always said he wasn't interested."

"I know. And I never pushed him, although I was always scared to death about his work in Special Forces. But now, well, he can't go back to that. Politics could be just the thing that brings him out of this slump. Do you think he has a chance?"

"A chance?! He could be Prime Minister tomorrow if he wanted it," he had said, half jokingly. "Seriously though, his candidacy would be a coup for Labor."

Labor was viewed as the party of doves; Eliav would help dispel that view. That might even put a damper on the growing strength of Likud. And it certainly would strengthen Shaeffer's prospects for Prime Minister.

"I will speak with him again," Shaeffer had continued. "But this time you must be more supportive. And there is something else. Some months ago, when the Knesset took up the issue of Chimæra, some of us were offered the therapy if we voted for introducing the therapy in Israel."

"I never heard of that," Ruth had said.

"No, my dear, we don't make a habit of discussing the bribes we are offered," he had said smiling. "As it turned out, we have indefinitely postponed our vote. However, I have heard that some members of the Knesset have received the therapy anyway. My point is this; if David joins us, well then he probably could get it too."

"I don't know," Ruth had replied thoughtfully.

"It would certainly aid his recovery. Do you mind if I ask you a personal question?"

Ruth had anticipated her father's question and had been about to object when he had interrupted.

"Has David been able to . . . you know . . . perform his spousal responsibilities?"

"Father! Just a few months ago he was almost killed!"

"I thought so. Look, I don't mean to get personal, but that could be adding to his depression. But, I won't bring it up again. I'll leave that for you two to discuss. Just know that it would be available if he decides to join us in Tel Aviv."

Ruth finished putting the dishes away and began to set cookies and biscuits on a tray. Her father and mother would be joining them for afternoon tea. She would have had them over for dinner, but David wasn't ready to spend that much time with anyone, let alone her parents.

"Hi Grandma! Hi Grandpa!" Esther exclaimed as she ran out of Ruth's sight. She saw her again momentarily escorting her grandparents to the front door. Ruth turned the heat on under the teakettle, and left the kitchen to greet them at the door.

"Mom and Dad are here. Could you turn off the TV?" asked Ruth.

"Is that a question or a command?" replied David.

Ruth frowned but decided not to respond. David knew he was being a jerk. He didn't really like the way he had been acting either, but anger and bitterness had dammed up inside of him. Sometimes it would sneak out in some subtle sarcastic remark, while other times he would explode in vitriolic anger. Some of this was directed at his doctors, nurses, and therapists. Not a few of them had thought that it might have been better had he died. They resented having their heroic vision of "Jonathan" blemished by his self-pity and bitterness. But, most of his cruel remarks were directed at Ruth who patiently endured in the hope that the "real" David would someday reemerge from the rubble of that dreadful day in Bethlehem.

"Hi Mom! Hi Dad!" Ruth embraced her parents and gave both of them a kiss on the cheek.

David had turned off the TV and rolled his wheelchair towards the foyer. "Douglas," David said, tipping his head. "Hi, Eloise. How have you been?"

"Fine," answered Ruth's mother, smiling. She bent down and kissed David on the cheek. She wanted to ask him how he was doing, but decided against it, figuring that her son-in-law would simply use it as an opportunity to complain.

"Why don't you all go into the living room, and I'll bring everyone the tea."

David led them into the living room and positioned his wheelchair opposite the sofa where Douglas and Eloise sat down. A couple of minutes of uncomfortable silence followed until Ruth appeared with the teacart. She sat down in a chair next to David.

"So Mom, I hear that Rubinsky is still ill. Does that mean there's a chance you might get tapped for the Mendelsson Concerto?"

Eloise gave an expansive grin and took a sip of tea.

"You got it?!" anticipated Ruth.

Eloise nodded.

"Oh, that's terrific!" exclaimed Ruth. "That will be this Friday, right?"

"Yes," replied Eloise. "Unless, of course, the maestra has a miraculous recovery. She's such a prima dona!"

"How much you want to bet she'll recover by Saturday for the Korngold Concerto? She'll be afraid that after your performance the management will realize they don't need to pay top dollar for her when their first violinist is even better."

"Well, that's nice of you to say . . . ."

"It's true," said Douglas. "You're twice the violinist Miss 'what's her name' is."

"I don't know about that," replied Eloise modestly. "But I am twice her size!"

Eloise Shaeffer was the superior virtuoso. But, live classical performances were not just about virtuosity. If all one wanted was virtuosity, one might as well stay at home and put in a recording of Itzhak Perlman. Concerts had to be a visually appealing experience too. And Miss Rubinsky not only bowed a nice fiddle, she was breathtaking in her deep-plunging black evening gown. But, there was a price she paid for being svelte: she was prone to illness.

"No," continued Eloise, "half the people at the concert will be there to see her, not to hear Mendelsson. But at least the other half won't be disappointed with me."

"So, Binur has gotten the Palestinian Authority back to the Peace Table," interjected David.

Douglas and Eloise stared at David wondering if his non sequitur was just the result of thoughtlessness, or if he was intending to be rude and boorish. Ruth knew it to be the latter, but it might also be a fortuitous opportunity for her father to discuss politics.

"Mom, why don't we go take a look and see what Esther is up to in the garden. We'll leave the men to discuss politics."

Eloise immediately grasped Ruth's intent and followed her outside with her cup of tea. David had indeed meant to be boorish, but he immediately realized that his remark had backfired and played into some scheme of his wife's.

"The Palestinian Authority knows it has nothing to lose with Binur. Even if they were to come to some sort of an agreement, it will be rejected by Likud."

"But if it's a good agreement perhaps Likud would sign on," replied David.

"No. A failure at the peace table, even if it's because of Likud, will hurt Binur and Labor. And ultimately what hurts Labor, helps Likud."

"Surely, you don't think they put the party over the interests of Israel?"

"The interest of the party and that of Israel are one and the same."

David was shocked at Shaeffer's candor.

"Don't look so surprised," continued Shaeffer. "It is not as cynical and self-serving as it sounds. Each party has its own vision of Israel. After a while you cannot help but identify your vision of the state with the state itself. You see, the party becomes the state. Before too long, you cannot even imagine living in the country that has become what the other party envisions. If need be, you will risk the state itself to prevent the state from becoming what the other party envisions."

"Thank you," said David.

"For what?" asked Shaeffer.

"For reminding me why I hate politics. We in the military were simply pawns in a game of strategy between opposing parties."

"Opposing visions. And it's not a game," corrected Shaeffer.

"Yes, I stand corrected," said David placing his hands on his paralyzed legs, "if I could stand."

"Why don't you join us?"

"Ha!"

"I'm serious."

"I know. Remember, this is not the first time you've dangled politics in front of your son-in-law. Besides, which party would I join? I seem to lack that sense of vision which brings such single-minded clarity to all of you in the Knesset."

"I'm not going to lie to you. I'd like to see you join Labor. And you are wrong. You do have a vision."

"No offense, but I couldn't care less about your vision for Israel; much less that of Binur's or Likud's."

"Exactly," said Shaeffer, "and that's what will make you such an attractive candidate. More important than that, it's what makes you just what Israel needs right now. You see, you're not so arrogant as to think that you have some right to impose your vision on Israel. You just want her to survive; that somehow she'll fulfill her destiny if she's just given the chance. In your own way, you have more faith in the promises given to Abraham than most of the rabbis I know. That's why you're in that wheelchair."

"I'm in this wheelchair because I screwed up!" said David angrily.

"Little pieces of my friends are scattered all over Bethlehem . . . that's what my vision of Israel has accomplished!"

"You know that's not true. But I'm not going to argue with you. If it were just you, I don't think I'd give a shit if you wanted to flush your life down the toilet. But you see, you just happen to be married to my daughter and you are the father of my granddaughter. And they love you, and you can't love them back when all you can do is hate yourself. And you cannot stop hating yourself until you give yourself."

"To what?"

"To what you've always given yourself—Israel."

"I've given enough," said Eliav, turning away as he began to roll his wheelchair out of the living room.

"No you haven't. Ferdman, Meisner, and Shansky—they gave enough."

"Get out!" shouted David. "Get out of my house!"

Shaeffer stormed out of the front door waving his arm in disgust in the direction of Eliav. He saw Ruth and Eloise looking at him with pained expressions.

"I tried," said Shaeffer. He grabbed his daughter by the arms, then kissed her on the forehead. "I wish things were different."

"Me too, Dad. I'm sorry."

"It's not your fault. Come on, Eloise. Let's go."

Shaeffer took his wife by the arm. Eloise looked at her daughter with sadness and kissed her on the cheek.

Esther had her arm around her mother's waist. She watched her grandparents leave then looked up at her mom and saw tears welling up in her eyes. She felt bad for being angry with her father. Her mother had told her not to be angry—she must be patient. "The explosion hurt more than Daddy's body," her mother had told her. "It hurt his heart, too." But, she had a hard time not being angry. She wasn't mad that he couldn't play soccer or any of the other games he used to play with her. She was mad because he was so unhappy, and he made everyone else unhappy. She hoped and prayed that things would change. Mommy had told her that maybe Grandpa could help fix things. She could tell from the way her grandparents had left and from the expression on her mommy's face that her Grandpa hadn't been able to fix Daddy. Out of the corner of her eye she saw her daddy wheel himself up to the screen door. Maybe she could cheer him up. She had worked all morning on the garden. Daddy loved his garden and hadn't been able to take care of it.

"See Daddy. See how I made the garden pretty again," said Esther excitedly.

David looked at the garden. Esther had pulled up some of the flowers that she must have thought were weeds; other plants she had pruned into a variety of misshaped forms.

"What the hell have you done?! You've ruined my beautiful garden, you stupid girl!"

Ruth spun around and stared at David in disbelief. Esther buried her head in her mother's apron and whimpered. As David watched his wife and daughter reel from his abusive remark, his words echoed back, piercing his heart with their cruel bitterness.

What have I become? he thought.

He wheeled himself away from the door and into the bedroom. He went over to the nightstand next to his side of the bed. He opened the top drawer trembling. He felt confused, possessed, dizzy; unable to focus. Yet, he felt compelled; drawn to the instrument that could end his pathetic existence. He didn't deserve to live. Any man who could hurt a little girl, his own daughter, for God's sake, wasn't worthy of life. He reached into the drawer; his hand shook as though he were reaching into a pit that hid a venomous serpent. He picked up the pistol. It already had a bullet in the chamber. All he had to do was stick the muzzle under his chin . . . . As he removed the pistol he saw a photograph of himself and his comrades. Ferdman was there with his two-year old.

I should have died in his place.

He continued to lift the pistol. Sharon Meisner was there with her boyfriend.

She never even had the opportunity to be a mother.

And there was Shansky. The goof off! He had turned around and mooned everyone!

How Shansky loved life! You wouldn't understand this would you, Joel?

The pistol was under his chin and his finger was on the trigger. He stared at the picture of his trio. It was as if they were forgiving him, or rather, he knew that they had never blamed him. But, if he pulled the trigger . . . now that was an act of betrayal and cowardice. There could be no forgiveness for that. Then the last words he had spoken with them came to mind,

But, a man dies as he lives. I want to die for Israel.

He began to struggle against the invisible force that was compelling him to pull the trigger. It was the hardest thing he had done, but he withdrew his finger from the trigger. Back from the precipice, he lowered the pistol, and trembling, pushed the button on the grip and watched the magazine drop out. He pulled back the cocking mechanism and ejected the bullet in the chamber. He put the pistol back into the drawer and closed it. The picture of his friends and comrades he left on the nightstand. He wheeled himself out of the bedroom into the foyer where his wife and daughter had just entered the house.

"I'm so sorry, Esther. Daddy's a jerk. Can you forgive me?"

Esther's mouth began to twitch as she tried not to cry. She wanted to be mad at him, but couldn't. She hugged her father and in a quivering voice whispered, "I love you, Daddy."

David smiled, all too aware of how unworthy he was of his daughter's love and forgiveness.

"Give me just a minute with Mommy, and then if you like, I'll go out with you and help you with the garden."

"I'd like that, Daddy," replied Esther, hoping that perhaps her father would be fixed after all. She went back outside to the garden.

Ruth looked at her husband bewildered.

"I want to give you something."

David held out his hands, but Ruth could not make out what they held. She held out both of her hands under his. He put into her hands the magazine and the single bullet that had just missed its deadly rendezvous. She looked down in horror at what her husband had just handed her. She grew pale at the thought of what had almost happened just moments before.

"I need your help, Ruth. I'm sorry . . . . I need your help . . . ."

A Great Mystery

For this reason a man shall leave his father and mother and be joined to his wife, and the two shall become one. This is a great mystery, and I mean in reference to Christ and the church.

~Ephesians 5:31,32

"Another cup of coffee, Detective?"

"Please," replied Lewis. "You're spoiling me with this good coffee of yours."

Mrs. Lefkowitz got up from the kitchen table and walked over to the coffeemaker. She brought back the pot and poured Lewis another cup. It had been nearly two years since the disappearance of her husband, Jimmy. Jimmy Lefkowitz had been a coroner. He had been working on a case with Detective Lewis. Shortly after doing an autopsy on Mrs. Maria O'Conner he had disappeared.

"And you, Miss Ryan?"

"Oh no," said Ryan, placing her hand over her cup. "If I drink any more, I'll have the jitters all day."

"I was hoping when you both dropped by that you would have some news for me about my Jimmy."

"I'm sorry. Every time I get a lead, it turns out to be a dead-end."

Ryan almost choked at his inappropriate metaphor. Jimmy Lefkowitz had been missing for well over two years now. His widow had long given up hope. Now, she sought closure. Lewis had hoped that he might be able to provide her with something, anything that might help her make sense of his death.

"I still believe," continued Lewis, "that the file holds the key. Are you sure you've thought of everything?"

"Yes. And I've looked everywhere. Nothing. I can't imagine where he might have placed it. Are you sure he said file?"

"Well, I thought he did. I'm beginning to wonder now."

"Maybe I should pray to Saint Anthony," said Ryan. "When I was younger, I'd pray to him whenever I misplaced things. He never failed."

Mrs. Lefkowitz smiled. Catholics, she thought, they have a saint for every problem and every occasion! "It's not right of me just to be thinking of myself and my Jimmy. How are things going with you, young lady? I heard you were in some trouble."

"Yeah, I've been in and out of prison. The last time was over that ridiculous charge of hate crime. So much for free speech. Anyway, it was a misdemeanor offense, so I was in and out. Actually, I'm getting kind of used to it. I figure it's about time . . . ."

Yap! Yap! Yap!

Mrs. Lefkowitz began to get up again from the kitchen table; her little poodle was barking at the back door.

"Little Joey needs to take care of business," said Mrs. Lefkowitz.

Ryan placed her arm on Mrs. Lefkowitz. "You sit. You've been jumping up and down all morning. I'll let him out."

Ryan walked through the laundry room. Joey was spinning in anxious little circles. Boy, thought Ryan, you really must need to go. She opened the door and Joey bolted out. As she was closing the door she noticed a mezuzah attached to the doorpost. It was tilted at an angle. She thought that perhaps she had bumped it. She grasped the mezuzah and tried to straighten it out. It wouldn't budge.

"I'm sorry," said Ryan as she sat back down at the table. "I think I bumped your a . . . little Jewish thing on the door post."

Mezuzah," Mrs. Lefkowitz said smiling.

"Yeah, that's it. I tried to straighten it, but it wouldn't budge."

"Oh, that's all right. I hung it that way."

"The one on your front door, if I recall," observed Lewis, "was straight."

"Yes, that's right. Jimmy hung that one. Some families hang them straight; others hang them crooked."

"Why is that?" asked Ryan.

"To be honest with you, I really don't know. There's probably a reason. One of Jimmy's friends brought it to me. It's one he had at his office."

Lewis' ears perked up. "Really?"

"A few weeks after Jimmy disappeared one of his colleagues packed up a few of his items and brought them to me. Wasn't that nice of them?"

"Do you mind if I look at it?" asked Lewis.

"Go ahead," said Mrs. Lefkowitz. As Lewis went to retrieve it, she continued, "I remember when Jimmy put it up in his office doorway someone complained. Church and state . . . you know all about that, don't you Miss Ryan? Well, it really got Jimmy mad, and eventually they made him take it down. So he hung it up where no one would see it, just to spite them. That's my Jimmy. I guess they were moving some furniture around, bookcases or something, when they found it. That's when Jimmy's friend brought it to me."

Lewis sat back down and placed the mezuzah on the table. He turned it over, inspecting it.

"There's something inside of it."

"Yes," said Mrs. Lefkowitz, "there's a tiny piece of paper with two scriptures from Deuteronomy written on it."

"May I take it out?" asked Lewis.

Mrs. Lefkowitz nodded. She was now curious as to why Lewis was so interested in the mezuzah. Lewis tried to remove the tiny papers inside, but his fingers were too big and clumsy to grasp them.

"Here," said Ryan. "Let me try."

Ryan grasped the tiny paper, pulled it out and handed it to Mrs. Lefkowitz. She opened the miniature scroll. Ryan and Lewis could see tiny Hebrew lettering on the paper.

"Yes, this is it," said Mrs. Lefkowitz.

Lewis looked crestfallen. He was hoping for something out of the ordinary.

"This is odd," said Mrs. Lefkowitz.

"What is it?" asked Lewis excitedly.

"Another scripture is written on the scroll. It looks like Jimmy's handwriting," said Mrs. Lefkowitz.

"What does it say?" asked Lewis.

"Wait a second," said Ryan pulling out her notepad.

"You'll have to forgive Ms. Ryan," said Lewis. "She's a journalist."

"You just never know what might be important," replied Ryan.

"It's from Deuteronomy," answered Mrs. Lefkowitz smiling at Ryan. "That's D-e-u-t-r-o-n-o-m-y. Chapter twelve, verse twenty-three: ' . . . for blood is life . . . . '"

"Is that it?" asked Ryan.

"Yes, that's all Jimmy wrote," answered Mrs. Lefkowitz.

"If Jimmy did write that, do you have any idea what he meant by it?" asked Lewis.

"I have no idea," replied Mrs. Lefkowitz. "But there is a stain next to the scripture he wrote. It looks like a blood stain."

"Really?!" said Lewis excitedly. "May I look at it?"

"Certainly," said Mrs. Lefkowitz, handing Lewis the scroll.

"It does look like a blood stain," exclaimed Lewis. "Would you mind if I kept this piece of paper? I'd like to have this stain analyzed."

"Certainly, if it would help," said Mrs. Lefkowitz.

"I think it might. I know someone with a lab that can help us out. He owes me a favor."

"Is there anyone around this city who doesn't owe you a favor?" teased Ryan.

"Not that I can think of."

A brief drive across town brought Lewis and Ryan to the medical labs of Mr. Adnan Getender. Mr. Getender was an industrious, well-educated Indian, who had set up a practice in an affluent suburb of

Washington, D.C. Most of his staff were family and friends he had brought over from India.

"And you want this when?"

"Today," said Lewis

"Impossible! Look around. See how busy everyone is. But, I tell you what I'll do for you, soon as . . . ."

"Today," repeated Lewis.

"I heard you retired."

"From the Force. I didn't retire my brain, Adnan, or my memory. But I like you. That's why I am going to ask again. Today."

Adnan Getender frowned. He took the small scrap of paper from Lewis and walked over to a microscope mumbling to himself. "See, this is what happens when you try to make a better life for your family. I set up a medical laboratory, employed family and friends, all trained in the best schools in India, mind you, and what do I get . . . harassment."

Lewis smiled at Ryan. "We're actually good friends," he told her. "This is a little ritual we have to go through every time I ask a favor of him."

"Favor!" exclaimed Adnan. He had now placed the scrap of paper under a microscope. But, Ryan saw that this was not the kind of microscope she had used in high school, a purplish light shown on the scrap of paper. "I am a busy man. Do you care when you come by and say, 'Adnan do this! Adnan do that!" Adnan turned knobs to adjust the focus.

"Mr. Getender was giving kickbacks to doctors," explained Lewis.

"Kickbacks! Nonsense. I was simply showing my gratitude to doctors who referred patients to me. This is an ungrateful country," replied Mr. Getender, peering into the microscope. "Yes, this is blood. Remarkably well preserved, I might add. I see some well-formed red and white cells. How old did you say this sample is?"

"About two years," replied Lewis.

"No. That is not possible. The cells would have lysed."

Lewis watched as Ryan pulled out the ubiquitous notepad. "You would have made a good detective."

Ryan smiled. "What was that again? Lysed?" asked Ryan.

"Yes, that's right. Burst or broken up because of dehydration. No, these cells are fresh." Adnan removed the paper from the microscope and held it up to the light. "It is dry, though. It is a puzzle. Where did you get this?"

"So what else can you tell me?" asked Lewis, ignoring Adnan's question.

"Blood type, DNA profile perhaps."

"Yes. But, I don't want the sample destroyed."

"I just need the tiniest sample of it." Adnan walked over to another apparatus, sat down in front of a monitor and typed in some instructions. "You are lucky that the technology for this type of analysis has advanced," he continued. "There was a time when this would have taken weeks. You, being an impatient man, would no doubt have been annoyed." He took a tiny stainless steel needle and pushed it through the outer edge of the bloodstain. He then placed the needle into a holder in the machine and closed a little door. "Now I just type a few more instructions for the computer to disregard the cellulose and other plant material in the paper and . . . ." he grabbed the mouse ". . . click analyze. Now we wait."

"How long?" asked Lewis.

"A few minutes. We'll get the blood type first. The DNA profile takes longer. I suppose we are following the usual protocols. I can discuss this with no one."

"That's right," replied Lewis.

"Haven't I seen you before, Miss Ryan?"

"Probably," she replied as she continued to jot down notes.

"That's right. In the newspaper and on TV. You had something to do with . . . . Oh no, you're not getting me involved in all that are you?" he asked Lewis.

Lewis put his finger to his lips, indicating that Adnan was better off not asking any more questions.

Adnan shook his head and muttered something in Hindi that neither Lewis nor Ryan understood.

"Here we go," said Adnan. Results were appearing on the monitor. "What you have here is actually two blood samples."

"No, that can't be right," said Lewis.

"Look," said Adnan pointing to the monitor. "You see, there are two blood types, BB and AB. A person cannot have two types of blood cells."

Lewis looked over at Ryan. She shrugged.

"Well look, here comes some more data," continued Adnan. "You see, this has to be two blood samples mixed together. We have two completely different karyotypes." Adnan typed a few more commands into the computer. The monitor showed groups of chromosomes paired together. "See," he said pointing to the monitor. "On the left, that is the karyotype of a woman; there, see the XX. Now on the right side here, there's an XY. What you have here is the blood of a woman and a man mixed together."

Lewis and Ryan looked at each other perplexed. "Why would Jimmy mix Maria's blood with someone else's?" asked Ryan.

"Can we be sure that this is Maria's blood?" asked Lewis.

"Here's the DNA profile," said Adnan, pointing to the monitor again. What appeared to Lewis and Ryan as an indecipherable series of colored bars made perfect sense to Adnan. "There are a few genes here on the male that the computer cannot identify. They are not part of the human genome database. Huh, maybe a glitch or perhaps contamination. Wait a minute. Some of these genes are part of the woman's genome also. It would seem that these two individuals were related, perhaps siblings? If you know who these individuals are I would like to run another sample to check to see whether there is a problem with the analysis."

"No, I'm afraid not. I thought we knew who the woman was. But, we don't have any other blood samples from her," said Lewis.

"Wait a minute!" exclaimed Ryan excitedly. "Would hair work?"

"Yes, we can do a DNA profile from hair if there are any cells present within the sample."

Ryan pulled a locket out from under her blouse, lifted it over her head and reverently placed it on the counter. She opened the locket. Inside was a small braid of brownish-black hair tied with a tiny purple ribbon. She withdrew several strands of hair from the braid and handed it to Adnan.

"I cut off a sample of Maria's hair the day she died," she said as she closed the locket. She then kissed the locket and put it back over her neck.

"Yes, I remember," said Lewis.

Using forceps, Adnan placed the hair in a tiny test tube. He inserted a stopper in the test tube and connected a tiny plastic tube to a needle that stuck out of the stopper. He placed this in another compartment of the analyzer and typed in some more instructions.

"This will take a few minutes. What I will do is compare the DNA profiles of the woman from the blood sample to the DNA profile from the hair. We'll know for certain if they are from the same person. Now, while we wait. I probably should not get involved with this . . . ."

"Probably not," interrupted Lewis.

"But some of my people," continued Adnan, "believe Maria O'Conner is an incarnation of Shiva."

Ryan looked perplexed.

"You see, many in my community believe Chimæra is bad karma. It is only through death and rebirth that we can hope to attain union with Brahma. Shiva, they say, had to reestablish the cycle of death. So, she was incarnated in your friend, Mrs. O'Conner.

"Is Shiva with an 'e' or an 'i'?" asked Ryan, pen poised over her notebook.

"An 'i.'" answered Getender. "Here we go," he said pointing to the monitor. "On the right is the DNA profile of the woman taken from the blood sample. On the left is the one from the hair. Yes. They are the same person."

Lewis clenched his fist. "Yes!" he exclaimed.

"Praise God!" said Ryan.

"This is odd," said Adnan. "The genes that we could not identify that were in her blood sample are not present in the hair sample."

"How do you explain that?" asked Lewis.

"I'm not sure. Perhaps the genes transferred from the male sample to the female when the blood was mixed—some kind of transposon[54] phenomenon. I do not know. You have a mystery here."

"Yes," replied Ryan as she spelled 'transposon' to herself as she wrote it down. When she was finished she looked up and said, "The ways of God are often mysterious."

Resubstantiation

Nothing was beyond his power; beneath him flesh was brought back into life.

~*Sirach 48:13*

"This is one helluva party, Hans! One hell of a party!" said President Pearson not knowing exactly how to describe the event he was witnessing.

The entire Obermann estate had been transformed into a carnival. There were death-defying performances, magic shows, wild animal acts, and booths for the kiddies to play games and win toys. The event was even being televised worldwide—everyone was enthralled by the child whose birthday was being celebrated today.

"A remarkable party, for a remarkable young man," said Colin.

The trio slowly walked around the periphery of the "event." They would rejoin the party after they had discussed a few "details" that Obermann wanted clarified.

"So how old is he?" asked Pearson. "I mean, I know that this is his second birthday, but, you know what I mean, what do the doctors say?"

"Dr. Richardson and her team say that, physiologically, he is about thirteen years old. Intellectually, he absorbs his books and lessons at a rate that far exceeds any and all criteria. But, social maturity . . . , that's been a problem for him. You see, he outgrows his friends so quickly. Fortunately, he has a few friends like Diego," Obermann placed his arm around Colin's shoulder. "Diego has become like a little brother to Frederick."

Colin smiled sheepishly. He hoped that Obermann's "perception of angels" did not allow him to perceive just how terrified Diego was of Frederick. It wasn't that Frederick had actually done anything to Diego. Diego couldn't explain why he felt the way he did when he was around Frederick. Colin was sure that he was just imagining things. But, he had somehow convinced Cynthia that there was something wrong with Frederick. She would always argue with him about sending Diego over to the Obermann's to play with Frederick. But, he would remind her that Diego was his son, and that she should stop interfering. This probably would have eventually led to a crisis in their relationship, but as Frederick got "older" he wasn't asking for Diego as much. In fact, today was the first time Diego had been with Frederick in months. Cynthia assured him that she would stay with him all the time, in spite of Colin scolding both of them for being "babies."

"He's different, and that can be difficult," continued Obermann. "It's not that he doesn't like being different. He does. I've made sure he realizes that his uniqueness is a gift; a gift to humanity. But, it can be trying at times for him. You know he didn't want his birthday to be televised, but when letters from all over the world poured in expressing their disappointment, well, he conceded. That's just the way he is. Always putting the needs of others first. But, back to business, right gentlemen? I think things seem to be progressing splendidly. Six new Chimæra Distribution Centers opening within the next few months, more and more Tree of Life communities springing up, hate crime legislation in place protecting Chimærics . . . . Why, there's even a sit-com starting this Fall where one of the characters is a black, gay, Chimæric. Now that's what I call diversity!"

The trio rounded one of the estate ponds and proceeded through a grove of elms as they began their trek back towards the birthday festivities.

"I don't want to rain on your parade," began President Pearson.

"Russia?" inquired Obermann.

"Yes. It seems that they are dramatically increasing their oil production, and they have managed to keep at least portions of the Alliance together. Our effort to establish a resistance movement against Goricsan's reforms has met with minimal success. Up until recently, Russia had the lowest birth rate of any European nation. They were well below replacement level. This, you might remember, was part of the West's plan to help restrain Russia's imperialistic tendencies. Now, Goricsan has given significant tax breaks to married couples that have more than two children. Russia, which used to have the highest rate of abortion in Europe, now has the lowest. He has this whole cultural revolution thing going on. They call it 'conversion.'"

"This is a phenomenon," interrupted Colin, "that I have some familiarity with. You no doubt remember how the Ayatollah of Iran was fond of calling the West the Great Satan. Such rhetoric seems to be spreading not only throughout the Islamic world, but also in the Christian East. I have also heard the reports coming out of Russia. There is a growing national Messianism occurring in Russia."

"Yes that is true," continued the President. "And there is no reason to believe that they intend to keep this movement within their own borders."

"Of course, gentlemen," interrupted Obermann, "you have yet to grasp the big picture. This is the *raison d'être* of the Great Alliance. The control of world oil is a secondary, albeit an important, objective. Conflict is likely inevitable. But, in the meantime we will continue to promote Chimæra and the New Era, while tightening the economic noose around our adversaries. We will grow stronger while they grow weaker. And who knows, perhaps as they slide into economic ruin they will turn over their newfound messiahs to us for thirty pieces of silver. It's happened before. Why not again?" Obermann said with a wicked grin. "But now, I must join my son. Ah, there he is!"

Colin looked over at the crowd of young children watching what appeared from a distance to be some type of magic show. Several rows of chairs were arranged in a semicircle around a stage. As they approached the performance, Colin could see an attractive young woman take her position against a backboard, her body was outlined by balloons. A man dressed as a Gypsy tied her hands to hooks that were connected to the backboard. The woman appeared to be in her late twenties. Her costume accentuated her curvaceous figure. She had a dark complexion and shoulder length black hair. Colin thought she might be Latina or perhaps Italian. She reminded him of Maria. The man stepped away from the stage and walked about ten paces to where a small table and wooden box had already been set up. He then dramatically removed large knives with shiny polished blades. He laid the knives out carefully on a small table to his right. Colin spotted Diego. He was seated to the left of the performers. Cynthia was next to him.

Pop!

The audience squealed with delight. There was some clapping and nervous laughter. The man had thrown the first knife, and it had pierced the balloon next to the woman's right hand. Colin moved through the crowd. Obermann was already standing next to his son who was seated a few seats from Diego and closer to the stage. He seemed to be thoroughly entranced by the performance. Diego looked up as he saw his father approach.

"Daddy, this scares me," said Diego.

Cynthia looked up when she heard Diego speak. She had been unaware of Colin's arrival. She frowned at Colin. She didn't have to say a word. He could read from her expression that she was not pleased with the performance. No doubt, she thought it was inappropriate for the age group. But, she is too protective of Diego, thought Colin. And besides, it is Frederick's birthday party and he was . . . more mature.

Pop!

"Don't worry," said Colin reassuringly. "It's a trick. They don't use real knives. No one will get hurt."

Pop!

The man dressed as a Gypsy reached down for another knife. He looked at the young woman who was his wife. Their eyes met. Now was the time. The man picked up the knife. He flipped it several times grasping the knife each time by the handle. There was a clear line-of-sight between him and Obermann's son. What a glorious honor to be a martyr for the true Successor! What a glorious honor to be chosen to slay the beast!

Frederick sensed something was wrong. Perhaps it was the delay between the popping balloons. Perhaps it was the expression on the face of the woman who appeared almost pinned against the stage backdrop. No, it was the inner voice that warned him of danger. Obermann sensed it too. But it was too late. The knife had been hurled with tremendous force and speed and in less than a blink of an eye it would strike its target burying itself fatally deep into Frederick's skull. Too late to duck; too late to cry out. Father and son's eyes met in a moment of desperate helplessness. But, as immediate as their awareness of the impending disaster was the unseen intervention that deflected the blade from its deadly mission.

Sclunck!

The sound of the blade piercing flesh and blood, muscle and bone were followed by a low, guttural groan and the exhalation of a final breath. The knife had broken through the sternum, had driven itself all the way to its hilt, and split open her heart. Her head slouched on her chest, the young performer hung lifeless, a bizarre cruciform parody outlined by gaily colored balloons.

Some of the audience screamed in horror while others just stared in disbelief. A few clapped, thinking that this was part of the show. Diego buried his face in his hands. Colin looked at the scene in bewilderment. Cynthia was now standing with her hands covering her mouth and her eyes opened wide. The knife thrower just stood motionless, expressionless, in shock.

Obermann looked at his son. How? Obermann thought.

Frederick did not answer but raised his hand slightly as if to say, Wait, all will be answered soon enough.

Security personnel finally converged on the scene. Some took their places next to the Obermanns; the others to the woman who hung lifeless on the stage. A doctor emerged from the audience and pushed his way through the security personnel surrounding the woman. He felt for a carotid pulse while examining the wound. There was nothing that could be done. He shook his head. Now the full impact of the catastrophe finally overwhelmed the woman's husband. He fell to his knees.

"He's the devil's child," the man shouted, pointing to Frederick. "He is responsible . . . ."

The two security guards who were standing next to the man now seized him, recognizing for the first time that he might be a threat to the Obermanns.

"Wait," exclaimed Frederick loudly. "This is my party and my birthday. Today, this woman will be born anew!"

All eyes were on the young Frederick as he walked over to the dead woman. The security personnel stepped aside so that Frederick could approach; even the doctor gave way. Frederick stood before the woman. There was not a sound to be heard as everyone's attention was focused on what young Obermann was doing. Frederick reached out with his left hand and placed it on the woman's upper torso near the right clavicle. He pushed the body hard against the backboard. Then with his right hand he grasped the handle of the knife firmly and with a steady and deliberate force pulled the blade from her chest. A ghastly sucking could be heard as the blade came out, and the crowd gasped at the sight and the sound of Frederick's action. Frederick now held the bloodied blade out in front of him. Puzzled eyes watched not only from the audience but from homes across America where people stared dumbstruck at their television sets. Frederick withdrew his left hand from the woman and held it close to the knife's razor-sharp edge. He then drew the knife's blade across his palm, making a quarter-inch deep incision in his hand. People in the audience jumped and screamed, but Frederick did not flinch. He ripped open the woman's blouse and pressed his bleeding hand against the still oozing wound in her chest. He stood motionless pushing hard against her chest so that blood was forced from his hand into her wound. Frederick felt an odd, inexplicable excitement coursing through his body as his hand pressed against the warm flesh of the woman's breasts.

Several minutes passed. Not a sound could be heard; all were transfixed by the spectacle before them. Obermann began to hear the nonverbal mutterings of minds nearby. What is he doing? She's dead, there's nothing anyone can do for her. Why doesn't somebody stop him? This is just making a horrible tragedy worse. Obermann began to wonder as well.

Suddenly, a sucking of air could be heard from the direction of the stage. The woman's head lifted, and her chest rose as it filled with air. She coughed several times spitting up blood. Everyone in the immediate vicinity took a step back, except for Frederick. He removed his hand from her blouse and then took the knife and cut loose the bindings that had held her against the backboard. He caught her body as she fell forward. Again, he felt the perplexing sensation as her body slumped into his arms and her breasts pressed against him. He was both relieved and annoyed as others moved forward and helped to support her.

"Bring her to the house," said Obermann who now stood next to his son. "And bring him also," he said, pointing to her husband who was being held by security personnel.

"Have the woman taken to my room," whispered Frederick to his father. "I would like to be alone with her for a few minutes."

Obermann nodded. He beckoned the President with a wave of his hand. Although Jack Pearson was still white faced and shaky he trotted over dutifully to Obermann's side. "Say something appropriate," said Obermann. "The party's over."

It didn't take long for Obermann to ascertain what had happened. A few moments alone within the husband's consciousness revealed that the knife had indeed been intended for his son. It did not surprise Obermann that this assassination attempt was associated with Bishop

Entremont and the Congregation of Saint Pierre. He did, after all, already have personal experience with them. But this assassin, Elliot Hoffman, was not a Catholic. He was a member of an Evangelical sect that had formed some sort of confederation with the Congregation. Obermann found this disturbing. The Congregation had been secretly supported by Obermann and the Administration to help create division within Christianity. Indeed, the Congregation had even been used by the President in Obermann's assassination. Since then, efforts were being made to rein in the Congregation's influence. Now it appeared to be forming alliances with a variety of religious groups. The fact that they were almost able to carry off another assassination, this time against his only son, was an unacceptable development. Something had to be done.

Obermann wanted to extract more information from the man. He could have, but such a penetration would have revealed his presence. Then he would have had to kill him. No, thought Obermann, there might be a way to use him as long as he does not suspect that I know his identity and mission.

"I want to see Elaina," Hoffman demanded. "I want to see my wife now!"

"You will," replied Obermann. "But I know something about coming back. It can be a traumatic experience. My son is helping as she returns to you from the Penumbra Realm."

Obermann said all of this in a most reassuring way, yet he, too, was beginning to wonder what was taking so long. Why had his son not returned with the woman? He began to worry. The man had, after all, tried to kill his son. Perhaps his wife would try to finish the job! He didn't sense any danger, but then again, he had not sensed it earlier. Not until the last moment when it was too late to respond.

"I will bring her to you," said Obermann.

As Obermann left the room he signaled for a security guard to remain with Hoffman. Obermann walked briskly down the long hall and jogged up the stairs. Although he didn't sense any immediate alarm or urgency there were still many questions he was anxious to ask his son. How had Frederick deflected the knife? How was he able to bring the woman back to life? He figured that somehow his unique Chimæric cells had something to do with it. But, how did he manage to return her soul to her body? He reached his son's door. It was closed.

Obermann opened the door. His mouth dropped in disbelief. Frederick lay naked on the bed propped up by pillows against the headboard. The once dead woman, also naked, straddled his son's legs. Frederick used his finger to draw concentrically smaller circles around one of her breasts.

"Father!" exclaimed Frederick delighted to see him enter the room. "I had no idea! How come you never told me about sex?"

Obermann was dumbfounded. Tell him about sex?! He'd just turned two today! Granted his physiology was more like a thirteen-year old, but he had no idea that his son was ready for anything like this! And the woman! Moments ago she and her husband had risked everything to kill his son. Now she was making love to him!

"I . . . I . . . ," stammered Obermann.

"Oh, that's all right, Father," replied Frederick. "Elaina showed me everything!"

"Everything?" repeated Obermann.

Now, for the first time the woman turned her attention away from Frederick and faced Obermann. Obermann's knees nearly buckled at the force of lustful passion projected in the woman's expression. She took Frederick's hand, extended one of his fingers, and inserted it in her mouth. She slowly withdrew it, never taking her eyes off Obermann.

"Everything," she said breathlessly.

Obermann took a couple of steps back.

"Come, Father, join us. I know you want to."

He did want to. That's what surprised him. The idea of participating in an orgy with his young son was repulsive, yet he felt drawn by the powerful seduction of the woman. Finally, he shook off her enchantment.

"No. Get dressed. Both of you."

The woman crawled off Frederick, stood by the side of the bed, bent over and kissed him on the cheek.

"We'll have to do that again sometime," she said.

"I hope so!" said Frederick exuberantly.

The woman grabbed her clothes that were scattered at the foot of the bed. She walked over to Obermann holding the clothes over her abdomen. Obermann could see what appeared to be a faint scar and patches of dried blood between her breasts. She stood shamelessly in front of him.

"I wonder if the father is as good as the son?"

"The bathroom is over there," said Obermann, pointing to the adjoining room. "Why don't you take a shower. Take a look in the dresser. I believe you'll find a shirt that will fit you. You can't wear that," he pointed to the bloody shirt.

She smiled and walked towards the bathroom exaggerating the motion of her hips. Obermann couldn't help but watch. His son had been pulling up his pants stopped and watched Elaina leave the room.

"You disapprove?" Frederick asked, as he buttoned his pants.

"I don't know what to think," said Obermann.

"Oh, it was amazing! You should have told me!"

"I had no idea that you were ready for anything like this. You're not like other children."

"You're right, Father," said Frederick, as he sat at the end of the bed lacing up his shoes. "I'm better. I can do things that no one else can do, not even you."

"So it would seem. I have many questions I need to ask you. Some can wait. But, others I need to ask now."

"Sure, Father. You know I keep nothing from you."

"Perhaps," said Obermann, "but obviously there are things about you, things that you can do, that, I did not know you could do."

"Like what?"

"Like how you brought that woman back to life. I know something about coming back to life, after all."

"My blood, Father," replied Frederick. "You know my blood has life."

"I know that. But I did not know that it would work on another person."

"Neither did I. I have tried it on my pets, and it worked."

"You mean you've killed your pets?!"

"Yes, and then I bring them back to life."

"But people are different. They have a spirit, a spirit that leaves the body at death. That woman, Elaina, is not a Chimæric. Her spirit must have left her body when she died."

"It did," replied Frederick nonchalantly.

"But . . . she has consciousness."

"You don't see them, do you, Father?" Frederick had suspected that his father could not perceive this realm. He had always been able to see them. He had thought everyone could, until one of them had told him that only he could see and communicate with them. But, Frederick knew that his father was special. He had traversed the Penumbra Realm and had the "perception of angels." He had thought at first that this meant that his father could perceive angels. Now it was clear that he could not.

"See who?"

"The Incorporeals."

"You mean like angels and demons?"

"You don't believe me?"

"Oh, trust me, I believe you. Remember I met one and it wasn't a very pleasant experience. But I don't see them. Sometimes I am aware of another consciousness when I am alone."

"That's them."

"And you see them now?"

"Yes, you have several that have been assigned to you."

"And you can communicate with these . . . Incorporeals?"

"Yes. There are some that are against us and some that are for us. They are always whispering in peoples' ears."

Obermann rubbed his chin. This was a fascinating and unexpected development. He had been given the gift of the "perception of angels" in the Penumbra Realm. With this gift he could see the image of a man, and the extent to which he had yielded to this image. He had also learned how to enter the consciousness of another. Selfishness, lust, hatred, any vice, were like windows left open through which his mind could crawl entering their secret thoughts. But, Frederick's perception was different, complementary. He would have to reflect on this more deeply. But, there were more immediate issues at hand.

"So what do these incorporeals have to do with the woman?" asked Obermann.

"After I restored the body, I invited an incorporeal to occupy it. The incorporeal spirit gave life to the body," replied Frederick.

Obermann stared at his son in awe. Frederick had resubstantiated a body with a demon! It all made sense now. This woman, Elaina, had been part of the conspiracy to kill his son. Now, she had introduced him to the joy of sex! The woman appeared from the bathroom having showered and now wearing one of Obermann's shirts. As she walked towards them she slowly buttoned the shirt. She relished the power of being able to mesmerize them with her sexuality. Obermann stared intently at her as she approached him.

"Can you behave yourself?" Obermann asked finally.

"That depends on what you mean by behave," replied Elaina coyly.

"What I mean is, can you behave like Elaina, the woman who was married to the man who tried to murder my son? Or are you going to act like some out-of-control nymphet?"

Elaina uttered a sinister laugh that sent a chill down Obermann's spine. "Of course I can control myself. This is not the first body I've possessed. But, thanks to your son . . ." She turned her attention to him and stroked his cheek. "I have a body all to myself. No other wills to contend with, save that of the Master whose will it is that I serve you."

"Do you have a name?" asked Obermann.

"My name is Legion . . . just kidding. Why don't you call me Elaina. Less confusing. Now that I have served master Frederick, how may I serve you?"

"Return to your husband," said Obermann.

"Uhmm . . . He is terribly religious. You know, I learned most of what I showed Master Frederick from uptight religious folks. I remember one time . . . ."

"Later," interrupted Obermann. "Your husband is waiting and I don't want him to become any more suspicious than he already must be. I want you to go to him and act like his wife, everything back to normal, the way it was before she died. Can you do that?"

"Yes. Her engrams are still intact. Who she was, I will be . . . well, maybe a bit more mischievous."

"I want you to infiltrate the Congregation of Saint Pierre. They were responsible for my assassination, and now they have made an attempt on the life of my son. I already tried to extract information from your husband but was not very successful. Either he was kept in the dark or he has a way of blocking my access to parts of his consciousness."

"It is both," replied Elaina. "Information was deliberately denied both of them for fear that you might be able to extract it from them through the abilities given to you by the Master. But you are right. I sense there is more they know, but not even I seem to be able to detect what it is."

"You must find out everything you can. How will I be able to communicate with you?"

"Through your son," replied Elaina. "Frederick, when your father wishes to see me, just communicate with an Incorporeal and he will let me know."

Frederick nodded. "And if I would like to see you again?"

"You will talk with me first," said Obermann.

Obermann, Frederick and Elaina entered the den where her husband had been waiting for her. When they entered the room Elliot stood up, but did not advance towards her. He examined her from a distance, silently looking for a sign to indicate that the woman who stood before him was still actually his wife.

"Mr. Hoffman," Obermann finally said. "Your wife," he now gently pushed Elaina towards her husband, "needs you now. We'll leave you two alone for the moment." Father and son left through the door by which they had entered.

Hoffman took a step back, stumbled and fell into the chair. Elaina went over to him; knelt on one knee, and took his hands into hers.

"It's me, Ellie," she whispered. Only Elaina called him this, and only during the most intimate of circumstances.

"Is it really you?"

"Yes, my dear, it is."

"But how?"

"Don't worry about that now," she whispered. "They think they control me, but they can't. They'll take me into their confidence. Then when they least expect it . . ."

Elliot understood her meaning.

"We won't disappoint Bishop Entremont next time," she continued.

"Quiet," Hoffman rebuked her, "Do not mention his name."

"Don't worry my love. No one heard me." Elaina kissed her husband. They were the familiar, warm, moist lips of his wife. Yet . . . he felt as if something was being sucked from him. A momentary suspicion flashed like lightning across his consciousness, but just as quickly it was evaporated by the heat of pleasure that radiated back to him through her.

Dr. Richardson was working in the lab when she received a call from Dr. Yarelis, a physician in the employ of Chimæra, Inc. He had been one of the physicians attending Maria O'Conner after she had been injected with Chimæric stem-cells. He had been attending Frederick's party and witnessed the terrible accident that had occurred and the remarkable "resurrection" performed by Obermann's son.

"You'd better get over here right away!"

"You mean the birthday party?" inquired Richardson, surprised by the note of alarm in Yarelis's voice. What could go wrong at a birthday party? she thought.

"Yeah! Obermann wants you here right now. Don't you know what's happened?"

"What are you talking about?"

"Jeez, I thought you'd at least be watching the party on television!"

Richardson had, of course, been invited to the party. She had found an excuse for not going. She didn't particularly like Frederick. She couldn't put her finger on it. It wasn't that he was Chimæric and had demonstrated remarkable physiological and intellectual abilities. And he certainly was polite, even gracious. No, she just couldn't put her finger on it. There was something about him that just made her uneasy. Sometimes, Richardson wondered if she hadn't made a mistake when she had complied with Obermann's request to implant a Chimæric embryo in the womb of his dead wife. She tried to suppress these thoughts, not only because her rational scientific mind told her that she was being illogical, but also because she was concerned that Obermann might suspect her misgivings about Frederick. That is why she had wanted to avoid the birthday party.

"No, I wasn't. Is everything okay?"

"My God! I can't believe you missed it. Frederick just raised some woman from the dead!"

"What?!"

"That's right! And Obermann wants you down here right now!"

Richardson was shown into the room where Obermann and Frederick had been monitoring Elaina and Elliot Hoffman.

"What's this I hear about . . ." started Richardson.

"Almost an hour ago," Obermann interrupted and pointed to the monitor, "that woman had a six-inch knife blade buried in her heart. She was dead, and Frederick brought her back to life."

"How?"

"We will discuss that later. In the meantime, I would like to introduce you to them. And I would like you, and Dr. Yarelis, to give her a quick exam and then maybe later you could give her a more thorough examination."

"She should be admitted to our clinic for . . ."

"No. Trust me. She's quite fine, isn't she Frederick?"

"Oh yes, very fine indeed!" replied Frederick.

Richardson turned and stared at Frederick. He had said it in such a tone of voice that she immediately caught the sexual connotation.

"That brings me to the other thing I wanted to discuss with you. I would like you to examine Frederick."

"He was just in a week or so ago. He's not due for a checkup for another couple of weeks."

"Things have changed," replied Obermann.

"I look forward to the examination, Dr. Richardson," said Frederick with a wry, even a seductive grin.

Elaina pulled her lips away from her husband. He sat numb, trembling, with his eyes closed and his lips still slightly extended.

"Take me home," she said. She stood and pulled her husband up. He was surprised by her strength, especially considering what she had just been through.

Yes, home, he thought. How very much he wanted to take her home and be alone with her. Obermann, Frederick and Richardson entered the room.

"Excuse me," said Obermann gently, "I am sure that you would like to go home. You have both been through a traumatic experience. But, I believe it would be best, Elaina, if you were examined by Dr. Richardson. She is our head of research at Chimæra."

"I want to be with my wife," said Hoffman.

"Yes, of course," replied Obermann. "Dr. Yarelis will be joining you. He is a medical doctor. It won't take long, and then I will have someone take you home. I would also like to give you something for your . . . inconvenience?" Obermann handed Hoffman a check for a hundred thousand dollars.

"This is not necessary," said Hoffman surprised by the sum. He attempted to hand it back, but Obermann refused.

"Don't be rash. Think about it. If you decide you don't want it, tear it up. If you change your mind, well then, you have enough to get some training in a less risky profession."

Elaina snatched the check from Hoffman's hand and shoved it into her shirt pocket. Richardson then took Elaina by the arm and led her and Hoffman out of the den.

"Dr. Yarelis is waiting for us in the clinic," said Dr. Richardson. "It is in another building on the estate. It's just a few minutes walk through the garden."

As the trio left the Obermann residence, they could see that most of the guests had already gone home. Those that had not, stared at them as they passed. As they walked by the stage where the "accident" had happened, Elaina stopped. Hoffman shuddered at the sight of the bloodstained stage. Elaina smiled wickedly.

Obermann and Frederick were left alone in the den. Obermann went over to the mantel, opened the humidor and removed a cigar.

"So, Frederick," Obermann momentarily paused to light his cigar, "what I want to know is how that knife was redirected from you to Elaina? You didn't do it, did you?"

"You're right. It took me by surprise, too. But of course the Incorporeals were aware of it."

"You mean one of them redirected the knife?"

"Yes. In fact, the incorporeal that I placed in Elaina is the one that saved my life. That's his job, to guard me."

"You mean like a guardian angel?" asked Obermann.

"Yes, but they work for the Other, my guardians work for the Master."

"Do I have a guardian?"

"Yes, he is with you now. He is always with you. But he is not able to protect you as mine protects me. I am fully Chimæric. I am one with them. They serve me. With them, I am indestructible."

Obermann frowned. As remarkable as his son was, his behavior now seemed too self-assured, even cocky. Yes, he had thought that way too, once. But then that bastard Father Pietro had shot him in the head and killed him. He didn't need his son to become overconfident and make the same mistakes he had made.

"You don't believe me?" said Frederick, as he walked over to his father's desk.

"It's not that, it's just that . . . ."

Frederick opened the drawer and removed the revolver that his father always kept loaded.

"What the hell are you doing?!" cried Obermann. But before he even had a chance to intervene his son had placed the revolver in his mouth.

Bang!

Obermann fell into the chair horrified. He had expected to see the top of his son's head blow off. Instead, his son slowly removed the barrel of the revolver from his mouth. He then placed it back into the drawer. He walked around the desk and stood in front of his father. Frederick held his clenched left hand in front of him. Trembling, Obermann held out his right hand. Frederick dropped the bullet into it.

"What I am, you can be."

12/02 NEWERA

Soul-Companion

You have been my helper against my adversaries. You have saved
me from death, and kept back my body from the pit, from the clutches of
the nether world you have snatched my feet. . . .

~Sirach 51:2

Madrina and *ahijada*[55] walked down the riverbank with bundles of
clothing on their backs. It was time for the weekly wash. Ahead of
them they could see Mayan women squatting near the shore, pounding
their dirty clothes against flat stones, scrubbing them until their
whiteness and colors became vibrant as if new. A few of the women
had waded out into the river and were bathing. Of course, they were
fully dressed. They would wash themselves under their clothes, pull on
a clean skirt and then, and only then, would they remove their dirty
clothing. No respectable Mayan woman would ever completely disrobe,
not even in the presence of her husband.

It was only a few months after Father Suarez arrived that a most
terrible offense had occurred. One evening, Santiago was overcome by
a spirit of perversion. While he and his wife, Xunka, lay in bed, he

quietly reached for a flashlight. He crept under the covers, lifted up his wife's clothing and looked at her naked body. She awoke, catching him in the despicable act. Horrified, Xunka fled from the house in the middle of night and sought sanctuary with Rosario. After listening to Xunka's story, Rosario knew there could be only one course of action that could restore Xunka's dignity. In the morning they would call the elders together and she must sue for divorce.

"Divorce!" protested Mateas, overhearing his mother's conversation with his friend's wife. "This is ridiculous. Santiago loves Xunka."

"This is our way," corrected Rosario. "When a man lusts with the eyes, the love of the heart will eventually wax cold. And then, when his wife becomes older and he sees prettier flesh . . . ."

"No man in the highlands or in the Lacandon is likely to see the flesh of any woman. Only God knows what the women around here look like naked."

"And that is how it should be. That is why God clothed man and woman."

"But divorce is too extreme."

Father Suarez and several of the elders agreed with Mateas and Santiago. Father Humberto Suarez had never heard of this tradition and was surprised to discover that Mayan women were so modest.

"Please, try to understand," pleaded Father Suarez, "a man has certain desires. I know these things. I have heard many confessions. Is it not better that these desires be directed towards one's wife?"

"These are not the normal desires of a husband," insisted Rosario. "Santiago is an animal!"

Santiago, who sat with Mateas, hung his head in shame. Mateas placed his arm around Santiago's shoulder. "My life is ruined," Santiago said. "I will lose my Xunka. I will be cast out of the community. And the women will never tire of telling the story of the animal, Santiago."

Fortunately, these things did not occur. Father Suarez made it clear that the Church would not grant an annulment for such a "trivial" offense. In fact, he insisted, such a custom was contrary to the conjugal responsibilities of a wife. Father Suarez threatened that if Rosario and Xunka persisted with the divorce he would have to preach about such responsibilities from the pulpit. Rosario could not let this happen, so eventually a compromise was achieved in which Santiago was appropriately chastised. Thus began Rosario's relationship with Father Suarez, in which the two disputed, agreed, and compromised for the good of the Mayan community.

That event had occurred several years ago, yet it was still the favorite topic of gossip during laundry. Santiago had been right about that. When Xunka was present, the women would offer her sympathy as if she were a widow. How scandalized they would all be if they knew that Xunka now willingly kept a flashlight by the bed for her husband!

Rosario and *Ch'ucha'* approached the women expecting to hear, another telling of "Santiago the Animal," a story that had become more elaborate with each telling. Instead, Rosario heard one of the children recite a song that *Ch'ucha'* had been singing the day before.

> *iii iii iii laa laa laa*
> *You are small and plain.*
> *Happy not to be noticed;*
> *Content to be the least of birds,*
> *Little Sparrow.*
> *But another keeps his eyes fixed on me.*
> *Your tail is long,*
> *Your legs are strong,*
> *Your whiskers stand on end.*
> *Why are you looking at me black animal, black jaguar?*

"That child!" a woman said derisively. "Does she think she is better than our children? Does she really believe that the jaguar, the lord of animal spirits, is her soul-companion? Rosario is a wise woman, but I believe the child has bewitched her."

"I've seen her do odd, magical things with the white woman," said another woman, pounding her laundry with a stone. "The white woman is training her as if she were a warrior of *Chaan-Muan*![56] I saw them fighting with sticks like they were swords."

"She is only two and a half, yet she looks like she's eight years old!" said another woman, laying out her clean laundry on bushes to dry.

"The evening before last," said a young woman who was bathing, "when Mateas was in Palenque, I saw a spook enter Rosario's house. Maybe her soul-companion is not a jaguar but a spook?"

That last comment got everyone talking at once, speculating as to the possibility that *Ch'ucha'* was possessed by a demon. And if that was so, then perhaps Rosario's judgment should no longer be trusted. Anyway, it was not natural for the village to have a woman for a shaman. It might be time for a change.

Foolish women, thought Rosario, they are no better than cackling hens. Rosario did not know how much *Ch'ucha'* had heard of the gossiping. Was she aware of the whispering and stares? If she was, she had said nothing. Yet, as Rosario looked down at her goddaughter, her eyes, the eyes that were as blue as the Agua Azul, betrayed her pain and her anger. The pain she would have to bear. But *Kos*[57] help her, prayed Rosario, she must control her anger.

"No one likes her," said the child. "Sister Margarita makes us play with her, but no one wants to."

Rosario and *Ch'ucha'* emerged from the trail just as the young girl, *Ch'ucha's* "friend," had finished speaking. The women looked up embarrassed and perhaps a little frightened. *Ch'ucha'* ran into the forest, tears streaming from her eyes.

As *Ch'ucha'* ran sobbing, a few of the animals of the forest turned to watch the little girl. Birds flitted from branch to branch following *Ch'ucha'* as she ran. A squirrel ran along behind her. Two reflective eyes watched from a tree as *Ch'ucha'* ran beneath him. Finally, she arrived in a clearing where the forest canopy opened and a brilliant blue sky shone above her. She fell to her knees and covered her ears with her hands.

Send fire from heaven upon them!

She pushed harder against her ears as if to prevent the voice that spoke to her anger. It was no use. The voice resounded in her mind; her heart pounded and her body shook with rage. She stood and raised her arms with clenched fists. The prophetic words were forming in her throat and were about to be released in a terrible judgment against her persecutors . . . .

"No! *Mija.* You are *Batz'i Kristiana,*"⁵⁸ said Rosario placing a hand on her shoulder.

Ch'ucha's arms fell to her sides. She unclenched her fists, took a deep breath, and looked up at her *madrina* trembling; beads of sweat drenched her face. Rosario looked into her eyes and smiled sympathetically at her. *Ch'ucha'* bent over and convulsed. Rosario knelt down and held onto her tightly as she vomited several more times. When she was done, Rosario reached under her *huipil* and removed a handkerchief. Rosario wiped her mouth and bloody nose then held her head against her chest. *Ch'ucha's* trembling finally subsided.

"You are being tested," Rosario said.

Ch'ucha' looked up at her *madrina*; tears streamed down her cheeks. "Why?" she whimpered.

Kos desires to grant you more powers."

"No," replied *Ch'ucha'* angrily. "No more powers! I have prayed that He take away the powers I already have, but He will not."

"These powers have been given to you to serve the people," explained Rosario. "You need help in wielding these powers."

"Who? The Ancestors? *Kos*? They made me this way. I know this; I have dreamt it."

There was no disputing the dream world. Rosario knew that it was so for she too had dreamt it even before *Ch'ucha'* and Ludmelia had arrived. She was the child. Now that *Ch'ucha'* had dreamt, it meant that the time was near for the next phase of her development. If she were to defeat the Lords of *Xibalba* she would need the help of her soul-companion.

"You see him watching you, do you not?" asked Rosario.

"Who?" replied *Ch'ucha'*, although she suspected who her *madrina* was speaking of.

Kos has given each Maya two souls," Rosario began to explain. "The *ch'ulel* is the soul that Father Suarez speaks of. It is crafted in the image of God and is immortal. But, *Kos* has given the Maya another soul, a mortal soul, the *chanul.* It is our animal soul, and He has placed an identical *chanul* into the animal that is destined to be our soul-companion. Our soul-companion is our helper, our protector. He helps us to fulfill our *ch'ulel* destiny."

Ch'ucha' was fascinated. She knew that every Mayan had a soul-companion, but this was the first she had heard that she had two souls. She suspected that Sister Margarita would not be teaching her this in catechism class.

"Your soul-companion will be revealed to you in your dreams," continued Rosario. Rosario looked up at the sky noting the position of the sun. It was getting late; soon it would be evening. "That is enough for now," said Rosario, realizing that the best instruction leaves the pupil wanting to learn more. "And the laundry can wait for tomorrow. Come home and help me prepare dinner."

Ch'ucha' nodded and together they walked through the fields of maize carrying their unwashed laundry. As they walked, *Ch'ucha'* thought about all that her *madrina* had told her. She wished that the little sparrow were her soul-companion. It woke her every morning with its joyous carefree chirping. Its littleness and frailty were guarantors of its insignificance and therefore, freedom. But, as they walked towards Rosario's house, *Ch'ucha'* sensed other eyes watching her from the jungle, eyes that frightened her although she did not understand why.

* * *

"A man cannot live without tortillas," said Rosario. She placed the pressed corn dough onto the hot clay griddle that rested on three hearthstones that circled the fire. This was the morning ritual of Mayan women: to get up early, start the fires, and to prepare the fresh tortillas.

"Mateas is a grown man. He should be able to make his own tortillas," replied Nizhniya.

"That is not our way. A man depends on his mother, or his sisters for tortillas. When he is married, then his wife will make them for him. If she dies and he has no family then he must quickly find another wife. A man without tortillas . . . that is no man at all."

Nizhniya shook her head incredulously. "Why do you women put up with this?"

Rosario smiled. "There are always men who need tortillas. Our men are well fed, and our women are never lonely. Do you really think there are people that are happier than the Mayan?"

"Perhaps not," laughed Nizhniya.

Mateas walked into the house. He had had sentry duty during the early morning hours. "*Buenos dias*, Ludmelia. What brings you here so early in the morning?" he asked. "Are you here to learn how to make tortillas?"

"Certainly not!" said Nizhniya emphatically.

Rosario laughed.

"What? Did I say something wrong?" asked Mateas bewildered

"Never mind," said Rosario.

"I am here because *Ch'ucha'* insisted. She said she had a dream last night and that she had to weave a *huipil*."

"I saw her working away at the loom on the porch," said Mateas. "I have only seen such craftsmanship among the most accomplished weavers. You have taught her well, Mother."

"I have not taught, but prayed, to Santa Luciá.[59] *Ch'ucha'* has learned with her heart."

"As she seems to do with all her studies," replied Nizhniya. "Sister Margarita tells me that she is having to use high school curriculum with her. And I am already teaching her calculus."

"And how are her martial arts instructions proceeding?" asked Mateas.

"She does not like them. Guns are loud and scary, she complains. But, she does like playing with our wooden swords. Perhaps she does not understand what real swords are for. And I would prefer that she would never have to learn."

"She must learn the way of the jaguar," insisted Rosario. "This is why God has given her to you. She is reluctant to learn because she is afraid of what she might do with the knowledge and strength you are teaching her. She must embrace her soul-companion."

Ch'ucha' ran into the house proudly holding up the little *huipil*. She had embroidered the same little green frog that had been on her *huipil* when she was a baby.

"That is beautiful," said Nizhniya. "But it is very small. Who could wear such a tiny *huipil*?"

"This is for Saint Miguel. He spoke to me in a dream last night. He said he wanted a new *huipil* for Christmas. And since Christmas is tomorrow, I thought I better start working on it right away."

Rosario took the little *huipil* from *Ch'ucha'* and walked over to the statue of the archangel. Miguel had always been their household saint. It was not fitting that a saint should have to wear the same huipil for several Christmases. Rosario was pleased that Miguel would have a new one this Christmas. She removed the old *huipil* from the statue and placed the newly woven one on him.

"I will bring you fresh flowers a little later that you can lay next to him."

While all of this was happening, Nizhniya stood mesmerized. Mateas had seen her look this way before. This occurred whenever thoughts or images emerged from the depth of her amnesia.

"What is it?" asked Mateas.

"I saw an angel once," she said.

"You?!" Mateas said surprised.

"Yes, it surprised me to . . . . I remember now. A man touched my eyes. A priest, no, a monk . . ." Then she remembered the other priest, the one who wore the large Byzantine cross. He held his arms out to her. "No," she said falling back into a chair.

Rosario knelt down next to her and placed her arm around her shoulder. "You must try to remember."

"It hurts," said Nizhniya.

"I know," said Rosario reassuringly. "You learned to bear the pain once before. You must bear it again."

"Why? Why can't things just continue as they are?"

"Because that is not your destiny. You must remember. *Ch'ucha'* needs you to remember. You must go back to the memory, quickly, before it slips away."

Nizhniya closed her eyes. The priest reappeared in her mind. He held his arms out to her. She stood hesitantly before him. The arms beckoned. She stepped slowly, tentatively towards him.

Father?

Nizhniya's father grasped her in his arms. He whispered in her ear. Remember.

I don't have the strength to remember.

Yes, you do my little milka. I will hold you. I will always hold you.

Nizhniya yielded, trusting in her father's love. Immediately, a flood of memories poured in on her. She felt her knees buckling, but he held her firmly in his loving embrace. She watched as her life was reassembled before her. As the parts were fitted into place she felt joy, sorrow, anger, and the desire for revenge. But, ultimately what emerged was a sense that her life had been committed to another. It was this commitment that had enabled her to endure the pain.

"Are you okay, Mommy?" asked *Ch'ucha'*.

Nizhniya blinked a couple of times as she re-entered the time and space of the present. She then smiled and embraced *Ch'ucha'*. "Yes, my little *milka*, I am fine."

Milka?" asked *Ch'ucha'*.

"My sweet darling girl," replied Nizhniya. "My father called me his little *milka*. I loved it when he would call me that."

"Then I want you to call me your little *milka* too."

"You remember?" asked Rosario.

"Yes. Not everything . . . yet. But, enough. And I know whom I can go to when I am ready to remember more."

"Your father," said Rosario.

"Yes, how did you . . . ."

"Know?" interrupted Mateas. "Remember, my mother is a shaman who speaks with the Ancestors."

Rosario wondered if this was the time *Kos* had ordained for *Ch'ucha'* to learn the truth of her mother and herself. "Did you remember *Ch'ucha's* ancestor?"

"Vaguely," replied Nizhniya.

"Do not talk about her. You are my mother!"

"No, little *milka*, I am not your mother. I am your guardian," said

Nizhniya now remembering her conversation with Father Nikitas. "I do remember that your mother was a *yurodivyi*."

"What is that?" asked Rosario.

"A fool, a fool for Christ," replied Nizhniya.

"And I am fool's child. It is her fault that I am the freak that I am!"

Rosario looked keenly at *Ch'ucha'*. It was a look that *Ch'ucha'* had seen before. This was the look that she gave Father Suarez, or perhaps her son when she was saying something important; something that needed to be listened to. Such a look had never been directed at her by *Rina*. "Your mother," said Rosario, "was the jaguar, but became a sparrow. You, *Ch'ucha'*, wish to be a sparrow, but in your heart you are the jaguar."

* * *

Ernesto Aguilar sat alone on the wooden bench. No one would sit next to him. He didn't want anyone to sit next to him. He rubbed where the wooden prosthesis was strapped to the stump of what remained of his leg. It had been two and a half years since his leg had been amputated. Once he had wished that he had been in the helicopter with Zokoroff; death had seemed a better alternative than being a crippled prisoner of the pathetic Mayans. But, his loathing of his captors and desire for revenge had restored purpose to his life. Someday, he assured himself, he would inflict a terrible revenge on his captors. Suffering and death is what they deserved for what they had done to him.

Father Suarez had insisted that he join the community for the Christmas celebration. The fool priest was always trying to save him. He had already made him attend Christmas Mass in the morning. Now he had to suffer through some ridiculous Christmas play put on by the dirty, ignorant Indian children.

In the courtyard of the Mission a little manger had been set up. In Mexico City, where Aguilar had grown up, he remembered seeing many a manger scene during the Christmas season. They were quaint remembrances of a bygone era. But here at the Mission de las Casas a manger scene blended seamlessly with the primitive environment. It was all pathetically ironic. Two children dressed as Mary and Joseph knelt by the manger wearing *huipiles* woven specially for the holiday. A handmade baby Jesus doll lay between them in the manger. Two young girls with angel wings stood on either side of the manger singing,

"Glory to God in the highest! Peace to men of good will!"

Aguilar watched Nizhniya, Rosario, and Mateas sit down together on a bench not far from the manger. Aguilar and Mateas' eyes met. They shared a mutual hatred for each other. There was no way of knowing whether it was Mateas' bullet that had shattered Aguilar's knee. It didn't matter. As far as Aguilar was concerned, Mateas was responsible. And so was the bitch that sat next to him. Had she not shown up when she did, he and Zokoroff would have gotten away. Then there was the old witch next to her. Damn her and her cryptic remarks! She had never done anything to him, but she represented everything that he found disgusting about the Indians. He remembered the conversation he had had with Zokoroff the day they flew into Chiapas to 'rescue' the child from her grandparents. Yes, he remembered, if I were the ruler of Mexico I would exterminate these useless Indians once and for all.

Children dressed as shepherds and shepherdesses entered the courtyard. Each child came with an animal to pay homage to the baby Jesus. Some of the children carried little pets in their arms; other had them on leashes. One of the last to enter was *Ch'ucha'*. Aguilar's eyes narrowed when she entered. This was the person who was ultimately responsible for his suffering. She was the cause of the loss of his leg and his imprisonment in the Mission. He reserved a special hatred for her. He had never been told whom Zokoroff worked for, only that he was employed by an international consortium. But, it was evident why they wanted the child. She was a freak. She was only two and a half years old, and yet she looked almost ten. And he had heard stories; stories of special powers. Normally, he would not have believed any of the nonsensical stories the Mayans conjured, but he suspected that the stories about *Ch'ucha'* were true. It was said that she had powers over nature and that she could communicate with animals. Some day, he thought as she approached the manger, he would get his revenge on her too. But he wouldn't kill her. No, that would be too good for her. He would complete the mission that he began with Zokoroff. He would capture her and deliver her to whomever it was who had employed them. No doubt there would be considerable remuneration for his efforts. Maybe they would put her in a cage and do experiments on her. Yes, he nodded to himself, quite pleased at the thought of how miserable she would be.

Ch'ucha' approached the manger. During the entire procession she held her hands cupped loosely together. When she arrived in front of the crib she knelt down. She opened her hands. A little sparrow stood in her open palms for a moment and then flew out of her hands. The little bird flew two circles around the courtyard and then perched itself on the manger as if it too were paying homage to the doll that lay there.

Aguilar surveyed the audience and noted the look of astonishment on the faces of everyone present, that is, except for Rosario who seemed to watch as though she had witnessed this event already. Then a collective shriek made Aguilar jump. He turned around to see people jumping off their benches and running to the far end of the courtyard. Aguilar stood up to see what had terrified everyone. It was hard to see over the people who were pushing past him. He could see Mateas standing with his pistol drawn pointing down in the direction where the children had just processed into the courtyard. His gaze followed the direction of Mateas' pistol. A formidable black jaguar emerged, walking slowly towards the manger. Why doesn't he shoot it? Aguilar thought. He looked again at Mateas. His mother had placed her hand on his pistol and had pushed it down so that it pointed towards the ground. The large cat continued to walk towards the manger. *Ch'ucha'* was standing looking at the jaguar. It was no more than three feet in front of her. Aguilar was amazed by her lack of fear as the powerful beast stood before her. In a blink of an eye it could pounce on her and rip her throat out. Everyone watched terrified wondering what the animal would do, but it too just stood motionless watching *Ch'ucha'*. Finally, she waved it away with her arms.

"Shoo! Go away. Go back into the forest where you belong. Leave me alone."

The jaguar stared at her for another moment and then turned aside. It looked at Aguilar who stood mesmerized by its ferocious stare. It then emitted a low resonating growl that seemed to make his very bones vibrate. It was as though it spoke to him,

I know your smell. My eyes watch you from the dark. My claws and teeth eagerly await your flesh.

The jaguar then ran back into the forest.

Deliverance

And We will deliver those who guarded (against evil), and We will leave the unjust therein on their knees.

- The Holy Qu'ran 19.72

General Malik groaned as the phone rang. It took considerable effort to turn his body so that he could reach the phone on the nightstand.

"What fool is calling me at this time in the morning?" grumbled Malik.

He looked at his watch. The luminescent dial showed that it was four forty-five. The young boy curled up next to him whimpered as the General complained and maneuvered to reach the phone. The boy repositioned himself so that he embraced his companion from behind. His arms could barely reach around Malik's ponderous body.

"Yes," said the General in an irritated tone. "Who the hell is this?"

"Sir, this is Major Mazarul. Radar is picking up over a hundred aircraft coming in from the north!"

"What?! Is this some type of mistake? A malfunction?"

"No sir. We have confirming reports from *Ad Dammam* and *Buraydah*. Also, we could not contact our bases in *Kaf, Al Bi'r, Badanah* or *Rahfa*."

"Have you been able to identify these aircraft?"

"That's just it. Their electronic signatures indicate that these planes belong to our own air force."

"Damn!" exclaimed Malik and he swung his large body with surprising speed so that his legs now rested on the floor. He threw the covers off exposing his morbidly obese body.

"What is it?" said the effeminate boy in a frightened tone.

Malik ignored him. He stood up and placed the cordless phone between his ear and shoulder. His mind raced to consider the possible scenarios that might be unfolding. Were they being invaded? By who? His crazy brother? Possibly. But that didn't explain why these aircraft had Arabian Air Force signatures, signatures that were designed to prevent loss due to friendly fire, signatures that were a closely guarded military secret.

"Scramble our fighters!" said Malik as he began to dress himself.

"We've done that. They've already shot down four; no, I've just been told, seven, of our aircraft. "

"Well shoot back, goddamn it!"

"We've tried. But, our radar won't lock on them because they show up as being our own aircraft."

"What about surface to air?" asked Malik.

"Same problem."

"It's a damn coup!" Malik mumbled.

"What?" asked the Major.

"Nothing," said Malik. "Has the King been informed?"

"We were about to call him."

"Don't bother. I will. You're in charge until I get back in touch with you."

"But what am I suppose to do?"

"Just keep doing what you've been doing." Malik hung up the phone. What was the point? If this was a coup, and it had all the markings of one, then there must be high-ranking members of the military who were participating in it. Malik had his suspicions, but he wasn't sure. Captain al-Sharif was probably in on it. Perhaps even Queen Miriam. If that was true, then there wasn't any point in trying to contact his father. He was probably already dead. The best thing he could do now, would be to try to save his own skin.

"What's the matter?" asked the boy, who could tell that his lover and benefactor was distraught.

"I am sorry," said Malik as he reached into the nightstand drawer. "I have to leave. We have had an exquisite time together."

Malik couldn't imagine sharing his young lover with whoever might have him after he left. He drew a large knife from the drawer. The young boy looked neither surprised nor saddened. He had always known that it would come to this. He lay passively on the bed as he had many times before for his lover. Malik placed his big, fat hand over the boy's face and pressed it down into the pillow exposing his soft, tender neck.

"You understand, don't you, my dear boy?"

*   *   *

The Arabian military was a composite, or rather a menagerie, of foreign technology. The lack of integration of this technology continued to pose a significant threat to Arabian security. During its brief time in the Great Alliance, Russian military experts had begun the task of integrating the country's air defenses so that the Arabian Military could distinguish various disparate components of its air force from that of a potential adversary thereby reducing the risk of friendly fire casualties. The task had not been completed when King Saïd broke the Alliance, at least that is what the commanders of the Arabian military had been told. What General Masud had learned during the planning stages of the coup was that the project had indeed been completed and that the Russians had retained capabilities that could now work in Prince Abdullah's favor. Even so, General Masud knew that it would only be a matter of time before the Arabian Military Command saw through the subterfuge. There was no massive air assault. In fact, the Russians took advantage of their integration technology to make the handful of MiGs and helicopters, provided by Goricsan, appear more formidable than it was. It also made them indistinguishable from the Arabian Air Force giving the impression of a coup while also making them secure from anti-aircraft missiles.

General Masud reflected on the *jihad,* which had started to take shape several months ago after the meeting with the enigmatic envoy of Czar Goricsan. They had concluded that it would be unlikely that the Prince would be able to raise a substantial enough army to overthrow his father, King Saïd. Jihad must rely on deception and the ensuing confusion that would arise from the breakdown of communication and leadership within the Arabian Military Command. Commandos had been positioned weeks in advance ready to strike centers of communication and defense. If all had gone well, these commandos were now enjoying their rewards in Paradise. As for the breakdown in leadership, Masud expected that the cowardly dog, General Malik, would flee at the first sign that the government might be overthrown. However, this command vacuum would not last long. The plan was for Prince Abdullah and his forces would be in or, at least approaching, Mecca.

Masud sat strapped into the seat of the Russian Hind assault helicopter, accompanied by Prince Abdullah and other leaders of the jihad. Four of his commanders sat facing him with laptop computers that were receiving updates on the progress of the coup. The information they had received so far had been promising. Masud glanced over at the Prince who was speaking passionately into a microphone announcing the jihad to his countrymen throughout Arabia. Masud marveled at the young Prince's zeal, and understood why so many of his followers believed him to be the Mahdi. When the Prince had heard that the King was planning on making his *hajj*[60] to Mecca during Ramadan he had been outraged.

"It is an incomparable blasphemy that the Chimæric King should enter the holy city," said the Prince into the microphone. He exhorted his fellow citizens to rise up and punish the King and all his supporters.

The jihad would need all the popular support it could get. The Prince had insisted on beginning the jihad as soon as he heard that the King was going to Mecca.

"This is not wise, Sahib," exhorted Masud. "We will be better prepared if we wait a few more months." But, Abdullah had refused to listen to reason.

"I would rather have a single angel of *Allah* join us in preserving the Holy City from the stain of Chimæra than to have a thousand man-made war machines." When Abdullah had revealed his plan to the men of the camp there was much rejoicing, for they saw in this a recapitulation of the *Hegira*.[61] Prince Abdullah, the Mahdi of the Kingdom of Truth, would fly over the footsteps of the Prophet through Medina and on towards Mecca, a path that he would not have taken had the coup waited until the return of King Saïd to the capital. Masud hoped that Abdullah was right. They would need angelic assistance to make it all the way to Mecca! Indeed, he was surprised that they had made it past Medina without enemy engagement. And if they did make it all the way to Mecca . . . well, he hoped that their intelligence had not exaggerated the support of the populace for the young Prince. The one hundred and fifty warriors accompanying them in the five-helicopter fleet would hardly be sufficient to defeat the security forces that guarded the holy city. And with the King present, Masud anticipated these forces would be substantially reinforced.

Masud saw a flash of light in the small window across from him. Almost immediately a terrific explosion followed. He unbuckled his seat belt and ran to the cockpit.

"What's going on?" he shouted.

The pilot pointed out the windshield at the black streak that raced overhead.

"A Harrier. It came out of nowhere," said the copilot. "Buckle yourself in. It's going to be a rough ride."

Masud ignored the copilot's orders. "Where's our escort?"

"They're ahead," said the pilot, pointing to the two distant helicopters ahead of them. Suddenly, one of them exploded.

Govno!" exclaimed the pilot. "Hold on!"

Masud gripped the backs of the pilots' seats as the helicopter took a sharp dive to the left. He looked back. Abdullah was working his way up towards them. Masud waved him back. There was a terrific bang and the helicopter shook violently.

"Have we been hit?" asked Abdullah, as he grabbed Masud's arm.

"No," replied the co-pilot. "But you've lost another helicopter."

"There!" said Abdullah pointing down towards the earth. "The canyons of *al-Darith*. Fly into the canyons."

"No," said the pilot. "It's suicide."

The remaining escort ahead of them exploded.

"Ah, shit!" growled the pilot. He pointed the helicopter into a steep descent directly into the canyons. The helicopter shook again. The pilot crossed himself as he leveled the helicopter off some fifty feet above the ground.

"Can't you do something about him?" said Masud, referring to the fighter.

"No," said the co-pilot. "He's too fast. If I could see him long enough . . . ."

The helicopter weaved in and out of rock formations and up over sand dunes. The two remaining helicopters kept in close pursuit. Clouds of sand and dust engulfed the helicopters, obscuring visual observation from above.

"We can't stay here for long," said the pilot. "Our engines can only take so much of this. I can barely see where I'm going."

"Can we shoot him down?" asked Abdullah.

"Yes," said the co-pilot. "If we can get a visual on him long enough."

"Tell the other pilots to fall back and put some distance between us. And tell them to have their fingers on the triggers!"

"What are you planning?" asked Masud.

"Never mind, just do it!" demanded Abdullah.

The co-pilot communicated the message.

"How much distance is there between us now?" asked Abdullah.

"About a kilometer."

"Take us up."

"We'll be sitting ducks!"

"A decoy. Now do it!"

No sooner had the pilot brought the helicopter above the cloud of dust and sand then . . . .

Bam! Bam! Bam! Bam! Bam!

We've been hit!" shouted the co-pilot. "We're going . . . ."
Another explosion rocked the helicopter. Masud was sure that they would soon be engulfed in a fireball and would momentarily be joining their companions in Paradise.

"They're going up!" said the pilot of the other helicopter.
"Follow them!" said Jafar who was now standing between the pilot and the co-pilot.
"What? So that we can be blasted?!"
Jafar leaned over and grabbed the controls. He yanked up on them, hurling the helicopter upward above the dust."
"You crazy son-of-a-bitch!" shouted the pilot.
"There he is!" shouted Jafar, pointing in front and above the pilots. The gray silhouette streaked by; flashes of light blazed from the jet as it fired its twenty-five mm cannons at the helicopter ahead of them. The copilot instinctively grabbed the machine gun control, locked the machine gun on the stealth fighter visually and started firing. The stealth exploded in an orange ball of fire. Jafar swung his fist and let out a yelp of victory as pieces of the fighter could be seen falling from the fireball.
"Where's the Prince" shouted Jafar.
"They must have been hit!" said the pilot.
"Take us down. We must find them!" said Jafar.

"Brace yourself," shouted the pilot.
Masud grabbed the Prince and dragged him to the floor of the helicopter. He pinned himself against the Prince in an attempt to shield Abdullah against the inevitable explosion. The pilots struggled to land the helicopter, but they were losing control. Abdullah could hear shouts of panic and prayer over the sputtering and clanking of the helicopter. The helicopter hit the ground with a tremendous thud and began to

tip. As it did, the larger blade dug into the sand making a horrific blast and causing the entire helicopter to spin around violently. Finally, it came to stop, but the machine still groaned around them.

"Are we dead, Sahib?" asked Masud whose body still pinned Abdullah's to the floor.

"I think not, General," said Abdullah as he pushed Masud off him. "My idea of Paradise is not you laying on top of me!"

*　*　*

"Your Highness, we have been unable to contact your son, General Malik," said Captain al-Sharif. "We fear the worst. The insurgency has spread to the capital and . . . ."

"There is no insurrection!" the King barked back as he adjusted his seamless white garment. "Today I will begin my circumambulations around the *Kaaba*."[62]

"But your Highness . . ." Captain al-Sharif began to protest.

"I have just spoken with Major Mazarul," interrupted the King. "And he has informed me that the coup has been crushed. There were no hundreds of aircraft from the north. Only a handful of jets and helicopters, and the last of those were shot down just south of Medina."

"Even so, it might be wise to wait a day or two," cautioned al-Sharif.

The King placed his hand on the captain's shoulder. "You are like a mother, al-Sharif. You worry too much. My presence among the throng of pilgrims will demonstrate to the few enemies I have left that I have no fear of them. My son, their Mahdi, is dead! I am king and will be forever! Now go inform the Queen that I am ready."

Al-Sharif saluted and left the King. As he walked towards the Queen's quarters he felt conflicted. His heart was with the young Prince Abdullah, yet duty required that he protect the King and Queen. The day that he had allowed the Prince to flee the country he had hoped that he would stay in hiding and forget the old sheik's prophecies. But, al-Sharif had heard of Abdullah's plans for jihad. He had little expectation that he would be successful.

Captain al-Sharif started to knock on the queen's door but hesitated. They had known one another in their youth. He loved her still, but he could never reveal his love. He wondered if she still retained some small affection for him. He shook his head. Such thoughts were nonsense! She was as high above him as the stars. He was the servant; she was the Queen of Islam's mightiest country. In his eyes, she was the Archetype of queens, indeed of all women.

It was with considerable sorrow that he had watched the transformation of Queen Miriam after she had received the Chimæric therapy. She now seemed as intolerant and as unmerciful as her husband. Perhaps the young Prince Abdullah had been right. Perhaps, she was possessed by a *jinn*. He knocked on the Queen's door. Perhaps, he thought, it would have been better had she died of her disease.

The door opened a crack and the Queen's elderly lady servant peered out. The "Mistress," as she was reverently called by the household staff who no longer remembered her Christian name, had been in the service of the Queen since she had been her wet nurse nearly forty years ago. When the Queen's mother had died, Mistress had been there to console her and raise her to womanhood. Mistress was a Copt. Generations earlier her family had not been able to pay the *jizya*[63] and had been sold into slavery. Purchased by the Qudama royal family, they had been treated with justice and allowed to practice their ancient Christian faith discreetly. Mistress was the last of this family of bondservants. Yet, her commitment to her charge, Miriam, had transformed servitude to loving service. Through word and deed, Mistress had demonstrated to the young princess that *Allah* is the father of *dhimmi* and *ummah* alike. Mistress, more than anyone, was pained to see this sweet date of Arabia despoiled by the technology of the West.

"Who is it?"

Captain al-Sharif heard the queen's voice call from within the room.

"It is Captain al-Sharif, my Lady,"

"Show him in," replied the Queen.

"But my Lady . . . ."

"Do as you are told!" barked Queen Miriam.

Mistress lowered her eyes from Captain al-Sharif, feeling the shame of her chastisement. She opened the door so that he could enter. As he entered the room he looked down at the elderly woman sympathetically. She looked up at him, their eyes met, and in that instant her eyes begged for forgiveness.

"You wanted to see me?" asked the Queen.

Captain al-Sharif looked up. The Queen stood next to the window so that the morning light passed through her nearly transparent garments. She was as exquisite as he remembered her! He averted his eyes. She walked over to him, and grasping his face with her hands she turned his gaze towards her.

"Afraid that you might succumb to temptation again, dear Captain?"

"My Queen, twenty years ago I succumbed to love. It is because of that love that I will not succumb to temptation."

"Ha!" laughed the Queen, releasing him. She turned and walked towards the window. She twirled around, holding her arms out at length. Once again, the morning light shone through the garments giving the appearance that her body was painted with flecks of sparkling gold. "The person that you loved so many years ago no longer exists. Would you rather love a dream or the woman who stands before you."

"I will continue to love the dream, my Lady, while serving the woman whom I pray will awaken from her nightmare."

"You sound like my son. He believes I am possessed by a *jinn*. But, I suppose, what he thought doesn't matter now. I have been informed that his coup attempt has failed, and his body will soon be the food of carrion."

"If this is so, then I mourn the death of your son, my Queen."

"Why should you mourn him? He was a traitor! You have sworn to protect your king and queen. If he had not died in the desert then perhaps you would have had to kill him yourself. That would be rich in irony!"

"Perhaps, but I can still mourn a man whom I have killed, especially if that man was a good man. I fail to see the irony in that."

"You would kill good to protect evil? Do you not find that ironic?"

"Perhaps tragic," replied Captain al-Sharif. "Then again, perhaps it is the will of *Allah*; death can, after all, preserve us from evil."

Queen Miriam understood his meaning, but chose not to respond to the obvious reference to her. "There could have been an even more delicious irony if you had known the secret, but alas, it will die with him."

Without warning, the Captain sprang towards the Queen and tackled her. He lay on top of her on the floor of her bedroom. She caught her breath and collected her startled wits.

"So perhaps you have changed your mind?"

The distant sound of helicopter blades slicing the air now reached the palace. Captain al-Sharif had seen the helicopter in the distance through the window behind the Queen. There were two now, approaching quickly. If they were remnants of the failed coup they could still launch missiles that could reach the palace in seconds.

"What is that sound?" asked the Queen.

"Helicopters. You may still get a chance to taste your delicious irony," said Captain al-Sharif contemptuously. Then standing he continued, "Remain here in your room. Stay away from the windows. I will be back."

Captain al-Sharif ran out of the room, but he had not gotten far when he heard Mistress call after him. He stopped.

"Yes, Mistress. Do not worry, your Lady will . . . ."

Mistress took him by the arm firmly. "Listen to me," she said. "It is rare that one is given an opportunity to undo an error that has caused a lifetime of sorrow and misfortune. We have been given such an opportunity."

"What error have I committed, Mistress?"

"It is not your error, but mine. And if you do as I say, all things can be set right."

By the time the two helicopters had reached the courtyard over a hundred heavily armed soldiers of the Palace Guard had already assembled, taking cover behind the colonnade and the low walls that partitioned the gardens. They were waiting for instructions from Captain al-Sharif, but he was nowhere to be found. One of the helicopters began to descend while the other remained hovering some fifty feet above it. The helicopter touched down.

"*Sahib*," pleaded General Masud. "I beg you to reconsider. Strafe the courtyard with machine-gun fire first!"

"No," said Prince Abdullah. "This is a holy place and violence must be avoided."

"Then let me and the others go out ahead of you," continued Masud.

Prince Abdullah ignored Masud's request and turned to Jafar. "Do you remember when this journey began you asked me whether I was the *Mahdi*?"

"Yes," replied Jafar. "You said that we would find out together."

"That time has come," said the Prince.

Guns on the ground were poised to fire while the helicopter machine gun turrets swept back and forth, yet not a single shot was fired on either side. Everyone held their breath, fingers on their triggers waiting for an order or for the other to make the first move. Finally, the door of the helicopter opened. A hundred guns pointed towards the opened door. A man emerged wearing a white robe pulled together at the waist by a wide black leather belt. Attached to the belt was a scabbard and in it the hilt of a sword glistened in the morning light. The man wore the traditional *kaffiyeh,* a part of which draped across his face. He stepped out of the helicopter alone; his fearlessness made him appear larger, more formidable, even glorious to the soldiers who had him in their gun sights. He took several steps towards them, then pulled the *kaffiyeh* away from his face. A gasp flowed through the Palace Guard: It is the Prince! Some looked up from their rifles, others took a couple of steps backwards. The Prince slowly removed the sword from its scabbard and raised it high over his head.

"It is the *sahib al-sayf!*" shouted one of the soldiers, recognizing the young Prince and his sword.

A groan of fear and awe rose from among the soldiers of the Palace. Some began to lower their rifles. They had heard the stories surrounding Prince Abdullah. Who had not heard the stories that the Prince was the *Mahdi*? What should they do? There was no one to give the command. And if the young Prince was the *Mahdi*, should not their loyalty be with him?

"Shoot him!" a man shouted as he emerged from the Palace. It was King Saïd! The King stood at the edge of the colonnade and the courtyard, some twenty paces from the Prince. He waved a pistol furiously towards the Prince. "He is a traitor! Kill him and all those with him!"

"Stand down!" shouted Captain al-Sharif as he emerged from behind the King.

"How dare you contradict my order," exclaimed the King angrily as he turned around to face Captain al-Sharif.

Now all the Palace Guard turned their attention to their commander and the King.

"You have sworn your loyalty to the King!"

"I have. And *my* son, Prince Abdullah, will be a nobler king than you," replied Captain al-Sharif.

"I knew it!" shouted the King. "That unfaithful whore!" The king fired two shots into Captain al-Sharif's chest and abdomen. The Captain fell to his knees. The King turned and faced the Prince. He aimed his pistol at the Prince.

"I am the King, and I will be King forever," he said as he began to squeeze the trigger.

A shot was fired. The King straightened. Another shot—this time the King fell to the ground. Captain al-Sharif dropped his pistol and fell onto his hands. Prince Abdullah went over to the King, reached down and turned him over. He was dead. The second bullet had shattered his skull. Soldiers began to emerge from behind the colonnade and garden walls, their rifles and pistols lowered. They watched as the Prince walked over to Captain al-Sharif who had collapsed to the ground. He knelt beside Captain al-Sharif, cradling his head in his lap. He was dying. al-Sharif gathered his remaining strength trying to speak as Abdullah bent close as the Captain's words were barely audible.

"My King and *my* son, restore the Kingdom. Restore your mother."

The Prince looked curiously at al-Sharif wondering what the dying Captain's words meant. Mistress now appeared from the palace. She had dragged the Queen from her quarters to the perimeter of the courtyard where together they had witnessed the scene that had just unfolded. Mistress now placed one hand on Captain al-Sharif's cheek, the other on Abdullah arm.

"Today," said Mistress to Prince Abdullah, "Your father will be wedded to the Queen in Paradise."

Captain al-Sharif closed his eyes in peace assured of the reward reserved for him by *Allah*. Abdullah looked over at Mistress bewildered. Then the Prince saw his mother approaching. She looked younger than he remembered, but not more beautiful. Abdullah gently laid Captain al-Sharif's head on the ground and stood as his mother approached him with outstretched arms.

"My son, what a joy it is to see you!" she said not showing any sign of grief at the death of the men that lay at her feet.

"Silence," said Mistress. She grabbed Queen Miriam's shoulders and pushed her to her knees. "You know what you must do," Mistress said to Abdullah.

Abdullah did know, but he did not know why he knew. He reached under his tunic and withdrew the stainless steel container that hung around his neck. He lifted it over his head, opened it, and removed the glass vial. When the Queen saw the vial and its contents she let out a horrific squeal that made all around her shudder. The Prince snapped the top off the vial and poured the red viscous fluid into the palm of his left hand. The Queen began to shake violently. Prince Abdullah knelt on one knee and rubbed the thumb of his right hand into the blood. Then he took his bloody thumb and anointed his mother's forehead with the precious liquid. She shrieked and began shouting curses. Then, as if an invisible skin were peeled away, her former radiance and serenity were restored. She looked over at the dead Captain and tears began to well up in her eyes. She crawled over to him, bent down, and embraced him. She whispered words into his ear that Abdullah could not hear. Obviously, they had shared a special relationship that he had been unaware of. Finally, Miriam got back on her knees and kissed his cheek. Then turning to her son she placed her hand on his cheek.

"My son, remember, . . . *be maintainers of justice, bearers of witness of Allah's sake, though it may be against your own selves or your parents or near relatives; if he be rich or poor, Allah is nearer to them both in compassion . . . ."*

The Queen began to tremble again as the old skin, the Chimæric skin, began to reassert and attach itself.

"Quickly," said Mistress. "If you are to release my Lady from her possession you must act now."

Abdullah stood and withdrew his sword from the scabbard. He wiped the blade of the sword across his left palm coating its razor sharp edge with the blood from the vial. Holding the sword with both hands he raised it over his head. His mother struggled against the Chimæric stem cells as they fiercely reasserted themselves against her will. She bent her head down exposing her neck. Abdullah stood motionless, straining with all his effort to do what he must. But he could not. The Queen's body began to shake violently again. Her head began to rise.

"Strike now!" insisted Mistress.

Abdullah could not.

Mistress reached over and took the sword from his hands.

"Go to your Captain now. He awaits you in Paradise."

Queen Miriam, with all the force of will she had remaining, grabbed the top of her own head and forced it down again, exposing her neck to Mistress. The old woman, feeble as she was, swung the blade with the force of a warrior. Abdullah turned away. General Masud grabbed and held the Prince. The Prince began to turn around but the General held his head against his chest.

"No, *Sahib*. Do not look. It is done."

Abdullah went limp in his arms and began to sob.

Mistress wiped the sword's blade on her skirt, then slipped the sword back into Abdullah's scabbard. She placed a gentle hand on his shoulder, and whispered,

"King Abdullah Mohammed al-Sharif. Your Kingdom awaits you."

Abdullah looked curiously at Mistress.

"That is right," said Mistress, "You are the son of Queen Miriam and Captain al-Sharif. You were conceived in the folly of their youth. Yet, God can use the fruit of our weakness to achieve His will."

Transference

Do you not know that anyone who joins himself to a prostitute becomes one body with her? For "the two," it says, "will become one flesh."

– 1 Corinthians 6:16

Obermann thumbed through the pages of the notebook that Dr. Richardson had handed him, then dropped it back down on the table.

"Just summarize it for me, Doctor. Is there anything wrong with my boy?" asked Obermann.

"No . . . I mean . . . I don't know . . . you see, he's different," stammered Richardson.

"I know that," replied Obermann, irritated. "But obviously there is something that concerns you, otherwise you would not have called me down here to the clinic."

"I wouldn't exactly say I'm concerned. Perhaps it would be better if I were to say I am surprised."

"Yes?"

"You wanted me to examine your son because of his, well uh, unexpected sexual activity."

"Yes, that was several months ago. I'm disappointed that it has taken you this long to report on your findings."

"I try to be thorough," replied Richardson somewhat defensively. "And the more I examined your son and his sexual contacts . . . ."

"There's been more than one?" asked Obermann.

"Yes, several. I thought you knew."

"No I did not! Who are they?"

"Well, of course, there is Elaina. He has had intercourse with her on a number of occasions. And there are several members of your household staff."

"What?!" exclaimed Obermann, jumping out of his chair.

"Female and male," Richardson sheepishly added.

Obermann paced back and forth furiously. This was intolerable behavior. It was not that he was prudish about his son's sexual activity, but it seemed that his son was out of control and acting compulsively. If Frederick were to fulfill his destiny alongside his father he would need to demonstrate self-discipline. He might be unique; he might even have the protection of the incorporeals, but that didn't mean that he couldn't self-destruct.

"Thank you, Doctor, for telling me," Obermann finally said after he had collected himself. "I will speak with my son immediately."

"Excuse me, Mr. Obermann," said Richardson nervously, "but there's more. I suggest you have a seat."

Obermann sat back down in the chair. Now, he did begin to worry. The information that the doctor had already shared seemed shocking enough, but he had a feeling she was about to reveal even more disturbing information. For the first time he felt like a patient about to be given the 'bad news' about a medical test. Richardson took the seat across the conference table from him.

"Your son has experienced remarkable maturation over the past year, especially the past few months. It is as though his physiology has been driven to have him achieve sexual maturity. Indeed, I believe it has. And I believe that this may also explain his behavior. It is as though his biological destiny is to inseminate."

"That's rather crude, Doctor," interrupted Obermann.

"I did not intend it to sound that way. I am, after all, a biologist, and there are many species of organisms that achieve rapid maturity just for that reason, so they can reproduce."

"So, in all of these sexual encounters that my son has had," said Obermann, "has he gotten anyone pregnant? I mean I'd sure like to know. Don't you think it would be good for me to know whether I we're expecting a little Frederick the Fourth?"

"Yes, of course. But that's just the thing I don't understand. Your son is sterile."

"What?" exclaimed Obermann. "Why?"

"It has to do with his gametes, his sperm. As you know, sperm has to be haploid, that is, it has to contain half the number of chromosomes; that way, when it combines with an egg the resulting zygote has a full complement of chromosomes. But, your son's sperm is diploid."

"Meaning?"

"Meaning that it already contains a full complement of chromosomes. There is no way his sperm can fertilize an egg."

"Is there anything that can be done to correct this?"

"Maybe. But, this is what I meant before when I said he was different. I'm not sure that this is supposed to be corrected. This may be normal for him. Maybe this is the way his reproductive system is supposed to function."

"Well that doesn't make much sense, Doctor. After all, a reproductive system is supposed to reproduce. And he can't. So how can this be normal, even for Frederick?"

"I wondered about that myself. Then I began to examine the individuals that he had had sex with. In each case, they had well established Chimæric Regeneration Systems."

"What?"

"That's right. Apparently, Frederick's sperm cells have the ability to pass through the host's reproductive system and enter the blood stream. Once in the circulatory system, they can create Undifferentiated Chimæric Colonies, just as we have done through implantation of Chimæric Stem Cells."

Richardson was expecting Obermann to have some sort of comment on this remarkable development, but he just sat stroking his chin as if he were trying to grasp a meaning beyond the physiological explanations that she had just articulated.

"That's not all," continued Richardson. "We examined egg and sperm samples from each of Frederick's sexual partners and in each case we found . . . Now this is what's really remarkable."

"Go on, Doctor."

"In each case, they were no longer making haploid gametes either. We did a DNA profile on the gametes of each of these individuals, and in each case their DNA had been replaced by Frederick's! This is not all, however. We have taken tissue samples from these individuals and have found snippets of Frederick's DNA even in their somatic cells. There may be systemic genomic alteration that is occurring within these individuals, but it is too early to be sure."

"Do any of these individuals know any of this?" asked Obermann.

"No, not yet. But it's only a matter of time. Whereas we had to administer drugs to control a Chimæric's reproductive ability, these new Chimærics are already sterile. I suspect that some of them will discover this soon enough. What's more, we discovered something remarkable during one of our examinations of Elaina. She seemed to know that something was going on with her body."

"Yes, I suspect she would," muttered Obermann.

"Well, since she seemed to know already, I asked her whether she and her husband were frequently intimate and she said they were."

Obermann's eyes grew wide anticipating where Richardson was going with this line of reasoning.

"I asked her if after they had sex she could provide me with a sample of her husband's semen without his knowing. She did, and we found that her husband's sperm had also been converted."

"*Mein Gott!*" exclaimed Obermann. "And does the husband also have a Chimæric Regeneration System?"

"That I'm not sure of. I was concerned about having him examined without first discussing this with you. However, my educated guess is that he does."

"This changes everything!" exclaimed Obermann. "We could lose complete control over Chimæra. The damn thing will be spread like some sexually transmitted disease, like HIV or something! All the millions spent on Chimæric Distribution Centers, all the hours spent in planning scenarios to phase in the New Era . . . ."

Obermann grew quiet again and paced back and forth.

"There's more," continued Richardson. "The Chimæric cells that Frederick has transferred do not possess the membrane proteins that allow us to either track or control them.

"I thought I understood how I was to proceed," Obermann muttered to himself. Then turning to Richardson he answered, "I will need your help."

"Yes sir," she replied. "How can I help you?"

"I need you to help me set up a meeting," replied Obermann.

"With whom?" asked Richardson surprised by a sense of apprehension, even foreboding, in Obermann's demeanor.

"With a man . . . clothed in light."

*   *   *

Obermann did not waste anytime seeking the interview with the so-called man who was "clothed in light." It was not that he was eager to seek his advice; it was that he feared the consequences of taking a misstep in the implementation of his will. It was only yesterday that he had learned about his son's ability to pass on his Chimæric stem-cells, now Obermann lay strapped in a hospital bed. He shook involuntarily; his skin was cold and clammy. He resisted the urge to vomit.

"Whatever I say or do, ignore me. You must let me die."

"It would be easier if you would allow us to use drugs," replied Dr. Yarelis.

"No," insisted Obermann. "In fact, I want you to secure me to the bed. I don't know what I'm likely to do as I begin to enter the Penumbra Realm."

Dr. Richardson watched as assistants attached restraints to Mr. Obermann's arms and legs. She was somewhat bewildered by his behavior. Certainly, she could understand his anxiety about dying, but on the other hand, he had spoken so glowingly about the Penumbra Realm; she had expected that he would be looking forward to the reunion. Even if he didn't "make it back," he had said earlier that he never wanted to return to the "clumsy world of the flesh." Perhaps, Richardson thought, it was too great a strain to see the beauty of the Penumbra Realm only to leave it again. Yes, that must be it.

Dr. Yarelis completed attaching the electrodes to Obermann's chest. A small voltage would be delivered, stopping Obermann's heart. It would only take a few minutes—he would then become unconscious and die. His Chimæric stem cells would help to prevent brain damage during the relatively short duration of hypoxia. The medical team had been instructed to revive him ten minutes after the EEG showed no activity. Obermann believed that this would give him enough time to communicate with the "man clothed in white." Then he would return. Obermann was quite insistent that they should not delay. Again, Richardson assumed his insistence must have been for fear that he might find it more difficult to return if he remained longer in the joy of the Penumbra Realm.

Frederick gripped his father's hand. "Who can compare to my father?" he asked rhetorically. "Who can wage war against him?"

Richardson looked over at Dr. Yarelis who gave her a curious glance. The exchange between them made it clear that they both thought Frederick's remark was a strange one.

Obermann nodded to Yarelis. "I am ready," he said calmly.

Dr. Yarelis turned his attention to the cardioverter. He examined Obermann's EKG one last time. He made a final adjustment and then pushed a button, which delivered the prescribed amount of electricity to Obermann's heart.

Obermann's body became tense. "Ah, shit!" he exclaimed, more out of surprise and panic than out of pain. He felt an odd hollowness in his chest, but other than that nothing too extraordinary. In fact, he wondered if the procedure had worked. He looked over at Yarelis questioningly.

"Relax," said Yarelis. "It will only be a few minutes now."

It had worked. He could begin to feel it now. He felt he was starving for air. He started to breathe heavily. It made no difference. This is what it must feel like to drown, he thought. He instinctively started to panic.

"Stop! Stop!" Obermann cried out.

"I told you we should have used drugs," exclaimed Yarelis to Richardson.

Obermann felt cold and dizzy. He couldn't focus his eyes any longer. He knew it would be only a few more seconds and he would be unconscious.

"Stop," he cried out again. "For God's sake, stop!"

"I'm going to start his heart!" said Yarelis. "I didn't think this was a good idea to begin with."

Richardson just stared at the almost surreal scene unfolding before her. Her mind flashed back to when she had witnessed the death of another Chimæric—Maria O'Conner. She *didn't* come back. And her death was different. There was something tranquil, even beautiful about the way she had died. It was a holy death.

Obermann struggled against his restraints. Yarelis' hands trembled while he attempted to adjust the cardioverter to deliver a shock to restart Obermann's heart.

"Leave that alone!" insisted Frederick. "My father gave explicit instructions to ignore his request to reverse this procedure. We must let him die."

Yarelis stopped. He was incredulous that Frederick could be so calm while watching his father dying and crying out for help. Yarelis looked over at Richardson.

"He's right," Richardson said. "Let him go."

Obermann's struggling became less intense. He was no longer calling out. His face took on a ghastly, ashen hue and his breathing became shallow. His body relaxed. A single, final gurgling exhalation passed out of his body. Obermann was dead.

KD McMahon

The first time Obermann had experienced death he hadn't understood what was happening. There was no life after death, or so he had believed. He had been murdered, and he had been shocked that he was aware of his own death. In that moment of entering eternity he had understood how terribly he had miscalculated. He had seen for the first time that the entire cosmos was filled with Presence and Promise. But, this newfound realization was no longer available to him. Something had gone horribly wrong. He had wanted to "run" to it, but he had been yanked back as if he were on a leash. He had been trapped within his body, and the horror of his eternal entombment gnawed his very essence. He had wondered how he would endure the nightmare of knowing that humanity had been destined to embrace all in love, but he had chosen to be reduced to an eternal finitude of self. Then he had discovered that he was not alone. An ancient presence had made itself known to him. It was the personifcation of self-interest. Indeed, he had understood that all self-interest flowed from the abyss of this polluted well. Obermann could taste its regret made bitter by the choosing of malice and vengeance over repentance and reconciliation. Obermann had been offered this "salvation" too.

Ensnare humanity in its garments of skin and together we will empty the Cross of its power. Their lust for eternal carnality will deliver to me the Key of Death and then when they seek it I will not open it to them. And I will establish my kingdom, and humanity will be conformed to my image. Together we will sit on the thrones of the New Era; you at my right, and your son at my left.

Obermann had been careful to carry out all the instructions he had been given in the Penumbra Realm by the "angel of light." But, the recent developments with his son, his ability to transfer "the ensnarement" through sex was unexpected. Now he did not know how to proceed. And he dared not err in his mission; the consequences were too terrible to take such a risk. He had to consult with Lucifer.

Obermann did not wait since there was no time in the Penumbra Realm. However, he did think, and to the extent that his thoughts were linearly fashioned, he held on to some idea as to the continuity of existence. But, as with a dream that conveys a complexity of thoughts and emotions in an instant, so too was the Penumbra Realm. There was no way he could know whether an instant or a millennium had passed. In the dark solitude of despair he began to panic. *What if something goes wrong? What if they can't revive me? What if I am left here forever?*

Then he reached out with his consciousness and perceived Doctors Yarelis and Richardson as they stood vigil over his corpse. He could read from their consciousness that everything was proceeding as planned. But, he also perceived that they had doubts; doubts that he had not been aware of when he was alive. Somehow his corporeal senses had dulled his "perception of angels." When he returned to the living he would have to deal with this, especially in Dr. Richardson. There was still the lingering effect of Maria O'Conner in her consciousness. He was considering how he might rectify this when suddenly he was engulfed by a massive presence. It was as if a giant bird of prey had swooped down on him unexpectedly, seized and then devoured him. He felt as if he were in the belly of the Great Dragon.

Master, thought Obermann fearfully, *I have come to you so that I may know how you wish me to proceed.*

I would have thought that it would be obvious. I have overestimated you.

I am sorry, my Lord, replied Obermann, trembling yet surprised that Lucifer was not omniscient.

Unbelievers are rarely of any use. They know nothing of the realm of spirit or its operation. A Believer, on the other hand, who has turned aside from the Way knows how to manipulate the truth in his service to me. So it is I who must now instruct you in the ways of the spirit. Do you not know that it is through sex that two become one? And when this truth is perverted, the sin of one is transferred to the other, ensnaring them both.[64] *But, it is not enough to ensnare men, you must so enslave them through their passions that they love their bondage. In this way humanity will be transformed, first into the image of your son, then ultimately to mine.*

When the Dragon had completed all that he had to instruct him he regurgitated him back into temporal existence. Obermann drew in a deep breath and coughed several times while struggling against his restraints. He became aware of Yarelis and Richardson's frantic activity around him.

"Enough!" Obermann reprimanded. "How long have I been dead?"

"Only for a few moments," replied Dr. Yarelis. "We did not even begin the procedure to revive you. How did you . . . ."

"The *man clothed in white* . . ." replied Obermann without further explanation. "Disconnect me," continued Obermann as he pulled an electrode off his chest.

"I think we should monitor you for just a little while," said Dr. Richardson, "Don't you agree, Dr. Yarelis, you know, just to be on the safe side?"

"Nonsense, I'm fine. Besides, there is much to do. I have the answers that I need." He looked over at his son who was seated in a chair in the corner of the room. "Frederick."

"Yes, Father?"

"Contact Elaina. Have her meet us at the estate tomorrow morning. You too, Dr. Richardson."

*   *   *

"It's a pleasure to see you again, Hans," said Elaina with a wink. "And it's always a pleasure to see you again, Freddie." She gave Frederick a kiss on the cheek. "Maybe if we have a little time . . . ."

"I'm sorry," interrupted Obermann, "but there will be no time today. Please have a seat." Obermann pointed to the chair across the table from him. Elaina walked around the table and seated herself. "I have met with the Master," Obermann continued.

"So I have heard," replied Elaina. "All the incorporeals are talking about it."

"Then you already know?"

"No. But, I assume that this somehow involves me."

"That is correct," replied Obermann. "Let me give you a little background. When we were in the developing stages of Chimæric technology, we recognized that we might want to be able to control our stem cells once they were introduced into human subjects. We incorporated into the membrane of these cells a protein that would allow them to absorb certain substances. We developed a number of substances that allowed us to monitor, even destroy our Chimæric stem cells."

Obermann stood up, walked over to his desk and opened a drawer. He removed a small stainless steel cylinder. It looked like a small oxygen tank. He walked over to Elaina and placed it on the table in front of her.

"Inside that container is a substance which, when released into the air, is capable of destroying Chimæric stem cells. It is harmless to non-Chimærics."

"What will happen to the Chimærics?" inquired Elaina.

"In the few test cases we have tried, the Chimæric stem cells agglutinated, causing fatal embolisms."

"I see. So if I were to open this container, you and Freddie would die?"

"Elaina, Elaina," exclaimed Frederick, wagging his finger at her, "you're such a naughty girl. If that were true, then you would die too."

"Oh, I suppose you're right."

"Frederick is immune. His Chimæric stem cells do not contain the membrane protein that is necessary to absorb the chemical. You are too. Your Chimæric Regeneration System was established as a result of your having sex with Fredrick."

"So then, it would only be you, Hans, that would keel over if I opened this container."

"No," interjected Frederick. "I converted Father yesterday. Didn't I, Father?"

"Yes," mumbled Obermann. "We don't need to discuss it."

"Hmm, I would have liked to have been there for that," snickered Elaina. "We could have made it a threesome!"

"Enough!" exclaimed Obermann. "Now I want you to deliver this cylinder, and four others like it, to the Congregation of Saint Pierre. You have their confidence, don't you?"

"They've had their suspicions. But, I believe I have convinced them that I am their spy. And, you know, most of them are a bunch of horny old men; I think they just like having me around."

"You haven't done anything, have you?" asked Obermann.

"No, I've been good. Just like you ordered. So you want me to give them the cylinders. Why?"

"So they can perpetrate an act of terrorism against Chimærics," replied Obermann.

"And why would you want them do that?"

"So that I can kill several birds with one stone," replied Obermann. "First, there are already several thousand Chimærics in this country. I want them converted. They'll be motivated when many of them start dropping like flies. And when we show that religious groups are responsible for this heinous act of terrorism, we will finally get the support we've needed to outlaw all religions that are not affiliated with the Tree of Life."

"Brilliant! Isn't it?" said Frederick rhetorically.

"Yes," answered Elaina. "I trust that the Master has approved your plan?"

"He is its author."

*   *   *

It was getting dark when Elaina left the Obermann estate with the five cylinders that she had been given to deliver to the Congregation of Saint Pierre. Dr. Richardson recognized her as she drove away from the estate. She wondered why Obermann had wanted to meet with her. And why had they postponed her appointment to later? Probably another sexual liaison with Frederick, she thought. She had originally been disgusted by Frederick's obsession with sex. She now began to understand that his behavior was driven by some sort of biological imperative to spread his Chimæric seed. We do, after all, have this drive to procreate, she had concluded. Maybe it was entirely appropriate, even necessary that Frederick behaved as he did. It was difficult to judge him, after all, if his behavior were genetically determined. Besides, she was nearly as responsible for his existence as Obermann and Fletcher had been.

As she pulled into the driveway, she thought about Elizabeth Fletcher. She hadn't thought about her in some time. She wondered what she would have thought about all this. She probably would not like it. She parked, stepped out of the car and walked up the stairs to the front door. She rang the bell. No, she thought, she wouldn't have liked it a bit!

To her surprise, Obermann opened the door.

"Come in, come in," said Obermann.

Richardson thought, almost instinctively, about finishing his greeting with "said the spider to the fly," but did not.

"Finally, an opportunity to talk to you alone," said Obermann, putting his arm around her shoulders. He began walking with her towards the den. "You know, we've been so busy there just hasn't been the time. I've been neglecting you. I'm sorry."

"Oh, I understand," said Richardson somewhat perplexed by Obermann's comments and demeanor. "You have so much you're responsible for. Why just yesterday you were . . . huh . . ."

"Dead," replied Obermann with a slight smile. "Exactly, and it was while I was in the Penumbra Realm that I realized that I needed to connect with you better. I haven't been as sensitive to your needs as I should have been."

Richardson hadn't thought that she needed anything in particular from Obermann, but as he said it she began to believe that perhaps she did. She remembered how she felt when he had returned from the Penumbra Realm the first time. It was as though she had discovered a father, a father who truly appreciated her.

"Yes," continued Obermann as he showed her into the den and pointed to one of the luxuriously soft leather chairs. "I need to tell you more often how much I appreciate everything you've done. A thousand years from now students will be learning about you in their schools. What am I talking about; you'll be the guest of honor!" Obermann laughed.

As much as Richardson enjoyed Obermann's compliments she suspected that there was more to this meeting than his having an opportunity to praise her. Obermann poured her a glass of white wine, a delicate and sweet Muscat of Alexandria and handed it to her. She took a sip. It was warm and fruity, perhaps with a hint of an herbal flavoring. Obermann poured himself a brandy and sat across from her.

"I have been concerned, though," he continued, "that perhaps you've been having some doubts about Chimæra, myself . . . Frederick."

Richardson squirmed imperceptibly in her chair. She had been having her doubts. Had it been obvious? They weren't really doubts. Seconds thoughts?

"No, no, . . . not doubts . . . not exactly. I guess it's just that everything has been happening so quickly."

"You're right. Things are happening even quicker than I expected. But, you have to expect that with a revolution. Everything is changing. And those that don't change, they'll become the fossil remnants of a past era of human evolution. They won't survive in the New Era. Not even you."

"But, I'm a Chimæric," replied Richardson.

"Yes, I thought that would be sufficient too. That is, until I visited the Penumbra Realm and talked with the *man clothed in white*. You see, he exists outside of time. He sees in an instant that which was, is, and will be. He *knows*. And what he revealed to me was that everything that we have done was not so that we could inject transgenically altered stem cells into people so that they could live for five hundred years. No, it was to restore humanity to its original undefiled state of perfection. Frederick is the first fruit of this perfection. It is his destiny to plant the seed of this perfection in as many as possible. We in turn must spread the seeds."

"I don't understand," said Richardson.

"I know it's difficult for you to grasp. You're a scientist. You're not trained to see the universe except through the lens of a microscope. But, I must ask you now to look through the lens of your heart. You must trust me."

"Trust you for . . . what?"

"Trust me to receive the seed of transformation."

It finally dawned on Richardson what was being asked of her. Obermann wanted her to have sex, sex with his son! She recoiled at the idea. Obermann sensed her reluctance, even disgust at the prospect. He had anticipated this response. This is why he had widened his access to her through his previous conversation; she was a woman in desperate need of acceptance and approval.

"Trust me, Charla. Once the seed has been implanted in you and you are transformed; you will understand."

"But he's a child!"

"He is *the* man-child."

"I don't love him!"

"The New Era transcends the limitation of human love and its monogamous bondage."

"But I won't be able to have my own children," she protested.

"You will have his. We will all have his. We will be the patriarchs and matriarchs of the New Era.

"I . . . I . . . don't know."

The doubt that he had perceived in Richardson while in the Penumbra Realm was evident to him now. She had indeed spent too much time with Maria O'Conner. She was the one who had planted the seeds of doubt in her. He couldn't allow these doubts to continue; Richardson was too valuable. He pushed his psyche more deeply into her consciousness than he had ever done previously. There, he saw the wound. In every person he had penetrated, there was a wound, and that wound became the gravimetric center of their being. Each individual kept a tight orbit around this wound. Their hopes and ambitions were directed at escaping the pull of this wound. Pride and self-esteem were the illusion that they were free from its influence. Fear and its compulsions were the acquiescence to its ultimate and inescapable power. Obermann saw reflected in Richardson's wound his response to his own woundedness. He had no illusions that he could escape it. The recognition of his own powerlessness had redirected itself towards ruthlessly dominating others. So be it, he thought.

As he penetrated more deeply into Richardson's psyche, he observed the superficial healing of her wound. Underneath it, lay the still festering pustule of paternal conditional love. This was the key to manipulating Richardson. He had used it before, but now by entering the pus-filled pocket his thoughts would resonate with the voice of her father. *Be obedient! Do not disappointment me or I will not love you!*

Richardson's shoulders slumped, and she lowered her head. He had broken her. "All right," she muttered.

"Wonderful!" exclaimed Obermann. "Trust me, it will be easy." Obermann reached his arms out to her. She extended hers reluctantly. He grasped her hands firmly and pulled her up out of the chair.

"Come. My son is waiting for you. Just yield to him. Then everything will be made clear to you. You will know what you must do."

*   *   *

Dr. Charla Richardson did indeed yield to Frederick Obermann. But, it was not the brightness of clarity that she experienced. During the climax of their intimate union his soul was naked before her. And in that terrible instant she saw the unfathomable dark of nothingness within him. For evil is *nothing* and it seeks to suck the order of God's creation into its chaotic vortex. Richardson was seized by the terrifying recognition that the horror that she was instrumental in creating had now implanted itself in her. And she knew the secret. She saw *him* lurking in the recesses of Frederick's soul. He was not clothed in light, but wrapped in dark nothingness. And she had felt the strangling darkness penetrate her. It was only a matter of time before the malignancy would engulf her entire being.

She knew that she must maintain her composure; to reveal that she knew their evil secret would jeopardize her even more. It was early morning when she attempted to leave the Obermann estate. She was hoping to leave without being noticed, but Obermann stopped her at the door.

"Why don't you stay until morning?" he asked probingly.

"I . . . I . . . don't feel very well," she stammered, trying to give herself enough time to consider what she would say next. She couldn't let on that she just wanted to flee from Frederick's disgusting presence. "Perhaps it's the transformation."

Obermann nodded. "Yes. Your report said that it occurs very rapidly. In a couple of days the gonadal transformation should be complete. Is that correct?"

"Yes," she said looking down. "Then I will be able to spread Frederick's seed."

"Good! I'm having a dinner party the day after tomorrow. Several important people will be present. I would like you there."

Richardson looked up at him. She understood his meaning. Matriarch of the New Era? What a joke! I'm his whore, enslaving humanity through my spread legs!

She wasn't quite sure how she made it home. Her mind was as blurred as her tear-filled eyes. She had almost driven off the road. But, she had instinctively saved herself, although she wasn't sure why she should bother. She threw her stuff dispiritedly on the entryway table. She was exhausted, but going to bed knowing that he was growing inside her, changing her, making her him . . . how could she sleep? She stumbled into the living room.

Thump!

She bumped into the bookcase. Books tumbled off the shelves onto the floor.

"Damn," she muttered. She turned on the lights, bent down to pick up the books, and then began to laugh. The irony of trying to maintain orderliness against the inevitable chaos—it was laughable! She spied one of the books sprawled open on the floor—her old biochemistry book. A piece of paper had fallen out of it. She picked it up. I know this! she thought.

> *To see a world in a grain of sand*
> *And a heaven in a wild flower,*
> *Hold infinity in the palm of your hand,*
> *And eternity in an hour.*

She remembered Maria O'Conner quoting this poem to her when she was preparing her for the Chimæric stem-cell therapy. She held the poem in her hands and began to cry.

Maria, you were right. Chimæra is evil. If only I had listened to you. Now it's too late. Soon I'll be transformed and he will be my master.

Then Richardson remembered. The autopsy had showed that there were no Chimæric stem cells in Maria's body. All their efforts to implant them had failed. And her blood! Now *that* was a mystery! She had type BB blood, yet she had also had a considerable amount of type AB blood in her body. Where had it come from? Why had her antibodies not caused it to agglutinate? And what was the unknown antigen on those AB blood cells? She had believed that the antigen might have had something to do with preventing the Chimæric stem cells from operating properly. She had never been able to complete her analysis because Obermann had ordered that O'Conner's body be cremated and all her tissue and blood samples destroyed.

But, one sample of Maria O'Conner's blood remained. Richardson had not deliberately disobeyed Obermann. A small test tube containing a blood sample had accidentally fallen into a lab drawer. She had found it about a month later. When she had picked it up, and seen that it was an O'Conner blood sample, her first thought had been to destroy it. But, then she had noticed that it was still liquid; it hadn't coagulated. And the tube had felt warm as though its contents had just been taken from Maria's body. She had known she should destroy it, but she could not do it. It was a curiosity and, after all, she was a scientist. Perhaps someday she would have time to study it. Until then, she had decided she'd bring it home. She hadn't wanted to take the chance of having it discovered at the lab.

Richardson got up off the floor, and taking the poem back into the biochemistry book, walked over to the adjoining study. She opened the middle drawer of her desk in which were assorted items, from pens to paperclips.

Where is it?

She pulled the drawer almost completely out. She shoved papers around uncovering what lay beneath them.

There it is!

She removed the test tube filled with the red, viscous fluid. It was still warm! Body temperature! Richardson carried the test tube into the bathroom. She set it down on the counter while she rummaged underneath the sink. Her mother had visited her a few months ago. She had been an insulin dependent diabetic until she had received

Chimæric therapy. Richardson had arranged that. Her mother had
stayed with her just before the treatment. She could have sworn that
her mother had brought insulin and a syringe with her. Where was it?
That's it! Richardson removed a small black, leatherette case. She
unzipped it. It still contained insulin and several disposable syringes.
She sat on the toilet lid and rolled up her left sleeve.

I'll be your whore, she thought.

She plunged the needle into the rubber stopper of the test tube,
and pulled back on the plunger, drawing blood into the syringe until
she had emptied the tube. She withdrew the needle from the tube,
tapped it a couple of times while pushing on the plunger, until a drop
of blood appeared on the top of the needle.

*And I will sow seeds of destruction. I will destroy the monster I have
created.*

She felt above her left forearm for the brachial artery, palpated it,
and then pushed the needle into it. She grimaced as she pushed the
plunger down, forcing the contents of the syringe into her circulatory
system. Almost immediately her arm became as hot as fire. She cried
out in agony as the pain moved from her arm to her chest. She felt that
she might burst into flames! When the intense heat reached her face
she was overwhelmed and passed out.

When she woke up later that morning, she was surprised to find
herself lying on the bathroom floor. Then she remembered what had
happened earlier. Sleep had given her a momentary respite from despair.
She was drenched with sweat, but she no longer felt warm. In fact, she
felt remarkably well, all things considered. There was a little swelling
and tenderness in her right forearm, but other than that it appeared
normal. Perhaps the O'Conner blood sample had done nothing after
all. Richardson picked herself up off the floor, undressed and stepped
into the shower. The shower beat down on her; she wished it could
wash away the impurity that Frederick had implanted in her. Then a
wave of pulsating heat radiated from her groin. She felt it course through
her body as her heart rate accelerated and her breathing quickened.
She had an overwhelming desire to be with a man.

Oh God! It's taking me over!

She turned off the hot water and leaned against the wall as the icy cold water poured over her. Her head began to clear. Finally, when she felt that she had regained her composure, she turned off the shower, grabbed a towel, and stepped out of the shower. After she had dried herself, she took her towel and wiped off the mirror. She threw the towel over the shower door and looked back into the mirror. She drew a deep breath. Her brownish-black eyes suddenly turned blue, but then returned to their normal color.

Perhaps I should just kill myself.

She opened the medicine cabinet; perhaps there was something she could overdose on. There was nothing. She had thrown out all her medicines a few months ago. She hadn't been sick, not even a head ache since she had become a Chimæric.

My mother's insulin!

The black bag was still lying on the counter. She opened it and pulled out a couple of bottles.

If I inject myself with all of it that would probably do it.

No! she thought.

Suicide was not an option. She had resolved last night to do what she could to stop the menace that she had helped to create. She would go to the lab and examine herself to determine what, if anything, Maria's blood had done to alter the course of her transformation.

She arrived at the lab later than her usual time. As she went in the lab several of her staff, noticing her late arrival, asked her whether she was all right. She assured them she was fine and attempted, as best she could, to look cheerful.

She stepped into her lab. Good, nobody is in here, she thought. She closed and locked the door behind her and went over to a cabinet and took out a phlebotomy kit. Sitting down on a stool, she tried to tie the elastic tourniquet around her upper left arm. She pulled one end of the tourniquet with her right hand while using her teeth to pull the other end. It wasn't working.

"Damn it!" she exclaimed.

"Maybe I can be of some assistance?" said a voice from the other end of the lab.

Richardson looked up startled. She had thought she was alone.

"Dr. Yarelis! I didn't know you were here."

"Finishing up on some work," he replied. "But what are you doing?"

"I'm drawing a blood sample."

"I can see that. Here, let me help you." Yarelis tied the tourniquet snugly around Richardson's arm. He palpated a swollen vessel in her arm, stuck the needle into it and pulled back on the syringe filling a tube of blood. "How many tubes did you want?"

"Just one," said Richardson.

"Here you go," he said, handing her the tube. He then withdrew the needle and placed a bandage over the puncture.

"Charla," said Yarelis, "we've been friends for a while. You can trust me. Are you in some sort of trouble?"

Richardson studied Yarelis, wondering if he could be trusted. Maybe she should take a chance. The burden felt too great to bear alone. She respected Dr. Yarelis. She had even sort of liked him at one time. But that was before Obermann came back from the Penumbra Realm the first time. After that, everything had changed. She had been too busy to think about a relationship. Yarelis had even asked her out a few months back, but she had said no. Now it was too late. He wouldn't want anything to do with her after she had been with Frederick. And the last thing she would want to do would be to infect him with Frederick's pestilence. As she thought about what might have been, but now would never be, her heart broke. She started sobbing. Dr. Yarelis put his arm around her. Finally, she wiped her eyes and took several deep breaths. She would take a chance.

"I was with Frederick," she said, looking down at the floor.

"Oh," said Yarelis. He was disappointed, but that's the way things were going to be from now on, he thought. "I guess that's to be expected. I suppose we all will be with Frederick one way or the other."

"You talked to Maria O'Conner a few times, didn't you?" she asked.

He was surprised by her question. How could Maria have anything to do with this?

"Yes, I did," he replied.

"What did you think of her?"

"I'm not sure. Everyone said she was nuts. Her husband thought she was nuts."

"Yeah, but what did *you* think?"

"She seemed nice enough. I was even trying to make arrangements with an OB to help her deliver her baby. That was before the abortion."

"Really! I never knew that. You weren't authorized to make those arrangements. You were taking a chance. Why would you do that?"

Yarelis shrugged. "Maybe because she was also a Mexican-American like myself. Maybe because I was raised Catholic too, not that I go to Church anymore."

"Maybe because there was some tiny part of you that thought that she was right?"

Dr. Yarelis stood up and took several steps away from Richardson. Then, turning around, he asked, "What are you suggesting?"

"I'm not suggesting anything," said Richardson, looking down at the forearm from which Yarelis had drawn blood. Then, looking up at him, she said, "I'm telling you. She was right!"

Yarelis just stared at her, not knowing what to say.

"She was right all along," continued Richardson. "And I was given a chance, but now it's too late for me?"

"What do you mean?"

"The day she died. I saw them."

"Who?"

"I don't know who. But, they weren't like you or me. They were like angels; they were supernatural. They came for Maria. But, I convinced myself that I was hallucinating. I, with my scientific method wouldn't allow myself to accept anything that wasn't reproducible in a test tube. And now I'm screwed!"

Richardson laughed at the pathetic irony of her last comment.

"What does this have to do with Frederick?" asked Yarelis.

"Do you know what I saw when he . . . he . . ." Richardson couldn't bring herself to speak of the hideous act she had had to submit to. "I saw him. I mean I saw *him*. He's evil."

"You mean he's a bad person? He's different, but I don't know whether I would . . . ."

"No," Richardson interrupted. "I mean he *is* evil. And he has impregnated me with his evil. And he and his father want to spread his evil seed throughout humanity."

Yarelis shook his head. "Dr. Richardson, no one has more respect for you than I do. But, all this is just too unbelievable. You're asking me to accept that Maria was some sort of saint, and that she was taken to heaven by some angels, and then you tell me that Mr. Obermann and his son are what? Devils? Charla, do you think that maybe you've just been under too much stress, or perhaps you're feeling guilty about your, you know, experience with Frederick?"

"So you won't believe me?"

"Well, come on, Charla. It is all a bit farfetched!"

Richardson grabbed the tube of her blood that Dr. Yarelis had placed on the counter. "Then maybe you'll believe this!"

"A tube of blood? How is that going to prove anything?"

"Last night I injected myself with a sample that I had kept of Maria's blood . . . ."

"You did what?!" interrupted Yarelis. "That was a stupid thing to do! Christ! She was infected with virulent HIV. And besides, it might have clotted up and caused an embolism. Shit! I can't believe you did that!"

"Let's analyze it together. Right now. Then you go ahead and tell me whether you think I'm crazy."

Richardson handed him the tube of blood. Dr. Yarelis held the still warm blood in his hand. It looked just like any other blood sample, but then he didn't expect it to look different.

"All right." Yarelis brought the tube over to the analyzer, lifted the lid, and inserted the tube into the holder. Then he pushed a tiny stainless steel capillary tube through the rubber stopper and immersed it in the blood sample. The apparatus would draw blood up through the tube to be analyzed.

"So, what I am I looking for?"

"Here, let me." Richardson sat down at the keyboard and typed in several sets of instructions into the analyzer. She spoke the instructions out loud as she typed. "*Chimæra Profile Panel* and *blood type*."

"What are you expecting to find out?" asked Yarelis.

"I'm not sure. I'm hoping that there will be some Chimæric parameter outside the normal range."

"That's it. You injected yourself with O'Conner's blood to see if somehow you could reverse your Chimæric Regeneration System. Why not just inject yourself with the Apoptosis substrate?"

"That's not going to work now that I'm being converted by Frederick. Besides, that's not what I'm trying to accomplish here."

"Then what are you trying to do?"

"Did you ever read *Frankenstein*, Doctor?"

"Yeah, a long time ago in high school. I saw the movie not that long ago though."

"Do you remember what Dr. Frankenstein had to do at the end?"

"Yeah, he tried to destroy the monster he created."

Dr. Richardson didn't respond. The machine was already printing out the results of the analysis. She pulled the printed report out of the machine and quickly scanned it. She closed her eyes, took a deep breath and nodded a couple of times, as though affirming a question she had posed to herself.

"What is it?" asked Dr. Yarelis.

Richardson handed Yarelis the report. He read over the Chimæric profile results. "Chimæric hormone C589. The concentration seems to be significantly reduced. What do you make of that?"

"C589 is responsible for helping to integrate the various Undifferentiated Chimæric Colonies into a functioning body system. We are not sure how it works, and it may do other things as well."

"And what's the consequence of lower than normal levels of this hormone?"

"I'm not sure," replied Richardson, "but it can't be good."

Yarelis looked back at the report. "Oh, wait a minute. There must be something wrong with the equipment. Look here," he said pointing to the blood type report, "it says that you have three different types of blood cells, AO, BB, and AB. That's impossible."

"My blood type is AO. Maria O'Conner's blood was BB and . . . ."

"Are you suggesting that the BB blood cells here are the ones you injected into yourself from Maria's blood sample? That's ridiculous. Those cells would have been destroyed almost immediately. And even if they weren't, they would have been diluted down to almost nothing. And this report suggests that approximately ten percent of your blood cells is BB. How could that be, especially since red blood cells can't reproduce themselves? And what about the AB blood? Whose blood is that?"

"You still don't get it do you? We're not talking about things that can be explained by science."

"What? You think something supernatural is going on within you?"

"I read that Maria believed that the battle with Chimæra was being fought in her own body. She was right. And now it will continue in mine."

*   *   *

Cynthia James watched Dr. Richardson from the other side of the spacious banquet room at the Obermann estate. It wasn't that long ago that the Nobel laureate had had her picture on every magazine and newspaper cover in the country. But, fame was not the reason James watched her now or why so many men kept their eyes glued on her as she *paraded* herself around the estate. Even Colin was behaving pathetically like some horny sailor waiting impatiently for the next port-of-call. Richardson was an attractive woman, but the tight dress with the deep plunging neckline, the makeup, the hair . . . it was all so inappropriate, thought James. And then, there were the coy little seductive glances. She had even made one at Colin!

"This is some party, isn't it!" said Colin enthusiastically to Cynthia.

"Hrrmph," she replied. She was not at all impressed by the various government officials, business leaders, and heads-of-state, gathered around Richardson as if they were adolescent boys around a girlie magazine.

"Now what's the matter?"

"What's the matter? Look at those guys falling all over themselves around Dr. Richardson. How pathetic is that! Isn't that Bishop Worthington? Look at him! Christ! He's staring at her breasts!"

"Oh, that's ridiculous. You're making things up again!"

"Really?! I saw the way you looked at her!"

"Well, maybe if you dressed a little more . . . interestingly . . . men would look at you too; wouldn't hurt your ratings either."

Cynthia was astounded at Colin's last remark. It was true that her television program, *The Early Bird Show,* had fallen into second place in the morning time slot. She felt terrible about that. She didn't need Colin throwing that in her face right now. He had obviously said what he did just to get a rise out of her. He had.

She pursed her lips angrily and poked Colin on the chest with her finger. "If you want to be with the Chimæra skank, why then, go ahead!"

"Keep your voice down," said Colin. "People might hear you."

Cynthia turned around in disgust. She needed to find a place alone where she could calm down. She remembered where the bathroom was from her first visit to the Obermann estate. She had been in the bathroom with Diego when Obermann's son, Frederick, had walked in on them. Where was that freak anyway? she thought. He hadn't been around all evening. Cynthia finally found the bathroom; she closed the door behind her. She looked into the mirror and checked her makeup.

What is he talking about? I look fine. In fact, I'm better than fine. Cynthia tugged at the tiny crows feet around her eyes and then pulled back on the skin under her chin. I am getting a little older. Damn, that little bitch on *Wake Up America!* At first, everyone thought she had had a facelift. Now the word was that she had received Chimæric therapy. Just the other day, Cynthia's producer had suggested to her that she get the treatment. After all, she shouldn't have any difficulty securing it since her boyfriend was the head of the Office of Justice and Tolerance. Maybe he's right, thought Cynthia as she pushed up on her bosom. I'm not getting any younger.

The bathroom door opened.

"Excuse me," said Cynthia indignantly. "I'm . . ." she stopped. She could hardly believe who had just walked in on her.

"Listen," said Richardson, closing the door behind her, "I don't have much time to explain."

"What are you talking about?"

"I will be having sex with most of the men here this evening."

"What?!" exclaimed Cynthia incredulously.

"Including Colin."

Cynthia just stared, dumbstruck.

"Chimæra will now be spread through sexual relations. It starts here tonight. And from here it will spread throughout world."

"Why are you telling me this?"

"Because you must protect yourself."

"I don't understand."

"You must not have relations with Colin. If you do, then you too will be infected."

"Infected? With Chimæra? Why would that be bad, after all, you created it."

"I can't explain now. Trust me, Obermann and his son, they're evil. You must get away."

"You expect me to leave the man I love, my job, everything I know and become a fugitive or something . . . just because you come in and tell me some nonsense about evil? How do I know you just don't want me out of the way so you can have Colin? Shit . . . you said it yourself. You're going to sleep with him. Well, I'll be damned if . . . ."

While Cynthia was talking, Richardson had been looking through her purse. She pulled out a silver ring and held it in her palm. It was stained with blotches of red, perhaps blood.

"What's that?" asked Cynthia. She realized that there was no point in arguing with Richardson. She was obviously following her own agenda.

"Maria O'Conner's ring. I took it off her body during the autopsy. You should give it to Diego. Maybe she can protect him."

"Why didn't you give it to Colin? It should go to him."

"No! He doesn't deserve it."

"She was his wife. What do you mean . . . ."

Someone knocked on the bathroom door.

"I'll be out in a minute," replied Richardson.

"Ah, I was looking for you," replied Obermann. "I will be needing your services soon. You know where I'll be."

"I'll be there in a few minutes," said Richardson, eyeing Cynthia as if to say, 'you see, I told you so.'

"That could mean anything," whispered Cynthia.

"I've done what I could to warn you. If you go home with Colin tonight, he will want to make love to you. Actually, *want* is not the right word. *Compelled* would be better. You will not be able to resist him just as those men out there will not be able to resist me. I am sorry."

Richardson placed the ring in Cynthia's hand and then left the bathroom. Cynthia was stunned as she continued to face the door that Richardson had closed behind her. Finally, she turned back to the mirror. What am I going to do? Does she really think that I'm going to give up everything because she comes up with this way out story? She must have cracked!

Even so, the whole incident with Richardson was unnerving. She had spoken with Richardson on a number of occasions, and she had never behaved like this before. She seemed like a changed woman— terrified, but also as if oddly reconciled to carrying out some sort of twisted mission. And she had to agree with Richardson, at least to an extent. There was something she didn't like about Obermann or his son, Frederick. But evil? She had known lots of bad people, but she wouldn't characterize them as evil. That was a word reserved for people like Hitler, Stalin, and Pol Pot.

If there were some way of knowing for sure, she thought. Some way of confirming her story. The tabernacle! She remembered the disturbing conversation she had with Obermann regarding the tabernacle.

"You sense that something important is inside," he had said to her. *"Something that may give you insight into the man who owns it."*

She had shuddered when he had said that to her. She hadn't known why. She still didn't know why the thought of it continued to terrify her. But, somehow, she knew that if she could see what was inside the tabernacle, she would know for certain, one way or the other, if Richardson were telling the truth.

She stepped out of the bathroom and walked briskly down the short hall that led to the den. She looked behind her to see if anyone might be watching. There was no one. Arriving at the door to the den, she found it closed. She held her breath, and she turned the doorknob, hoping that Obermann, or God forbid, Frederick was not inside. She opened the door slowly. The room was dimly lit, illuminated only by the smoldering embers from an earlier fire. She stepped into the room and closed the door behind her. The only sound she could hear was that of her heart pounding. She wanted to leave the room, get out before she was discovered. Then she saw it, the tabernacle, its bronze finish reflected the dim light. The tabernacle was as she remembered it—cylindrical, ornately decorated, and not too large—but large enough that something dreadful could be in it. She had a sudden urge to run, but she fought against it. She had to know what "dark secret" Obermann kept hidden inside it.

She walked over to the tabernacle. She felt around the front of it looking for a latch or button, which would release the doors. Nothing. Then she noticed a keyhole in the front base of the tabernacle. But where was the key? She looked around the pedestal. It was not there. She stepped over to the mantelpiece and looked over the length of the mantel, opened a couple of boxes, peered into a vase. Still, no key. This was taking too much time. She should leave before someone found her.

I'll check the desk. If it's not there, I'll leave, she thought.

She stepped behind the large mahogany desk and moved the chair back so she could pull out the middle drawer. She opened the drawer and was startled to find a revolver inside. It was too dark to make out anything else in the drawer, but she didn't want to turn on the light for fear it might draw someone's attention. She pushed her hand into the drawer and felt around. Pens, pencils, a letter opener, paper clips, small notepads—what was this? It felt like a key. She pulled it out. It was a key. But was it *the* key?

She brought the key to the tabernacle and attempted to insert it into the keyhole. Her hand was shaking so much she couldn't even find the opening of the hole with the tip of the key. Finally, she grasped her right hand with her left to steady it, then pushed. It fit! She stood for a moment. An awful sense of foreboding engulfed her. Her heart beat fiercely as she turned the key. The door slid silently open. She stared into the cavernous tabernacle. She could see nothing. It was too dark. She went back over to the mantel, removed a taper from a small vase and lit it from the fireplace. With her hand she cupped the small flame that flickered at the end of the taper as she brought it back to the tabernacle. She held the taper in front of the open door of the tabernacle, and then she removed her hand. Two dull eyes looked back at her as they reflected the flame from the taper. She screamed!

Suddenly, the lights went on. She spun around. It was Obermann. He had entered through another door. He locked it behind him. Cynthia stared at him trembling as he calmly walked over to a small bar and poured two glasses of sherry. He handed her a glass.

"Do you recognize my friend?" he asked her with a sinister smile.

Cynthia was afraid to look back in the direction of the tabernacle.

"Go ahead. Look. He won't bite."

Cynthia stood frozen unable to move.

"Look goddamn it!" Obermann shouted.

Cynthia slowly turned around and faced the open tabernacle. Her hand shook so much that Sherry slopped over the rim of the glass. The remarkably well-preserved head of a man sat on a small pedestal in the tabernacle. The mouth was open, slack-jawed as at the moment of death. But, it was the eyes that were the most frightful. They were not at all sunken in as one might expect. They were open and glistening, as if they were still moist, still living. They were cast down and had the appearance of hopelessness.

Cynthia wanted to cry out, but she could not make a sound. She wanted to run, but her body would not obey her mind. Richardson was right. Maria had been right. She was in the midst of incomparable evil. And now it was too late to extricate herself from it.

"You didn't answer my question, Ms. James. Do you recognize my friend?"

She did. It was Father Pietro. The man, who had been tried and convicted for the murder of Obermann and his wife.

"No," she finally replied. She wasn't exactly sure why she lied. Perhaps, she thought, if I say I don't recognize him I'll be in less trouble. It was a preposterous notion.

"I think you do," said Obermann. "And I think you understand my motive."

"Revenge," said Cynthia contemptuously.

"Very good! And let me assure you . . . ," he said, walking over to the tabernacle, placing his hand inside and then ruffling the hair of his victim as if he were stroking a pet cat, ". . . it's far sweeter than you could ever imagine."

"You're barbaric!" she exclaimed.

"Ha! You think so? And you know only the half of it! I'm going to tell you the rest so that you can fully appreciate just how barbaric I really am."

"I'd rather not know," replied Cynthia, now more disgusted than scared. "Besides, I'm sure Colin will be looking for me soon."

"Oh, Colin. Well, I wouldn't count on him coming around very soon. He's . . . how shall I say . . . indisposed at the moment. So now, have a seat, and together we will penetrate the dark secret of Hans Obermann."

Cynthia took a seat that was not facing the tabernacle. She nervously played with the glass of sherry. She had known that she was in peril as soon as she had decided to try opening the tabernacle. Now that Obermann was disclosing his secret she realized that her situation had become desperate. But what could she do?

"Death can be an amazing conversion experience," began Obermann. "When I was alive, the first time that is, I was an atheist. I thought all that business about God, the devil and the soul were just the product of a lot of wishful thinking. Boy, was I ever wrong!"

Obermann walked over to the mantle and took a cigar from the humidor. While snipping the end of the cigar, he continued.

"I used to believe that our bodies were just biological machines; that life was just the inevitable result of biochemical complexity. It's not though. It is the soul that animates the body. The soul and body form an intimate union, a union shattered by death. It is the departure of the soul that causes physical death and bodily degradation."

Obermann took a taper from the vase, bent down and ignited it from the embers that continued to glow in the fireplace. He lit his cigar, taking several puffs, while rolling it between his thumb and fingers to make sure it was evenly lit. He removed the cigar from his mouth and examined it.

Cynthia wondered why Obermann was telling her all of this. She knew the more he revealed the greater her jeopardy.

"You're curious as to why I'm telling you this," said Obermann, now turning his attention away from his cigar and staring at her. A shiver went down Cynthia's spine. "You're a journalist. I thought you might like to know."

"I'd rather not."

"Oh, it's way too late for that, Miss James. Now, as I was saying, a funny thing happened on the way to hell; I didn't get there. In fact, I didn't go anywhere, my soul that is. It seems that bitch Maria O'Conner was right. Damned if my soul wasn't stuck in my body. Don't ask me how, but it seems that death, rather than separating the soul from the body, simply broke the interface between the two. So there I was, caught between heaven and hell; a solitary confinement within a universe of self. You don't really appreciate what social animals we humans are until you're alone like that."

Obermann drew in the aromatic smoke from his cigar. He seemed to be enraptured by the experience. He followed this with a sip of Sherry. Cynthia looked over at the door. Perhaps she could escape? No. Even if she could get away she wouldn't get far. Obermann's reach was too great.

"Then there is the sensory deprivation," Obermann continued. "You cannot imagine what it is like not to taste, not to smell, not to feel. The soul aches to experience these things. It was maddening to be in the body while being denied access to its sensations."

Obermann took a large mouthful of sherry and swished it around in his mouth. "I can assure you, Miss James, you cannot imagine a more horrific experience."

"So why would you want to inflict that horror on the rest of humanity?" asked Cynthia.

"That's easy. It was part of a deal that allowed me to return. Trust me, anyone would do, what I have done. Even our holy Father Pietro did," Obermann said, motioning towards the head in the tabernacle.

"It's remarkable how well-preserved his head is, isn't it?" asked Obermann rhetorically. It was evident that he was proud of his trophy. "It is probably due to the lingering effects of the soul."

The gun! The gun in the desk drawer! thought Cynthia. *Maybe I can work my way around his desk. I'll send the son-of-a-bitch back where he belongs!*

Cynthia stood up and sipped her sherry. *Perhaps I can distract him by asking questions.*

"I don't understand. What deal did Father Pietro make?"

"I told him that if he didn't implicate Cardinal McIntyre in my assassination I'd inject him with Chimæra."

Cynthia continued to move closer to the desk trying not to give the impression that she was going in that direction for a purpose.

"He also believed all that *garments of skin* business. He knew what the consequences would be if he were injected, so he sold out the good Cardinal.

Cynthia was now behind Obermann's desk.

"After he testified against the Cardinal, I had him injected with Chimæra anyway. And the sweetest possible revenge is that he's still with us. His soul is trapped in his head; locked away in my little tabernacle prison." Obermann approached the tabernacle, bent down and came face to face with the head of Father Pietro. "How do you like that, you piece of shit!"

Cynthia quickly reached into the drawer and pulled out the revolver.

"Go to hell where you belong!" exclaimed Cynthia.

Obermann looked up. He saw the barrel of his revolver pointing directly at him.

Bang!

The gun recoiled so violently that it flew out of Cynthia's hand. Obermann grabbed his chest dropping the glass of sherry to the floor.

I shot him! I shot him! Cynthia could hardly believe it. But what else could she do?

Obermann smiled. He walked towards the desk and drew his hand away from his chest. He opened his hand. The still warm bullet rested in his palm.

"A little something I picked up from my son," Obermann scoffed. He picked up the phone and pushed a button. "Yeah, nothing to worry about. I'll take care of it."

Cynthia had reached back into the drawer while Obermann was on the phone. She grabbed the letter opener, hid it behind her back, and stepped away behind the desk.

Obermann set the receiver back in its cradle. "When you become a Chimæric you'll be more compliant," he said, placing a hand on her shoulder. "Otherwise, perhaps you'll join good ol' Father . . . ."

Cynthia plunged the letter opener into Obermann's chest. She pushed him away and he fell back onto the desk. He stared down at his bleeding chest, hardly believing what had just happened to him. How could she do that to me? he thought. Where was his incorporeal guardian? Why hadn't he stopped the blade as he had the bullet? He was so perplexed by the object sticking out of his chest he hardly noticed the pain or the fact that it could be a serious injury. He hadn't even noticed Cynthia as she ran to leave the room.

As Cynthia reached the door, she thought she heard a voice, a voice in her mind. *Help me! Deliver me from my captor!* She turned around. Obermann still sat on the desk, transfixed by the wound she had inflicted on him. She looked over at the tabernacle. She was not sure how she knew, but something inside her told her the voice was *his*. She walked over to the tabernacle and looked at the ghostly eyes as if an answer resided within them. She opened her purse, reached inside, felt around and removed the ring that Richardson had given her moments earlier. She withdrew the ring and held it in her clenched fist.

"What are you doing?!" asked Obermann whose attention was now drawn to the activity in front of the tabernacle.

Cynthia ignored Obermann's question. She reached out her hand, holding the ring with her fingers.

"What is that?" Obermann sounded alarmed.

Cynthia pressed the ring against Father Pietro's forehead. She thought that she detected something change in the eyes.

Thank you.

"Damn you! What have you done?" Obermann began to stand but fell back down into the chair. He had lost a considerable amount of blood. His injury was more serious than he had thought. He reached for the phone to call for help. Cynthia ran over, grabbed the phone cord and yanked it out of the wall. Obermann slumped back into his chair unconscious. Cynthia picked up the heavy brass desk lamp and raised it above her head. Her intent was to bring it down on Obermann's skull to crush it. Her arms trembled as she tried to deliver the lethal blow. She could not do it. She turned and ran out of the room.

Her mind was racing nearly as fast as her car's engine as she sped home. Her situation was hopeless. *If Obermann survives, God knows what he will do with me. May be I'll become another trophy!* Even if he did die, Cynthia knew that Frederick would wreak some horrible punishment on her. Finally, after what seemed to be an eternity, she pulled into her driveway. She jumped out of the car and ran for the door. As she fumbled with her keys trying to open the front door, a voice called from inside,

"Who is it?" inquired Lucia, the nanny.

"It's Cynthia. Please open the door!"

"Certainly." Lucia opened the door. Lucia was a Latina in her mid-fifties. Colin had hired her shortly after the death of Maria to help take care of Diego. She had continued to live in the O'Conner household even after Cynthia had moved in. Lucia was pleased at how "motherly" Cynthia had become. She frequently remonstrated Colin for not marrying Cynthia.

"A better mother for your *mijo* you will not find," Lucia had told him in her thick accent.

"Once was enough," said Colin despairingly.

"You were unworthy of the saintly Maria, may she pray for us," Lucia muttered in Spanish, crossing herself.

"What?" asked Colin.

Lucia didn't bother to translate.

"What is the matter, *Señorita* James?" Lucia could see that Cynthia was distressed.

"No time to explain, Lucia. Is Diego in bed?"

"*Sí*, he is asleep."

"If anyone calls, do not tell them I am here." Cynthia began to walk down the hall towards the bedroom.

"All right, Miss Cynthia, but is there something I can do to help?"

Cynthia walked back and took Lucia by the hand. "For me, nothing. Promise me you will continue to look after Diego."

"Of course. But, you will be here, will you not, *Señorita*?"

Cynthia gave Lucia a sad smile and then turned away. She walked down the hall and entered Diego's dimly lit bedroom. Maria had bought the night light for the nursery even before Diego was born. It was a little statue of the Virgin Mary. Colin had wanted to get rid of it, but Diego had protested so vehemently that Colin relented. Cynthia sat down on the bed next to Diego. She unlatched a gold chain from around her neck. She slid the lone pearl that was suspended from it. She then reached into her purse and removed Maria's wedding band. She ran the gold chain through the ring, clasped it around Diego's neck and then tucked the ring under his pajamas. Diego stirred and murmured something unintelligible.

"Your mother will have to protect you now," she whispered as she bent down and kissed him on the forehead. She then left Diego's room, went into the bathroom, and locked the door.

It was about two hours later when Colin arrived home. He was accompanied by two gentlemen, one in a policeman's uniform. Lucia greeted the trio at the door.

"Is there a problem?" asked Lucia.

"Where is Cynthia?" asked Colin sternly.

"She was taking a bath, *Señor* O'Conner. Perhaps she is in bed now," replied Lucia.

Colin turned around and spoke with the officers. "Please, let me have a moment with her before you take her away."

The officers nodded.

"Take her away?!" shrieked Lucia. "I knew there was a problem."

"Never mind," said Colin. "Take care of Diego. I will probably be gone the rest of the night."

Colin went into their bedroom while the policemen waited in the living room. Cynthia was not in their bed. Colin turned the doorknob to the bathroom. It was locked.

"Cynthia, it's me, Colin. I need to talk with you."

There was no answer.

Colin reached into his pocket and removed his keys. The bathroom door could be unlocked by any key. He opened the door and stepped in.

"God Almighty!"

Cynthia lay in the tub up to her chin in blood red water. Her eyes were closed as if she were asleep. She had a serene expression on her face. Cynthia was dead.

Colin sat down on the toilet seat and stared at Cynthia and shook his head.

"Why?" he asked her rhetorically. Obermann had told Colin that Cynthia had confronted him about Colin having sexual relations with Dr. Richardson. He had said he had tried to assure her that it had nothing to do with Colin being unfaithful to her; that this was the means by which Chimæra would now be spread. But, he said Cynthia wouldn't listen. She had become so enraged that she had stabbed him with a letter opener. Fortunately, Obermann continued, the attack did not damage any vital organs or sever a major artery. His Chimæric stem cells promptly healed the wound without medical intervention. Obermann assured Colin he would not press charges. "It's my fault," confessed Obermann magnanimously. "I should have been more sensitive. Some people still cling to the old ways of thinking about sex."

Colin picked up a note that was on the counter. It was from Cynthia.

My Dear Colin,

Yes, I stabbed Hans Obermann. I hope he's dead. If he is, then I have done you, and the world, a favor. If he is not, then at least, I have inflicted on him some measure of pain for which he is deserving. In either case, I am beyond his reach and the reach of his evil son. But, you are not and neither is Diego. If you love your son, keep him away from the Obermanns and under no circumstances allow him to become infected with Chimæra! May God have mercy on me!

-Cynthia

Colin sat and stared at the letter incredulously. It's happening all over again, he thought.

The detective appeared in the doorway of the bathroom; he could see Cynthia in the tub.

"Is she . . ." asked the detective.

"Dead?" finished Colin. "Yes, it appears to be suicide."

"We'll determine that," said the detective, bending down to examine the body. He straightened up, "Who else is here besides the housekeeper?"

"My son."

"I'd like to speak with him," pulling out a small notepad from his pocket.

"No," replied Colin forcefully. "He's just a boy. He's going to be very upset to find out that Cynthia is dead. I will speak with him when the time is right. If he knows anything that might be of help to you I will let you know."

The detective nodded. "There's going to be a lot of activity around here, Mr. O'Conner. Forensics, the coroner. I don't think you will want your son to be around."

"You're right," said Colin going to the sink. As he was washing his hands he continued, "My son and I will stay at a hotel for a few days until all this gets cleaned up."

"Oh, there is one more thing. Mr. Obermann said that she had something in her possession. He wasn't sure what it was, but it was small. Small enough to put in her purse. He thought it might be important in our investigation. Do you mind if I look in your wife's purse?"

"Go ahead. I think I saw it on the bed."

"Thanks."

The detective found the purse and dumped its contents onto the bed. Colin was right. The purse looked as though it had been hastily thrown on the bed: keys, cell phone, makeup, change purse, wallet . . . nothing unusual here.

The detective stepped back into the bathroom.

"I'd like to take these with me," said the detective.

"Sure," said Colin. "I'll contact her family. What about the producer of her TV show?"

"We'll make an announcement to the media." Then the detective reached into a pocket and took out a card. He handed it to Colin.

"If you find anything unusual around the house, call me."

Colin looked down at the card.

"Detective Reilly. Yes. I will," he said as he shoved the detective's card into his pocket.

"Daddy! Daddy!"

"It's my son," said Colin stepping out of the bathroom. He turned back to the detective. "Let me leave with my son before you call in your crew."

Detective Reilly nodded.

Colin stepped out of the bedroom and into the hallway. Lucia was heading towards Diego's bedroom.

"Lucia, pack a suitcase with some of Diego's things. We'll be spending the night, maybe a few nights, at a hotel."

"Should I pack some things for you, too?" asked Lucia

"No. I'll take care of that myself."

"And *Señorita* James?"

"Daddy," called Diego, exasperated. "I have to tell you something."

"Yes, Diego. Just a second." Colin turned back to Lucia. "Just pack Diego's things. I'll explain everything in just a moment. Let me . . . ."

"I saw Mommy!" exclaimed Diego excitedly.

Colin entered Diego's bedroom and turned on the light. "You mean, Cynthia?" asked Colin.

"No, I mean my real mommy. You know, the one in the hallway. The one without an arm."

This had been Diego's only remaining memory of his mother. Colin had tried to eradicate every memory of Maria from his son. He had thrown out nearly all of her pictures, and everything that had once belonged to her. But, he could not erase this particular memory, so powerfully had the experience embedded itself in Diego's mind. He had hoped that Diego would accept Cynthia as his mother and that eventually, even this memory would fade.

Diego was sitting up in bed. He was holding something in his hand that was attached to a chain that was around his neck. Colin stooped down to see what Diego was holding. Diego opened his hand. It was a ring.

"Mommy gave it to me," said Diego.

Colin recognized Maria's wedding ring!

"Where did you get this?!" exclaimed Colin.

"I told you, Daddy," said Diego startled by his father's response. "Mommy gave it to me."

"No she didn't. Your mother is dead. Cynthia gave it to you." Then Colin realized that this must be what Cynthia had that Obermann wanted.

"Give it to me!" said Colin angrily.

Diego was alarmed by his father's reaction. He tucked the ring back under his pajama shirt and fell back onto his bed. "No Daddy. Mommy gave it to *me*!"

Colin leaned over Diego and ripped open his pajama shirt.

"No, Daddy! No!"

Colin was about to reach for the ring when he noticed a glistening red drop appear on its surface. He watched as the drop slid off the ring onto his son's chest where it penetrated his skin and then disappeared.

"No!" shouted Colin. Somehow he knew that Maria had reached across the veil of death to touch *his* son. How dare she! He grabbed the ring with the intent of yanking it off his son's neck. As he held the ring in his hand it became hotter and hotter until it seemed on fire. Although his fist was closed around the ring, he could see that it was glowing. Light emanated from between his fingers; his hand glowed red, and he could see the outlines of his bones. His hand began to ache. He could hear the sizzling and popping of his burning flesh. He tried to open his hand and let go of the ring, but he could not. Unbearable pain radiated up his arm.

"Let me go! Let me go!" he cried out.

The ring would not release him. Colin fell to his knees. His hand burst into flames. The flames continued up his arm.

"Oh my God! Oh my God! Help me!"

The flames spread to his chest and head. His entire body was engulfed in fire. He felt the protoplasm of every cell boiling and their membranes bursting. The pain was beyond what anybody could experience physically. Why am I not dead? He wanted to scream out, Let me die! He could not. He no longer possessed the organs for speech. He burned in an unquenchable fire.

"Daddy, please let me keep Mommy's ring."

Colin came to himself and found he was standing over his son, his hand still holding the ring. He looked at his hand. It was not on fire! He was not on fire! Colin stood shaking. His hand, almost involuntarily, released the ring. He looked down at his palm. There was a dark reddish-black mark where the ring had branded his palm. A slight stench of burnt flesh emanated from the wound.

"Are you okay, Daddy?"

Colin said nothing, but understood. He rubbed his hand and stared at the ring that seconds ago had seared his flesh; it now lay harmlessly on his son's chest. This was the judgment that awaited him. He had betrayed and destroyed everyone who had loved him. But, it wasn't God judging him. It was his own guilty conscience that had set him ablaze. There was no hiding from it. Not anymore. Self-deception could not disguise what he had just experienced. Besides, he bore the indelible mark of guilt on his palm as surely as Maria had borne the stigmata. Cynthia's words echoed in his mind. *Maria was right!* Yes! She was right. He had always known it. Colin breathed a heavy sigh. It is not too late to love my son, he thought. He sat down next to Diego.

"I'm sorry if I scared you. You did see your mother. Do what she told you. Keep the ring with you. She's right. She was always right. The ring will protect you." Colin kissed his son on the forehead. "Try to go back to sleep. Perhaps your mom will come to you again. If she does, tell her for me that I'm sorry."

Colin kissed his son and stood. He motioned to Lucia to follow him. They went into Colin's office, and he closed the door.

"I want you to take Diego away from here. I want both of you to stay with my parents. It will be better for Diego."

"How long do you want us to stay there, *Señor*," said Lucia.

"Indefinitely. I'll call them and make the arrangements. They'll love having you."

"I don't understand, *Señor* O'Conner. He should be with his father."

"You think so? No. If it were possible I'd send him away, and he would never see me again. But that would make Obermann suspicious and that would be dangerous for Diego. Besides, I think you understand me perfectly, Lucia. You see, I know about your phone calls and meetings with Madison Ryan. And I know why you did it. You and Miss Ryan were trying to protect my son. Probably, some last request of my wife. That is why I am entrusting my son to you. But I'm not sure how long I'll continue to see things this way. That's why you must leave immediately. Also, and this is very important, if I should want my son back, or if I make arrangements for him to become a Chimæric, you must flee with him, and do not let me know where you are taking him."

Colin took his keys out of his pocket and unlocked a desk drawer. He took out a metal box and opened it with another key. He pulled out a wad of bills.

"Here's some money. You'll need a few things. I'll send more, but my parents will also help you. I suppose I should ask whether you'd be willing to do this."

Lucia smiled. "For Blessed Maria, I lay down my life."

"Yes," smiled Colin. "I thought you might."

"Maybe it's not too late for you, *Señor* O'Conner? Pray to your wife, she will help you," said Lucia.

"I doubt it. Besides, it's not about me anymore. It's about Diego."

Colin reached back into the metal box and pulled out a picture. It was the last remaining picture he had of Maria—taken on their wedding day. He started to tear the picture.

"I did everything I could to get Diego to forget his mother. It was me he should have forgotten."

Colin handed the torn picture to Lucia. Lucia looked at the picture of Maria. She was beautiful. "He will remember his father," she said.

Colin tossed the remaining half of the picture—himself—back into the box. "It would be better for him to forget me."

"Every night, I make sure that he prays for you, *Señor*. It was Maria's wish."

"Well, then perhaps there is hope," replied Colin. He reached into the metal box again and removed a silver band that matched the one that Diego now wore. He placed the ring in the center of his palm over the still throbbing wound. "Maybe there is still time to pluck a brand from the fire."

Nightmare

For nightmares come with many cares, and a fool's utterance with many words. When you make a vow to God, delay not its fulfillment. For God has no pleasure in fools; fulfill what you have vowed. You had better not make a vow than make it and not fulfill it.
—Ecclesiastes 5:2

The chapel was dark; the still air was cool and moist. The sweetly pungent odor of incense lingered in the atmosphere from some earlier liturgy. Statues appeared to move as they reflected the reddish hues cast by flickering candles enclosed in ruby-red votive lamps. Soft, repetitive chanting could be heard in one corner of the chapel. A lone figure knelt before a statue of the Blessed Virgin. The meditative quiet was broken as footfalls announced the arrival of another in the chapel. This new arrival wore a robe, a rope for a belt, and sandals. He placed his hand on the shoulder of the cleric who was kneeling.

"They are here, your Eminence. They are waiting for you in your office."

The man slowly stood and crossed himself. "Lead me to them, Brother Andres," replied the shadowy figure.

The two men walked through the dark labyrinth of hallways until they arrived at a large, heavy wooden door. The monk opened the door, and the older man entered the room. It took a few moments for their eyes to adjust to the brightly lit room. The man and woman who were seated in front of a desk turned around towards the opening door. They wore blindfolds.

"Remove the blindfold," said the elderly cleric.

The young monk walked over to the man and removed his blindfold. The man rubbed his eyes while they adjusted themselves to the light. The woman's blindfold was also removed. She stared at the older cleric.

The man jumped out of his chair, fell to his knees, grabbed the cleric's hand, and kissed his ring.

"Your Eminence, it is an honor to meet you."

Bishop Entremont placed his hand on Elliot Hoffman's head. "Have a seat." Mrs. Elaina Hoffman began to stand up. Bishop Entremont raised his hand to indicate that he wanted her to remain where she was. He didn't speak for a moment. He had never seen a woman in such a way as the one that stood before him now; or rather, he had never looked at a woman such as he looked at Elaina. He felt a primordial passion that he had thought he had rooted out of his psyche through years of ascetic practice. Now he struggled to gather his wits.

"I hope you understand," Entremont finally said, "why I took the precaution of having you blindfolded. Few know of this old French monastery and those that do, believe it to be a retirement home for aging religious. If the beasts and their nephilim hordes were to discover my whereabouts, all would be lost."

"Surely you don't think . . . ." began Hoffman.

"I am not sure what to think," interrupted Entremont. "Personally, I thought it was too risky to meet with you. However, my advisors believed that what you had to offer was potentially of such great value it was worth the risk." Bishop Entremont sat down at his desk facing Elliot and his wife Elaina. "I will be frank with you. It is you, Elaina, that I do not trust." Although he said these things, and meant them, he felt powerfully drawn to her. He wondered if she knew what he was thinking. He remembered the scripture where David looked down and saw Bathsheba taking a bath. He knew he should avert the eyes of his heart, but he could not.

"Your Eminence?" asked Elaina coyly, feigning surprise and disappointment at Entremont's apprehension.

"You should not be surprised. After all, it was Frederick, the beast, who restored your life. How can I be sure that you do not now owe your allegiance to him?"

"I was never really dead," said Elaina. "They just wanted people to believe that I was. I played along with them to earn their trust."

"Hmm." Entremont rubbed his chin. "Even so," he said, shaking his head indicating that he was unsure of their loyalty to himself and the Congregation, "how can I be sure?"

Elaina nodded to her husband. Elliot reached down into a box that was on the floor next to his chair. He removed a shiny stainless steel cylinder.

"Because of this," said Elliot, placing the cylinder on Entremont's desk.

"Is that the toxin I was told about?" asked Entremont.

"Yes," replied Elliot. "This canister alone has enough toxin to kill a city full of Chimærics. All that needs to be done is to release it into the air. It will remain in the air for days, perhaps weeks. The particles are smaller than a virus. They enter the body either through the respiratory system or through the skin. A Chimæric has no defense against it."

"And what effect does it have on non-Chimærics?"

"It is harmless," replied Elliot.

"And how did you come into possession of these cylinders? Are you expecting me to believe that you just walked out of Chimæra with these deadly poisons? They must have been carefully guarded."

"When I was there for an examination, I was approached by someone in the facility," replied Elaina. "They were part of the team working on the toxin. Not everyone who works for Mr. Obermann is sympathetic to his evil objectives."

"Assuming for the moment that what you are telling me is the truth, why would they even make such a toxin?"

"I was told that during the initial stages of the program, Obermann was concerned that the Chimæric cells might mutate or the technology could fall into the wrong hands. They wanted the ability to destroy Chimæric stem cells and their hosts."

"And how come there hasn't been an announcement that these deadly poisons are missing?"

"I suspect that they are doing everything they can to locate them," said Elliot. "But, if they were to go public, I'm sure it would cause panic among the growing Chimæric community."

Entremont nodded. "So what do you propose I do with these cylinders?"

"You have operatives throughout North America and Western Europe. Release the toxin in the major metropolitan areas where there are Chimæric Distribution Centers. Think of how many Chimærics we could destroy. People considering Chimæric therapy will think twice when they recognize how vulnerable they are."

Entremont picked up the cylinder and examined it. "A provocative plan," he said, standing up. "If it were released during a public event, such as when Obermann and his demonic son, Frederick, are present we could kill them and scores of their nephilim in a single stroke."

"Exactly," said Elaina.

"If it actually does what you claim it can do. Then again, it could be a trap—a trap to expose members of the Congregation, including myself. You see that's the problem. And besides, how can I be sure that it will do what you claim?"

Entremont placed the cylinder back on his desk in front of Elaina. Elliot was disappointed. They had come all this way and risked so much to deliver these cylinders to Bishop Entremont. Elaina picked up the cylinder that had been placed in front of her. She smiled sadly at her husband.

"You are right," said Elaina to Entremont. "Although Frederick did not restore my life, his blood did enter my body. I am now a Chimæric."

Entremont took a step back, while Brother Andres began to approach Elaina. Elliot just stared at her perplexed. "But you are wrong if you think I owe my allegiance to him. I can however understand why you would find it difficult to trust me. Perhaps this will convince you."

Elaina grabbed the regulator valve of the cylinder and gave it a twist. Immediately, a hissing sound could be heard emanating from a tiny hole as it released a colorless and odorless gas into the air.

"Stop!" exclaimed Elliot as he reached for the cylinder.

Elaina pulled the cylinder to her chest and held onto it tenaciously as Elliot tried to pry it from her.

"Leave her be!" commanded Entremont.

Elaina started to shake violently. She began to wheeze and cough. Blood and saliva foamed from her mouth. Her head slumped to her chest; the shaking subsided. She was dead in a matter of seconds.

Elliot sat in shock. Entremont was stunned as well, but also relieved that he would no longer experience the temptation of Elaina's presence. He placed his hand on Elliot's shoulder.

"There are some who believe that Maria O'Conner's death was the defeat of Chimæra," said Entremont. "What we have just witnessed is the true defeat of the Chimæric menace. The whole world will know of the sacrifice your wife made this day. When I am Pope, I will have Elaina Hoffman declared a saint."

Entremont then turned to the monk, "Brother Andres, have some of the sisters prepare Elaina Hoffman's body. She died a martyr's death. Her body should lie within the chapel until the morning. We will then have a funeral Mass for her.

Brother Andres left to speak with several of the resident nuns about the arrangement Bishop Entremont had ordered. Elliot, emotionally shattered yet encouraged by Entremont's words, stayed with the body of his wife until the nuns arrived. Bishop Entremont retired to his room. Before he went to bed, he knelt before the crucifix that hung in his room. He pleaded for forgiveness for the lust he had experienced when he saw Elaina. He felt embarrassment and shame as he recalled his thoughts and feelings about the woman he now believed to be a saint. Finally, he went to bed, not convinced that God had forgiven him.

It was early in the morning when the sisters had completed their preparations. Elaina's body was laid out on a table covered with lace, her head resting peacefully on a silk pillow. She was clothed in a white nightgown, which was strewn with sweet smelling flowers from the convent's garden. A garland of wildflowers was placed on her head. Her hands were folded over her chest. There was no longer any sign of the traumatic death that she had experienced just a few hours earlier. She looked peaceful, even angelic.

The chapel was dark save for the flickering of the many small candles that outlined Elaina's body. In the candlelight a lone figure could be seen keeping vigil; he knelt next to the body of his wife. Elliot's arms rested against the table. He had been in the chapel most of the night. It was nearly three in the morning, and he was overcome by fatigue. The Funeral Mass was scheduled for nine in the morning. He did not want to leave his wife, yet he knew that he should try to get some sleep. He struggled to stand up. He had been kneeling for so long his muscles had nearly cramped. Bracing himself against the table he pushed himself into a standing position. Elliot looked down at his wife. She looked so serene, almost as if she were not dead, but asleep.

"Just one last kiss my beloved," he whispered. "Until we meet again."

He bent down and gently kissed her lips. Suddenly, the tongue of the corpse shot between his lips and into his mouth. Elliot jerked back terrified, but as he retreated, Elaina's right hand reached out and she grasped his neck in a vice-like grip. She dug her fingers deep into his throat, nearly wrapping around his trachea. Elliot's eyes bulged as he gasped futilely for air.

"You fool," exclaimed Elaina, sitting up on the table and maintaining her superhuman grip on Elliot's throat. "I am not Elaina. And you will not be seeing her again. While your beloved is in heaven you will spend your eternity trapped in the solitary confinement of your rotting flesh."

Elaina then squeezed her hand so tightly that her fingers penetrated Elliot's throat. His knees buckled, and he would have fallen to the ground, but she held him upright until she saw his eyes roll back into their sockets. She then gave a terrific yank ripping out his trachea and esophagus. He crumpled to the floor, dead. Elaina tossed the organs onto the ground and laughed.

Bishop Entremont was having a fretful sleep. His guilty conscience could not extricate Elaina from his mind. And while he dreamt, she appeared to him. She was wearing a white nightgown and there was a garland of flowers resting on her head. She held a candle with her left hand and with her right she began to unbutton her gown. Entremont watched feverishly as Elaina's breasts were gradually exposed.

"No!" said Entremont, attempting to muster enough strength of will to resist the temptation.

"It is only a dream," said Elaina, as she approached the Bishop's bed. The gown now slipped completely off; revealing to Entremont what he thought must be the most desirous being in all creation. She climbed up on the bed, her naked body straddling his. Her breasts hung tantalizingly before him.

"My vow," he said. "My vow." And as he repeated these words one more time, he felt their binding power loosening their grip upon his soul.

"Shhh." She leaned down and kissed his lips, her breasts rubbed against his chest. "It's only a dream. What harm can there be in dreaming?"

PART III

Half a Time

And we all, with unveiled face, beholding the glory of the Lord, are being changed into His likeness from one degree of glory to another . . . .
~ 2 Corinthians 3:18

This is our *raison d'être*, the transformation of the *image* imparted to us at the first moment of our being into His *likeness*. It is our lifelong mission. Indeed, it may extend even into eternity itself, for to share in the Divine Nature is to participate in the Eternal. It is also our lifelong conflict. This is a war that began in the Garden when Satan offered an alternative path to the realization of this goal. "You shall be like god," he said. Our first parents were deceived because the false path was pleasing to the eye. The true path is not. Our attitude must be that of Christ: He emptied himself and obediently accepted death, death on a cross. So it must be with us. We must surrender our limited images of ourselves and yield to the cross of His transforming love.

Do not be unbelieving and fearful! Do you not know, oh heart, what God has prepared for you? My reason questions, "How can these things be?" My heart responds like the Virgin, "Behold, I am the handmaid of the Lord. May it be done to me according to your word."

~Saint Maria Theresa O'Conner (Journal)

Entertaining Angels

Do not neglect to show hospitality to strangers, for thereby some
have entertained angels unawares. Remember those who are in prison,
as though in prison with them; and those who are ill-treated, since you
also are in the body.

-Hebrews 13:2,3

"I'm sorry, your Eminence, I should have visited you sooner." "There is nothing to be sorry about," replied Cardinal McIntyre. "You've spent enough time in places like this. And please, Madison. Call me Father Bill, that's what everyone calls me around here."

"I don't know . . . ." began Ryan.

"She's as stubborn as Maria," said Sister Francis.

"Really?" replied Ryan. "Why thank you."

Sister Francis and Cardinal McIntyre joined in a hearty laugh. This was also the first time Sister Francis had had an opportunity to visit the Cardinal since his imprisonment. She had been recalled to the Mother House by her Superior shortly after Bishop Kavasilas had replaced the Cardinal as Vice-Postulator for the Cause of Maria's beatification. Mother Josephina had decided not to allow the independent-minded Sister Francis to continue to work with Kavasilas. In her opinion, Sister Francis lacked the prudence that the high profile case required. The Order simply didn't need the notoriety that Sister Francis might provoke. Mother Josephina was having a difficult enough time keeping the Order solvent, so she felt she didn't need to be harassed by the Tree of Life or the Office of Justice and Tolerance.

"And how's your imprisonment, Sister?" joked McIntyre.

"This place looks more cozy than the Mother House," replied Sister Francis sarcastically. "And I suspect the warden is more amiable than Mother Josephina! I'm going to go nuts if I stay there much longer. They're all too good for me."

"Nonsense," replied McIntyre. "You just have a different type of goodness. Cranky goodness."

Ryan laughed. Sister Francis scowled.

"All right. That's enough of that," said Sister Francis. "So, how are you enjoying your little vacation?"

"I never get a moment's peace around here," replied Cardinal McIntyre. "In fact, it makes me a bit suspicious."

"How so?" asked Ryan pulling out her note pad.

"I wouldn't bother. The guards will just take it away from you before you leave," said McIntyre, referring to her notebook. "You see those two guys over there?" McIntyre motioned with his head to two "gentlemen" sitting some distance from them watching television.

"Yeah?" asked Ryan.

"They're my roommates."

Ryan examined the two men. One looked particularly unsavory; he was the younger of the two. His head was shaved and as far as she could tell he was completely covered with tattoos. McIntyre's other roommate was well groomed with an impeccably manicured mustache and beard. He appeared to be in his early forties. The younger man turned around and looked right at Ryan. The hair on the back of her neck stood up. Then the man gave a broad, friendly smile and waved.

"That's Jaime," said McIntyre, smiling and nodding towards the inmate. "He's serving two life sentences. He'll get out before I do," McIntyre chuckled. "The other man is an interesting character. His name is Percy, Percy Collins. He was a professor of English literature."

"Really?" said Sister Francis who used to teach literature years ago.

"Yes. He can, at times, be interesting to talk with. He frequently quotes Keats, Dickens, or Browning, or some other poet or author. I try to guess whom he's quoting. I get it wrong most of the time. Then he scolds me, good naturedly, of course."

"And if you get it right?" asked Sister Francis.

"Then he says, *Just so*, with just a hint of an English accent."

Ryan laughed. "So what crime is he in here for?"

"He wrote an anthology of poems. Some critic gave it a scathing review. The word is he beat him to death."

"Now I can understand why you don't have any peace—not with these two guys around," observed Ryan.

"You have to expect to meet fellows like Jaime and Percy in a prison," said McIntyre. "What's unnerving is that I never get a break from these guys—they're always with me. And they're always bickering and fighting. I can't get through two decades of the rosary without them interrupting me."

"You said you were suspicious?" asked Ryan.

"Well, I might be just imagining things," replied McIntyre, "but I can't help but think that Obermann has something to do with these two characters being with me all the time."

"Why would he do that?" asked Ryan.

"Just in case I become inconvenient. It wouldn't be very difficult for them to do me in if Obermann gave the order."

"Oh my God!" exclaimed Ryan.

McIntyre placed his hand on Ryan's arm. "I'm sorry. You shouldn't worry. I'm in God's hands. But, enough about me and my situation. So tell me, any word from Rome yet about when they'll meet with you and Kavasilas?"

"Not yet; the wheels of the Church grind exceedingly slow," replied Ryan.

"And fine. Well then, I have some news. I got a letter from Father Nikitas."

"Really! What did he have to say?" asked Ryan excitedly.

"Not too much. I suppose he couldn't, even if he wanted to. As you know, they read all my mail. Anyway, he said that I was exactly where God wanted me."

"Prison? I hope God doesn't want me in here again!" replied Ryan.

McIntyre laughed. "No, I don't think so. He has other plans for you. Tell me about yourself and what's going on."

"Is it okay to talk freely?" asked Ryan.

"Yeah, I think so."

"Well then, you already know how Obermann tried to pull those shenanigans with the fraudulent journal. You couldn't ask for better publicity. Most everyone saw right through it except, of course, those that wanted to be deceived."

"And there are always plenty of those around," interjected Sister Francis. "You should have heard good ol' Bishop Worthington and his little tart Hampton go on about it!"

"But on the positive side," continued Ryan "when Maria's journal did come out, we could barely keep them in print. Mostly we made it available on the internet in an electronic format so that people could download it. Just about the time the Office of Justice and Tolerance would shut down one of our sites, we'd just move to another."

"Speaking of the Office of Injustice and Intolerance, how's Colin doing? Any word?"

"Yes. That's the main reason I came. I talked with Colin."

"Really!"

"You know how I had Lucia keeping an eye on Diego?"

"Yes. She was the nanny and helped around the house, right?" asked McIntyre.

"Yes. Well, a few weeks ago, Cynthia James, Colin's girlfriend came home from a party that was given by Obermann. Lucia knew something was wrong, but Cynthia never said what it was. I guess a few hours later, Colin showed up with the police. They found Cynthia dead in the bathroom. She had committed suicide."

"Oh my . . . . may God have mercy on her soul."

"Amen," replied Sister Francis.

"Yes. Well, after that, something happened to Colin," continued Ryan. He insisted that Lucia leave with Diego. He sent Diego to live with his parents."

"Wow, that is a turn of events."

"There's more. I called him. I told him that he should seek reconciliation with God and the Church."

"And?"

"He said no. He said that he knew that what he had done was wrong. But, then he said that the offense had to come. 'Each of us,' he said, 'has a destiny to fulfill.' He talked about Judas and how Jesus said that it would have been better if he had never been born; yet he was anyway."

"Such things must come, but woe to the one through whom they come!"[65] quoted Cardinal McIntyre.

"Hey, Father Bill," a voice called out from the other side of the room. It was the tattooed man that Ryan had observed earlier watching TV. "It's that guy they said you helped murder and he's with some priest and a woman priest. Hey, I didn't think we had women priests. You ought take a look at this!"

"Not now, Jaime," McIntyre called back. "I'm with friends. You watch it for me, and you can tell me later if they say something important."

"Okay Father, but they're kind of using big words. I'm not sure I get it all. Percy," Jaime said turning to the other man sitting next to him, "you're edumacated aren't ya?"

"Educated, I believe is the word you're looking for," replied Percy.

"Help me remember what this guy's sayin' so I can go tell Father Bill later."

"If you do not cease from your tedious soliloquization, I will not be able to hear what they are saying!" exclaimed Percy.

"Are you sayin' shut up?" said Jaime, raising his voice and standing up.

"I think that feeble mind of yours has managed to extract the essence of my remark,"

"Excuse me a minute," said Cardinal McIntyre to Sister Francis and Ryan.

"Are you sure that's wise?" asked Ryan.

"Do it all the time." McIntyre began walking over to the men. The two men were posturing and cursing at each other. McIntyre was just hoping he'd get things under control before either one of the men said something about the other man's mother. One of the guards began to move forward gripping his sidearm. McIntyre made a slight motion of his hand. The guard nodded and stepped back.

"Boys, I wanted you to tell me what's happening. You can't do that for me if you keep making all that ruckus!" McIntyre had learned that the best way to prevent an altercation was to not intervene directly, but to distract the combatants.

"I'm sorry, Father," said Jaime.

"*Mea culpa*, Father," added Percy.

"Well, have a seat boys. Since I'm here, I might as well see what bad ol' Obermann is up to."

"If I was out of here, I'd take him out for you, Father," said Jaime.

"Please be silent," pleaded McIntyre.

"Better to remain silent and be thought a fool than to speak out and remove all doubt," quoted Percy.

"Keats?" inquired the Cardinal who couldn't resist trying to guess the author of the line Percy just quoted.

"Abraham Lincoln," replied Percy, with a slight hint of disdain.

"Oh you think you're so smart . . ." began Jaime, getting up out of his seat again.

"Enough!" exclaimed McIntyre, placing his big hand on Jaime's shoulder and pushing him down in his chair. Jaime was surprised by the old man's strength.

"See that nun over there," said McIntyre, pointing to Sister Francis, "if you guys don't behave yourselves I'll have her come over here and she'll box both of your ears! Now let me hear the TV."

"Yes, sir," said Jaime, crossing himself.

"Good!" McIntyre turned his attention to the television. Obermann was now leaving the podium. "Darn it!" continued McIntyre, "I missed what he was saying."

The camera pulled back. It was apparent that the news conference was being held in an old gothic-style church. McIntyre recognized it as Saint Mary Magdalene's, Reverend Hampton's stomping ground. A woman in liturgical vestments came to the podium. Ah, the vicar herself, thought McIntyre.

"This is truly a breakthrough for all humanity," she began. "Chimæric therapy will now be available to all persons, no screening, no lotteries, no expenses! You will all soon be able to drink freely of the water of life! You will all be born anew, not from perishable but from the imperishable seed![66] What is this seed? It is a Chimæric seed that once implanted in you will blossom and transform your garments of skin into garments of immortality. And you too will become a source of this new life, capable of spreading this seed to your brothers and sisters . . . ."

McIntyre signaled Ryan and Sister Francis to come over.

"What's going on?" Ryan asked.

"I don't know. They're always speaking such gibberish it's hard to figure it out. But, I suspect that things will get worse."

"And from whom does it originate? Frederick! Yes, that's right! The son of the father is implanting his immortal seeds within his children. As he is, so shall you be!"

Hampton suddenly stopped talking. She turned around to look at something outside the view of the camera. Violent coughing echoed throughout the cathedral. Several calls for help, along with indistinguishable cries could be heard. The camera panned back. McIntyre could make out several people who were sitting in chairs flanking both sides of the altar. There was Obermann, Frederick, President Pearson, and Colin O'Conner on the right of the altar. On the left sat Bishop Worthington, Rabbi Elias, and another cleric whom

McIntyre didn't recognize. President Pearson was shaking and grasping his throat. The cleric that McIntyre had not recognized had slid off his chair and was writhing on the floor. Plain-clothes security men ran into the sanctuary and surrounded the President. Bishop Worthington and Rabbi Elias were attempting to help their fellow cleric. A reporter began to describe the panic that was unfolding at the Cathedral of Saint Mary Magdalene as the camera panned over the congregation and other invited guests and dignitaries. McIntyre could see that there were numerous people stricken by this horrific malady.

"My God, what's happening?" exclaimed Ryan.

"I don't know. Whatever it is, it happened without warning," replied McIntyre.

"Perhaps a poison gas?" said Percy.

"Yes, maybe," said McIntyre. "But it doesn't appear to be affecting everyone. Let's say a prayer for them, all right?"

Everyone nodded and bowed their heads. Cardinal McIntyre reached into his pocket and pulled out a rosary,

"Our Father who art in heaven, hallowed be Thy name . . . ."

Sons of Abraham

And though a man might prevail against one who is alone, two
will withstand him. A threefold cord is not quickly broken.
~Ecclesiastes 4:12

David Eliav shook his head in disbelief as the Land Rover in which
he was a passenger bounced along the dusty roads of *Tell al-Muqayyar*,
a medieval village on the edge of the *al-Hajar* desert in Iraq. The dirt
streets, the dilapidated buildings, the ruins of past civilizations gave
him the impression that he had traveled back in time. There was not
much to remind the visitor that they were still in the twenty-first century
aside from the occasional vehicle that spit and sputtered down a narrow
street or a television antenna that protruded from a roof. He was
experiencing *Tell al-Muqayyar* with all his senses in the open-air Land
Rover: the dust, the smell of the bazaars, the blistering heat of the *al-
Hajar* desert, and the clamor which was drowned out by the cursing of
his Iraq driver.

"Get out of the way, you fool!" the driver screamed, shaking his fist at a man leading a donkey and a cart through a narrow passage ahead of them. The man ignored him. Eliav looked at his watch, he was two hours late! He was incredulous that such arrangements had been made for such an important meeting, a meeting that could change the fate of Israel.

There were now over twenty political parties in the Knesset. Each one had its own narrow constituency, axe to grind, or prophetic vision to fulfill. As Eliav stared out the window of the Land Rover he thought back on the events of just a few days ago, watching his father-in-law, Douglas Shaeffer, futilely attempt to call the assembly to order. The coalition they had assembled to secure his victory was fragmenting. Usually, it was relations with the Palestinians or Israel's Arab neighbors that led to a vote of no confidence. Who would have guessed that political instability and realignments brought on by a biotechnological crisis would be the undoing of the Labor government?

But, the entire West was in turmoil. And although Chimæra had not prominently figured in Israeli politics, the ripple effect of the terrorists' attacks on Chimærics had hit the country like a tidal wave. Thousands of Chimærics had died in more than a dozen assaults that took place over several months. Many notable world leaders, including Jack Pearson, the President of the United States, were victims of the attack. Anarchy erupted in many cities in Europe and the United States. Martial law was imposed. New leaders were appointed or elected. Individuals who had spoken out against Chimæric technology were arrested, and often imprisoned. Religious groups that had been opposed to Chimæra became targets of retribution by Chimærics and their sympathizers. Numerous churches, synagogues, and mosques that did not display the Tree of Life logo were burned. And in the midst of this turmoil, a new Chimæric emerged, one that was immune from the toxin released by anti-Chimæric terrorists. They were known as Transformed Chimærics and the Sons of Frederick, who was also called the "New Adam" by adherents of the Tree of Life. The Sons of Frederick were sought out since they could pass on the "seed of life." Chimæra was spreading rapidly throughout the West. Humanity would soon emerge, like the Phoenix from the flames of turmoil, and return to the pristine life of the Garden from which it was exiled so long ago. Or so said the leaders of the Tree of Life.

But, the "Sons of the New Adam," as they were also known, were not welcomed everywhere. Some countries, especially those of the Alliance, closed their borders in an attempt to prevent the "Sons of Cain" from entering and spreading the "curse" into their countries. Even so, Transformed Chimærics spread throughout the world. Joachim Binur, Prime Minister of Israel, had decided to take a neutral policy towards Chimæra, believing that this would appease the various factions in the Knesset. It did not, and his government received a vote of no confidence. Seizing the opportunity, Douglas Shaeffer, with the assistance of his son-in-law, David Eliav, won the election for Prime Minister. But, now he had the untenable task of building and maintaining a coalition government. His political survival depended on it. Indeed, Israel's survival depended on it. To achieve this end, Shaeffer had agreed to send his Defense Minister, David Eliav, on a remarkable mission.

"I know a shortcut," said the driver veering into another narrow passage to his left shaking Eliav out of his reverie. They hadn't traveled twenty meters when, they encountered a shepherd leading perhaps twenty sheep down the passage. Again they came to a halt.

"Arrgh!" exclaimed Eliav. What's the use! he said to himself. He leaned his head back and moved around in the seat trying to get comfortable. His eyes closed. He immediately opened them. But the heat, the droning of the engine, the bahs of the sheep were all too much for his tired body to resist. His eyes inadvertently closed again. He fell asleep and began to dream.

In his dream the sun had just dipped beneath the horizon. The reddish hues of the lower horizon blended almost seamlessly with the hills of *al-Hajar*. Looking higher into the atmosphere, he noticed the sky progressively turning to deepening shades of purple. Stars broke through the amethyst veil, and immediately the darkness of night blanketed the desert. Eliav felt utterly alone and vulnerable. He sensed evil lurking in the darkness. Something in the distance began to move towards him. He shifted his eyes slightly to the right as he had been trained, so as to employ the more light sensitive rods in his retina. He saw a bull with large horns and fierce red eyes; it snorted angrily as it approached him. He stood motionless, wanting to flee, yet unable to move. Finally, when it was about five meters in front of him, it stopped. Then just as suddenly, a narrow beam of brilliant white light erupted from the top of the beast's nose. The light traveled up over its head and between the great horns. The light leapt a good half-meter as it dissected the animal's spine until it reached the tail, then the light was extinguished. The bull stood motionless for a moment, and then the two halves of the animal, cut clean by the brilliant light, fell, one to the left and the other to the right. The two halves smoldered and reeked of seared flesh. As Eliav stood, bewildered and terrified, he heard footsteps behind him. He turned around. Two men, he could not distinguish their faces, passed on either side of him. They approached the carcass, stopped momentarily, and then passed between the two halves. When they were on the other side, they turned around. Eliav still could not see their faces, yet he knew that they were looking at him, waiting for him to pass between the halves and join them.

"Captain Eliav," said the driver shaking him. "We are here."

Eliav shook himself, rubbed his face with his hand, and let out a muffled groan. "Oh man, what a dream," he muttered, half to himself.

"Ah," said the driver. "This is a land of dreams and visions. Perhaps an angel from Allah is trying to tell you something."

Eliav was about to make an imprudent comment to the driver when a tall, thin man with a long beard and wearing the robe of a monk approached the vehicle.

"Captain David Eliav," the monk said while opening the door of the car. "Let me help you."

"Thank you," said Eliav, handing the monk his crutches.

The monk took the crutches and leaned them against the car. He offered Eliav his hand and helped him out of the car. Eliav was surprised at the strength of the seemingly frail monk. The monk supported him as Eliav grasped one of the crutches. The monk handed him the other.

"Thanks, I can take it from here," said Eliav. "You must be Father Nikitas."

"Yes, I am. Now if you will come this way, the others are waiting for you."

Nikitas pointed to the entrance of a building which could only be reached by what looked to be about ten fairly steep stairs. Eliav was irritated. First, he had to come to this god-forsaken village, been driven by a moron, had a disconcerting dream, and now he had to clumsily maneuver himself up these damn stairs. After considerable effort Eliav finally made it to the entrance. Nikitas opened the doors for him. He was about to thank Nikitas when the monk pointed to another set of stairs.

"Is there an elevator?" asked Eliav, exasperated.

"Oh no," said Nikitas, as though such a question were too absurd to ask. "There are no elevators in these old buildings."

Eliav muttered something under his breath as he began to work his way up another flight of stairs.

"If your condition troubles you, why do you not receive Chimæric therapy?" asked Nikitas.

Eliav stopped. That was it! "Because if I did, all holy hell would break loose! That is, after all, what we're trying to prevent here, a damn jihad against my country."

"I'm sorry," said Nikitas, "that is not what this meeting is about. This is not about preventing anything. War is inevitable."

They now reached the top of the stairs. Nikitas lead Eliav towards an open door. "No, this is about the resealing of an ancient covenant," continued Nikitas. Eliav now stopped in the doorway. He could see Constantin Goricsan and King Abdullah Mohammed al-Sharif seated across from each other. They were laughing.

"They thought Nikitas was what?" asked Goricsan.

"That he was a jinn," replied Abdullah. "I am quite serious. Well, you do have to admit, he is a bit strange."

"I can attest to that!" exclaimed Eliav as he entered the room.

"Enough now, Gentlemen; you are talking about my staretz, my spiritual father. If you utter another harsh word against him, he will make me do a horrific and humiliating penance."

"You all have difficulty enough ahead of you without my adding to it," said Nikitas. He bowed and left the room.

"A grim fellow," said Abdullah.

"Speaking of which," interjected Eliav, "threatening my country with jihad . . . I would call that a bit grim."

"Good," said Goricsan. "I like that. Cut through the diplomatic and political bullshit and get right to the point. Nikitas said that you would be a man we could work with."

"I am not a politician," replied Eliav, "I am a soldier."

"Yes, and as a soldier you know that if I call for *jihad* it will not be another seven-day war," said Abdullah.

"And all this because of Chimæra?" asked Eliav incredulously. "You are willing to risk mutual destruction if we allow Chimærics into the country?!"

"The destruction will not be mutual. And I have no intention of destroying Israel. I will protect it. The Holy City must be protected from the Shayâtin."

"Satan?" asked Eliav. "How can you be sure that Satan has anything to do with Chimæra? Besides, this is the twenty-first century. If there are evils in this world it is because of man, not because of imaginary demons."

"This is not imaginary. I have had personal experience with *Shayâtin*," said Abdullah with irritation.

Goricsan watched as Abdullah became increasingly agitated. It had not been that long since his mother had been delivered from Chimæra through death. It still weighed heavily on the young ruler.

"We are not here to have a theological debate," interjected Goricsan. "You may believe what you wish. But, believe this with certainty, the Arabian Empire is convinced that Chimæra is demonic. If you allow Chimærics to enter Israel, they will declare war on Israel."

"We will fight back."

"You will be fighting two wars," said Abdullah. "Do not think that we are unaware of what is happening in your country. The Orthodox Shas Party is building an anti-Chimæric coalition that includes not only Israeli Jews, but Muslims and Christians as well. If your Knesset allows Chimærics into your country you will be facing not only a war with Arabia but a civil war."

King Abdullah was right. Shaeffer and Eliav were aware of the anti-Chimæric coalition. They were also aware that Israel's allies were occupied with their own troubles and were not in a position to come to their aid. If events led to war, the most likely scenario would be a victory for Arabia and the establishment of a protectorate through the Israeli anti-Chimæric coalition. This is why Shaeffer had sent Eliav to the summit with Czar Goricsan and King Abdullah. He knew that he had to work the best deal for Israel; one that guaranteed its freedom and independence.

"So what are you suggesting?"

"We are offering you," said Goricsan, "membership in the Great Alliance. The future of humanity lies here in the East. The West has sold itself into slavery. The godless secular state is bankrupt spiritually and biologically."

"We are not the only countries of the East," replied Eliav. "What of China?"

"We will all have to watch and see how things sort out in China," said Abdullah. "As I am sure you know, most of the high-ranking Party officials and military leaders were Chimærics. There was a release of toxin in Beijing. Many of the Central Committee members were killed. We shall see who fills the power vacuum."

"We Christians have a saying," said Goricsan. "'The blood of the martyrs is the seed of the Church.' The totalitarian regime in China has planted many seeds in China, not only Christian, but Buddhist and Muslim as well. We shall see what grows in China."

Goricsan handed Eliav a document. "This is a draft of the treaty that incorporates Israel into the Great Alliance. I know that you will want to look this over. Discuss it with the Prime Minister. Communicate with us regarding modifications. Then I hope that you will present it to the Knesset and the people of Israel."

"Even if Israel were to align itself with the Great Alliance," said Eliav, "how can you reasonably expect to keep Chimæra out of the country. Has any country been able to keep AIDS or any other sexually transmitted disease from entering its borders?"

"That is precisely the reasoning of the Man of Sin," said Nikitas, entering the room. He carried with him a small wooden box and set it down on the table next to Goricsan. "And that is why the West will do nothing when you join the Alliance. Time is their ally. They know that Chimæra will spread insidiously until every land is infected by it."

"They are right," said Eliav. "There is no stopping it now."

"No," replied Nikitas. "You are looking through natural eyes. You must see with the eyes of a heart that knows that with God all things are possible. That is why we are here in *Tell al-Muqayyar*."

Eliav shrugged. It made absolutely no sense to Eliav why this meeting was being held in this pathetic dust hole.

"Perhaps you know it as Ur of the Chaldees," said Abdullah.

Ur of the Chaldees, Ur of the Chaldees, thought Eliav. Why does that sound so familiar? "Didn't Abraham come from Ur of the Chaldees?" asked Eliav.

"Yes," replied Nikitas. "It is said that it is in this very place that God made his covenant with Abram and with his sons. The wickedness of the Amorites is now finally reaching its full measure. All the Sons of Abraham, Isaac, Ishmael, and the sons by faith, must covenant together to defeat them."[67]

As Nikitas finished speaking, Eliav felt an almost mystical power moving among them. It was as though the Patriarch himself was with them. He recalled the dream he had had earlier. An intuitive awareness had quickened within him. He was not sure how or why this had happened, but a latent ability that he knew was part of his heritage as a Son of Abraham had somehow been activated. He knew that they were at a nexus ordained since the foundation of the world. Yet, his rational mind struggled with his inexplicable certainty.

"Gentlemen, I respect your conviction," said Eliav. "And I must add that there is something about this place that . . . that almost makes me believe. But . . ."

"But you have your doubts," said Goricsan.

"Indeed. There will be those in the Knesset whose opposition to Chimæra will lead them to support the Alliance. But there are others, myself among them, who bear the wounds of history."

"We all have wounds," interjected Abdullah. "I give you my word that all Islam will recognize the legitimate sovereignty of Israel."

"Yours is not the only voice of Islam, King Abdullah. How then, am I to convince the Knesset of the good faith of the Alliance?"

Abdullah nodded. He was not offended by Eliav's reservations. He knew Eliav had good cause to be skeptical. Years of terrorism and threats from their Arab neighbors necessitated prudence. Abdullah stood and walked towards a door that led to an adjoining room. When he reached the door, he stopped, turned, and faced Eliav.

"The ancient covenants were sealed in blood," said Abdullah. He now opened the door. An Arab sentry appeared and stood at attention.

"Bring the prisoner," ordered Abdullah.

The sentry saluted and disappeared. Moments later he reappeared followed by two other sentries. These two men each gripped an arm of another man. The prisoner's arms were tied behind his back and a canvas sack had been placed over his head. The lead sentry pushed the bound man forward. Abdullah walked over to him.

"Prisoner!" commanded Abdullah.

The prisoner raised his head and "looked" in the direction from which the voice came.

"You have been tried and found guilty of murder and blasphemy against Allah, and His Prophet. I, King Abdullah, will now execute the sentence that has been pronounced against you."

Abdullah withdrew his sword. It made a dreadful sliding sound as it left the scabbard. Abdullah reached over and removed the sack from the prisoner's head. It was Ali Hossein!

Eliav struggled to his feet. His heart was pounding. In front of him stood the criminal responsible for the death of thousands of innocent people—responsible for the death of his comrades and the shattering of his own life. At last! Eliav thought. The bastard gets what he deserves.

"Death to infidels!" shouted Hossein. "Death to the Alliance!"

"It is you, perverter of the True Path, whose blood will seal the covenant between the Sons of Abraham!" exclaimed Abdullah, raising the sword over his head.

"No!" shouted Eliav.

Abdullah lowered his blade. "You wish me to spare him?"

"No. I wish him dead, as you do. But, if you release him to me, to Israeli authority, the Knesset might look more favorably on the Alliance."

"No!" shouted Hossein. "Kill me now. Do not turn me over to dogs."

Abdullah nodded and motioned with his head for the prisoner to be removed. He slid his sword back into its scabbard.

"It shall be as you request."

Father Nikitas had been standing towards the back of the room and had watched with satisfaction at all that had happened. He was confident now that the Sons of Abraham would unite. Soon, he thought, the daughter of Abraham would join her brothers.

*   *   *

"Ladies and Gentlemen," Shaeffer had shouted. "Never has the security of the State of Israel been under greater threat. We are surrounded by those who have promised to unleash *jihad* upon us. And if that were not enough, there are those among us who seem to be determined to bring us to the brink of civil war. The decisions that we make today will determine whether Israel will continue or whether there will be another tragic diaspora."

Eliav was pleased to see that the fractious assembly had now quieted down. It was not because Shaeffer was employing hyperbole to gain their attention. Everyone in the Knesset knew that the Prime Minister was speaking the truth. On this at least they could agree and they hoped that Shaeffer would be able to deliver on his promise to plot a course that would guide the ship of state through the tumultuous seas ahead.

"What I have here," said Shaeffer, lifting a portfolio, "is a treaty which I believe can guarantee the continuance of our nation. It is a severing of ties with old allies, and a strategic realignment with former adversaries."

The members of the Knesset began to whisper among themselves. Eliav strained to hear what they were saying. Which adversaries? It's all about that Chimæra business. He better not open the borders to

Chimærics or there'll be civil war! He's not suggesting we make a treaty with the Muslims?

"The Minister of Defense, David Eliav, has worked tirelessly at my request to make this treaty possible. Copies of the treaty are now being distributed for your examination. I hope that you will agree that the future of Israel lies with the Great Alliance."

The Knesset exploded with shouting, clapping, hissing, arguing, cursing, cheering . . . a cacophony of confusion. Eliav shook his head. How odd, he thought, that he should feel more camaraderie with foreigners than with his own countrymen. There was a forthrightness in the men with whom he had hammered out the treaty. He knew where they stood. He knew what to expect, peace or destruction. Here in the Knesset, machinations would eat away at the state like the teeth of little foxes that chewed at the vines. He hoped that the Knesset would act with as much integrity as Czar Goricsan and King Abdullah had when he had met with them a few days earlier.

"I would now like our Minister of Defense, Captain David Eliav, to discuss with you the details of the treaty," continued Prime Minister Shaeffer.

Eliav stood up, using his crutches for support. All the members of the Knesset stood and clapped for the retired Captain. They did not clap in approval of the Treaty; they were undecided about that, but they were not undecided about the man. Since his injury and the subsequent revelation that he was the heroic "Jonathan," Eliav had enjoyed enormous popularity and influence. Eliav thought it was absurd. Yet, he had been willing to use his popularity to help his father-in-law win the election. And he would use it again to lead his country towards a new future.

"Ladies and Gentlemen of the Knesset," began Eliav. "The future of Israel lies in the East . . . ."

12/03 NEWERA

Heart of the Temple

Do you not know that your body is a temple of the holy Spirit within you, whom you have from God, and that you are not your own?
~1 Corinthians 6:19

"It has been too long," said Rosario. *Ch'ucha'* knew that Rosario was not speaking to her, but to the forest and ruins, and the spirits that dwelt within them. *Ch'ucha'* had never been to this part of the jungle. They carried lanterns, although *Ch'ucha'* did not know why. Rosario had assured Nizhniya they would be back before nightfall. She would not have approved such an adventure had she known where Rosario was taking her. This made it all the more exciting.

Ch'ucha' was surprised by the old woman's vigor. They had been steadily ascending a low, deeply forested hill. Everything around her was living. The rocks were blanketed with thick layers of moss; the air was filled with the clatter of insects and birds and the aroma of flowers. *Ch'ucha'* felt the life of the forest permeate her. This is what it must be like to be fully alive, she thought. She could not imagine living anywhere else.

"Only the Maya know of this place. It is our most carefully guarded secret. My husband, may his soul rest in peace, suspected it, but never asked, so great was his respect for our traditions."

Finally, Rosario stopped in front of a thicket of dense vegetation.

"Only the shaman can enter," said Rosario, as she pushed aside the vegetation to reveal a dark opening in the hillside.

"Oh," said *Ch'ucha'*, disappointed. She was fascinated by Mayan antiquity. Although she was not Mayan, *Ch'ucha'* had adopted the culture as her own. She dearly wished to enter this secret Mayan sanctuary.

"It is time," said Rosario. "You are of age."

Ch'ucha' looked at her quizzically.

"When a girl becomes a young woman such as yourself . . . ."

Ch'ucha' looked down embarrassed. It had been a difficult few months. Puberty can be a challenge for any girl; it had been trauma for *Ch'ucha'*. One week the boys teased her, the next they couldn't take their eyes off her. In a month she had developed into a beautiful young woman. *Ch'ucha'* was well aware of her rapid development and was concerned that she might just as quickly become an old woman like Rosario. Rosario tried to assure her that this was not the case.

"It is necessary that the time is cut short," said Rosario, "that is why you have become a woman so quickly. You are now what God needs you to be."

Ch'ucha' did not know what to make of the comments made by her *Rina*. But in the past few weeks she had not witnessed any other changes in her body. *Ch'ucha'* wouldn't admit it, but she was pleased with the way she was now and hoped that she would remain like this, at least for a while.

". . . new worlds open up to her. It is time that you are introduced to the world of the shaman. Light the lamps."

Ch'ucha' dutifully removed the matches from a little satchel she wore around her waist. She lifted the glass and lit the wick of her lamp. She did the same for Rosario's lamp.

"Come," said Rosario, stooping down and entering the dark opening.

"But you said . . . ."

"Come."

Ch'ucha' watched Rosario enter the yawning darkness. She took a deep breath, bent down and followed. She tingled with excitement. It never occurred to her that she should be frightened, that the denizens of this thick darkness might include poisonous spiders or venomous snakes. She knew they were there. She was too exhilarated by the adventure to care. Where was Rosario leading her? What might be hidden within this sacred Mayan hill? What did she mean by 'being of age'?

Rosario and *Ch'ucha'* descended the passage. *Ch'ucha'* could see in the dim light that the sides of the passage were constructed out of massive blocks of rock. This was not a tunnel in a hillside but a corridor that descended from the top of some ancient Mayan temple buried by the forest for centuries. *Ch'ucha's* heart began to race. A Mayan temple! Perhaps there were ancient artifacts, skeletons, and treasure!

Rosario led *Ch'ucha'* through a labyrinth of rooms and corridors. It would be easy to become lost down here, thought *Ch'ucha'*. Finally, Rosario stopped. They had arrived at the very heart of the temple. Rosario stepped through the doorway. *Ch'ucha'* followed, holding up her lantern to reveal a large, cathedral-like chamber. *Ch'ucha'*, slowly turned around, holding her lantern as high as she could so that she could examine her surroundings. Giant bas-relief Mayan figures, kings, heroes, gods, and dragons decorated the walls and ceiling. When *Ch'ucha'* had finished this initial examination she walked towards the center of the chamber. The room was empty! No artifacts, no skeletons, no treasure. She bent down and picked up an old Conquistador sword with a broken blade. What was so special about this? thought *Ch'ucha'*. Why should the Mayans care about keeping this a secret? There is nothing of value here!

"I thought that, too, when I was first brought here," said Rosario.

Ch'ucha' turned around, startled, and saw Rosario seated on one of the blocks near the center of the great chamber.

"Come, sit beside an old woman." Rosario patted the spot next to her on the stone block.

Ch'ucha' dutifully sat next to her. She placed the lantern beside her.

"When my uncle, who was shaman before me, brought me here, I was very disappointed. I expected to find the Heart of the Temple filled with treasure. 'You are looking with your natural eyes,' he told me. 'You must look with the eyes of your heart.'"

"And do you see the treasure now?" asked *Ch'ucha'*.

"Yes. It is a vast treasure of incomparable wealth."

"Like this?" asked *Ch'ucha'* skeptically as she held the broken sword in front of the lantern for her godmother's inspection.

"Yes," replied Rosario. "I shall tell you a story."

Ch'ucha' ears perked up. No Mayan can resist a story.

"When the Conquistadores conquered our homeland they treated the Maya with great cruelty. We were no more than animals to them. They used us as beasts of burden. But, *Kos* sent us Bishop Barthtolomé de las Casas. He reminded our conquerors that we too had souls and were loved by God. He excommunicated the entire Spanish population of Chiapas for their unchristian behavior towards us. So enraged was the conquistador governor that he sought to kill the blessed de las Casas. But, our people hid him, here, in the Heart of the Temple," said Rosario motioning with her hand indicating the great chamber they were now in.

"Did he find him?" asked *Ch'ucha'* excitedly.

"Yes," replied Rosario.

"What happened?"

"His soldiers seized the blessed de las Casas. They made the holy bishop kneel." Rosario took the sword from *Ch'ucha'* hand. "The governor withdrew this very sword from his scabbard. He raised it over his head and swung it down fiercely striking the innocent neck of Fray Barthtolomé de las Casas."

"Then what? Then what?"

"Blood splashed upon the blade and with it, *K'awil*."

Ch'ucha knew that *K'awil* was a spiritual force imparted by a Saint or Ancestor into material things. *K'awil* imbued objects with tremendous power.

"The blade shattered." Rosario handed the sword back to *Ch'ucha'*. *Ch'ucha'* turned the sword over and inspected it with awe.

"And the blessed bishop was unharmed. You see, *Ch'ucha'*, the sword understood."

Ch'ucha' looked up at her godmother. "What did it understand, *Madrina*?"

"That the power that had been granted it was only to be used for justice."

"So it broke rather than be misused?"

"No," replied Rosario. "It broke so that it could be used rightly."

"I do not understand," said *Ch'ucha'*.

"When the time comes, you will. But now, this is not the only treasure that is here in this temple.

Ch'ucha' looked around again. She strained to see, but even with her imagination she could not perceive anything of interest, let alone, treasure.

"Each shaman must add to the treasure by bringing one special gift to the Temple."

"And what have you brought, godmother?"

"I have brought you."

"Me?! I am no treasure!"

"Yes, you are. You will be the sword in the hand of *Kos*; with you He will defeat the Lords of *Xibalba*."

"No," replied *Ch'ucha'* handing the sword back to her godmother. She stood and walked away from her godmother. "*Kos* must choose another. I am a weaver."

"And as a weaver you know that I speak the truth."

"I do not," replied *Ch'ucha'* defiantly.

"In your heart you know it, but your mind refuses to believe. It is your heart that is speaking while you weave. Do you not know that your *huipiles* foretell your destiny? Every weaver knows this. She does not weave just to decorate, she captures the Mayan cosmos with her yarn. She weaves the past, present, and future of her people into each *huipil*. Do you not weave on your own *huipiles* the little green frog that becomes a great saint? It is an ironic Mayan story. How can a lowly frog become a saint? With *Kos,* all things are possible. But, you will have to obtain *Itz* from *Xibalba*."

Ch'ucha' looked at her curiously.

"*Itz* is magic; a power reserved only for the jaguar shaman. You must travel the Black Road to *Xibalba*."

"But *Xibalba* is the underworld. One can only travel that road in death," replied *Ch'ucha'*.

"Dying is easy. The jaguar shaman, however, must enter the deepest regions of death."

Ch'ucha' shook her head. "No. I did not ask for these things. All I ask is to be like other Mayan women, to sit at the loom, weave, and gossip with friends . . . ." her voice trailed off. "If I had friends," she added quietly.

Rosario placed her arm around *Ch'ucha'*'s shoulders. "You see, I have brought you to the right place then."

Ch'ucha' looked curiously at Rosario. She respected Rosario, she was a wise woman but sometimes her paradoxes tried *Ch'ucha'*'s patience.

"What friends am I likely to meet in a place like this?"

"The Ancestors."

"The Ancestors!" exclaimed *Ch'ucha'*. "Here?"

"Yes, you must learn their voices so that you may seek their counsel and their prayers."

"So the Ancestors live here? In the temple? Is that the treasure you were talking about?"

"Yes and no. It is the treasure. But, they do not live here in this temple."

"I don't understand. Why did you bring me here then?"

"The Ancestors live here," said Rosario placing her hand on *Ch'ucha'*'s chest over her heart. The temple is a place of silence. It is only in silence that you will learn to enter your heart. Once you learn this, the Ancestors will be with you and you will never feel alone again."

"Never feel alone?" asked *Ch'ucha'* incredulously. "How can I not feel alone? Who is like me? Just a few weeks ago I was a little girl; now I am a young woman. No one understands."

"She does."

Ch'ucha' spun around. Rosario did not have to mention who "she" was. *Ch'ucha'* knew. "Do not speak of her," said *Ch'ucha'* angrily.

"You have met her, have you not?" asked Rosario.

"Yes. In my dreams. I begged my mother to let me be as the other children. She ignored me."

"No," answered Rosario. "She was traveling the Black Road ahead of you."

"Enough of the Black Road!" shot back *Ch'ucha'* angrily. "I am not *Hunahpu* or *Xbalanque*, neither do I desire to be."

"That medallion you are wearing," said Rosario.

Ch'ucha' was startled by Rosario's non sequitur. She reached down and pulled out the medallion from under her blouse. She had always worn the medallion, for as long as she could remember.

"Do you know what it says?" asked Rosario.

"Yes, it is in Russian. Ludmelia taught me. It says, '*But the Lord Almighty thwarted them, by a woman's hand he confounded them.*'"

"Together, you are the woman. And together you will confound the Lords of *Xibalba*."

"I am sorry," said *Ch'ucha'* exasperatedly. "I do not want to be a hero twin. Just let me weave. I want to go home."

Rosario nodded then slowly stood up. "We will go. But know that this place . . ." Rosario motioned with her arm indicating the cavernous temple chamber, ". . . and this place," now she placed her hand once again on *Ch'ucha's* chest, ". . . will be here waiting for you."

*   *   *

Nizhniya sat on her patio with pieces of her AKS-92 assault rifle on the table in front of her. She was cleaning and lubricating each piece. Later this afternoon, when *Ch'ucha'* and Rosario returned from their walk, she would have *Ch'ucha'* assemble the rifle. She already knew what *Ch'ucha'* would say, "Oh, not again!" The AKS-92 was a complex rifle, but *Ch'ucha'* could break it down and assemble it without difficulty. This time, thought Nizhniya, I'll make her assemble it blindfolded. You never know when you might have to do that in the dark. Nizhniya knew she was grasping at straws. She felt obligated to teach her everything she knew about weaponry, military tactics, and the martial arts. *Ch'ucha'* learned, but not willingly. Besides, Nizhniya had taught her pretty much everything she could here in the Lacandon of Chiapas. She was now resorting to assembling rifles blindfolded. She thought she heard someone whispering to the left of her.

"My friend," whispered Santiago, "I see you are still languishing in unrequited love."

"It is true," said Mateas despondently.

"I have had enough," said Santiago. "A woman has reduced my best friend and the commander of the Zapatista Army to a weak-kneed coward."

Santiago began to walk out of the thicket. Nizhniya saw him out of the corner of her eye. She could see a hand grab him by the collar and pull him back. Nizhniya, who was not afraid of anything or anyone, now felt an uneasy knot in her stomach. It was Mateas.

"All right," said Mateas.

"Do not tell me all right. Say something or I will. I will be listening to make sure you do."

"The hell you will! Now go!" Mateas said, waving his hand in the opposite direction of Nizhniya's home.

Santiago began to walk backward but wagged his finger at Mateas as a warning that he would not tolerate anymore of his friend's pining after the Russian woman. Mateas waved him on and then stepped out of the thicket.

Nizhniya turned around, acting surprised, as if she were unaware that Mateas and Santiago had been standing there watching her.

"Good morning, Mateas. What a surprise it is to see you. Why did you not come up the path?"

"Ah . . . well . . . I . . ."

"I thought I heard something over there earlier, maybe a jaguar," said Nizhniya, smiling as she offered Mateas an opportunity to extricate himself from an awkward situation.

"Yes, yes. I thought I heard something too. That's why I was in the brush."

"Thank you, Mateas. I always feel so much safer knowing that you are always watching me . . . I mean watching out for me."

Mateas' shoulders slumped. She had seen him in the bushes. She had probably seen him with Santiago. Maybe she had even heard their conversation.

"It is true. I do watch you. And when I am not watching you, all I can do is think about you."

Nizhniya looked up at him with her beautiful blue eyes. Her blond hair, which she usually wore in a tight bun on the back of her head, hung loosely over her shoulders. It draped itself softly over the intricately woven *huipil* that *Ch'ucha'* had woven for her. Under this she wore standard-issue Zapatistan combat fatigues and boots. To the people of the village, Nizhniya was a bit of an oddity; they called her the half-woman, half-man. Mateas had to acknowledge that there was a bit of truth to this. He knew the man. Now he longed to know the woman.

"Why don't you help me reassemble my rifle," said Nizhniya as she fiddled with the pieces on the table. "I was going to have *Ch'ucha'* do it blindfolded. Stupid idea, huh?"

"Yeah," said Mateas, pulling up a chair and sitting uncomfortably close to Nizhniya. "I really don't want to assemble your rifle, or discuss military tactics or security. I wanted to talk to you . . . ."

"You know," interrupted Nizhniya, hoping to avoid the conversation, "with everything that we've heard that is happening in the United States and Europe, we've probably been just given a respite. We will still need to keep diligent watch . . . ."

Mateas grasped her hands. She released the trigger mechanism and looked at him. What woman wouldn't be attracted to him? He was handsome, intelligent, and brave. He was the epitome of the virtuous man. Yet . . . .

"I love you," said Mateas.

Nizhniya lowered her eyes. After a moment she lifted them up and looked into his eyes. Mateas felt as if he might melt like wax under their intense gaze. He then heard what he feared most.

"I love you too. As a friend and comrade."

Mateas released her hands, and was about to stand up and leave. There was no point in staying and humiliating himself any further. But, Nizhniya grasped his hands and would not release him.

"I know of no man I would rather love than you."

"Then why?"

"Because of a memory; one that still lingers in the mist of my amnesia. Yet, this I know with certainty. My heart belongs to another."

"And what if that memory never comes back to you? And even if it does, what are the chances that you will ever be with that man to whom you have given your heart?"

"It does not make a difference. Once the heart is given, it can never be taken back."

Mateas nodded. This he understood all too well. He stood, and she released his hands. "Then I will continue to consider it an honor to be your friend and comrade. And should the circumstances change . . . ."

Nizhniya stood, placed her right hand over her brow. She saw a cloud of dust in the distance. A vehicle was approaching. "Father Suarez has returned. Perhaps we will learn more about what is happening up north. Shall we go?"

Nizhniya offered Mateas her hand. She grasped his firmly; like a man, thought Mateas.

*　　*　　*

Father Suarez drove his old truck down the dirt road towards the Mission. Several children, spotting the cloud of dust that announced his arrival, shouted excitedly. Father Suarez had promised to return with gifts. By the time he pulled into the Mission, twenty to thirty children surrounded the beat-up old vehicle. As he stepped out, swarms of children engulfed him, nearly knocking him back into the truck. What a delight it was to see the children and return to the simple Christian life of his Mayan flock, he thought. He was convinced that his month of meetings with the bishops, and their staffs should gain him an indulgence.

"Children, children!" scolded Sister Margarita. "Move away from the truck. Father has had a tiring journey!"

The children made a narrow path so that Father could make his way from the truck to the rectory. But it was narrow. The children were not going to let him get away, not until they had learned about their gifts! Some of the children peered into the back of the truck. There were several boxes! Filled with toys, thought the children.

"Children," exclaimed Father Suarez joyously. "How happy I am to see you."

"Are those our toys in the back?" asked a young boy who could no longer restrain his enthusiasm.

"Toys? What toys?" feigned Father Suarez.

The children just laughed. They knew Father would not forget them.

"Okay, okay." Father leaned over and opened one of the boxes in the back of the truck.

"Why don't you wait until later, Father," suggested Sister Margarita. "You must be exhausted."

"And risk a riot?" laughed Father Suarez. "No, children come first. Perhaps, though, Sister you could help me pass the toys out. I placed little tags on the toys with their names on them."

"You went to a lot of trouble, Father," said Sister Margarita, opening another box.

Father and Sister proceeded to pull toys out of the boxes and called each child to collect his or her toy. In each case, the child shrieked with delight. Sister Margarita marveled at Father's ability to select the ideal toy for each child. As the children received their gifts, they scampered off to show their families and friends. Finally, there was one remaining toy in the box, a beautiful ceramic doll. She looked like an Indian princess, dark skin, but with keen blue eyes.

"Where is *Ch'ucha*?" asked Father. "Why was she not with the other children?"

"Because she is not a child anymore."

Father looked quizzically at her.

"You've been away for over a month. That's a long time for *Ch'ucha*'. She's entered puberty; she's a young woman now. I don't think you'll recognize her."

"Plants grown up in their youths," said Father Suarez.

"I'm sorry?" Sister Margarita asked, not understanding what Father was alluding to.

"Psalm 144," said Father. He reached into his jacket pocket and pulled out a small New Testament and Psalms. He flipped through the pages. "Ah, here. 'May our sons in their youth be like plants full grown, our daughters like corner pillars cut for the structure of a palace.'"

"I'm sorry, Father. I'm afraid I'm still not following you."

Father Suarez reached into the truck and pulled out his briefcase from the passenger seat. "Is there anything to eat?" he asked.

"Yes, fresh tortillas from this morning. Some meat, beans, and rice."

"Good," said Father Suarez, as he began walking over to the rectory. "Walk with me, Sister. I have a theory about our mysterious, not so little girl, *Ch'ucha'* . . . . Oh, '*ola*' Luis. I did not see you there."

Officer Luis Aguilar had been pulling weeds in the vegetable garden, and he was nearly invisible behind the towering tomato vines.

"Hello, Father," said Aguilar standing. "I trust you had a pleasant journey. How was Mexico City?"

"Dirty, noisy, congested. I'm happy to be back home."

"Home. We all wish we could be back home," said Aguilar.

"Yes, I know. I am sorry. But, you know that I cannot let you go. Perhaps some day."

Aguilar nodded. Of course, he expected that response. This was a conversation they had on frequent occasions. In fact, Aguilar had brought up his release because he didn't want Father to know that he had overheard his conversation with Sister Margarita. He had never learned from Zokoroff why they were trying to recover *Ch'ucha'* or who it was that Zokoroff worked for. Any piece of information he could obtain might someday help him to achieve what he longed for more than anything else, even more than his freedom. Revenge. Revenge on *Ch'ucha'*. Revenge on the miserable Mission, its village, and the Mayan people. He blamed them all for his imprisonment and for his crippling injury. But mostly, he blamed *Ch'ucha'*. Aguilar had overheard conversations. He had learned a few things, but not much. Ludmelia Nizhniya had remembered that she was the child's guardian and that she had to prepare her. Prepare her for what? Even she did not seem to know. But, he watched her 'train' the child in the art of war. He had even witnessed *Ch'ucha'* do inexplicable things. And then there was her uncanny relationship with animals.

Father and Sister Margarita entered the rectory office. Father Suarez put his briefcase on the table. They were unaware that Aguilar had silently crept behind them and was standing next to the open window listening to their conversation.

"Take a look at this," Father Suarez said removing a magazine from his briefcase. He handed the magazine to Sister Margarita.

"*Hans and Frederick Obermann . . . Prophets of a New Era?*" Sister Margarita read the magazine headline. "This is about Chimæra, isn't it?"

"That's right. All the bishops were talking about it. But we'll talk about that a little later. Right now, I want you to take a look at the boy. How old do you suppose he is?"

"He looks to be about nineteen, maybe twenty," answered Sister Margarita.

"He's three and a half years old!"

Sister Margarita raised her eyebrow, anticipating Father's theory. "Are you suggesting that *Ch'ucha'* is a Chimæric?"

"Yes, and perhaps more than that. This boy is reported to have powers," said Father, pointing to the picture of Frederick. "As far as I know, Chimærics do not have any special powers except for their ability to physically regenerate. Our little *Ch'ucha'* has some extraordinary gifts."

"And what type of powers does this Frederick supposedly possess?"

"It has been said that he raised a woman from the dead."

"Oh that is ridiculous!" exclaimed Sister Margarita. "Besides, *Ch'ucha'* has not raised anyone from the dead."

"No. I suppose you are right. But, if I recall, you said that Ludmelia's recovery was miraculous."

"True. But, how does that have anything to do with *Ch'ucha'*?"

"Remember the afternoon Mateas and Santiago brought her in? I had gone out to get my things to administer the last rites to Ludmelia, and you were examining Aguilar. When I came back, Rosario was performing an ancient Mayan bloodletting ritual."

"You never told me that!" said Sister Margarita.

Father shrugged. "I never made much out of it. I just thought it was another one of Rosario's bizarre antics. That is, until I read the account of how Frederick apparently restored the woman's life. He cut himself and pressed his bleeding hand against her fatal wound so that some of his blood entered her body."

"And what has that to do with *Ch'ucha*?"

"Rosario punctured *Ch'ucha's* tongue with a thorn she got from the garden. She then let *Ch'ucha's* blood drip into Ludmelia's wound."

"My God!" muttered Sister, shaking her head.

"That's not all. Take another look at Frederick's picture."

Sister held the magazine at the perfect distance so that she could make a careful examination of the picture. "The *Agua Azul!* He has *Ch'ucha's* eyes! You are not suggesting that . . . that . . . ."

A noise outside the window stopped Sister Margarita in mid sentence. Father Suarez went over to the window and looked out. At first, he saw no one there, then he saw Mateas and Nizhniya walking up the path towards the rectory. Sister Margarita went into the kitchen to get Father's meal.

"*Hola!* Come in! Come in!" shouted Father Suarez.

"Hey, Father," shouted back Mateas. Nizhniya waved.

"Where are *Ch'ucha'* and Rosario?" asked Father as they drew nearer.

"They went for a walk. They should be back soon," replied Nizhniya.

Mateas opened the door for Nizhniya. She entered and gave Father a hug.

"We've missed you, Father."

Mateas shook Father's hand. "So what has been happening out there in the rest of the world?" asked Mateas.

"Much. I'm glad you are here. I wanted to talk to both of you."

Sister appeared from the kitchen carrying a plate of food. "First you must eat!" demanded Sister.

"Ah, *gracias*, Sister. Forgive me, but I am starving. Can I offer you something to eat?"

"No, thank you, Father," said Nizhniya.

Mateas shook his head. "So, tell us. What is happening? We hardly know anything since Mother forbids almost all contact with the outside world. I don't know why you let her get away with it, Father. No radios, no televisions."

"She fears the corruption of Mayan culture," said Father. "She may be a bit extreme, but overall I believe she is right. But, I don't think there is anything that can be done to prevent the onslaught that will be coming from the North."

"What onslaught?" asked Nizhniya.

Father pointed to the magazine resting on the table. "Take a look at that."

Nizhniya picked up the magazine. The man on the cover, Hans Obermann, looked familiar. Nizhniya flipped through the magazine, found the cover article and began to peruse it.

"Of course, we've all heard about Chimæra," began Father, "and all the Chimærics that were killed in the Saint Pierre Massacres. Needless to say, all hell broke loose after that. The head of The Office of Justice and Tolerance, Colin O'Conner, declared martial law."

"He can do that?" asked Mateas.

"Apparently," replied Father. "The Secretary of State assumed the presidency, but from what I heard, The Office of Justice and Tolerance has secured enormous power over domestic affairs in the U.S. In any event, there's been understandable anger against the Congregation of Saint Pierre. The Office of Justice and Tolerance is claiming that religious groups that are not directly responsible for the attacks are still culpable because they have created an atmosphere of intolerance. They are demanding that all religious organizations affiliate with the Tree of Life or they will be closed down."

"So are the churches doing it?" asked Sister Margarita.

"Most are, some are not," replied Father. "Denominations are being split, some parishes are choosing to affiliate while other are not.

It's a real mess. We are witnessing a wave of persecution, the likes of which haven't been seen since the days of Stalin in Russia and the Cultural Revolution in China."

"But the article says here," interrupted Nizhniya, "that Obermann, his son Frederick, and a few other Chimærics were immune to the toxin released in the attacks."

"Yes, now the story takes on an even more sinister twist," continued Father. "Frederick is supposed to be the true Chimæric; there's even an American Catholic bishop, a guy by the name of Worthington, who calls Frederick the New Adam."

"That's heresy!" exclaimed Sister Margarita.

"That's true, and he's been excommunicated by the Pope. Anyway, Frederick's Chimæric cells are different from the others that were first developed. They are not affected by the toxin. Not only that, he can pass on these Chimæric cells to others."

"How does he do that?" asked Sister Margarita.

"Oh my God!" exclaimed Nizhniya reading, "It's passed on by having sex! It says here that once someone has received these new Chimæric cells through sex not only do they develop a Chimæric Regeneration System, but their reproduction system is altered so that they no longer produce sperm or eggs. They produce Chimæric cells which they can now pass on to others through sex."

"I told you it was sinister," said Father. "I've heard that the damn thing is spreading like wildfire. Apparently, the libido of these Chimærics is so voracious that they can have sex several times a day!"

"It says here," interrupted Nizhniya, "that if the transformation continues at its current rate, most of the citizens in the U.S. and Western Europe could be converted within a few years!"

"That's horrible!" exclaimed Sister Margarita.

"Yes, and it all started with Frederick." Father held out his hand to Nizhniya. She handed him back the magazine. He closed it and pointed to the picture of Frederick on the cover.

"My God! Those are *Ch'ucha's* eyes!" Nizhniya said with

astonishment. "How can that be? You don't suppose they're related, do you?"

"That's what I was thinking," said Sister Margarita.

"No," replied Father Suarez. "I promised Rosario that I wouldn't tell, but I think it is time that you knew. *Ch'ucha'* is the daughter of Maria O'Conner."

"What?!" exclaimed Sister Margarita. "Blessed Maria O'Conner?"

"That's right," said Father. He removed a book from his briefcase. "This is her *Journal*," he continued. He handed the book to Nizhniya. The book had a picture of Maria on the cover.

"I know this woman," said Nizhniya. She sat down at the table, closed her eyes, and struggled to remember the woman.

"I thought you might," said Father. "You see, Maria gave birth to a baby girl, a girl she named Theresa. The baby was taken by Maria's mother . . . ."

"Gabriela!" exclaimed Nizhniya remembering.

"The woman with Francisco Serrano," added Mateas.

"Exactly! How you fit into all this I'm still not sure," Father said to Nizhniya.

"I was trying to protect her from . . . Zokoroff and Hans Obermann," said Nizhniya. "I always knew I needed to protect her, now . . . now I remember.

"Here they come," said Mateas seeing *Ch'ucha'* and his mother approaching.

"I don't think *Ch'ucha'* should be told any of this. At least not yet," said Nizhniya.

"I agree," said Father. "However, we will have to tell *Ch'ucha'* sometime."

"Tell me what?" said *Ch'ucha'* as she entered the rectory.

"Ah . . . ," stammered Father, trying to think of something. "Ahh . . . bout the Weaver's Festival in San Cristobal a few months from now."

"Really? Can I go? Oh, I know if I enter my *huipiles* I'll win for sure."

"Just wait a minute," said Nizhniya. "I don't know if that's such a good idea."

"That's what you always say," protested *Ch'ucha'*. "I'll never get away from this place."

"Actually, it might not be such a good time," said Father. "It's going to be crowded, lots of security. You see, that's the other thing I needed to talk to you about. President Bustamonte will be there."

"*El Presidente?!*" exclaimed *Ch'ucha'*.

"Why is Bustamonte coming to San Cristobal?" asked Mateas suspiciously.

"He talked with me personally about the government's relations with the Mayans and the Zapatistas. The President would like to meet with you. He says that it's time for peace."

While everyone was talking about the President, Rosario had picked up the *Journal* that had been lying on the table and began to read it. Nizhniya watched her as she paced back and forth flipping pages and tracing a squiggling line down each page with her finger. Finally, she closed the volume and held the book in front of her between her palms. She looked up and closed her eyes. Rosario's expression was one of exultation; it was as though she had finally found the missing piece of a complex puzzle that had vexed her for years. Her reverie was broken by Father's comment about it being a "time for peace." She set the book back down on the table.

"*El Presidente*. Perhaps he would even see my weaving!" said *Ch'ucha'* excitedly.

Nizhniya knew that it would be unwise to venture beyond their refuge in the Lacandon. San Cristobal was not a large city, but it was always busy with tourists. And with the President there . . . no, it was out of the question.

"I'm sorry, *Ch'ucha'*, but . . ."

"It is time for *Ch'ucha'* to venture out," said Rosario.

Nizhniya was shocked. Up until that instant she had been confident that Rosario was in complete agreement with her. She was about to protest when Rosario continued.

"We can no longer deny the destiny *Ch'ucha'* has chosen for herself. She is, after all, a gifted weaver. The entire Mayan community of Chiapas should be allowed to admire her work."

Everyone just stared at Rosario in disbelief. She, more than anyone, had insisted on the necessity of protecting *Ch'ucha'*, that there were evil forces that were determined to destroy her. Now that they had confirmation of her fears, Rosario seemed no longer concerned.

Ch'ucha' ran over to Rosario and hugged her.

"*Gracias, Gracias,*" exclaimed *Ch'ucha'* as she squeezed Rosario. "May I, please?" *Ch'ucha'* continued looking over at Nizhniya while she continued to embrace Rosario.

"Well, maybe."

"It is necessary that she go," added Rosario.

They all looked at Rosario. She seemed so adamant, so confident in her conviction. They had trusted her even when they had little cause, and now they knew that she had been right about *Ch'ucha'* all along. Nizhniya looked over at Father Suarez. He shrugged. Mateas, seeing that Nizhniya was looking for advice offered, "It's time she got out of this little village and began seeing the world."

"Well then, all right," said Nizhniya. "But . . ."

Before Nizhniya had the opportunity to finish her sentence, *Ch'ucha'* released Rosario and ran to embrace her "mother." She squeezed Nizhniya with such a tight embrace that all the air was forced out of Nizhniya's lungs, and she couldn't finish her sentence.

"*Spasibo! Spasibo!*"[68] exclaimed *Ch'ucha'*.

Nizhniya gently patted *Ch'ucha's* back. "I can't breathe," choked Nizhniya.

"Oh, sorry," said *Ch'ucha'*, loosening her embrace. As she pushed herself away from Nizhniya she glanced down at the table and saw the magazine that was lying on it. She stared at the young man on the cover. He appeared to be only a little older than she, and they both had the same deep-blue eyes. A dark shadow came over the joy that just moments before had illumined her face. She was gripped by a nameless fear. Somehow she knew that he was like her; perhaps the only one like her. She felt both drawn to and terrified of the young man. Rosario saw and understood. It was necessary that the time be cut short.[69]

Sin of Presumption

So the all-seeing Lord, the God of Israel, struck him down with an unseen but incurable blow . . . he was seized with excruciating pains in his bowels and sharp internal torment. . . . Thus he who previously, in his superhuman presumption, thought he could command the waves of the sea, and imagined he could weigh the mountaintops in his scales, was now thrown to the ground and had to be carried on a litter. . . . The body of this impious man swarmed with worms, and while he was still alive in hideous torments, his flesh rotted off, so that the entire army was sickened by the stench of his corruption.

- 2Maccabees 9:5-9

Colm O'Ryan had been the Secretary of State during the Pearson administration. He was now the President of the United States. Those who had been in the line of succession ahead of him had all been Chimærics and all had perished during the Saint Pierre Massacre. O'Ryan had been recently "born again" through the "imperishable seed" transferred to him by Judith Goldman, the Secretary of Health and Human Services. She had been a Chimæric but had been "converted" prior to the massacre. O'Ryan, Colin O'Conner, Hans and Frederick Obermann sat in the President's Oval Office for a weekly briefing. This was Frederick's first participation in these meetings, which had been scheduled to keep Obermann abreast of international and domestic developments.

"I received a call this morning from our Ambassador in Israel; after two months of wrangling the Knesset has just approved the Treaty making Israel the third member of the Great Alliance."

Obermann shrugged. "We expected that. What else is new?"

"We are still attempting to assess the situation in China," said the President, who was somewhat surprised by Obermann's seeming lack of concern about the Great Alliance. "From what we have ascertained there appears to be a concerted effort to decentralize the government by establishing five or more provincial governments to form a Confederation of Chinese States."

"I trust that your people have made contact with the Provincial governors and have communicated that we would continue to offer them Most Favored Nation Status provided that they continue to issue our people visas."

"We have, and the Great Alliance has been courting them as well. You must remember that many of the former Communist government officials were Chimærics who were killed during the Saint Pierre Massacres. Non-Communists have filled the power vacuum. It would seem that many of them are sympathetic to the Great Alliance."

"And what's this I hear about the World Court?"

"Yes, the World Court in the Hague," said the President, "is considering bringing charges against Vatican officials who they believe might have been involved in the Saint Pierre Massacre. If they successfully prosecute the Church, it may lead to imprisonment of prominent clergy and confiscation of property."

"Yes, I am aware of that," said Obermann. "And I am also aware that Goricsan said that Russia would not tolerate the interference of the World Court in Church affairs."

"You don't actually believe he would go to war over that, do you?"

"He might. Anyway it's not worth it. Tell the Court to back off."

"I have to say, Mr. Obermann, I am a bit surprised by your somewhat phlegmatic approach to this news. I would have thought you would have been more concerned," said Colin.

"Politics, saber rattling, treaties and alliances . . . . none of it really matters anymore," replied Obermann. "All we have to do is bide our time. There is not a country in the world where we are not smuggling in young, attractive Chimærics. The sexual revolution of the late twentieth century paved a smooth highway for Chimæra. No one says no to sex anymore. What percentage of married couples remain faithful?

How long do you think it will be before all these anti-Chimæric countries are transformed? Why even some of our most ardent adversaries will become Chimærics before they even know it! No, we must not do anything precipitous. Let us wish the Great Alliance and all those against us peace and prosperity. And while they are unaware, they shall become our brethren. Isn't that right, Frederick? Frederick?"

Frederick did not respond. In fact, he hadn't been listening at all. Instead, he seemed absorbed by something.

"Frederick!" exclaimed his father.

Frederick shook himself out of his reverie. "What? I'm sorry. Were you talking to me?"

"Yes," replied Obermann. "You asked to participate in these briefings; at least you could pay attention."

"I was, but then something happened. I've never experienced anything like it. It was . . . ."

"Wait just a moment," said Obermann. "Gentlemen, if you would excuse us for a moment.

The President and the Minister of Justice and Tolerance nodded, stood up and left the Oval Office. When the President had closed the door behind him, Obermann motioned with his hand for his son to continue.

"It was extraordinary. It was as though someone were aware of me. Looked at me and then through me."

"An incorporeal?"

"No. That's just it. I don't know who it was. But, I had the overwhelming sense that . . . that . . . it was a person . . . like me?"

"There is no one like you, Frederick. At least, not any more."

"Not any more? I don't understand."

"There was a woman, you've heard me speak of her, Maria O'Conner."

"Yes, of course."

"She was pregnant. She was injected with Chimæric stem cells."

"Yes, I know that too, Father. She was O'Conner's wife. She gave birth to a child, a girl. The child was abducted and never heard of again."

"The child was killed. I didn't want the child killed. We wanted to study it. We had reason to believe that the child had powers, not unlike your own."

"What kind of powers?"

"An abortion was attempted on the fetus. The doctor swore that the scissors he was using to attempt to open the child's skull flew out of his hand."

"And you think that it was the baby trying to protect herself?"

"There is no way of knowing. We did some experiments where we injected pregnant women with Chimæric stem-cell and then aborted their fetuses. In all of those cases nothing out of the ordinary occurred. We also allowed some children to be born. They were Chimærics but possessed no powers other than their normal regenerative abilities."

"Then it would seem likely that this child also would not possess any special abilities. The doctor might have been imagining things."

"I would tend to agree, but the whole situation with Maria O'Conner was rather extraordinary."

"I have read the accounts. So you believe that she was a *yurodivyï*?"

"I do. She also bore the stigmata. She was a threat to the Master's plan, but not anymore. She is dead and so is her child."

There was a knock on the door.

"Yes, come in," replied Obermann.

The President stepped in. "There is a phone call from your secretary. She says it's urgent. You can use my phone."

"Thank you," said Obermann as he stood up and walked behind the President's desk. He sat down in the President's chair. The President scowled and was about to protest, but then thought better of it. Instead, he pointed to the phone and said, "Line three."

Obermann pushed the button and picked up the receiver. "Yes, Miss Hayes, this is Obermann."

"I'm sorry to interrupt your briefing with the President, but I thought you should know."

"Yes, Miss Hayes, go ahead."

"Dr. Charla Richardson has fallen ill."

"What? That's impossible!"

"I know. That's why I thought I should call you."

"How ill is she?"

"She's in our intensive care unit. The doctors say she's pretty bad off. They said it's liver failure."

"That can't be! Listen, I'll be there as soon as I can. You tell those doctors I want answers when I arrive!"

"Yes sir."

Obermann slammed the phone down.

"What's the matter?" asked the President.

Obermann ignored him and turned to his son. "Frederick, we're going back to Chimæra. I'll explain on the way."

Obermann, followed by Frederick, burst into the Intensive Care Unit of the Chimæra Hospital and Research facility. Father and son walked briskly to where several doctors had surrounded a bed. Over a dozen nurses and physicians were either examining the patient or scrutinizing monitors, obstructing their view of the patient. When Obermann reached the crowd surrounding the patient he pushed some of them aside. To his astonishment Richardson was sitting up in bed, smiling.

"What is going on here?" demanded Obermann. "I got a call just a couple of hours ago telling me that Dr. Richardson was dying of liver failure."

"We're at a loss to explain it ourselves," said one of the doctors.

Obermann recognized Dr. Raymond Kwan. He had been with the Chimæra project from the beginning. After sharing the Nobel Prize for Medicine with Charla Richardson he had decided to pursue a lifelong dream of becoming a medical doctor. Obermann had consented. Richardson was more than capable of heading up Research and Development, besides Kwan had proven himself to be a security risk on more than one occasion.

"Dr. Kwan, you seem to have returned to us at our time of need."

"Actually, I was doing rounds at Boston General when Miss Hayes, your secretary, contacted me."

"That was resourceful of her. I'm sure that you'll be of great assistance to us in helping Dr. Richardson. So what do we know?"

"Dr. Richardson was found unconscious in her lab early this morning. She was rushed to intensive care. Blood tests were run which showed elevated serum ammonia, SGPT, AST, and SGOT."

"Translation please," said Obermann.

"These are indications of liver disease. An MRI of her liver was performed. Two-thirds of her liver was necrotic."

"Necrotic? You mean dead?"

"My Chimæric stem cells are eating me from the inside out," interjected Richardson.

"What?!"

Kwan shook his head. "I think that is unlikely. In fact, when I arrived, the MRI was being performed, and although I could see that her liver was extensively damaged, we could also see that Chimæra stem-cells were beginning the process of regenerating her liver. It was not long after that that she started to come around. We were just about to do another MRI to check on the progress of Regeneration when you and your son arrived."

"Okay, but then what caused the liver disease?"

"We don't know yet," replied Kwan.

"Don't you see," said Richardson, "it's the judgment of Prometheus."

Obermann looked at Richardson curiously. He remembered something about the story of Prometheus; something that made him uneasy. Perhaps Richardson knew more about her illness than Dr. Kwan was willing to accept. Obermann probed her psyche, something he had not done for some time. He regretted that now. There was something definitely going on with her. She was not as easy to penetrate as she once had been. He perceived a secret, one that she had been guarding. He perceived it now, only because she was willing to reveal it to him. The smile on her face was not because of relief or gratitude for the restoration of her health. Rather, it was the malevolent satisfaction of a predator, who after having stealthily stalked its prey, now held its victim in her grip.

"I would like everyone, except Frederick and you, Dr. Kwan, to leave us with Dr. Richardson for a while."

As the doctors and nurses began leaving the room he noted that Richardson kept her gaze on Dr. Yarelis who had also been attending her. Yarelis seemed especially concerned. Obermann noted the exchange between them. He would consider that later. After the staff left the room, he turned his attention back to Richardson.

He sat on her bed and gently took her hand. "Tell me, Charla, tell me about Prometheus," said Obermann.

"Prometheus loved humanity," began Richardson, "and he wanted to give humanity something special, something from the heavens. He gave them fire."

"That's what you did, isn't it, Charla? You gave humanity the fire of divine life."

"Yes. But it was not mine to give. As it wasn't Prometheus' to give either."

"So what happened to Prometheus?" asked Obermann.

"Zeus had him tied to a great rock. And every day, a giant eagle would swoop down from the heavens and eat his organs. But then, during the night his organs would grow back. The next day, the eagle would devour his organs again. His judgment was an endless, excruciating cycle of being devoured and restored, only to be devoured again, and again."

"A harsh penalty to impose on someone who just wanted to do good for humanity, wouldn't you say?"

"It is a warning. The things of heaven can only be given and then only when humanity is ready to receive them. To steal them is to unleash destruction upon humanity."

"That's all very interesting, Dr. Richardson. But, why would you think that such a terrible thing would be happening to you?"

"I've been monitoring myself for nearly a year now and I've observed this cycle of necrosis and regeneration many times already. It began almost imperceptibly at first, but now it has progressed to where I can even feel them inside of me. The hungry little parasitic Chimæric stem cells inexplicably choose an organ to feast upon. Then they swarm around it, embed themselves into it, and devour the tissues. But just before the organ completely fails, the stem cells reverse themselves and regenerate the organ. Then they wait a little while, give me time to recover; perhaps, I think, I'll even get better. Then it starts all over again. And the pain! The pain! It's indescribable. But, worst of all is the awareness that this is my eternal destiny. I can assure you, Mr. Obermann, my life was never in danger. I wouldn't have died even if I hadn't been discovered in the lab. I'm chained to the rock, never to escape my judgment."

Obermann looked over at Kwan.

Kwan shrugged. "It is true that we did nothing to reverse her liver failure. The stem cells regenerated her liver. But, we have no evidence of the cyclical necrosis and regeneration that Dr. Richardson has described."

"I have the evidence," said Richardson.

"Why did you not share this with us?" asked Obermann. "Maybe we could have helped you sooner."

"There is nothing you can do to help me. And besides, I wanted to make sure the judgment had time to spread."

"Spread? You mean throughout your body?"

"No. Throughout yours and every Chimæric!"

Obermann stood up and looked down at her. He probed her consciousness with his mind. She was telling the truth. At least she was telling him what she thought was the truth. But how could it be? How could she have altered the stem cells so that they behaved in such a manner? How could she then effect this change in all Chimærics? After all, Chimærics now directly or indirectly received their stem-cells from Frederick's insemination. Unless . . . .

"That's right," replied Richardson, who sensed what Obermann was beginning to perceive. "It was when Frederick 'converted' me that I knew that I had made a mistake. And I became determined that I would destroy the monster I created."

"So what does that make me, Frankenstein's monster? Gee doc, you're hurting my feelings," Frederick said with a wicked smile.

Richardson ignored Frederick's comment. "That's when I remembered I had kept one sample of Maria O'Conner's blood."

Obermann, who had been pacing, now stopped and stared at her with a ferocious anger.

"Yes, that's right. I kept a sample. It was just too much of a scientific curiosity to destroy it. Why did her blood not agglutinate even though it contained both BB and AB blood cells? What was the mysterious molecule that evaded all our efforts to identify it, a phantom molecule that seemed to exist outside our normal time and space? Yes, you see, I've thought about it."

"The only thing I see is that you're quite mad," said Obermann. "I feel sorry for you."

"That's not what you're feeling. You're afraid. No, terrified! And you don't even know the half of it, yet!" Richardson was now enjoying seeing Obermann squirm. "So let me tell you. After I came home from having sex with your demon seed, I injected myself with the blood sample."

"You what?! You're lucky it didn't kill you!" exclaimed Obermann.

"I didn't know what would happen. Maybe it would kill me. Maybe it would somehow free me of the Chimæric stem cells as it did Maria. But it did neither. Instead, you know what it did?"

"Do tell," said Obermann, narrowing his eyes in a stern, malicious frown.

"What I learned was that the Chimæric Regeneration System is under the control of a small but critically important Chimæric Master Gland located near the corpus callosum. Somehow, the phantom molecule severed the communication between the Chimæric Master Gland and the rest of the Chimæric Regeneration System. Without that communication the Chimæric stem cells run amok. I think you know what happens after that."

"That's a very interesting story. Fortunately, Dr. Kwan has returned to us and will be able to help us determine if there is any truth to it. But, one thing you have not explained. You said that you kept this secret so that this cyclical necrosis would spread to all Chimærics? I don't see how this is possible. Furthermore, I haven't heard of any other Chimærics developing this problem."

"It's only a matter of time. After all, I am patient zero. But in regard to it spreading; it spreads sexually, right along with Frederick's Chimæric gametes."

Richardson watched the blood drain from Obermann's face. The night of the party, he thought. The night he had been stabbed by that crazed girlfriend of Colin's. Richardson had been there for the express purpose of helping to spread Frederick's Chimæric gametes. If it were true, then virtually everyone who was a Chimæric would also be infected with Maria's blood! Even he had had sex with Richardson that evening.

"You remember, don't you? We had sex that evening. I made a particular point of seducing you. It wasn't that difficult. But I can see; you have some lingering doubts." She turned to Dr. Kwan, "Take a sample of Mr. Obermann's blood."

Obermann nodded to Kwan. Kwan proceeded to open several cabinets and drawers. He found a phlebotomy kit.

"Why don't you have a seat over here," Kwan said to Obermann.

Obermann removed his jacket, rolled up his sleeve, and laid his arm across the counter.

"Did you ever have sex with Richardson again?" he said to his son.

"No, Father. Only the first time as you instructed."

"What about someone who has already been converted?"

"I'm not sure. I tend to focus my attention on non-Chimærics or the few remaining Chimærics in need of conversion. Most of these, of course, are VIP's."

Kwan removed the needle from Obermann's arm and pressed a cotton ball over where he had removed the needle.

"Draw Frederick's blood. We might as well know for sure."

Kwan proceeded to draw a sample of Frederick's blood. "So what am I looking for?" he asked Richardson.

"It would take too long for me to describe how you would detect the phantom molecule. Even then, you might not. Just check the blood type. That will do it."

Kwan removed a small medical analyzer from his lab coat. He inserted the needle from Frederick's blood sample into the analyzer. The device began to do a routine assessment of his blood chemistry.

"Nothing out of the ordinary with your son's blood sample, Mr. Obermann," said Kwan.

"Excellent." Obermann now turned his attention back to

Richardson as Kwan flushed the analyzer and prepared it to receive the sample of Obermann's blood. "Okay," continued Obermann, "assuming what you said is true and not just a fantasy from your deranged mind, what is it that you hope to accomplish?"

"I've already told you. I want to destroy Chimæra."

"And I don't suppose that there is anything that can be done to get you to change you're mind?"

"No, nothing," replied Richardson.

"I wouldn't be so sure," said Frederick.

"This is odd," interrupted Kwan. "Perhaps there's something wrong with my analyzer."

"What is it doctor?" asked Obermann.

"You have type AA blood, don't you?"

"Yes."

"Well, the sample shows AA, but also BB and AB blood types."

"Damn!" exclaimed Obermann. "I have *her* blood in me!"

"Yes," said Richardson. "You're infected. Everyone that I have had sex with is infected. And everyone they had sex with, and so on and so on, like dominoes. It's only a matter of time, and they'll be experiencing the Promethian judgment just as I am. You can't stop it. I brought fire from heaven, and I will extinguish it!"

"Your blood analysis is indicating an elevated BUN and creatinine," said Kwan.

"What does that mean?" asked Obermann.

"Early stages of kidney failure."

Reverse what you've done! Obermann pushed his psyche fiercely into her consciousness. Her body shook, and her eyes rolled back into their sockets.

No! She responded.

"She's having a seizure!" exclaimed Kwan. "We need to get some help!"

She fought to prevent his mental rape of her innermost consciousness. But he was too strong. He ransacked her mind like a burglar, tossing the contents of drawers across the room; knocking over cabinets . . . he'd find the cure he knew she was hiding.

Richardson's shaking had stopped. Kwan felt desperately for her carotid pulse. There was none.

"Christ! We're losing her!" shouted Kwan. Kwan ran out of the room. "We have a code blue down here, Stat!"

"Father! You're killing her!"

Obermann didn't hear his son. Instead he pushed deeper. She had conceived of a possible cure! He followed the thread. Original Chimæric stem cells might act as antagonists against the renegade stem cells! Obermann felt exhilarated at the prospect of hope. No! She had destroyed all of the remaining supplies of Chimæric stem cells. He looked around her consciousness. She could no longer resist him, but now her mind was growing dark, the mental landscape confusing. He had never entered another's consciousness so deeply. He wondered what effect it might have on his own consciousness. He felt as if the boundaries between Richardson and himself were beginning to blur. What if he could not extricate himself from her consciousness?! Then he saw what appeared to be a narrow hallway. He knew that it led to another possible solution. But did he dare push further? He had no choice. He entered the hallway, but as he did it began to contract. He felt a horrific claustrophobia press in on his own consciousness as Richardson's mind began to implode from the pressure of his psychic intrusion.

Two nurses pushed open the door and ran into the room with the crash cart. Kwan pulled it next to the bed, opened it and removed an intubator, which he inserted into Richardson's mouth and down her trachea to open her airway. He then climbed up on the bed, straddled her, and began compressing her chest while another nurse injected her with epinephrine. Her heart would not start beating.

Kwan jumped off the bed, ripped open Richardson' gown, turned on the defibrillator, grabbed the paddles and placed them on her chest.

"Everyone, stand back!"

"No! Not yet!" shouted Frederick, not sure what effect this might have on his father.

Obermann squeezed and pushed his way through Richardson's collapsing mind. Finally he reached his destination. *If there were another sample of Maria's blood an antidote might be prepared by . . . .*

Frederick grabbed his father's mind and yanked it back. Obermann stumbled and Frederick caught him and helped him into a chair.

Richardson's body convulsed as the electricity jolted her body.

"Why did you do that?" asked Obermann. "I almost had the answer."

"I had to get you out of there! I didn't know what might happen to you."

Richardson's body convulsed again. Kwan's attempts to resuscitate Richardson were failing.

"Is she gone?" asked Obermann.

"Not yet," replied Frederick. "But I have an idea."

Frederick grabbed the doctor's arm. "Stop! Given me those!"

"These are dangerous," protested Kwan. "Do you know what you're doing?"

"Give them to him!" commanded Obermann.

Kwan reluctantly handed the paddles over to Frederick. Frederick then turned the voltage regulator knob to maximum.

"Stop, that's too high! You could kill . . . ."

But before Kwan could finish his sentence, Frederick had pushed the paddles against Kwan's chest. Before he even had a chance to pull away Frederick fired off the powerful jolt of electricity throwing Kwan across the room. The nurses stood back in horror.

"What the hell did you do that for?" asked Obermann

Frederick didn't answer. If his plan were to work, they would have to act quickly. "Place the body in the chair, here!" commanded Frederick.

The two nurses picked up Kwan's body and placed him in the chair next to Richardson's bed. Frederick placed his left hand on Richardson's head and his right hand on Kwan's. He closed his eyes and stood there quietly for several minutes. Finally, he removed his hands.

"Start his heart," said Frederick standing back from the bodies.

The nurse pulled Kwan's body out of the chair and laid it flat on the floor. They pulled open his shirt. Burn marks showed where the defibrillator had discharged its lethal voltage. One nurse checked his airway while the other readjusted the defibrillator, placed the paddles on Kwan's chest, and jolted him. Immediately, his heart began to beat again.

"We need to monitor him; make sure he's okay. He's not out of the woods yet."

"They'll be fine," said Frederick.

"*They?*" asked Obermann.

"Yes," replied Frederick, smiling. "You always said they worked better as a team."

01/04 NEWERA

Shortening The Days

If the Lord had not shortened those days, no one would be saved;
but for the sake of the elect whom he chose, he did shorten the days.
~Mark 13:20

Six hours of driving on bumpy dirt roads was enough to exhaust anyone, but not *Ch'ucha'*. She could contain her excitement no longer. She stood up in the back of the truck as San Cristobal da las Casas came into view. Her mouth fell open in astonishment. Never had she seen anything like this. The city itself looked as if it were alive. Brightly colored buildings looked like jungle flowers blooming. And they were so much larger, and closer together then she had expected. And the people! There were so many of them. San Cristobal reminded her of the large anthills that dotted the Lacandon.

"Oh, I wish Rosario was here!" exclaimed *Ch'ucha'*, leaning down into the cab of the truck.

"She has been to San Cristobal many times over the years," replied Mateas who was driving the truck. "She doesn't like the crowds."

Nizhniya looked over at Mateas and frowned. She knew that his response would not satisfy *Ch'ucha'*. She had begged her *Rina* to come. She wanted Rosario to share in the excitement as she displayed her *huipiles*. *Ch'ucha'* had been surprised and hurt when Rosario had told her that she would be staying behind.

"But nearly everyone is coming," *Ch'ucha'* had pleaded.

"I promised Father Suarez that I would make sure that Aguilar was taken care of," Rosario had replied.

Ch'ucha' argued that those tending the livestock could take care of Aguilar. But, Rosario reminded her that they were too busy to attend to his needs.

"You can tell Rosario all about the festival when we get back," Nizhniya said, trying to alleviate *Ch'ucha's* disappointment. "And I'm sure you will have many ribbons to show her."

"I hope so," said *Ch'ucha'*. She wondered what people in the city would think about her weaving. Sure, at the Mission everyone had praised her work. But, the Festival at San Cristobal drew weavers from all over Chiapas. The finest weavers would be displaying their *huipiles* and other handiwork. How would her weaving compare to theirs? She was filled with both excitement and anxiety at the thought of the upcoming competition. Even so, underlying these emotions she felt an inexplicable foreboding. As they entered San Cristobal she tried to fill her senses with the sights, sounds, and smells of the city in order to push back the dark thoughts. But, her mind kept going back—back to the dark and mysterious hidden Mayan temple which Rosario had taken her just a few weeks earlier. Then her eyes caught sight of what appeared to be hundreds of *huipiles* out on display. They were beautiful! Her heart swelled with pride and hope; none could compare to what she had woven!

While *Ch'ucha'* thought about the Festival, Mateas and Nizhniya kept a vigilant eye open for any suspicious activity. Santiago and a contingent of ten other Zapatista soldiers had been sent ahead of them with Father Suarez. Santiago had radioed Mateas that they, along with three of the President's Cabinet, were now at the *Hostal Flamboyant Español*. The President had reluctantly agreed to allow the Zapatistas to hold a Cabinet minister hostage while negotiations were held with

Commander Valdez at the Bishop's residence. The hostage would remain at the Hotel for the duration of the negotiations. It was only after Mateas had received the okay from other Zapatistas that they entered the city. As Mateas surveyed the city looking for Federales he hoped that Father Suarez's faith in the President's goodwill was not misplaced.

"When is your meeting with the President?" asked Nizhniya.

"We will have dinner at five with the Bishop and Father Suarez, an informal affair, an opportunity for us to get to know one another. According to the President's agenda, we will not start negotiations until tomorrow morning. We shall see," added Mateas with a decided note of skepticism.

"He is meeting you on your turf. There is something to be said about that."

"This is true," said Mateas smiling. "This place is crawling with Zapatistas. If he were planning to betray our trust, he would pay dearly for it. Ah, here we are!"

Mateas pulled the truck into the driveway of the *Posada Diego de Mazariegos*.

"Let's go see all the *huipiles!*" exclaimed *Ch'ucha'*.

Nizhniya groaned as she stepped out of the truck. She massaged her lower back and stretched. Five hours of being jostled around in the old truck as it traveled down the bumpy and potholed roads between the Mission and San Cristobal was enough to wear down anybody. Where does she get her energy? Nizhniya thought.

Mateas laughed, "She's all yours for the next few days."

Ch'ucha' grabbed Nizhniya's hand. "Let's go!" she said.

Nizhniya thought her arm would be wrenched out of its socket, *Ch'ucha'* had pulled so hard.

"Whoa, wait a minute," exclaimed Nizhniya. "We must put our bags in our room."

"Okay, but then we can go out?"

"Yes, yes," replied Nizhniya.

"Come on," said Mateas. "Let's check in." He was beginning to think that negotiations with the President would be easier than Nizhniya's task of being with *Ch'ucha'* for the next few days.

Mateas checked them in and asked for someone to help bring their bags and the boxes from the back of the truck. A young porter piled bags and the three boxes of *huipiles* woven by *Ch'ucha'* onto a cart. He then proceeded to lead the trio to their rooms. Mateas was sharing a room with a couple of fellow Zapatistas. He knocked on the door.

"*Quien?*" said a voice from inside.

"It's Mateas!"

The door opened. A small, dark-skinned Mayan appeared at the door, smiling broadly exposing perfect white teeth. The little man grasped Mateas in a tenacious hug. Ludmelia struggled not to laugh at the sight of Mateas straining to free himself from the grasp of the little Zapatista.

"Anselmo, enough!"

"No," replied Anselmo. "It has been too long. Why have you been hiding at the Mission?"

Mateas finally freed himself from Anselmo's grip. "I have not been hiding. I've been busy . . ."

"Ah," said Anselmo, nodding his head finally seeing Ludmelia and *Ch'ucha'*. "Now I know why Commander Valdez has been so busy!"

"No, no. It's not what you think. She's . . . a . . . This is Nizhniya. She's staying with Sister Margarita. She's thinking about becoming a nun."

Nizhniya raised her eyebrows in surprise at Mateas' remark.

"Oh, I see," said Anselmo, with a note of skepticism. "And who is this?" he continued, nodding towards *Ch'ucha'*.

"I'm her daughter," replied *Ch'ucha'* smiling at the thought that she had just made Mateas' story even more unbelievable.

"Ladies," said Anselmo, bowing, "I hope that we will have the opportunity to spend more time together. But now, I must speak with Mateas. I want to hear more of his fanciful stories!"

Mateas frowned as Anselmo pulled him into the room. Nizhniya and *Ch'ucha'* shared a hearty laugh as the porter showed them to their room. He knocked on the door. There was no answer.

"Sister Margarita must be out," said Nizhniya.

The porter opened the door with a key and showed them in. He then deposited their bags and boxes in the room. As Nizhniya tipped him, *Ch'ucha'* caught eye of the television set in the room.

"Is this a TV?" asked *Ch'ucha'* excitedly.

"Yes," replied Nizhniya. "Just don't tell Rosario that I let you watch the television."

"What do I do?" asked *Ch'ucha'*.

Nizhniya walked over to the television and pushed the "on" button. Immediately, the black screen became alive with colorful images and sounds, and voices."

"Wow!" exclaimed *Ch'ucha'*.

There were no televisions at the Mission or the surrounding village. Father Suarez had brought a television with him when he had first arrived, but Rosario had forbidden it. She was convinced that it would have a corrupting influence on the community. It was a sacrifice, Rosario had insisted, which would demonstrate Father Suarez' commitment to preserving Mayan culture. "But . . . but . . . my soccer games!" Father Suarez had protested. There would be no compromising with Rosario. He had finally honored her demands, albeit, reluctantly.

"Push this button and you can change the stations."

Ch'ucha' just watched in amazement as the various images flickered across the screen when Nizhniya changed the stations. Maybe Rosario was right, thought Nizhniya, noting how enthralled *Ch'ucha'* was. Then again, it wasn't right to keep her totally isolated from the world. It was time for *Ch'ucha'* to experience more of life in spite of the risks.

"Why don't you watch some television while I take a shower. I haven't had a real shower in four years! When I'm done, we'll go check out the competition. What do you say?"

"Ah uh," replied *Ch'ucha'* mindlessly as she stared at the television.

Nizhniya shook her head as she went into the bathroom. She closed the door behind her and smiled to herself with a sense of almost perfect contentment as she looked at the shower. She turned on the hot water. It was warm today, but it didn't matter. The idea of being soaked in *hot* water was irresistible even if the ambient temperature was ninety degrees and the humidity was nearly a hundred percent. Steam began to pour out of the shower. She disrobed and stepped under the water. It stung her skin; it was absolutely delicious!

As she washed, her hand passed under her left breast. She could feel the slight scar from the nearly mortal wound that she had received four years ago from Aguilar. Everyone had attributed her healing to a miracle. What else could it have been? She had never discounted that explanation, but she had always felt there was more to it than divine intervention. Now it all made sense. The conversation she had had with Father Suarez helped fit the final pieces of her fragmented memory together. *Ch'ucha'* was Chimæric, exposed to stem-cell treatment *in utero*. But, she was not an ordinary Chimæric, not that any Chimæric is ordinary by normal standards. Somehow her very early exposure to the stem cells had endowed her not only with a unique physiology and development, but also with extraordinary abilities. It was *Ch'ucha's* Chimæric stem cells that had healed her; stem cells introduced directly into her mortal wound during Rosario's bloodletting ritual. Nizhniya glanced at the slightly discolored scar tissue as the steaming water drenched her. She wondered if she were now a Chimæric also.

Will my soul be trapped in my *garment of skin* if I am killed? she thought. She turned off the water. She pulled back the shower curtain, grabbed a towel and began to dry. There's enough to think about, she thought. Someone else will have to worry about my soul.

She put on some clean clothes and wrapped her hair up in a towel. She stepped out of the bathroom and saw *Ch'ucha'* sitting on the floor watching the television intensely.

"What's the matter?" asked Nizhniya who could see that *Ch'ucha'* was upset.

"Why doesn't somebody stop them?"

Ch'ucha' had been watching a news program that was showing footage of some war-torn area of the world. Nizhniya watched as the camera panned over a bomb-ravaged village; soldiers were patrolling the bloodstained streets. One of the soldiers turned over a body. Immediately, an arm emerged from the seemingly lifeless body, reaching out for help. An accompanying soldier responded by putting a bullet in the hapless victim's head. Nizhniya reached over and turned off the television. She closed her eyes and held onto *Ch'ucha'* tightly. She wanted to protect her, to keep her from the horrors that she was all too familiar with herself. She knew, though, that this would be impossible.

"It's not that easy," replied Nizhniya.

"Then why don't they just leave; find somewhere safe to live?"

"Sometimes evil comes looking for us."

"Like Mateas? The bad people came for his father. He tried to rescue his father, but it was too late."

"Yes, he was too late for his father. But, he and the other Zapatistas were able to rescue many others who had been taken to the mines. And now the mine is closed and the Federales leave our villages alone."

"And your family? They were murdered too, weren't they? I heard you speak with Mateas about that. What did you do?"

Nizhniya lowered her head and looked down at the floor. "I did nothing. There was nothing I could do. I was a child."

"But what if you *could* have done something?"

Ch'ucha's question brought the pain and anger of her childhood back to the surface and then lanced it like a boil. Yes, she knew what she would have done. She would have made the separatists' wives widows and their children fatherless. Nizhniya studied *Ch'ucha'*. She suspected that *Ch'ucha'* was asking more than a rhetorical question.

Ch'ucha' nodded, recognizing that Nizhniya understood the full import of her question.

Nizhniya drew a deep breath. She placed her left palm on *Ch'ucha's* cheek and her right index finger to her lips. "Ssh . . . that's enough for now. We're here to have fun. Now let's go show off some of those *huipiles* of yours."

They left the hotel room both wearing *huipiles* that *Ch'ucha'* had woven. *Ch'ucha's huipil* bore the distinctive green frog that had become her trademark, whereas on Nizhniya's *huipil* *Ch'ucha'* had woven a beautiful Virgin of Guadalupe. They decided not to bring the other *huipiles* until they knew exactly where they were supposed to set up their display.

Ch'ucha' had never seen so many people before. They had to squeeze their way through the narrow streets crowded with people and tables displaying their crafts. *Ch'ucha'* was excited as well as overwhelmed by the sensations that were smothering her senses. Buildings were painted in colors that she would have never expected—bright green, earthy reds, and the lavender of jungle flowers. The Plaza was filled with the cacophony normal when hundreds of people gathered. A common enough experience for any city dweller, but *Ch'ucha'* became exhausted as she instinctively tried to distinguish one conversation from another. And then, there were the smells of the city. The acrid smell of *ocote* which the women used to start their morning fires, the sweat of so many people jammed together, and the obvious inadequacy of proper sanitation, all made *Ch'ucha'* want to cover her nose with her *huipil*.

"How can people live this way?!" asked *Ch'ucha'*.

Nizhniya laughed. "Oh this is nothing! I have been to cities much, much larger than San Cristobal."

"Really!," exclaimed *Ch'ucha'* hardly believing that such a thing was possible. "Then you must really love living at the Mission."

"Yes, I have. I have found peace there. But, mostly," Nizhniya said, placing a fond arm around *Ch'ucha's* shoulder, "I have you."

Ch'ucha' smiled and kissed Nizhniya on the cheek. They made their way through the labyrinth of tables until they finally came to an empty booth. A woman in her early thirties was laying out *huipiles* and other crafts on the table next to the empty booth.

"Excuse me," said Nizhniya. "Is anyone else using this table?"

The woman looked up and then stared at Nizhniya and *Ch'ucha'*. Nizhniya knew that they made a conspicuous couple, she with her fair skin and blonde hair; *Ch'ucha'* with her light brown skin and luminescent blue eyes. Nizhniya began to wonder if coming to San Cristobal had been such a good idea after all.

"Grandma," exclaimed the woman. "Come and take a look at these *huipiles*! I have never seen such craftsmanship!"

Nizhniya relaxed when she realized that it was *Ch'ucha's* skill as a weaver that was drawing attention and not their persons. The grandmother had been facing the other direction and had been looking through a box of crafts when her granddaughter called her. She slowly straightened up and walked over to them. She examined them closely.

Then the old woman's attention was drawn to the exquisite *huipiles* that *Ch'ucha'* had woven.

"Did you weave these," asked the old woman, "or did Santa Lucia come down from heaven and weave them for you?"

Ch'ucha' smiled broadly. "I did," replied *Ch'ucha'* modestly. "But with Santa Lucia's help. I pray to her daily that she will guide my fingers."

The old woman nodded approvingly while continuing to study *Ch'ucha'*. "I know you," said the old woman. "I know I've met you before."

"I don't think so," replied *Ch'ucha'*. "This is the first time I have been to San Cristobal."

"No. I am certain." The old woman turned to her granddaughter. "Do you not recognize her?"

The younger woman leaned over her table of crafts to get a closer look at *Ch'ucha'*. "She does look familiar. It is her eyes."

"Yes, that is right," said the old woman. "Would you mind turning around?"

Ch'ucha' looked over at Nizhniya, wondering what to do. Nizhniya wasn't sure either. What harm could it do? If she protested it might create more of a stir than if she consented. Besides, how could the old woman have met *Ch'ucha'*? Better to put the question to rest. Nizhniya nodded.

Ch'ucha' turned around. Immediately, the old woman leaned across the table and lifted *Ch'ucha's* hair exposing her neck and the back of her head. A small scar was visible just above the hairline. The old woman let *Ch'ucha's* hair fall back.

"It is you!" exclaimed the old woman.

Ch'ucha' turned around and looked questioningly at the woman.

"But how can this be? You were a baby. Now you are a beautiful young woman. And it was only four years ago!"

Nizhniya was now alarmed. "Perhaps we should be leaving?" she said to *Ch'ucha'*. *Ch'ucha'* looked crestfallen.

"No," replied the old woman. "Your secret is safe. If the Earthlord himself were to visit me in my dreams, he could not force me to reveal the identity of the Lord's Anointed."

Ch'ucha' had no idea what the old woman was talking about. It didn't matter to her anyway. She wanted to display her *huipiles* now more than ever. "Please let me stay," *Ch'ucha'* pleaded.

Nizhniya didn't know what to do. She had been so careful up until now. *Ch'ucha'* would be disappointed if they left. And Rosario had been insistent that they come to the festival.

"All right," said Nizhniya.

Immediately, Ch'ucha' threw her arms around Nizhniya. While *Ch'ucha'* squeezed her tightly, Nizhniya hoped and prayed that Rosario knew what she was doing.

*   *   *

"Well, good morning, Rosario. Come to feed the caged animal?" asked Aguilar in his most acerbic tone.

It was eight in the morning. Nearly everyone in both the Mission and village had left for the festival in San Cristobal. Only a few remained and they were too busy tending to their flocks to come to the Mission.

Rosario unlocked the apartment door that had been Aguilar's 'prison' for the past five years. Aguilar was free most of the time to walk around the Mission grounds. After all, where could he go? Flee into the jungle? He would not get far. Either Mateas and his men would track him down, or he would fall prey to a jaguar or some venomous serpent. The Lacandon was a prison without walls.

Rosario entered the apartment. Aguilar sat in a chair and was glancing at a magazine that Father Suarez had left him. To his surprise Rosario did not bring with her a tray of food. She walked towards him and placed a set of keys on the table. Now he was curious. What was the old hag up to? he thought. She placed a thick wad of cash next to the keys. He grabbed the money and flipped through the bills.

"There is over six thousand American dollars here!" Aguilar exclaimed.

"Go," said Rosario dispassionately. "Ludmelia's motorcycle is in the Mission garage. Take the road south to Guatemala. You will come to the village of Kaputec. Ask for *Señor* Oscar Trujillo. He will take you to Guatemala City. I believe you will know what to do when you arrive."

Aguilar stood and snatched up the keys from the table and limped towards the door. He could hardly believe it. In fact, he wouldn't have believed it had anyone else offered him this opportunity to escape. He would have assumed it was just an excuse to kill him. But, Rosario was such an eccentric she was capable of any type of lunacy, even this. Nevertheless, he was curious to understand what twisted reasoning was behind her releasing him.

"Why?" he asked.

"Because the time must be cut short," she said matter-of-factly, as if this should be obvious to him.

Aguilar laughed. The old fool, he thought. But, she had given him an inspiration. "It is you, old woman, whose time will be cut short."

He went back to the table, picked up the heavy brass lamp, and raised it above his head. To his surprise, Rosario did not cry out or make any attempt to flee. She just stood patiently as if this was all part of her insane scheme. He laughed again as he swung the lamp striking her on the head. She fell dead, her skull crushed by the terrific impact. Aguilar tossed the bloodied lamp to the floor.

"Good riddance, old witch!"

As he left his apartment, he laughed to himself. The old soothsayer was right in her own twisted way, he thought. The time would be cut short for the Mission and the whole damn village. He'd finish the job that he and Zokoroff had begun four years ago. But, this time he'd take care of the little bitch himself.

The Nephilim

When men began to multiply on earth and daughters were born to them, the sons of heaven saw how beautiful the daughters of man were, and so they took for their wives as many of them as they chose.

Then the LORD said: "My spirit shall not remain in man forever, since he is but flesh. His days shall comprise one hundred and twenty years." At that time the Nephilim appeared on earth (as well as later), after the sons of heaven had intercourse with the daughters of man, who bore them sons. They were the heroes of old, the men of renown. When the LORD saw how great was man's wickedness on earth, and how no desire that his heart conceived was ever anything but evil, he regretted that he had made man on the earth, and his heart was grieved.

~ Genesis 6:1-6

When Kavasilas, Ryan and Milton Lewis had been led into an ornate conference room within the *Palazzo del Governatorato* in the Vatican, Lewis had been awestruck by the frescoes, tapestries, busts, and baroque furnishings. But after an hour and a half of waiting, even the beautiful surroundings could not assuage his irritation. As the trio waited for the arrival of the Postulator-General Lewis was briefed by Bishop Kavasilas, on the latest political maneuverings within the Vatican.

"There are forces within the Curia that are not at all pleased with the Holy Father's unification efforts with the Orthodox," said Kavasilas. "These same factions are also pressing him to be more conciliatory towards the Chimæric West and schismatic Tree of Life Catholics. They will do anything to block the canonization of Maria, which they rightfully see as solidifying both the Church's opposition to Chimæra and unity with the East. What is perplexing to me is that the Postulator-General, who had been very sympathetic towards the cause of Maria's beatification, now seems to be dragging his heels."

"Do you think the opposition has gotten to him?" asked Ryan.

"I think he is a politician. Perhaps he recognizes that the Holy Father's influence over his bishops has faltered along with his health. I wouldn't be surprised if he has his eye on the papacy himself."

"Sounds like inside the Beltway," said Lewis, recalling his days in Washington, D.C.

Kavasilas nodded sadly. "'Fraid so. Flesh is flesh. It hardly makes any difference if you dress it up in a cassock or a three-piece suit."

Finally, Cardinal Bosch, the Postulator-General, entered the room with his secretary, Father Duran. Bosch offered a vague apology and then sat down across from the trio. Bishop Kavasilas, as vice-postulator for Maria's cause, greeted the Cardinal and introduced Ryan and Lewis. Bosch knew Ryan, and although he had heard of Lewis he had never met him. Lewis shook the Cardinal's hand politely while scrutinizing him as if conducting a lineup of suspected criminals.

"I want to thank, your Eminence," began Bishop Kavasilas, "for your efforts in successfully expediting the beatification process of Blessed Maria O'Conner. I am confident that we can continue to count on your . . . ."

"I am sorry to inform you that we are considering reversing Mrs. O'Conner's blessed status and reinstating her as a Servant of God."[70]

"What?!" exclaimed Ryan aghast. "You can't be serious!"

"This is unprecedented!" protested Kavasilas. "On what grounds?"

"We have received numerous remissorial letters from bishops *in partibus*[71] all requesting that we reevaluate Maria's beatified status."

"Remissorial letters are not even required for the beatification of a martyr," replied Kavasilas.

"Some have raised doubts as to whether her death was genuine martyrdom. After all, it was those whom you claim were responsible for her death that were also trying to save her life."

"That's outrageous!" exclaimed Ryan. "I was there, damn it! I should know."

Bosch ignored her outburst and continued. "And then there is the *Processiculi diligentiarum*,"[72] he continued.

"We've been through this process before. Maria's Journal was found to be theologically orthodox by the Congregation," said Kavasilas.

"The question is, 'Which Journal is authentic?' As you know, there are two versions of Mrs. O'Conner's Journal."

"Indeed, I do know," replied Ryan. "Maria gave me the Journal herself."

"Yes, but to what extent did you modify it?" At this point Father Duran tapped the Cardinal's shoulder and whispered into his ear. "And then, there is the issue of her sanctity," Bosch continued. "We have received reports calling into question your claims that she practiced the theological and cardinal virtues heroically."

Ryan was exasperated. She flung up her hands in a questioning gesture, indicating her frustration and disappointment. Lewis may have been mystified by the process of canonization, but one thing he knew for certain—Cardinal Bosch was stonewalling. He had to be part of the faction opposing the Pope, as Kavasilas had discussed earlier. And who was this Father Duran? Kavasilas, on the other hand, knew that he had to play out the hand he had been dealt.

"All right then, what is it that you want us to do?" asked Kavasilas.

"First of all," replied Bosch, "I would expect the Orthodox to honor the *Processe de non cultu.*"

"You want us to cease our veneration of Maria O'Conner?" asked Kavasilas. "She is a recognized Saint among the Orthodox. We are not under your jurisdiction."

"I see. Perhaps you do not prize unity with the Roman Church as much as your cult of the Saints?"

Kavasilas realized that Bosch had set him up. To agree to the *Processe de non cultu* would set back the process of Maria's canonization even further. But, if the Orthodox refused, it would hinder the process of unification.

"I don't think you appreciate what life is like for God-fearing people in the Chimæric West who refuse to bend the knee to the Tree of Life," said Ryan. "The people need an advocate to strengthen them during these horrific times of persecution."

"Do you really think . . ." began Bosch, but then stopped when Father Duran tapped him on the shoulder again. Bosch nodded a couple times as Father Duran whispered to him. Bishop Kavasilas and Lewis exchanged glances. Lewis raised an eyebrow. Kavasilas knew what he was implying. They were both wondering which of the two clerics was in charge.

"Are we not being a bit hyperbolic, Ms. Ryan?" continued Cardinal Bosch. "Some of this persecution we have brought upon ourselves by our intolerance. The assassination of the Obermanns and General Pierce, the Saint Pierre Massacre, and now there is evidence that we may have some culpability in the 'blood plague' that is devastating Chimærics worldwide."

"This is the worst lie of all," protested Ryan. "Do you know that now some countries, countries that had once prided themselves on freedom of the press and of expression, have declared it a crime to own a copy of Maria's *Journal*. Non-Chimærics are being raped and turned into Chimærics against their will. Increasingly there are stories of non-Chimærics disappearing. We have heard that their organs are being harvested to replace the degenerating organs of Chimærics."

"Fanciful rumors!" interjected Bosch.

"There have been stories of resubstantiation," continued Ryan.

"Resubstantiation?" inquired Bosch.

Father Duran leaned over and began whispering in the Cardinal's ear. Ryan, annoyed by Father Duran's whispering, interrupted them.

"Excuse me, I'll explain it to the Cardinal."

Father Duran sat up straight and looked menacingly at Ryan. Ryan was startled by his expression, but she continued.

"Non-Chimærics are murdered. It is reported that Frederick is capable of then transferring the soul of a diseased Chimæric into the corpse. What he does next is too disgusting to talk about, especially in this hallowed place. Let it suffice to say, that when he is done, the transferred soul now occupies a new, living and healthy Chimæric body."

"We have heard, there have been stories, it is reported," replied Father Duran in a cynical tone. They were all surprised to hear him finally speak. "Evidence, Ms. Ryan. Evidence," Duran continued. "You and Bishop Kavasilas have presented us with hearsay and rumors. Saints are not made of hearsay and rumors!"

Bishop Kavasilas stroked his long beard as he sized up the situation. It was now obvious that no amount of argument would promote Maria's cause with Postulator-General Bosch; that is, if the Cardinal were even in charge. He was beginning to wonder. Who was this Father Duran anyway? Kavasilas decided to take a more conciliatory approach and see where it might lead.

"Cardinal Bosch, we appreciate how difficult it must be overseeing this process. Never has the Church, in its long history, considered a more controversial individual for sainthood. I understand the need to proceed carefully. I will discuss the issue of *Processe de non cultu* with my fellow Orthodox bishops. In the meantime, however, what else can we do to regain the confidence of the Postulator-General?"

"When Mrs. O'Conner was beatified under the code of canon law for Martyrs, a second-class miracle was all that was required. We will now need evidence of a first-class miracle."

"We have already provided you with evidence of the miraculous deaths attributed to Maria O'Conner," explained Ryan. "Wouldn't these be considered first-class."

"Yes," said Bosch. "However, we have received additional testimony suggesting that these deaths could be explained naturally."

"Was this testimony provided by Chimæra doctors?" asked Kavasilas. "Surely, you don't expect them to be objective, do you?"

"No more than I would expect you and Ms. Ryan to be objective. We have to hear both sides. No, I'm afraid we'll need more tangible evidence."

"You want first-class evidence!" exclaimed Ryan. "Here's evidence!"

She opened her briefcase and pulled out a wooden box about twice the size of a deck of cards. She opened the box and removed a plastic bag that contained a strip of paper. She put the bag in front of Cardinal Bosch. Duran's eyes widened as he pushed himself imperceptibly away from the table. Lewis noted the curious, perhaps even suspicious, behavior.

"And what is this?" asked Bosch.

This was Lewis' cue; his forensic expertise would add credibility to the evidence. "This strip of paper contains a drop of blood, Maria O'Conner's blood," said Lewis.

"And what is your connection with this case? I've been told, Detective Lewis, that you are not even a Catholic."

"That is correct. How I became involved in this affair is a rather lengthy story. However, as a detective, or at least former detective, it's my business to get to the bottom of things. There are aspects of this case that defy a logical explanation."

"Presumably it has to do with this bloodstain," said Bosch.

"Yes," replied Lewis, "although there are many other inexplicable aspects to this case."

"I assume that you can prove that this bloodstain actually is from Maria O'Conner."

"DNA analysis has demonstrated beyond a shadow of a doubt that it is," replied Lewis.

"All right, then, so what is unusual about it?"

"I am sure you are well versed in the story of how Mrs. O'Conner was injected with Chimæric stem cells. In spite of this, she died."

"The doctors from Chimæra stated that Mrs. O'Conner died because her fetus was absorbing the stem cells, preventing them from performing their therapeutic tasks. That is why they attempted to perform an abortion."

"We do not believe that is correct," stated Kavasilas. "As you know, in the East, we have proclaimed Maria O'Conner a Passion-Bearer, one who . . ."

"I thought you all called her a *yurodivyi* or something like that?" interrupted Bosch.

"That is also true, although there are some within the Orthodox community who believe she does not fit the pattern of a 'Fool for Christ.' I for one believe that a *yurodivyi*, by their very nature, defy readily definable characteristics. Besides, what could be more foolish than to risk one's own salvation for the sake of humanity?"

"Hmm. Well, I suppose. But, I still don't see the connection between her being a Passion-Bearer or *yurodivyi* and this bloodstain and how all this has to do with her dying, defeating Chimæra, or being a help to anyone else for that matter."

"The stain shows that her blood contained mostly BB blood cells, which was her blood type, but also AB blood."

"Oh, I see where you're going with this now!" exclaimed Cardinal Bosch.

Lewis was taken aback by this comment. He thought it was unusual, probably the mystery that Jimmy Lefkowitz alluded to. Perhaps it had something to do with the fact that O'Conner wasn't healed by the stem cells. But, Bosch definitely seemed to be suggesting something that

Lewis was unaware of. And it appeared to Lewis that Bosch was already hostile to the idea.

"The Shroud of Turin, and the *sudarion*,[73] both contain blood that is AB. You're suggesting that Maria and our Lord's blood were somehow miraculously united, aren't you?!"

"In the East, it is enough to say that such things are mysteries," replied Kavasilas. "But such an idea is not extraordinary. We believe that *theosis*, the participation in the divine nature, will transform not only our souls but our *garments of skin* as well."

While Kavasilas was explaining the Eastern Christian perspective of salvation, Lewis continued to observe Father Duran's expression and fascination with the small strip of paper that contained the drop of blood. Duran looked up from the 'evidence' and stared as if he were looking at someone invisible to the rest.

"First of all," protested Bosch, "how can we be sure, that this blood stain is only from Mrs. O'Conner. It is possible, after all, that two separate samples were mixed to form a single bloodstain. Secondly, you seem to be suggesting that this blood of hers, if it is indeed hers, might have some miraculous powers. But, what good is one tiny dried-up drop of blood going to do for anyone? Have there been any miracles attributed to it?"

At that moment the door behind Cardinal Bosch and Father Duran opened. A thin, grim-looking monk strode into the room followed by two attendants such as one would hardly expect to see at the Vatican. They were tall, rugged, swarthy men. One had a thick mustache that curled upward on both ends; the other a wellgroomed beard. Each wore a long black robe, a thick leather belt around the waist, and a black *kaffiyeh* as a headdress. Large, jewel-handled scimitars were secured under their belts, and a single bandolier hung over the shoulder of each. The two guards carried between them an ornately carved wooden chest about the size of a large suitcase.

Bosch and his secretary spun around in their seats and stared aghast at the trio. Bishop Kavasilas stood, walked over and embraced the monk, kissing him on both cheeks.

"What is the meaning of this?!" exclaimed Cardinal Bosch.

"Allow me to introduce to you, Father Nikitas," said Kavasilas.

"Now I recognize you," replied Bosch. "You're that Russian monk. What is this, some sort of Orthodox conspiracy?"

"For he will bring to light what is hidden in darkness and will manifest the motives of our hearts,"[74] replied Nikitas.

Bosch turned to Kavasilas, "Does he always talk like this?" he asked sarcastically. "And who are these . . . these . . . ."

"They are the Guardians of the Holy Relic," replied Nikitas. "They, and the others who are stationed outside, have been provided by King Abdullah Mohammed al-Sharif. They would rather die than let an unholy hand touch this reliquary."

Bosch stood up. "I'm going to find out what Vatican official authorized this intrusion by this mad monk and his heathen henchmen!"

As Bosch walked towards the door another Guardian appeared blocking the doorway. This formidable Guardian stood stoically with his muscular arms folded across his chest.

"Have a seat, Cardinal. It was the Holy Father who authorized our being here with you. He wants two issues irrevocably settled, the canonization of Maria O'Conner. The other I have already explained."

"I don't see how *this* can settle anything," said Bosch, pointing to the reliquary chest while taking his seat again.

"I believe there was a question about the authenticity of the bloodstain," said Father Nikitas.

Kavasilas, Lewis, and Ryan exchanged glances. How did Nikitas know about the bloodstain? They hadn't discussed it with anyone. Perhaps he had overhead the discussion from outside the room.

"And, I believe, that I can demonstrate the miraculous power of the blood."

Nikitas motioned to the two Guardians to set the chest on the table. They put it down so that the front of the chest could be seen by everyone seated around the table. As Nikitas approached the chest he removed a key from around his neck. He inserted it into the base of the chest. A metallic mechanism clicked; this was followed by the sliding of a heavy cylinder. There was complete silence in the room, all leaned forward in anticipation. Father Duran pushed himself slightly away from the table, distancing himself from the chest. Nikitas grasped the handle in the front of the chest and pulled upward. The double-hinged door opened, revealing an inner glass and brass cabinet. Everyone stared in amazement.

"It's . . . it's . . . Maria's arm!" Ryan finally gasped.

In the glass cabinet, lying on a purple velvet cushion and secured by ropes of silk, was the incorrupt forearm and hand of Maria Theresa O'Conner; the limb that had been lost in the Hotel Metropol on the day that Goricsan reestablished the Czarist monarchy in Russia. The hand bore a wound, the stigmata of Christ. Under the hand was placed a crystal flask. Blood slowly dripped from the stigmata into the flask; approximately half a centimeter of blood covered the bottom of the vessel.

Cardinal Bosch, Bishop Kavasilas, Milton Lewis, and Madison Ryan were all standing, still staring at the arm. Kavasilas made a profound bow and crossed himself. Ryan held her hand over her mouth heedless of the tears that streamed down her cheeks. Lewis, stunned, his skepticism vanquished by the miracle before him, believed. Cardinal Bosch looked back and forth from the arm to Nikitas trying to find words, but said nothing. Father Duran retreated towards the door.

"You may analyze the blood if you wish," Nikitas said to Cardinal Bosch. "You will find that it matches the blood stain. But, this may not be enough to persuade you. And now is not the time for persuasion, but a demonstration of spirit and power!"[75]

Nikitas unlatched one of the sides of the glass cabinet. He reached his hand into the cabinet, and dipped his right index finger into the crystal flask. He spun around and lunged at Father Duran who was nearly out the door. Nikitas' finger touched the forehead of the priest anointing him with Maria's blood. Immediately Father Duran shrieked horribly. Steam rose from the spot of blood on his forehead. The smell of burnt and decaying flesh filled the room. Duran, or the being that now occupied his body, started cursing with a hollow, demonic voice. Everyone stood back in horror as the creature, now exposed by the blood, writhed in agony. Nikitas reached over and pulled a scimitar from the belt of one of the Guardians. Bosch raised his hand anticipating

Nikitas' action. Too late. Nikitas swung the blade decapitating the host body of the demon. The head fell to the ground smoking and sputtering like a steam-powered top. It finally came to rest. The flesh was so burnt and blistered that it was no longer recognizable as Father Duran. It continued to hiss and give off a horrific stench.

"My God! What the hell was it?" exclaimed Cardinal Bosch.

"A nephilim," replied Nikitas.

Ryan clung to Lewis trembling. Lewis, having been a DC policeman for forty years, had thought he had seen everything. He had just witnessed a gruesome killing, yet he was not prepared to call it murder. The creature that had just been executed was not human or at least it was no longer human. Lewis was not sure what to think.

"A nephilim?!," inquired Bishop Kavasilas. "Isn't that what Bishop Entremont was calling Chimærics?"

"Yes, but he is a false prophet," replied Nikitas as he wiped the scimitar's blade on the cassock of the dead cleric. "But a prophet none the less," he continued while handing the scimitar back to the Guardian who then slipped it back under his belt. "He has unwittingly become Obermann's Balaam. He correctly prophesied the return of the nephilim. But, their return is far more devious than even he imagined."

"How can this be?" asked Ryan.

"Frederick is recreating the race of nephilim, but there is no time for explanations now," said Nikitas as he removed the crystal flask from the reliquary. "Now that they know about the holy relic and the power of the blood, they will stop at nothing to capture it or destroy it."

"But how can they know?" asked Lewis.

"A nephilim is an incarnate demon. And he can communicate with his fellow fallen angels who are always around him and protect him. In the realm of spirit, messages are sent faster than if they traveled on a beam of light! Obermann and Frederick already know everything. There are undoubtedly many nephilim that have been stationed here in Rome. We must leave without delay. But before we do, I must anoint you with a drop of this blood."

Nikitas proceeded to dip his forefinger into the blood and to make a sign of the cross on Kavasilas' forehead with it. He then turned to anoint Bosch.

"No," said Bosch. "I'm not going to let you put that stuff on me. I don't even know what the hell is going on here."

"Fear is useless," answered Nikitas. "What is needed is trust. The blood has the power to protect you."

Bosch shook his head.

"Very well," said Nikitas who then continued to anoint the others. "No one who has been anointed by the blood can be transformed into a Chimæric unless they desire it. It has the power to release the souls of Chimærics from their *garments of skin*, but they must lay their life down at the moment of anointing. It cannot, however, prevent a body from being resubstantiated either with the soul of a Chimæric or a demon spirit."

Nikitas placed the crystal flask back into the reliquary and secured it. He then closed the chamber and locked the chest. The two Guardians picked up the chest. "If any one of us is captured," Nikitas continued, "we must not allow our bodies to become hosts for the nephilim. If two are together one must decapitate the other, then the one remaining must decapitate himself."

Kavasilas, Lewis and Ryan stared at one another incredulously. Finally, Ryan spoke, "I . . . I . . . I don't think I can do that."

"Then remain close to a Guardian," replied Nikitas. "He will assist you."

Nikitas walked over to the door, opened it and said something in Arabic. Two additional Guardians stepped into the room.

"Like cockroaches, the nephilim have hidden in the recesses of the Vatican," said Nikitas. "Even I did not anticipate such an infestation. The Holy Father is no longer safe here." Nikitas turned to Bosch. "Where would the Holy Father be now?"

"I suspect he is at his residence," replied Bosch.

"We arrived earlier this morning by helicopter. I will call for the helicopter to pick us up. It may be too dangerous to travel all the way to the heliport from here."

"Do you really think that they could mobilize that quickly?" asked Lewis.

"There have been rumors of the Holy Relic. I suspect that they have made plans to acquire it should it arrive in Rome."

"If you suspected this," said Kavasilas, "then why did you risk bringing it here?"

"Because the Holy Father requested it," replied Nikitas. "And it is necessary that we force the enemy into action. But enough, we will discuss this later. Go to the Holy Father," he said to Bosch.

"Me?! You want me to go?!"

"A Guardian will accompany you," continued Nikitas. "Tell him that he must leave with us. I noticed there was a clearing sufficient enough for the helicopter to land just south of this building. Meet us there."

"Only one Guardian?" asked Bosch. "But suppose it's dangerous?"

"Maybe I can help," said Lewis. "I've been known to be able to handle myself pretty well in a pinch."

Nikitas nodded.

Ryan grabbed his arm. "Are you sure?"

"I'll be fine," Lewis assured her. "Do you have a gun I could borrow?" Lewis asked the Guardian who would be accompanying them.

The Guardian started to hand Lewis his rifle.

"I'd rather have a pistol."

The Guardian reached under his black robes, removed a 9 mm automatic and handed it to Lewis. Lewis examined it. He smiled. It was a Mokorov. It seemed fitting. His introduction to this whole affair had started with an investigation of a killing that involved a Mokorov. He had a premonition that it very well might end with a Mokorov. He released the safety and snapped back on the bolt, loading a bullet in the chamber.

"Let's lock and load, Cardinal," said Lewis.

As Lewis, Bosch, and the Guardian sped down the hall, they heard Father Nikitas exhort, "Stay near your Guardian!" Lewis did not find that reassuring.

Nikitas pulled out a communicator from under his robes. He spoke to the pilot of the helicopter in Russian, instructing him where and when to land to pick them up.

A few minutes later Ryan heard the sound of the helicopter. She looked out the window and saw the helicopter begin its descent onto the *Largo Isqaurel Santo Stefano*. Ryan immediately knew that this was no ordinary transport. She had seen helicopters like this in action in Moscow during the coup almost five years earlier. This was the latest version of the Ka-57-3 Erdogan Black Shark, a joint venture of the Great Alliance.

"You were obviously expecting trouble," said Ryan.

"Yes," replied Nikitas. "Shall we go?"

The Guardians picked up the chest and followed Nikitas out of the room. Ryan was happy to leave the room that still reeked of sulfur and seared flesh. Kavasilas and Ryan followed as Nikitas led the Guardians through the long south corridor and down the stairs. They encountered very few people as they headed towards the rendezvous point. Indeed, the ease which they made their way towards the helicopter, which had now landed, was disconcerting to Nikitas. He had anticipated some resistance. This was all too easy. As they approached the helicopter, there was no sign of Bosch, Lewis, the Guardian or the Holy Father. They should be here by now, thought Nikitas. He approached the helicopter door, turned the handle, and slid open the door.

"*Bon jour*, Father Nikitas. I have been expecting you."

Nikitas gave Bishop Entremont a fierce gaze, but said nothing. The Guardians behind him withdrew their swords and pistols.

"Tell your Arab friends to relax," said Entremont. "As you can see, I am alone. Step in, I have a proposal that I think you will want to consider."

*   *   *

Bosch, Lewis, and the Guardian exited the Government Palace and then crossed through a thick grove of trees that lined the path to the papal residence. Although they did this without incident, Bosch did note with some apprehension that the usually bustling Vatican seemed uncharacteristically quiet. They arrived at the entrance of the papal residence; two Swiss Guards were stationed in front of the doors.

"I am Cardinal Bosch. We are here to see the Holy Father."

"I'm sorry," replied one of the Guardsmen. "The Holy Father is not receiving any visitors today."

"But it is of the utmost urgency that we speak with him," protested Bosch.

"Let me call my superior," replied the Guardsman. He started to reach down for his radio but then grabbed a concealed pistol instead.

Lewis saw the action of the Guardsman. He reached down to pull his pistol from under his belt—too late. The Guardsman raised his pistol and fired several shots at Lewis. Lewis stumbled back expecting to be shot. Instead, the bullets exploded in bright yellow-orange flashes in front of him. The Guardian stepped forward and decapitated the Guardsman. Lewis collected himself enough to fire off a couple of rounds at the remaining Swiss Guard. The bullets never reached the Guard but exploded in front of him. The Guard was beginning to withdraw his ceremonial sword when the Guardian spun around and struck his arm off. The Guard howled, but was silenced by another blow by the Guardian.

"What the hell just happened?" asked Lewis stunned.

"They were *majnun*, like the priest," answered the Guardian.

"You mean those neph' things that Nikitas was talking about?"

"Yes. They are protected by the *jinn*. Only the force of the human will uninterrupted by space and time can penetrate their *jinn* protection."

"Bullets can't hurt them?" asked Lewis.

"That is right," replied the Guardian as he removed a sword from the belt of one of the Swiss Guards.

"But what about me? The bullets exploded before they hit me? I'm not maj . . . neph . . . or what ever the hell those things are?"

"The blood from the Holy Relic imparts angelic protection. Here," said the Guardian handing Lewis the sword, "this will be effective against the *majnun*."

"I don't know how to use this," he was about to say, but Bosch had reached for the door and opened it."

"No, wait!" shouted the Guardian.

A hail of bullets greeted Bosch as he opened the door and he was flung back by the multiple impacts. He was dead before he hit the ground.

"Ready?" asked the Guardian.

"You're not serious?!" asked Lewis.

"It is a good day to die," replied the Guardian. He than ran through the door shouting, *"Allahu Akhbah!"*

"Ah Jesus!" exclaimed Lewis fervently as he followed the Guardian.

*　　*　　*

Father Nikitas stepped into the helicopter. Kavasilas, Ryan, and the Guardians remained just outside.

Bishop Entremont extended his hand to Father Nikitas. Nikitas saw that Entremont was wearing the Holy Father's ring, the symbol of his Apostolic authority.

"There has been, how shall we say, an Apostolic succession," said Entremont, continuing to extend his hand to Nikitas, "I am now the Vicar of Christ." Nikitas refused to kiss the ring.

"I thought that would be your response," Entremont said, pulling back his hand. "No matter. A pope is pope for life. Mine will be the longest papal reign in history."

"You are a Chimæric?"

"Yes," replied Entremont. "A lifetime of ascetic practice." Entremont shook his head. "Do you know that in my youth I would flagellate myself? I steeled myself against all impure thoughts. And if one should slip through, I would whip myself until I bled. I used to have scars on my back, mementoes of my former righteousness. They're gone now, Chimæric stem cells, you know. One damn momentary indiscretion! The very thing I had set myself to fight against has befallen me. And now the Beast, Obermann, believes he owns me. The papacy for the relic—that is what he offered me. Surprised? Yes, we suspected that it existed. There were rumors of the relic. It took months of planning."

"I suspected," said Nikitas.

"What do you mean, you suspected?! There is no way you could have known. And even if you did, why would you risk bringing the relic here?"

"Isn't it obvious? If you, of all people, can succumb to temptation, then no flesh will be left untainted by Chimæra. But, the blood of the relic has the power to release you. It is not too late for you, Entremont."

"Ah yes, I thought you might make me that offer. I have heard the stories of Queen Miriam, King Abdullah's mother. No, I'm afraid not. I still have much to accomplish. Obermann may think that he owns me, but he does not. My will is still my own."

"And that is precisely why you have fallen prey to the Evil One."

"Enough of this. Now that I am Pope, I am infallible. I am no man's prey. And to prove it to you I am allowing you, your company, and your holy relic to escape."

Entremont was disappointed that Nikitas did not demonstrate surprise at his announcement. So he continued, hoping to impress Nikitas with his independence and cleverness.

"You see, Obermann's power is diminished so long as you retain the relic. That makes my position as head of the Church more secure."

"And should he find out that you double-crossed him?" asked Nikitas.

"That is why I am talking with you alone. We don't need the listening ears of nephilim around, do we? And I trust you will not speak of it."

"Since you are being so bold as to defy Obermann, why not let me take the Holy Father back to Russia with me?"

"I cannot appear to be that incompetent to Obermann. He wants the Pope dead. For that matter, so do I. I can't say that I appreciated his excommunicating me. I declared him a heretic."

Entremont rubbed his chin looking thoughtful, then mused to himself, "I could bring back the Inquisition. Perhaps I'll have him burnt at the stake."

Entremont refocused his attention on Nikitas. "Oh, don't worry. He'll die of natural causes—maybe today or tomorrow. But, now it's time for me to go. It wouldn't be fitting for me to be seen with you. Nephilim might talk. You should leave immediately."

Nikitas glanced over his shoulder at the Papal residence. There was no sign of Bosch, Lewis, or the Guardian.

Entremont stood up, opened the door to the helicopter and stepped out. Kavasilas, Ryan, and the Guardians were waiting outside.

"You must leave immediately," said Entremont.

The Guardians loaded the chest onto the helicopter. They then helped Kavasilas and Ryan on board.

"What about the others?" asked Ryan, leaning out of the helicopter.

"They are dead by now, and if you don't leave immediately you will be too," said Entremont.

At that moment, the doors of the papal residence burst open. Lewis and the Guardian were running with the Holy Father between them. They were both struggling to support the Pope. Lewis and the Guardian appeared badly wounded.

The helicopter was approximately a hundred yards from the residence. Bishop Kavasilas jumped out immediately and ran towards them. One of the Guardians jumped off the helicopter and quickly passed him. He had almost reached them when suddenly, nephilim carrying guns and other weapons burst out of the *Piazza Santa Maria* and the Palace of the Tribunal.

"Sit down and strap yourself in," ordered Nikitas to Ryan.

"But . . . ," began Ryan.

Other nephilim appeared and were now charging the helicopter, firing weapons. Nikitas slammed the door shut; bullets ricocheted off the door and all the sides of the helicopter.

"Go!" Nikitas shouted to the pilot.

The pilot started the engine. The blades whirled faster and faster. Ryan peered out the window. As the helicopter began to rise, she pressed her hands against the window as if she could pluck her friends to safety. As the helicopter move away, Ryan watched the horde of nephilim close in on those left behind.

"No!" she cried pounding on the window again and again

Nikitas pulled her away from the window and held her to his chest.

"Oh God! Why? Why?" she whimpered.

Nikitas began to recite from the liturgy for the dead, "In the place of rest which is Yours, O Lord, where all your saints repose, give rest to the souls of your servants for You alone love mankind."

*   *   *

"They have escaped, father."

"What?!," exclaimed Obermann. "Entremont is an incompetent bastard! You heard that didn't you, O'Ryan?"

"Yes," replied the President.

Obermann and Frederick were monitoring the progress of their Vatican coup and the acquisition of the "relic," from Chimæra headquarters in Massachusetts. They were video conferencing with the President at the White House who was accompanied by members of the Joint Chiefs, Security Council, and Colin O'Conner.

"Are you tracking them?" asked Obermann.

"Yes," replied General Barkley. "They are flying southeast."

"Where do you think they're going?" asked Obermann.

"They will be over the Tyrrhenian Sea in a few minutes," replied the General, "unless they change course."

"Where the hell is that?" asked O'Ryan.

"It is the body of water bounded by Italy, Sicily and Sardinia," replied Frederick. "Jeez, I thought you needed to know some geography to be President." he said to his father.

Obermann rolled his eyes. "Are there ships in the vicinity?"

"No," replied General Barkley. "At least nothing that would accommodate a Ka-57-3."

"Then where could they be going?" asked the President.

"Don't know. What's the range of a Black Shark?" the General asked his aide.

The aide typed into his laptop and had the Black Shark's specifications in seconds. "About 450 km, assuming a full fuel tank," said the aide.

"Not at the rate they're traveling. We're clocking them at 425 kilometers per hour. I figure they have at most a 300-kilometer range. We have no evidence they refueled in Vatican City."

"They'll never reach land," said Obermann who had pulled up a map on his computer. "They'll ditch into the sea. There has to be a ship out there somewhere. When will our NATO planes intercept them?"

"In just a few minutes," replied the General.

"You can communicate with the Black Shark, can't you?" asked Obermann.

"Yes. We have tried this already. They are not responding."

"Can you patch me through?" asked Obermann.

The general turned to his aide. The aide nodded.

"Can do," said the General. "By the time you're connected our planes will have intercepted them."

"They have a radar lock on us," said the pilot of the Black Shark.

"You have your coordinates," said Nikitas.

"I have radar lock on them," said the copilot.

"Send them a message," replied Nikitas.

The artillery specialist fired the air-to-air missile from the helicopter.

"Son-of-a-bitch!" said General Barkley. "They just fired at one of our fighters!"

"Do they want to start a war?" exclaimed the President.

"Blow the bastards out of the sky!" exclaimed the General.

"No!" shouted Obermann. "I give the orders!"

"That's exactly what he wants to do," said Frederick. "He wants to start a war. Cut the time short."

"He may give us no choice," said Obermann. "Am I patched in, yet?"

"Yes," replied the aide.

"Nikitas, we got your message," said Obermann. "You can't possibly get away. We have too many fighters on your tail. But, I'll make you a deal. All we need is a sample of blood so that we can prepare an antidote for the blood plague. Turn around, land at the nearest airport. Leave us a sample. I promise you safe passage back to Russia."

"They just fired another missile at one of our jets," said General Barkley. "I think they just gave us their answer."

"Damn it, Nikitas," said Obermann. "You're giving us no choice!"

"Mr. President," said the Chief of Staff who had just stepped into the Oval Office, "The Russian Ambassador just called. He wanted me to convey to you that the Alliance is ready to respond with all the means at its disposal should NATO take any hostile actions against Alliance personnel or property."

"Shit! Are they mad?!" exclaimed the President. "They can't possibly be serious. Do they expect us to believe they'd go to war over some damn bloody arm?"

"They are deadly serious," said Obermann. "And so am I."

"Remember, Father. Time is on our side. Don't let your hatred for Maria O'Conner cloud your judgment."

"Hatred! You have no idea! That bitch strikes at me from the grave. Well, damn her again! General?"

"Yes, Mr. Obermann?"

"Blow them to hell!"

"Gladly!"

"Wait a minute!" exclaimed the President.

"Do it, damn it!" exclaimed Obermann.

The General conveyed Obermann's orders.

"Incoming missiles!" exclaimed the pilot.

Both of the Black Shark's 2A-42 quick-firing 30 mm guns automatically began firing at the incoming missiles. The pilot dove towards the sea.

Bam!

One of the missiles exploded before it could strike the helicopter. Another continued towards the helicopter. The pilot made a last-second maneuver. No use, the missile was on them. Then, at the last possible moment, the missile inexplicably missed its target and slammed into the ocean.

"What the . . . ?" exclaimed the pilot.

Nikitas pulled out a medallion from under his robe—the icon of Saint Michael, the warrior angel. He made the sign of the cross while holding the medallion and began to pray silently.

"We cannot outrun them!" said the copilot.

"Stay on course," reassured Nikitas. "Do not lose heart for the battle is not yours but God's."[76]

Several more missiles were launched towards the Black Shark. One by one they missed their target at the last possible moment.

"The missiles keep missing their target," the General informed Obermann. "I don't understand it."

Obermann turned to his son questioningly.

"Angelic protection," answered Frederick. "The incorporeals are resisting but . . . ."

"Barkley, tell your pilots to crash their planes into the helicopter!" ordered Obermann.

"What?!" exclaimed the General. "You mean like kamikazes? Are you mad?"

"Do it!" demanded Obermann.

"Mr. President?" inquired the General.

"Go ahead," replied the President. "Have the pilots eject just before . . . ."

"No," interrupted Frederick. "They must stay with their planes."

"You heard him, General. Give the order!" said Obermann.

"I can't ask these men to commit suicide!" replied the General.

Obermann turned to Frederick. *Are any of the pilots Chimærics?* he thought.

Frederick closed his eyes momentarily as he communicated with incorporeals. *Yes. Armstrong and Nevard.*

"Let me speak with Armstrong and Nevard," Obermann told the General.

Barkley was surprised that Obermann would know the names of the pilots. He told his aide to make the connection so that Obermann could speak with the pilots. "Go ahead, Mr. Obermann."

"Armstrong and Nevard, can you hear me?" asked Obermann.

"Yes," they replied. "Who is this?" asked Armstrong.

"This is Hans Obermann." Obermann used the connection to

press his psyche into the pilots. "I need you to do my son and me a favor."

"Yes sir?" replied Nevard.

"We need you to crash your planes into the helicopter. You may not eject. You will die. Do you understand?"

"You want us to do what?" exclaimed Armstrong incredulously.

"I understand," replied Nevard.

Nevard has been converted, Frederick informed his father.

Immediately, Nevard's fighter broke formation and dove towards the helicopter.

"Nevard! What are you doing?" shouted Armstrong. Nevard did not respond but continued to plunge towards the helicopter.

"One of the fighters is heading straight for us!" shouted the Black Hawk pilot.

"Evade him!" ordered Nikitas.

The pilot dove his plane closer to the ocean. The fighter stayed on his tail. The helicopter pulled up and starboard. The fighter countered. It was seconds away from the helicopter.

"*Govno!* I can't lose him," shouted the pilot.

Phush! Phush!

Streaks of light emerged from the waters underneath the Black Shark. Within seconds the fighter exploded.

Phush, Phush.

Two more fighters exploded. The remaining fighters began to pull back.

Nikitas peered out the helicopter window. He pointed down towards the waters below.

"There," he shouted to the pilot.

Ryan, who had her head buried in her knees, straightened up and looked out the window. The water beneath them was foaming. In the midst of the foam, the hull of a submarine broke the surface of the sea.

"Damn!" exclaimed General Barkley. "A sub just surfaced! We have a visual on it from satellite surveillance. We can target it."

"Don't bother! They won't work. Mr. President, you must order the pilots to crash their planes into the submarine," demanded Obermann.

"Shit! Are you guys crazy," said O'Ryan. "It's one thing to shoot down a helicopter, if we sink a sub, damn it, that's an act of war!"

"General," interrupted the aide, "look at these pictures we're getting from the satellite. This may be the secret Novgrod-2 submarine. Look at the size of it! And yet we had no knowledge of its location. That's state-of-the-art stealth technology. Not only that, look at all the foam around it."

"We're wasting time," said Barkley. "The helicopter is beginning to descend onto the sub's deck."

"Let him finish," said the President. "Make it quick."

"We've known for some time," continued the aide, "that the Russians have been working on supercavitation . . . ."

"What's that?" asked the President.

"What the hell difference does it make?!" interjected Obermann. "Give the order."

"Father, listen," said Frederick, placing his hand on his father's shoulder.

"Supercavitation places a bubble around the ship. It's like an underwater warp drive. Most subs are lucky to reach 35 knots. A sub employing supercavitation could theoretically reach speeds of nearly 200 knots. A fleet of supercavitating submarines armed with intercontinental ballistic missiles could change the balance of power."

"General," said the President, "Tell our fighters to stand down!"

"Balance of power?!," exclaimed Obermann. "The balance of power is shifting away from technology to the realm of spirit. This is now a battle between principalities and powers in a cosmic struggle for domination. We need that blood. And if we can't have it, then they must not have it either. Whatever the cost!"

Obermann looked into the monitor at the General. With all the force of his concentration he drove his psyche into the consciousness of the General. The General watched on his computer screen the images being sent by the satellite. The Black Shark had landed on the deck of the submarine.

"If we don't act now," said the General. "They'll dive back into the sea and we'll lose them."

"Give the order, General," demanded Obermann with his force of will acting on the General's weakened Chimæric consciousness, "Do it!"

The General was wavering between Obermann and his loyalty to the President.

"Excuse me, Mr. Obermann," said a voice on the intercom. It was Obermann's personal secretary. "I have a gentleman out here who says he has an urgent message to convey to you."

Obermann looked incredulously at Frederick. "Urgent?!" exclaimed Obermann. "Urgent?! I'm trying to start World War III and you're telling me that someone has something urgent to tell me?!"

"I'm sorry, Mr. Obermann," apologized Miss Hayes. "But he said he knows the whereabouts of your daughter."

"What?!" exclaimed Obermann. "I don't have a daughter. Have the son-of-a-bitch thrown out of the building."

"I'm sorry for the interruption," said Obermann as he turned back to the monitor.

Everyone in the Oval Office looked at each other perplexed by the absurdity of the conversation they had just heard over the phone.

"General," said Obermann. "Strike now before . . . ."

Obermann's office door burst in. A disheveled, unshaven man with straggly unkempt hair stumbled into the room.

"I am Officer Ernesto Aguilar," said the man recovering his balance. He continued towards them limping. "I was assigned by my government to assist Alexi Zokoroff in the apprehension of a baby girl."

Obermann and Frederick jumped out of their seats. They stared at the man speechless.

"I thought that the child might be your daughter. I guess I was mistaken. I do believe, however, she may still be of interest to you."

"She is alive?"

"Mr. Obermann," interrupted the General. "The submarine is beginning to dive. We will lose her if . . . ."

"Yes," replied Aguilar.

"Let the sub go," said Obermann.

The President leaned back into his chair and placed his hand on his forehead. "Thank God," he muttered.

Colin, who had been nervously sitting and observing everything that had transpired over the past few minutes, was stunned. Alive? he thought. Theresa is alive? He was about to say something when the connection between the Oval Office and Obermann was cut off.

"We received evidence that she was dead," said Obermann.

"An arm," said Aguilar.

"That's right."

"She has grown it back."

"Really?! Is there anything else remarkable about the child?" asked Frederick.

"Yes," replied Aguilar. "I have read that you are three-and-a-half years old."

"That is correct. I matured quickly."

"So has *Ch'ucha'*."

"*Ch'ucha'*?" asked Obermann.

"That is the name that was given her," answered Aguilar.

Frederick and Obermann looked at each other. They each knew what the other was thinking. *Just how similar were they? Did she also possess powers that could be comparable to his? Perhaps her blood . . . .* thought Frederick. *Yes,* thought Obermann. *It might be enough like her mother's to be used for a cure.*

"What else have you observed about her?" asked Obermann.

"Animals seem to have a peculiar attraction to her. I've seen her do some tricks. A ball can be thrown away from her, and then it appears to change direction and go to her."

Telekinesis? thought Obermann.

Angelic synergy, replied Frederick.

"Why have you not come to us before?" asked Obermann.

"I was being held prisoner."

"By whom?" asked Frederick.

"By the people who killed Zokoroff, who gave me this," Aguilar lifted his pant leg and showed his wooden prosthesis, "and who are protecting the child."

"And who are these people?" asked Obermann. "And where are they?"

"Well now, I have suffered greatly, as you can see. My escape was harrowing."

"You will be adequately compensated," said Obermann.

"I don't want money. I want revenge! Revenge and power!"

Obermann turned away and walked towards his desk. He could appreciate a man who knew what he wanted; who wasn't inhibited by an antiquated ethic from grasping at the things that gave life a sense of meaning. Revenge and power—these were, after all, the motives of the Master.

"Can you be," asked Obermann, facing Aguilar, "more precise?"

"Provide me with sufficient men and equipment and I will bring you back the child."

"Alive," said Frederick.

"I would prefer bringing you the little bitch in a body bag."

"She is more useful to us alive," said Obermann. "If it concerns you, however, I can assure you that her life with us would be most unpleasant. Draining her blood and performing experiments on her . . . I trust that would satisfy your need for revenge."

"Not entirely," replied Aguilar. "I want the entire village massacred and all the indigenous people from the surrounding territory exterminated."

These people had deceived me, thought Obermann. Extermination seemed like an appropriate punishment. "Very well," said Obermann, nodding slowly. "We can provide you with sufficient forces to accomplish your mission. Special Forces will oversee . . . ."

"No," said Aguilar. "I will oversee. I know what their plans are. I have been with them for nearly four years. I know their ways. They are clever. And they have remarkable leadership in Mateas Valdez and Ludmelia Nizhniya."

"Ludmelia Nizhniya?!" asked Obermann. "I had heard that she was on your heels."

"If it wasn't for her, Zokoroff and I would have escaped and delivered the child to you. She has been the child's mother these past three and a half years. And she has committed herself to teaching the child the art of war. But the child doesn't listen. She fancies herself a great weaver of the garments that these stupid Mayans wear."

Obermann and Frederick looked at each other again. *Knowledge and power,* thought Obermann, *She could be a significant threat. She might need to be killed. We can extract blood from her body.*

Frederick shook his head. *Send me, Father. Aguilar said she hasn't listened. Besides, she cannot possess the powers that I have.*

Perhaps, thought Obermann. *But, if there is angelic synergy . . . we must be cautious."* Obermann detected a slight hesitation in his son when he had thought about the possibility of having to kill Theresa, or *Ch'ucha'* as she was now known. He sensed a familial bond between them.

"I will make the arrangements for you to lead a military force, sufficient for you to carry out what we have discussed," said Obermann.

"We must do it quickly," said Aguilar. "They will be returning to the village today. They will find that I have escaped. Valdez and Nizhniya will make preparations. She may even attempt to flee with the child."

"We cannot allow the child to escape us again." Obermann opened the doors of his office. "Miss Hayes, see that Officer Aguilar gets whatever he needs."

Aguilar slowly walked to the door. Obermann put his arm around his shoulder. "We can take care of that leg of yours when you get back. Get cleaned up. Eat. You have two hours to do whatever else you might want to do. Then we will meet again."

"We haven't discussed my reward," said Aguilar.

"Revenge is its own reward," said Obermann. "However, how about the Presidency of Mexico."

"That will do," said Aguilar, stepping out of Obermann's office. Aguilar remembered a conversation he had had four years earlier with Zokoroff. Yes, thought Aguilar, I will be Mexico's Stalin. I will deal with the indigenous problem once and for all.

Obermann closed the door to his office.

"Revenge and power may give us access to his consciousness," said Frederick, "and you can provide him with men and firepower; but I should be there just in case."

"No," said his father.

"I can take care of myself," said Frederick.

"Of course you can. But first, you must know your enemy. There are some things that I have not told you about this child or her mother. If things go badly with Aguilar, you may have to finish the job. You may find in this information her Achilles heel."

"Surely father, you overestimate this *girl*!"

"If I have learned anything, it is not to underestimate the enmity of the woman; neither will I underestimate her seed."

*   *   *

The door of the helicopter swung open. The cool, moist sea air rushed into the helicopter. A tall, ruggedly handsome man wearing a heavy-wool Russian sailor's jacket stood in front of the opening. He pushed his damp hair back with one hand while extending his arm out to those in the helicopter.

"Hurry!" the man shouted. "We must be underway!"

Nikitas pushed Ryan forward. The man grasped her hand and helped her onto the deck of the submarine as she jumped off the helicopter. Ryan slipped on the wet deck and nearly fell. She was afraid that the blast of wind from the helicopter's blades might sweep her off the deck and into the ocean. But, the man kept a firm grip on her arm and pulled her to her feet. She got a better look at him now. Ryan recognized him—it was Czar Goricsan. It was now that she noticed the young man standing next to the Czar. He had a swarthy complexion, and he wore a serious countenance as if he had already lived a lifetime of trouble. He looked familiar. He was now helping Nikitas out of the helicopter.

"Take her below," Goricsan shouted to one of the sailors.

One of the sailors put his arm around her and led her to the Conning Tower. She struggled up the stairs. It was now, for the first time, that Ryan realized how exhausted she was. She struggled up the fifteen-foot ladder to the top of the tower. When she reached the top of the ladder, she stepped down onto the Conning deck. The sailor directed Ryan towards the hatch, which was located near the center of the tower. Ryan turned around and looked down at the deck below. The young man was leading Nikitas and the Guardian who were carrying the Reliquary Chest. The Czar was leaning inside the helicopter. He then slammed the helicopter door, gave the pilot thumbs up, and then ran to join the others. The helicopter's rotors began to roar; it did not take off until Goricsan had joined the others. As she watched the men race towards the tower, she thought of her friends, Lewis and Kavasilas, who were not with them.

"We must go below," said the sailor pulling Ryan's arm and directing her towards the hatch. Ryan nodded passively still thinking about her fallen comrades. She climbed down a few rungs, stepped through an oblong shaped doorway, and into the helm of the submarine. There were about ten sailors sitting or standing at their post monitoring gauges, and performing a variety of activities.

"This way," the sailor said. "The others will join you in the Captain's Stateroom."

Ryan followed the sailor through several more oblong doorways. They arrived at the Stateroom, and the sailor motioned with his arm for Ryan to enter. The room was a stark contrast to the rest of the ship, which was cold, gray and metallic with pipes and cables running the length of every corridor. The Stateroom was paneled with teak and was decorated with photographs, schematics, and maps. Two men who had been seated at the table in the center of the room stood. One was dressed in an officer's uniform.

"Welcome aboard! I am Vladislav Glivijsky, Captain of the Novgrod. Miss Ryan, I believe?"

There was a momentary pause as Ryan attempted to collect herself. She tried to speak, but the words were not forming. The room grew dark and began to spin around . . . .

"What happened?" asked Ryan who now found herself seated in one of the chairs that had been pushed away from the conference table. The man who had been seated with the Captain when she had entered the room now leaned over her. He held a cool, damp cloth against her forehead.

"You passed out," said the Captain. "Fortunately, Mr. Sagalovich caught you before you fell. You might have hurt yourself."

"Thank you," Ryan said.

Sagalovich smiled and nodded. "Given the harrowing experience you've just been through, Miss Ryan, I think it's quite understandable. I am sorry for the loss of your friends."

"As we all are," said Goricsan entering the Stateroom. He was followed by Nikitas and the Guardian who were carrying the Reliquary Chest which they placed on the table. The young man Ryan had seen on the deck with Goricsan now stepped into the room and stood next to the Czar. He now wore a *kaffiyeh*. Ryan recognized the young man as King Abdullah Mohammed al-Sharif.

"I see you have already met our Captain and Mr. Sagalovich who, it would seem, has a knack at being at the right place at the right time . . . again," said Goricsan noting the uncharacteristic display of attention Sagalovich was directing at Miss Ryan.

Ryan smiled. Sagalovich shrugged as if it were just another day in the service of the Czar.

Nikitas noted Sagalovich's attempt at bravado and raised one of his eyebrows in mild consternation knowing that far greater troubles lay ahead of them. "Indeed, Mr. Sagalovich is quite indispensable," said Nikitas with just a touch of irony. "In fact, we'll need you to contact some of your old friends in Guatemala."

Goricsan looked curiously at Nikitas.

"Captain, you must set a course for the Gulf of Honduras," Nikitas said and then turning to Goricsan and Abdullah he continued, "We must be in Guatemala as quickly as possible."

"But Captain Eliav will be expecting us in Saint Petersburg," said Goricsan. "Remember, you said you wanted another meeting with the three of us."

"There is another who must join you."

Ryan sat up in her chair. She had the sense that Nikitas was about to reveal something extraordinary. Sagalovich looked at her curiously. He had no idea what was going on. In fact, up until a moment ago, he had had no idea why he was asked to come along. Not that he minded getting a break from Siberia and the General.

"Who is in Guatemala that must join us?" asked Goricsan furrowing his brow at Nikitas. Goricsan respected Father Nikitas' spiritual authority and insight, but he did not appreciate the riddles and being kept in the dark about important matters.

Nikitas recognized Goricsan's irritation, smiled and placed a hand on his shoulder. "Actually you will be going to Chiapas, Mexico," said Nikitas. "There, you will find your Czarina."

Goricsan looked at Nikitas in wonder. Could it be? It was beyond hope. He dare not even speak it. He leaned against the chair in front of him to brace himself.

"Ludmelia Nizhniya lives," said Nikitas. "And so does *the child.*"

"Theresa?!" exclaimed Ryan.

"Yes," replied Nikitas. "The Daughter of Abraham is ready to join her brothers. But we must make haste. The Great Red Dragon will attempt to devour them again."

The Second Woe

Then I looked again and heard an eagle flying high overhead cry out in a loud voice, "Woe! Woe! Woe to the inhabitants of the earth from the rest of the trumpet blasts that the three angels are about to blow!"
-Revelation 8:13

Mateas, Nizhniya, and *Ch'ucha'* were all squeezed into the cab of the old truck. *Ch'ucha'* sat in the middle with her legs straddling the gearshift. In spite of the discomfort of having been nearly immobile for four and a half hours, she was convinced that nothing could diminish the joy and sense of accomplishment she had experienced over the past several days. Her *huipiles* had been judged the best displayed at the festival. *El Presidente*, himself, had praised her work and had bought several *huipiles* to give to his daughters. The greatest honor was when the old weavers had inspected her work. They could hardly believe that the *huipiles* were the work of such a young artisan.

"Surely, someone older and more experienced wove these garments," one old woman had said.

"But who?" replied another. "There is no one in all Chiapas that weaves as beautifully as this."

"Perhaps," began a third, "Saint Lucia herself has come down from heaven and has woven these fine *huipiles*."

Ch'ucha' reflected on these comments and many others like them as Mateas turned east on the road heading towards the Mission. They were nearly home. Soon, she would run to Rosario's house and tell her every detail of the adventure of the past few days.

Mateas too was tentatively optimistic regarding the prospect of peace between the Zapatistas and the government. The President seemed more willing to listen than most of his predecessors. Right at the onset of the San Cristobal negotiations, Mateas had presented their principal demand for land reform: collectivization of farm and pasturelands under the ownership of state-run agribusinesses had to cease immediately. This was to be followed by the return of all these lands to the original ownership of the indigenous peoples of Chiapas. To Mateas' surprise the President had been willing to discuss a timeline for restoring lands to the Mayan people. He had said that he would, of course, need to discuss the details of such a plan with his Cabinet and then with the Chamber of Deputies. The President had warned Mateas not to be inflexible with regards to timelines.

"Change must come slowly if we are to be fair to everyone," the President had insisted. "There are Mexican citizens who have invested everything in their lands . . . ."

"*Our* lands," Mateas had corrected.

"Not yet," the President had replied. "These are powerful men. They will need to be compensated if we return these lands. This will be an expensive proposition. I am not sure that the World Bank will approve. So as you can see, this will take much time and effort."

"Revolution takes less time," Mateas had reminded.

"Ah, yes, Revolution," the President had said. "Your father called for Revolution, didn't he?"

"Yes, and he paid for it with his life."

"And I do not want the same thing happening to you, young Valdez. I may be *El Presidente,* but that does not mean that I can protect you from forces that are even stronger than I am. Work with me, and perhaps we can achieve what is best for all our people."

Mateas pulled into the Mission leading a small caravan of vehicles, which included an old school bus driven by Sister Margarita. He pulled his truck up to the fence. The bus parked next to Mateas' truck and stopped. Father Suarez stepped off the bus and headed towards Aguilar's apartment. He still felt bad for not allowing Aguilar to accompany them to San Christobal. He hoped that the news he brought back with him would help make up for it. He had secretly made inquires about Aguilar's family. He had learned that Aguilar's oldest daughter had given birth to a baby boy. Aguilar was a grandfather!

Nizhniya stepped out of the truck, put her hands behind her head, and stretched. Mateas stepped out and glanced over at her when he heard several vertebrae snap back into place. He almost said something, but instead silently watched as her chest pushed forward as she arched her back. She then turned and caught Mateas looking at her.

"Ah . . . , I'll go and a . . . ." stammered Mateas, embarrassed, "check on Aguilar."

"I'll come with you," replied Nizhniya. She was embarrassed at having caught Mateas glancing at her. She knew he meant no harm. He was a gentleman, and she cared for him deeply. He was the kind of man a woman loves to love, strong, confident, and virtuous. And yet he was sensitive and vulnerable too, at least when it came to a woman he felt deeply about. She regretted that she couldn't reciprocate his feelings. If things were different . . . . she thought, as she had more than once before. But no, her heart belonged to another, although she knew that it was probably futile to hold on to this mysterious vision of a love that she did not fully understand. She sighed, thinking how unlikely it was that she would ever find her way into that embrace.

Ch'ucha' scampered out of the truck and immediately sprinted towards Rosario's house. Mateas watched the cloud of dust created by her lightning-fast feet and wondered how it was possible that a human could run so quickly.

"I'm going to find Rosario," Mateas and Nizhniya could hear *Ch'ucha'* shouting as she sprinted away.

Nizhniya laughed. "I've never seen her so happy. I guess Rosario was right after all. It was good for her to go to San . . ."

"Mateas, Ludmelia!" shouted Father Suarez. "Come here!"

He had been standing in the door leading to the hallway which opened to Aguilar's apartment. Mateas and Nizhniya rushed to him and entered the doorway. They gasped as the smell of rotting flesh hit them. Mateas was about to go into the apartment but Father Suarez blocked his path. Mateas knew immediately; his mother was dead.

Nizhniya entered the apartment. She saw Sister Margarita kneeling next to the body of Rosario. She pulled a handkerchief from her pocket and held it over her nose and mouth. It did not take long for the jungle to reclaim its own. It made little difference whether one died in the heart of the jungle or in a settlement. Sister Margarita looked up at Nizhniya.

"She was murdered," she said, pointing to Rosario's skull.

Nizhniya grabbed a blanket from the bed and covered the body with it. She then turned away and walked back towards the door. Father Suarez was no longer able to keep Mateas from entering the room. Mateas stared at the body of his mother covered by the blanket.

"I should have killed the bastard!," Mateas said, choking through his tears. "Why didn't you let me kill the bastard!"

"I'm sorry Mateas, but . . ." began Nizhniya.

Santiago had followed them into the room. He saw the body and had overheard enough of the conversation to gather what had happened.

He crossed himself, turned to Mateas, "Aguilar can't have gotten far. I'll take some men and hunt him down. We'll bring him back to you."

"No," said Sister Margarita commandingly.

"No?!" shouted back Mateas. "You want that son-of-a-bitch to get away with murder again!" He turned to Santiago, "Go!"

"No," said Sister Margarita. "That's not what I meant. What I meant was that he might not be that easy to find now. Your mother has been dead for at least two, maybe three days. And then there's this." Sister Margarita handed Mateas a note that she had found clenched in Rosario's hand.

Mateas read the note out loud.

> My son,
>
> I am sorry that you had to find me this way. It was necessary that I use Aguilar; the second woe must pass[77] . My voice will now join those under the altar crying, 'How long will it be, holy and true master, before you sit in judgment and avenge our blood on the inhabitants of the earth?'[78] I was wrong when I asked Father Suarez to pray for more time. Our Ancestors were right in their calculation of the end of history. Cutting the time short is the only way to save our people. Ludmelia has done well. Ch'ucha' is ready to be the jaguar, but she must obtain Itz from the Heart of the Temple."

"What is *Itz*?" asked Ludmelia.

"It is magic," answered *Ch'ucha'* returning from Rosario's house. She stood in the doorway carrying a huipil folded over her arm. Then she noticed the body on the floor. She started towards it, but Nizhniya grabbed her. *Ch'ucha'* pulled free and fell to her knees next to the body. She pulled back the blanket. The badly decomposed face was still recognizable. *Ch'ucha'* shrieked in horror and anguish. Nizhniya knelt beside her and covered Rosario's body again with the blanket. Nizhniya pulled *Ch'ucha'* to her chest and held her tightly. *Ch'ucha'* groaned *Rina, Rina* between her sobs. Finally, she pulled herself away from Nizhniya and turned back to the body of Rosario. She stroked the blanket.

"*Rina*," *Ch'ucha'* said tearfully, "My *huipiles* won every prize at the festival. I got this for you," She laid the *huipil* she had been carrying over the blanket that covered her madrina. "Saint Miguel the Archangel is embroidered on it. I knew you would love it. He is your patron . . . ."

She stared at the image of Saint Miguel. "He didn't protect you anymore than he protected your husband." She grabbed the *huipil* she had laid on Rosario's body and threw it on the floor. She stood and looked at Nizhniya, tears streamed down her face.

"This would not have happened if it were not for me," cried *Ch'ucha'*. "I am the cause of all this."

"Of course not," said Father Suarez, reassuringly.

"No, Father," said Nizhniya. She turned to *Ch'ucha'* and put her hand on her shoulder, "It is time you knew the truth. You have to accept who you are. I had someone do that for me. When I couldn't face the truth he held it in front of me. He made me look at it; that saved me."

Ch'ucha' jerked herself away from Nizhniya's hands. "No!" she exclaimed. "I will leave. I will go into the jungle. It will be better for everyone if I go away."

Nizhniya grabbed her arm forcefully. "It is too late for that. People who loved you have sacrificed all that they had, even their lives, so that you would live, so that you could fulfill your destiny."

"Then they died in vain," said *Ch'ucha'* angrily. "I am not what they thought. I am not what *Kos* thinks I am. And even if I were . . . all I really want is to be a weaver."

"But . . . ." Nizhniya began to protest when Mateas put his hand on Nizhniya's shoulder and frowned at her. Nizhniya understood the unspoken message: Enough! Let her be. Let her grieve.

Nizhniya nodded. "We can talk about this later," she said, placing her arm around her. *Ch'ucha'*, now emotionally spent, hugged Nizhniya, who held her tightly while she wept. After several minutes, Nizhniya finally whispered into her ear, "I must talk with Mateas now. Would you stay with Sister Margarita?"

Ch'ucha' nodded and wiped her cheek with her hand.

"Sister, can *Ch'ucha'* stay with you for a while?" asked Nizhniya.

"Certainly," she said. "But I will need to prepare Rosario's body. We should not wait too long."

"I would like to help," said *Ch'ucha'*.

"Are you sure?" asked Nizhniya.

"Yes. It is the least I can do for my *madrina*."

Nizhniya looked at Sister Margarita who nodded reassuringly. She kissed *Ch'ucha'* on the forehead and then beckoned with a nod of her head for Mateas to follow her outside.

Mateas and Nizhniya went outside to a quiet area in the courtyard and sat on a bench. Nizhniya held Mateas' hand.

"I'm sorry about your mother," she said. "But we must begin to prepare."

"For what?" asked Mateas.

Santiago came rushing over to them. "Your motorcycle is missing!" he exclaimed.

"You see," said Nizhniya. "Your mother set all this up. She arranged Aguilar's escape."

"But why?"

"I'm not sure," replied Nizhniya. "But I think we can be confident that Aguilar will be back."

"Revenge?" asked Santiago.

"Yes," replied Nizhniya. "But I think we should assume that he is trying to contact those who had employed him and Zokoroff to abduct *Ch'ucha'*. Aguilar may even be with them now. They may try to complete the mission they failed to complete three years ago."

"You and *Ch'ucha'* must flee then," insisted Mateas. "When they arrive, the nest will be empty."

"No, I don't believe that is what Rosario had in mind."

Nizhniya observed Mateas' look of consternation and continued before he had a chance to protest.

"Whether you want to admit it or not, your mother has been right. We will have to trust her now. Besides, there is not enough time. We wouldn't get far. Our place is here with you and the people."

"Then we should implement the plan we set into place months ago," said Mateas. "I will contact all the division leaders and have them bring as many of their commandos here to the Mission."

"No," said Nizhniya, firmly.

"But why?" interrupted Santiago. "If Aguilar returns to complete his mission, they will come here."

"I think that we should assume that Aguilar knows of our plans, and I think we should also assume that their objectives will be the same. That is to abduct *Ch'ucha'* alive if possible, kill her only if necessary. To accomplish this they will want to use ground troops to minimize the risk of killing her. A direct assault on the Mission and village would risk collateral damage."

"But how could they deploy the required troops?" asked Santiago.

"By troop-carrying helicopters," said Mateas, now grasping what Nizhniya had in mind. "Escorted by assault helicopters."

"Exactly," said Nizhniya.

Mateas dropped to one knee and began to draw a map of the surrounding area in the dirt. "There are several clearings in the jungle three to five kilometers from the Mission. Here, here, and here," Mateas made three indentations in the sand surrounding the Mission. Two were north of the Mission while the other was south. "If we were to deploy our commandos in the jungle just on the perimeter of these clearings . . . ."

"With Stingers," interjected Nizhniya.

"Yes," said Mateas. "We could surprise the hell out of them!"

"But who would remain here at the Mission?" asked Santiago.

"Ludmelia," said Mateas.

"But . . . ." Nizhniya began to protest.

"I am still the commander of the Zapatistas," said Mateas. "And you have just been drafted. You now must follow *my* orders. I will leave a contingent of commandos under your command, not many though. If we have any hope of pulling this off we will need every available commando at these clearings."

"This is damned risky," said Santiago.

"It's our only chance," said Nizhniya. "We need to start deploying our troops immediately. The assault could occur as early as this evening."

"So soon?" asked Santiago.

"Yes. The last thing they want is to risk *Ch'ucha'* slipping out of their grasp again. Mateas, make sure your commandos take positions under the jungle canopy. Have them cover themselves with foliage if necessary. This will obscure their infrared signatures. Santiago, have all the ranchers bring their livestock from the fields to the Mission."

Santiago looked at her curiously.

"Satellite reconnaissance. They'll pick up the heat of the cattle. They just might misinterpret them as commandos."

Santiago nodded and left.

"We have much to accomplish," said Nizhniya, looking at her watch. "We have about six hours before it starts getting dark."

Mateas said nothing. The two stood silently for a moment.

"Where will you be?" Nizhniya finally asked.

Mateas knelt down again and pointed to the indentation representing the clearing that was approximately five kilometers northwest of the Mission. Nizhniya knelt on one knee in front of him. She took his hand pointing to the map drawn in the dirt. He looked up. Nizhniya appeared to Mateas to be profoundly sad yet reconciled with her destiny. They both knew that they would very likely never see each other again. Nizhniya held Mateas' hand firmly and smiled.

Mateas nodded and understood.

Late that same evening, when most of the preparations had been completed, Father Suarez finally had an opportunity to sit down. With no real expectation of being able to relax, he collapsed into his favorite old chair. Perhaps he could rest enough to gather some strength to face what lay ahead. He closed his eyes and began to pray. As he prayed, Rosario's note to Mateas came back to him—. . . *the second woe must pass.* He vaguely remembered the scripture verse. It was from the Book of Revelation. Rosario had frequently referred to this book ever since the *child* had arrived. Since then, he had made a study of Revelation, if for no other reason than to keep Rosario from becoming over inventive with her exegesis. He had a pretty good idea where he could find her reference to the second woe; it was in chapter eleven. He reached over to the Bible that he always kept on the table next to the chair and thumbed through the final book until he found the chapter he was looking for.

*And I will grant my two witnesses power to prophesy for one
thousand two hundred and sixty days . . . .*

One thousand two hundred and sixty days . . . . Father Suarez
mulled over the number in his mind. About three and a half years, he
estimated. *Ch'ucha'* and Nizhniya had arrived in the Mission about
three and a half years ago. Father shook his head. Coincidence. He
continued reading.

*These are the two olive trees and two lampstands which stand
before the Lord of the earth. And if anyone would harm them, fire pours
from their mouth and consumes their foes; if anyone would harm them,
thus he is doomed to be killed . . . .* [79]

What did Rosario see in these scriptures that she was willing to die
to set into motion? Did she actually believe *Ch'ucha'* was one of the two
witnesses? She had compared her to one of the Hero Twins of Mayan
lore. Perhaps this was just another example of her syncretism? Was
Rosario just a crazy old woman or a prophetess? Father Suarez had an
inexplicable feeling that the events of the past three and a half years
were rapidly heading towards a climax. Whether it was the one that
Rosario had envisioned he was not sure. Neither was he sure that it
was a climax that any of them would survive. He set down his Bible,
reached into his cassock pocket, and took out his rosary. When in
doubt . . . he thought as he crossed himself with the crucifix.
Our Father who art in heaven . . .

*   *   *

"Sir, satellite reconnoissance has picked up significant infrared
activity surrounding the primary target," said the soldier, pointing to
an onboard computer screen.

Aguilar left his seat and examined the screen.

"You see that, Obermann," Aguilar said, tapping the computer
screen at the center of a mass of red images. Aguilar turned around

and faced a camera attached to the ceiling of the command helicopter. This, and many other cameras, provided Obermann, who was at the NSA command center, with visual access to the entire operation. "I told you what these *Indianos* would do. These precautions are unnecessary and a waste of time."

"We proceed as planned," replied Obermann. "There'll be no mistakes this time."

Mateas and about forty commandos surrounded the perimeter of the northwestern clearing. Hunkered down under brush, they waited. Mateas did not need to look at his watch to know the time. He was half Mayan and could read the sky like a clock face. The few stars he could see through the forest canopy were enough to tell him it was just after two. Perhaps the night would pass. His mind played through various scenarios. He did not have enough men. Neither did the other commanders stationed at the other clearings. Although he was not a believer, he found himself instinctively praying. While he prayed the ground began to vibrate. He looked up. His eyes met that of another commando, wide-eyed and full of alarm. Mateas nodded reassuringly.

"We fight for the people—our families," said Mateas.

The commando drew a deep breath and gripped his rifle. The sound of helicopters could be heard rapidly approaching from the north. Mateas pulled his communicator off his belt. All of the commanders had maintained radio silence. Mateas would break that silence once the first shot was fired. He knew that would be soon. The first helicopter appeared over the tree line, illuminated by the gibbous moon. Then two more appeared, flanking it on both sides.

"Stop," he muttered to himself. He feared that they might continue toward the Mission. But they did stop, with the leading helicopter hovering approximately 50 feet above the treetops near the southernmost edge of the clearing. The other two helicopters hovered midway over the clearing opposite each other. The canopy above the commandos shook as if a hurricane were passing through the jungle. Leaves and branches were flung to the ground with tremendous force by the vortex from the helicopter that was nearly overhead. Mateas looked back over his shoulder. Two commandos, covered with brush, began to move towards a shoulder-launch Stinger near them. Mateas signaled them to remain still.

After a couple of minutes, two large troop-carrying Chinook helicopters appeared over the trees, tracing the same path as the first three helicopters. The Chinooks were followed by another helicopter gunship. They all hovered thunderously over the clearing: the gunships forming a diamond over the clearing; the troop carriers hovering in the middle of the diamond.

Mateas turned around again and nodded at the commandos. They crept towards the Stinger. He saw one of them kneel on one knee while the other picked up the Stinger and secured it on his shoulder. He pointed at the lead helicopter. The commando got it in the Stinger's sight. The two Chinooks began to descend.

"Fire!" shouted Mateas.

The missile was launched; almost immediately the lead helicopter exploded in an orange ball of flame. Flaming debris crashed down around them as the helicopter plummeted to the ground. Mateas rolled several times to keep from being hit.

"Santiago, Carlos . . ." Mateas shouted into his communicator.

"Yes," said Santiago, "helicopters have just appeared over our clearing."

"Here too," replied Carlos.

"Fire!" said Mateas hastily, and then slipped the communicator back in his pocket. He looked over at the commandos who had launched the Stinger. One was covered by debris—dead; his companion was injured. Mateas crawled over to the Stinger, loaded another missile into it, and hoisted it on to his shoulder. He got one of the Chinooks in the sight and fired. The impact ripped off the rear of the helicopter. Without the stabilizing rear rotor the helicopter spun violently out of control. He saw soldiers falling out of the rear of the helicopter. As the mortally wounded helicopter careened aimlessly, it slammed into one of the gunships tearing it apart and the two helicopters fell as a single, flaming mix of metal and bodies.

Immediately, Mateas ran with the launcher under one arm and

another missile he had grabbed under the other. Machine-gun fire erupted from the helicopter gunships in the direction in which the Stingers had been launched. Mateas could hear the large caliber bullets whiz by. He wanted to stop to launch another missile if he could. The jungle behind him was being shredded into pieces by the machine gun fire. Missiles were now being fired into the forest. Large plumes of red and orange flames were erupting like volcanoes around the perimeter of the clearing. Mateas knew that his men could not survive such a bombardment. He stopped and shoved another missile in the launcher. As he hoisted the launcher on to his shoulder, he felt a burning pain in his left thigh. He had been hit. He gritted his teeth, trying to push back the pain while struggling to stabilize the Stinger on his shoulder. But, the helicopter kept darting back and forth firing at various locations around the perimeter of the clearing. He couldn't get a fix on it. The jungle was being obliterated around him as the gunship cannons fired relentlessly, aimlessly, at the perimeter. Finally, Mateas locked it in his sight and fired. The helicopter exploded, showering wreckage over the clearing.

"What the hell is happening?" demanded Obermann. Several monitors at NSA headquarters, where Obermann and Frederick were monitoring the mission, had gone blank.

"We're receiving heavy fire," said a panicked voice.

"Who's that?" said Obermann.

"It's the commander of the Southern force," replied General Barkley. "All three divisions are reporting heavy casualties."

"Damn!" shouted Obermann. He looked over at his son who was not watching any of the monitors. His eyes were fixed on some distant, invisible point. "What is it?" he asked his son.

"It's Michael," said Frederick.

Several officers who had heard Frederick now looked curiously at each other, wondering what he was talking about. But Obermann understood.

"Are you sure?" asked Obermann.

"Yes," replied Frederick.

Obermann turned to General Barkley, "Tell the remaining forces to regroup." Obermann then turned to his son. "He forgets who the Prince of this world is. We'll remind him!"

The remaining Chinook landed while the last of the gunships provided cover fire and troops began to deploy. Mateas wondered how many commandos, if any, were left to engage the soldiers as they took positions around the helicopter. To his surprise, machine-gun fire erupted from several areas around the perimeter. The soldiers in the clearing had little cover on the ground and insufficient air support. The remaining gunship rose higher in the sky, it made a wide turn, and headed back north over the trees. Mateas crawled through the brush and looked into the clearing. The Chinook's engines were powering up. Troops, who moments ago had exited from the helicopter, were now trying to get back on board. Only a handful did. The Chinook lifted off and followed the retreating gunship over the tree line.

Mateas pushed himself up, grimacing as he stood. Blood poured out of his left thigh. He looked over the clearing; it was illuminated by a smoky orange glow from the wreckage strewn across the fields. He heard the groans of the wounded. He removed his belt and fastened it around his thigh, and pulled it tight. The bleeding subsided. He saw a handful of shadowy figures emerge from the jungle, their rifles raised over their heads. Mateas limped towards where most of his men had gathered. He felt for his communicator. It was still attached to his belt.

"Santiago, come in. Santiago, Carlos. Do you read me?"

"This is Santiago. They've retreated."

"This is Manuel. Carlos was killed. The enemy has retreated here as well."

"How many men do you have left?" asked Mateas.

"Not many," said Santiago. "Very little ammunition."

"Same here," said Manuel.

"Mateas? Is that you? Are you all right?" a voice pleaded over the communicator.

"You were right," said Mateas. "We kicked their ass!"

"Thank God!" replied Nizhniya. "Are you all right?" she asked again.

"I'm a little battered up. We took many casualties. Listen, I can't talk now. We have to get the wounded back to the Mission." Mateas returned his communicator to his belt. As Mateas limped towards his men gathered near the center of the clearing, he heard them shouting.

"We did it!" exclaimed one.

"We sent them to Earthlord. May he devour their bones!" said another.

"It's Mateas! You're hurt," said one of the commandos, rushing over to him. He put his arm around Mateas to support him.

"Look for wounded," said Mateas. "We'll bring them back to the Mission. Tomorrow we'll come back for the dead."

"What about the enemy wounded?"

"Bring them too."

The men split up and began looking for wounded. Most were not difficult to find; they were either moaning or were shouting out for help. The commandos carried lanterns looking for wounded who were either unconscious or too weak to make their presence known. Unfortunately, the dead outnumbered the wounded. One of the commandos brought a truck into the clearing. The others lifted wounded onto the truck.

"You must sit," said one of the commandos to Mateas. "You are losing too much blood."

Mateas steadied himself against the truck. A commando took him by the arm and helped him into the cab. In spite of his best efforts Mateas could not remain alert.

I'll close my eyes for a moment, he thought, but passed out from exhaustion and the loss of blood. He was just beginning to dream that he was driving the truck with Nizhniya and *Ch'ucha'* back from San Cristobal when a commando shook his arm.

"They're back!" he shouted.

Mateas shook himself into alertness as the commando pulled him out of the truck.

"Everyone out of the clearing!" he shouted. "Back to the Mission."

He stumbled as he tried to run for the cover of the surrounding jungle, dragging his wounded leg behind him. The commando tried to lift him to his feet.

"No," shouted Mateas. "Go . . . go!" he waved to the commando. The commando reluctantly obeyed.

Helicopter gunships roared over the northern treetops. There were more of them this time, many more. He rolled over and watched them pass overhead. They were firing salvo after salvo into the clearing and into the surrounding jungle. This time the enemy would make sure they would not be forced to retreat.

He pulled out his communicator. The orange glow that had illuminated the jungle was dimming. The stars overhead began to fade. "Ludmelia?!"

"Yes," said the voice over the communicator.

"They're back." Mateas had lost too much blood; he was falling back into unconsciousness. The jungle grew deadly quiet. "I'm sorry," he finally said.

"Mateas . . . Mateas . . ." the voice called out from the communicator. There was no response.

Major Nizhniya turned to the handful of commandos who had remained at the Mission, "Wait here," she told them. "Come with me," she said to *Ch'ucha'* who was standing next to her. They walked together to the rectory where she explained the situation to Father Suarez and Sister Margarita.

"Gather the women and children," Nizhniya instructed Sister Margarita. "Head east into the jungle towards Guatemala. Go quickly." Nizhniya then turned to *Ch'ucha'*. "Go with Sister Margarita. Help her with the little ones."

"I want to stay with you," *Ch'ucha'* insisted.

"No. Do what I say. Sister Margarita will need your help."

Ch'ucha' hugged Nizhniya tightly. "I don't want to leave you."

Nizhniya pushed *Ch'ucha'* away holding her at arm's length.

"I know, little *Milka*. But you must." Nizhniya wiped a tear that rolled down *Ch'ucha's* cheek.

"What will they do to you?"

"Never mind." Nizhniya kissed *Ch'ucha'* on the forehead. "Now go. Sister Margarita is waiting."

Ch'ucha' grudgingly left with Sister Margarita. Nizhniya watched as they left. *Ch'ucha'* turned around several times to catch a final glimpse of her "mother."

Major Nizhniya now turned to Father Suarez, "Father, come and bless us for battle."

She led him out to the small band of Zapatistas and joined a gathering of old men and young boys who were waiting in the Mission courtyard. As Father approached the men knelt. Nizhniya joined them.

"In the name of the Father, the Son, and the Holy Spirit," began Father Suarez, making the sign of the cross over the small company and their commander. Father Suarez then absolved them of their sins. "Remember," he said to them, "it is appointed for you once to die. Live and die as a soldier of Christ."

Nizhniya stood and faced the men. "The enemy has broken through our lines. There is only us now. Tonight, if you fight valiantly, you will join the Ancestors, and your descendants will remember this night in song! Take your positions."

She walked towards the road leading to the Mission. Several old vehicles and a wagon now blocked the road fifty meters from the Mission entrance. She recognized it was only a symbolic barricade, but then, this final resistance would only be symbolic anyway.

"May I join you?" asked Father Suarez.

"You may walk me to the barricade," she said. "Then I think it would be best if you went back to the chapel. I suspect that your prayers will be more effective than our bullets."

When they arrived at the barricade, She removed the Mokorov from her shoulder holster, unlatched the safety, and loaded a bullet into the chamber.

"I'm sorry," she said to Father Suarez.

"What for?" he asked.

"For bringing so much trouble to your Mission. If *Ch'ucha'* and I had left . . . ."

"Nonsense," interrupted Father Suarez. "Besides, Rosario wouldn't have permitted you to leave."

Nizhniya laughed. "She was a strong-willed woman. I wish she were here."

"Perhaps she is."

There was a momentary silence. Major Nizhniya stared down the road waiting for what she knew would inevitably come.

"Your father was a priest," said Father Suarez making conversation.

"Yes," replied Nizhniya. She continued to stare down the road as she answered. "I remember we would have the poorer members of our parish over for dinner nearly every night." Nizhniya laughed, "We were so poor we should have invited ourselves. It was all right though. Those were the happiest days of my life." She faced Father Suarez, "Do you suppose I'll see them before the night is over?"

Father just smiled. Nizhniya nodded and removed the AKS-92 that had been strapped over her shoulder. She cocked it and lowered the rifle, resting it on the hood of the old car in front of her. Peering through the night scope, she could just make out shadowy forms in the distance, slowly making their way through the thick growth of jungle on both sides of the road leading to the Mission.

"I think it's time for you to go now, Father. We're going to be needing those prayers very soon."

Father Suarez placed his hand gently on her shoulder and nodded. He didn't say anything. What could be said? It was likely that this would be the last time they would see each other, at least, in this life. Then he turned away and walked back towards the Church.

Nizhniya leaned against the vehicle. *Guardian of the child.* The words of Father Nikitas came back to her. Ha! Nizhniya shook her head. In all likelihood she and the child would be dead by morning. She had always thought he was a *durak.*[80] The present circumstances now confirmed it.

Trust your angel; he is with you.

"What?! Who's there?!" Nizhniya exclaimed. She held her rifle out in front of her as she turned a full 360 degrees looking for where the voice had come from. She saw no one.

"I must be hearing things," she mumbled to herself. She remembered the medallion that Father Nikitas had given her. She felt it under her shirt. She grabbed the chain and pulled the medallion out. She looked down at it. She could just barely see the icon illuminated by moonlight and the orange-red glow that hung over the horizon—Michael the Archangel, the warrior angel. She held the medallion tightly.

She spun around as she heard the sound of vehicles. A convoy was making its way up the road. She peered through the riflescope. The once shadowy figures were now clearly recognizable—heavily armed soldiers. They were moving rapidly along the edge of the road. She listened for helicopters but heard none. She had been right. Troops would secure the Mission. They would avoid the use of heavy artillery and rockets. Minimize collateral damage. Take prisoners if possible; one prisoner in particular, *Ch'ucha'*.

Bap, bap, bap, bap, bap . . . .

Gunfire erupted from behind her. They were encircled. The convoy was now speeding up the road. Nizhniya looked in her sight, took aim,

Brrrip, brrrip . . .

The short burst from the AKS-92 brought down two of the enemy. Soldiers scattered. Nizhniya scanned through the scope looking for another target.

Brrrip, brrrip . . .

Another soldier fell.

Pang, pang, pang, pang . . .

Bullets struck the vehicle beside her. Nizhniya spun around and saw a flash from a rifle muzzle in the bushes.

Brrrp, brrrp . . .

The flashes stopped, but were immediately followed by others.

Pang, pang, pang, pang, pang, pang, pang, pang . . .

The vehicles, she was taking cover behind, were being shredded by high velocity bullets. She wedged herself between two vehicles trying to maximize her cover. The convoy in front of her had stopped. Troops were now exiting the trucks and running towards the Mission.

Brrrp, brrrp, brrrp, brrrp, brrrp, brrrp . . .

A half a dozen or more of the soldiers in front of her fell, others dove into the bushes, some clung near the trucks for cover.

Pang, pang, pang, pang, pang, pang, pang, pang . . .

The barricade was being torn apart. Nizhniya was being struck almost on every side by shrapnel. The lead truck revved its engine and charged the barricade. Nizhniya jumped just before the truck smashed into the barricade. She dove into a ditch on the side of the road.

"Mother! Mother!" shouted a voice from behind her.

Nizhniya spun around. It was *Ch'ucha*! Two soldiers were chasing her, two more emerged from the brush and seized her. *Ch'ucha'* flung one to the ground. The other two caught up with her and together the three grabbed her. They struggled to keep her in their grasp. Finally, the soldier that had been knocked down by *Ch'ucha'*, got up, pulled out a pistol, and held it to her head.

Nizhniya emerged from the ditch, holding her Mokorov in front of her as she ran towards *Ch'ucha'* and her captors.

Pow!

The soldier holding the gun to *Ch'ucha's* head fell to the ground with a bullet in his own head.

Pow! Pow!

Soldiers on the left and the right of *Ch'ucha'* fell. The remaining soldier stood behind *Ch'ucha'*. He had pulled out his own pistol and now held it to *Ch'ucha's* head. Nizhniya had not stopped running and as she was sprinting towards the two; the soldier peered from behind *Ch'ucha'*.

Pow!

Ch'ucha' felt the man release her. He fell over backward with a bullet through his forehead. Bullets continued to fly from every side. Nizhniya, still running, doubled over and slammed into *Ch'ucha'*; both went sprawling into the brush.

"I told you not to come back!" admonished Nizhniya as she lay on top of *Ch'ucha'*.

"I couldn't . . . ."

"Sister Margarita and the children?" interrupted Nizhniya.

"They're safe. I led them to a cave on the other side of the Usumacinta River."

"Listen to me," said Nizhniya. "Rosario took you somewhere. It was a secret place, right?"

"Yes. The Temple of the . . . ."

"Never mind. Go there, now! And stay there. Do not come out—no matter what! Do you understand?"

"Yes, but . . ."

"You will do this, for me?"

"I want to be with you. I don't care what happens to me!"

"I do," exclaimed Nizhniya hugging *Ch'ucha'*. "Please, go. Do it for me."

Ch'ucha' felt as if her heart would explode. She would rather die than be separated from Nizhniya. Yet, *Ch'ucha'* did not want to deny what might be Nizhniya's final request.

"What am I to do?" cried *Ch'ucha'*, burying her head within Nizhniya's embrace.

"Say *yes*," said Nizhniya softly.

Ch'ucha' looked up at Nizhniya. Tears streamed from her eyes.

"Yes," *Ch'ucha'* choked.

"Good," said Nizhniya smiling while she wiped the tears from *Ch'ucha'* cheeks. She released *Ch'ucha'* from her embrace. Then she dropped the clip out of her Mokorov and replaced it with a fully loaded clip. "Which direction?"

"Northeast from here," replied *Ch'ucha'* pointing.

Nizhniya and *Ch'ucha'* stood. She kissed *Ch'ucha'* on the forehead. "Go! Do not look back!"

Ch'ucha' stood frozen. Finally, Nizhniya smiled and swatted her on the rear. "Go!"

Ch'ucha' dashed off in the direction of the Temple of the Ancestors.

"There she is!" shouted a soldier, pointing in the direction of *Ch'ucha'*. Two soldiers leaped after her.

Nizhniya jumped out of the bushes.

Pow! Pow!

The two soldiers fell dead.

Nizhniya felt her legs give way before she even heard the explosion of the gun. She turned around. The soldier who had seen *Ch'ucha'* was pointing his pistol at her. He hesitated. That was all Nizhniya needed to fire off another round and kill him. She started limping towards the Mission. A smokey dawn was beginning to break. She could now clearly see soldiers leaving the Mission. They were dragging Father Suarez behind them. They threw him to the ground. She felt another bullet strike her other leg; then another bullet. She fell down on her back. She watched the leaves rustling overhead. She felt the ground begin to quake. The dark belly of a helicopter appeared overhead. Then everything vanished into the mists of unconsciousness.

Aguilar stepped out of the helicopter. He placed his hands on his hips. A triumphant victor, he looked with satisfaction over the vanquished. Four years of brooding. Now his dream of revenge was nearly complete! And Obermann was not about to spoil it!

Two soldiers dragged a wounded Zapatista over to him. Her head hung down, but he recognized her immediately.

"Water," said Aguilar.

A soldier handed him his canteen. Aguilar walked over to Nizhniya, grabbed her hair and pulled her head back. He poured water over her face. She opened her eyes.

"We meet again," said Aguilar smiling.

Nizhniya stared at him with glassy eyes.

"You've lost some blood. But you'll survive. Which is more than I can say for your friend here." Aguilar turned back to the helicopter. "Bring out the prisoner!"

Two soldiers dragged Mateas out of the helicopter and dropped his body in front of Nizhniya. He was conscious, but barely. He looked up at her.

"Ludmelia?" he whispered.

Nizhniya jerked her arms free from the soldiers who were supporting her. She knelt down next to Mateas forgetting her own pain. She put his head on her lap and stroked his forehead.

"Ssh, it's me," she said.

"Ah, now isn't this a touching scene," said Aguilar. He bent down close to Nizhniya. "The surgeon tells me that he can still be saved. But, he can't lose any more blood." Aguilar pulled a large knife from his belt and slid the blade under the belt that Mateas had used as a tourniquet. He sliced the belt; immediately blood began to ooze out of the wound. Aguilar shoved the blade into the wound, opening the artery that had coagulated shut. Mateas cried out in pain as blood squirted out with each heartbeat.

"You bastard!" shouted Nizhniya.

"Where is *Ch'ucha*?"

Mateas began whispering again. Nizhniya bent down to hear.

"What'd he say? What'd he say?" insisted Aguilar.

Nizhniya ignored Aguilar and pulled Mateas to her chest and held him in a tight embrace. Finally, Mateas' eyes rolled back. She closed his eyelids with her fingers and kissed him on the forehead. Then looking up at Aguilar, "He said, 'Go to hell!'"

Aguilar slapped her with the back of his hand knocking her to the ground.

"That's enough!" said the voice in Aguilar's earphone.

At least twenty different cameras, some attached to soldiers and others mounted on helicopters, had allowed Obermann, Frederick and NSA personnel to monitor every aspect of the operation.

"This is *my* operation," continued Obermann. "Remember, if we had done things your way, your body parts would have been scattered all over that clearing!"

"I know what I'm doing," Aguilar muttered into his microphone.

Nizhniya looked up and gave Aguilar a sarcastic smile. She had heard Aguilar's defensive remark. She knew whom he was answering to. "So now Obermann has you on a chain."

Aguilar was startled by Nizhniya's comment. Then collecting his wits, he knelt down on one knee and grabbed her chin. She stared at him with contempt.

"No one," he said, ripping the earphone and microphone off his head, "tells Aguilar what to do!" He turned to one of the officers nearby. "Gather all the prisoners in the courtyard." He then turned to the medic. "Fix her up," he said pointing to Nizhniya, "I don't want her dead, not yet."

"Shit! That dumb bastard!" exclaimed Obermann. "Aguilar is so blinded by his desire for vengeance that he doesn't even see how that Russian bitch is manipulating him."

"I told you, Father. You should have let me go with them."

Obermann nodded. He put his arm around Frederick's shoulder and walked him over to a quiet part of the room.

"Assemble twenty Resubstantiates. I will make arrangements for you to depart immediately for Chiapas."

"I will not let you down!"

Itz from *Xibalba*

For, although we are in the flesh, we do not battle according to the flesh, for the weapons of our battle are not of flesh but are enormously powerful, capable of destroying fortresses . . . . we are ready to punish every disobedience, once your obedience is complete.

-2Corithians 10:3-6

Ch'ucha' entered the Temple of the Ancestors. As she ran through the dark labyrinth she thought about what Rosario had said in the letter she had heard Mateas read. She said I was ready— ready for what? Ludmelia has trained me to be a warrior. But Rosario had said that I was destined to be a shaman. Perhaps, if I were these things, I could help Ludmelia. Perhaps I could save my people. But, I am only one against so many! Then she remembered Rosario's final words, I must get *Itz* from the underworld of *Xibalba*! But how?

She was surprised when she found herself in the great chamber, the heart of the Temple—even more surprised to find a single candle flickering in the darkness. She slowly approached the candle. It stood in the middle of the stone altar. *Ch'ucha'* was about to reach for it when she was startled by something moving next to the candle. It was *Henhen*,[81] the toad-master shaman and guardian of the gateway to the realm of the Earthlord. Its skin glistened with toxic secretions; if touched, the potent chemicals could cause visions and even death.

She leaned down and spoke softly to the toad, "*Henhen*, lead me to the gates of *Xibalba*."

Ch'ucha' took a deep breath, picked up the toad and held it in front of her face.

"Permit me, *Henhen,* to pass your threshold."

Ch'ucha' brought the toad to her lips and kissed it. Immediately, light exploded from *Ch'ucha'*. She felt her spirit ripped from her body. She floated upwards towards the cavernous vault of the temple. She saw her body collapse to the ground.

Ch'ucha' watched Rosario enter the yawning darkness. She took a deep breath, bent down and followed. Ch'ucha' tingled with excitement. It never occurred to her that she should be frightened, that the denizens of this thick darkness might include poisonous spiders or venomous snakes. She knew they were there. She was too exhilarated by the adventure. Where was Rosario leading her? What might be hidden within this sacred Mayan hill? What did she mean by being of age?

I am dreaming, thought Ch'ucha', about my past experience with Rosario in the Temple. Or perhaps that past experience had been a dream and I am redreaming the dream.

Ch'ucha' was not sure. But, she knew that she was re-experiencing everything but somehow it was different. She was now both experiencing and observing. As observer she could distinguish the two realities. As she descended into the inner Temple she entered deeper into the dream, until finally, they were once again in the heart the Temple. The two realities were now indistinguishably fused.

Ch'ucha' slowly turned around, holding her lantern as high as she could, so that she could examine her surroundings. Giant bas-reliefs of Mayan figures, kings, heroes, gods, and dragons decorated the walls and ceiling. When Ch'ucha' had finished with this initial examination she walked

towards the center of the chamber where there was a stone altar. On the
stone altar was Rosario's statue of Saint Miguel the Archangel. He was
wearing the tiny huipil that Ch'ucha' had woven for him for his feast day.
A votive lamp flickered on the right of the statue. In front of the statue lay
a beautiful Conquistador sword.

"This is the Itz you will need for the battle," said Rosario slowly
waving her arm over the altar.

Ch'ucha' looked curiously at Rosario.

"You must have Miguel and his angels accompany you into battle." She
touched her statue and then the medallion that hung around Ch'ucha's
neck. "You must have the fire of God's wrath." Rosario held her finger in
the flame until it caught fire. She then made the sign of the cross on
Ch'ucha's forehead with her flaming finger. "You must have the sword that
is broken," Rosario picked up the sword and handed it to Ch'ucha'. It was
no longer old, rusted, and broken. Rather, the sword's hilt glistened and its
blade was shinny and razor sharp as the day it was crafted centuries ago.
"Finally, you must wear the armor of His grace to shield you in battle."
Rosario lifted the huipil off the statue of Miguel.

"But it is too small for me!" exclaimed Ch'ucha'.

"Itz is a tremendous responsibility and it can be wielded only in
submission. Yield and you will grow into this huipil. Resist, and Itz will
betray you."

The vision evaporated and *Ch'ucha'* fell into a deep, dreamless
sleep during which time itself dissolved. Then she "awoke" and found
herself floating outside of the Temple of the Ancestors. It was not as
she had known it, covered by jungle over-growth, it was as it had been
ages ago, a mighty monument and shrine of her adopted Mayan
ancestors. She watched as centuries of history played out beneath her—
the rise of the Mayan civilization, the building of the great cities, the
collapse of the Empire, the coming of the Spanish. Fifteen hundred
years of history flew by in a few moments, yet somehow she had
experienced and assimilated all of it.

She was nearly back to the present when she heard the purring of
a great cat:

iii iii iii laa laa laa
Your skin is brown as the jungle tree,
Your eyes are as blue as the running stream,
Your legs are small,
And your hands are weak.
Why are you looking at me little girl, human child?
Are you my soul's companion?

Ch'ucha' saw herself, a little girl, twirling and dancing in her huipil. Crouched from behind tall grasses, she was watching herself. Then an explosion of light bombarded her senses again. She blinked her eyes several times to let her pupils adjust to the brilliance of the present. Now, she was looking through the same crouched eyes. The atmosphere was thick with smoke. Her nostrils flared to inhale every clue of human activity. There was much blood in the air; many human voices speaking an unfamiliar language. Shouting, screaming, cries . . . even from human children. She bounded up a tree and perched herself on a large branch. She surveyed the Mission below her. There were many bodies, torn apart and mutilated. Needless! Wasteful! Not for food but for destruction!

She scampered off the branch, and crouching low beneath the brush maneuvered closer to the Mission, following the smell of blood. As she approached a group of humans she recognized a scent. She peered through the brush. The white-skinned human female was tied to a fence like a domesticated beast. She was bruised, bloody, dying . . . ."

Ch'ucha' woke up with a start. She was still standing in front of the stone altar. Her heart was pounding. The hair on the back of her neck stood up. The smell of smoke and blood lingered in her nostrils. She felt a fierceness coursing through her body. She wanted to lash out; tear asunder She shook herself. Had she been dreaming? Her hand was warm and moist. She looked down at her clenched fist. Red and green fluid oozed from between her fingers. *Henhen* was crushed beyond recognition. As she wiped her hand on her *huipil* she saw Rosario's statue of Saint Miguel the Archangel on the altar next to the votive candle. In the cosmos of the shaman, the dream world and the world of consciousness are fused into a single reality. This had been Rosario's world. This is my world now, she thought.

She touched the huipil she had woven for Miguel, remembering Rosario's words. And the sword—it was as she remembered it, not in the dream, but when she had descended into the Temple with Rosario the first time. Broken. *Ch'ucha'* knew what she had to do. She grasped the sword and shoved the four inches of its broken blade under her belt. Then she moved quickly through the passages and up the stairway that led out of the Temple. As she approached the entrance, she could see the waning light of day; evening was approaching. She had spent most of the day in the Temple. When she stepped out of the Temple entrance a large, black jaguar was waiting for her, seated on his haunches.

"Come," she said to her soul-companion.

*   *   *

Soldiers dragged another young man and dropped him in front of Nizhniya. He, as well as many other young boys had refused to leave the Mission with Sister Margarita. They wanted to stay and fight with their heroes, the Zapatistas. He had been wounded in the fighting during the morning. Since then he had been 'interrogated,' that is to say beaten numerous times.

"We are all running out of patience," Aguilar said to Nizhniya while kicking the young man in the back. "Tell me where she is and I will end his misery quickly."

"I told you," choked Nizhniya, who had already been similarly interrogated several times, "I do not know where she is."

Angry and frustrated, Aguilar delivered a vicious kick to the boy's head. His neck snapped.

One by one, Aguilar had brought prisoners before Nizhniya, the old and the young, even Father Suarez and Santiago.

"Where is she?" he would ask.

"I don't know!" had been her reply.

He would then execute them. Then their bodies were dragged a short distance and piled in a heap in front of her. The body of the young man that Aguilar had just dispatched was thrown on the ever-growing pile of bodies.

"Bring me the others!" ordered Aguilar.

"The women and children are all that are left," replied the soldier.

"Bring them out here so they can see what misfortune this bitch and her kid have brought upon their people."

The soldiers left to carry out Aguilar's orders. He then kicked Nizhniya in the leg where she had been shot. She winced but stifled her desire to cry out in pain

"Did you really think they could escape us? I was only disappointed that our little *Ch'ucha'* was not among them."

Nizhniya could hear the crying of children and babies, and the wailing of their mothers, as they were driven by soldiers into the courtyard. They had been held in the church and were not fully aware of the carnage inflicted on their families. Now, they saw the mutilated bodies of their husbands, fathers, brothers and sons. Sister Margarita crossed herself. A sinister smiled crossed over Aguilar's face as he saw her. He walked over to her and grabbed her, then pushed her to the ground in front of Nizhniya. He pulled a large knife from his belt. It had a terrible serrated edge. He dropped to one knee and pulled up Sister Margarita's skirt, exposing her leg. He turned to Nizhniya.

"Watch as I perform the same surgery on Sister's leg as she did on mine. Then, when I'm done with her, I'll cut off the limbs of the children, one by one!"

Nizhniya struggled against her bindings. It was no use. She banged her head against the post in frustration. "Damn you, damn you!"

"Sir," interrupted one of the soldiers, "it appears that someone is coming up the road."

Aguilar stood up. Sister Margarita scrambled to her feet and ran back to the children. Aguilar could just barely make out in the growing darkness the figure that was still some distance from the Mission. The soldiers also strained to see the figure walking up the road. Sister Margarita motioned to the children to return to the church building while Aguilar and the soldiers were distracted. Aguilar grabbed a pair of binoculars from one of the soldiers near him.

"*Ch'ucha*," Aguilar muttered as a sinister grin edged up his lips.

"What is that walking next to her?" a soldier asked.

Aguilar lowered his binoculars. "A jaguar."

*   *   *

"Thank God!" exclaimed General Barkley who, along with Obermann and a few others, was continuing to monitor the progress of the raid on the Mission from NSA headquarters. "That Aguilar is a madman!"

"I cannot say that I approve of his methods, but let's not feign innocence either," said Obermann. "I am sure that the NSA has carried out missions in its colorful past, perhaps some even under your guidance, in which civilians were killed."

"Well . . . yes . . . but . . . ." stammered General Barkley.

"But . . ." continued Obermann for Barkley, "approve or disapprove, Aguilar is about to deliver on his promise. Ah, you see, there she is!" Obermann pointed to one of the monitors.

"I certainly do hope she has been worth all this effort, and so many lives," replied Barkley.

"Oh, you have no idea!" said Obermann. "Get a couple of choppers airborne. I want some overhead visual," he instructed the General. "You see her, don't you Frederick?"

"Yes," replied Frederick. Frederick and twenty of his resubstantiated demonic warriors were on a military jet heading towards Chiapas. They planned to land at the command center at *Ciudad del Carmen*, the launching point of Aguilar's invasion force. As *Ch'ucha* approached, Frederick could gradually see her more clearly on his monitor. There is something about her, he thought. She looks bruised and disheveled, but she carries herself with dignity. And her eyes! They reflect the light like those of an animal!

He felt a kinship with her. That did not surprise him. She did, after all, share some of his genome. So did all Chimærics. But, she was unique in that she had been exposed to his stem cells early in her fetal development. Had his genes become incorporated into her embryonic stem cells? If so, then every cell of her body would carry some of his genes. How much was she like him? Were they like brother and sister? Then it occurred to him. What about her gametes? Are they like mine too? What would happen if . . . ?

"I want you to proceed to the Mission. You should arrive there tomorrow morning. Aguilar will turn her over to you. Bring her to Chimæra headquarters."

Frederick assured his father that he would bring her back. As *Ch'ucha'* approached the Mission courtyard, Obermann felt apprehensive. It was unlikely that she possessed abilities anywhere close to Frederick's. But, Aguilar had suggested that she did possess some extraordinary powers. Even if she did possess some rudimentary abilities, she probably did not know how to exercise them, especially how to use them synergistically with incorporeals. But, he couldn't shake his uneasiness. She was, after all, Maria O'Conner's child.

"Aguilar, can you hear me?"

"He's not wearing his earphone," said General Barkley.

"Damn it! Who is?"

"Lieutenant Mathers."

"Mathers!"

"Yes, sir?"

Obermann was standing in front of a wall of monitors that were receiving video from the ground as well as the helicopters overhead. Night was falling. The helicopters were shining bright lights on the scene below. Obermann could see that *Ch'ucha'* had stopped and knelt down by the pile of bodies. Aguilar was in the process of untying Nizhniya.

"Mathers, this is Hans Obermann. Tell Aguilar that he is not to do anything provocative. He is to take the girl into custody without incident. He is not to harm her in anyway!" Obermann knew that no matter how much angelic synergy she was capable of achieving, if she willingly surrendered herself there was nothing her angels could do to intervene.

"Yes sir," replied Mathers.

Obermann watched as Lieutenant Mathers walked over to Aguilar and gave him the orders. Aguilar pushed him aside.

"Damn him!" exclaimed Obermann. "Damn him!"

Ch'ucha' was horrified by the carnage she had seen as she walked up the road towards the Mission. Now, as she approached the courtyard, she saw the pile of bodies. Many were barely recognizable they had been beaten so brutally.

"Hey, little *bruja*, are you looking for someone?"

Ch'ucha' recognized the voice. It was the murderer of her *Rina*, the butcher who had killed so many of her people. Aguilar! She slowly turned and faced him. Aguilar was startled for a moment. He had never seen her look this way. Her eyes were narrowed and focused. It was as if only he existed. As if he were prey.

He took a couple of steps back. Then he bent down and pulled up a body that had been lying near a fence post. He yanked the mangled body to its feet and held it out in front of him.

"Maybe you were looking for your mother?!"

Aguilar now pulled Nizhniya's head back. *Ch'ucha'* could barely recognize Nizhniya. Nizhniya shook herself to keep from falling back into unconsciousness.

"Oh, my little *milka*," choked Nizhniya as blood and saliva drooled from her mouth. She tried to break free from Aguilar's grasp but was too weak.

Ch'ucha' began to move towards Nizhniya.

"Stop right there," commanded Aguilar. "Before I give you back your mother, will you promise to be a good little girl and come with me?"

"Yes," said *Ch'ucha'*.

"Okay then," said Aguilar smiling, "here's your mommy." Aguilar pushed Nizhniya forward. There was a terrific bang. Blood exploded from Nizhniya's chest and splattered onto *Ch'ucha's* face and huipil. Nizhniya stumbled and fell into *Ch'ucha's* arms. Aguilar stood smiling with perverse satisfaction while holding his smoking revolver. *Ch'ucha'* gently brought her body to the ground and laid Nizhniya's head on her lap.

"Mother! Mother!" *Ch'ucha'* exclaimed.

"Little *milka*, do you see them?"

"See who?" asked *Ch'ucha'*.

"Angels . . . all around you," said Nizhniya haltingly. "They are . . . waiting . . . waiting for you . . . ."

Nizhniya's eyes rolled back. She let out a shallow breath, and her body went limp in *Ch'ucha's* arms. *Ch'ucha'* closed her mother's eyes, kissed her on the forehead, gently lifted Nizhniya's head off her lap and laid her on the ground. Nizhniya was dead. Still kneeling beside her mother, *Ch'ucha'* removed her own huipil and laid it over Nizhniya's body.

Aguilar had been laughing at the pitiful scene. *Ch'ucha'* felt the hair on the back of her neck stand up; her eyes narrowed, her heartbeat violently. A ferocious anger welled up inside her. This time, she would yield to it. She looked up at Aguilar. A deep guttural sound reverberated from her chest and throat. Aguilar stopped laughing, startled by the panther-like growl. She withdrew the sword from her belt, and jumped to her feet with cat-like speed while raising the sword over her head. Aguilar took a step back, and then saw the broken blade. He began to laugh again. Soldiers, who had now gathered around them, also began to laugh at the preposterousness of this young girl threatening Aguilar with an old, broken sword.

Ch'ucha' let out a scream that sounded more like a roar and swung the sword down. The smile was suddenly erased from Aguilar's face. It was replaced not so much by a look of horror and pain, as by surprise. Lieutenant Mathers looked at Aguilar bewildered as blood emerged on Aguilar's clothing forming a line that went from his upper right shoulder down to his lower left side. Then the upper half of Aguilar's body slid off; the lower half teetered and fell backward. The Lieutenant took several steps back in panic, groped for his pistol, pulled it out of its holster and aimed it at *Ch'ucha'*. He was about to fire when a nearly invisible black form leapt from the brush and pounced knocking him to the ground. Its jaws grabbed his throat and ripped it out.

Ch'ucha' flung herself at the soldiers who had gathered around to witness Nizhniya's execution. They were now firing recklessly at her.

The bullets exploded in yellow-white sparks before they struck her. *Ch'ucha'* slashed and stabbed with the sword that was now as it had been in *Xilbalba*. Limbs, and headless torsos fell to the ground. Some of the soldiers ran into the jungle to escape, but were dispatched by *Ch'ucha'* soul-companion.

Two soldiers jumped on *Ch'ucha's* back. She flung them away with such violence that their bodies broke against the surrounding trees. Machine gun fire blasted the ground around her. She looked up. One of the helicopters, overhead was firing its canons at her. She reached up with her hand. She grasped the air as if taking hold of the helicopter itself. The helicopter jerked and sputtered. The pilot tried to ascend. He could not release the aircraft from the invisible force that held it. He called desperately to the pilot of the other helicopter for assistance. The other helicopter began firing at *Ch'ucha'*. She closed her fist, crushing the helicopter. She flung the shattered machine into the other helicopter. Both hurtled to the ground, exploding in a giant fireball.

Sister Margarita had gathered all the women and their children into the church. Mothers were trying to quiet their children who were terrified by the many explosions and screams they could hear just outside. Sister Margarita looked out the window and marveled as she watched *Ch'ucha'*—marveled as the Israelites had done when the Lord vanquished Pharaoh and his armies by casting them into the sea. She began to recite Psalm ninety-one as she stood at the window watching. The women and children listened as Sister Margarita prayed.

> *You shall not fear the terror of the night nor the arrow*
> *that flies by day,*
> *Nor the pestilence that roams in darkness . . . . Though a thousand*
> *fall at your side, ten thousand at your right hand,*
> *near you it shall not come . . . .*
> *For God commands the angels to guard you in all your ways.*

The doors of the church burst open. Terrified soldiers flooded in. Each grabbed one or two children. The children kicked and screamed as the soldiers dragged them away. *Ch'ucha'* heard the cries of the children.

She stopped, placed her sword back under her belt, and strode towards the church.

The soldiers came out holding children in front of them. "Surrender yourself and we will spare the children!"

Ch'ucha' folded her arms over her chest. Her hands were clenched and bloody. She looked up to the heavens and closed her eyes. An eerie silence followed. Her still, solitary figure, illuminated by the fires that now burned throughout the Mission, looked anything but threatening. She looked innocent, angelic. She bowed her head. Then with a terrific roar that came from a depth of her being that even she did not understand, she flung her arms outwards. A circle of fire exploded from her and raced like a huge wave through the camp, sweeping away the remaining soldiers and leaving the children unscathed.

Ch'ucha' stood silent. Exhausted. Broken. She took a single deep breath, lowered her head, and walked back to the body of Ludmelia Nizhniya.

Sister Margarita led the remaining women and children out of the church. It was safe; no one was left now to hurt them. She saw *Ch'ucha'* was now kneeling beside Nizhniya's body. She placed her hand tenderly on *Ch'ucha's* shoulder as *Ch'ucha'* lifted the body of Nizhniya and cradled her in her arms. She and the women and children of Mission de las Casas, watched as *Ch'ucha'*, carrying the body of her guardian, walked down the road, the same road by which they had arrived nearly four years earlier. Just as they were about to disappear from view, she could see the shadowy form of a great cat join them. Together, they disappeared into the jungle.

*   *   *

Obermann had watched as one monitor after another had displayed static. Finally, Obermann and General Barkley stood in front of the only remaining monitor that continued to display live video of the operation. One of the soldiers still had a camera strapped to his helmet. Obermann watched the lone figure of Theresa O'Conner, *Ch'ucha'*, as she stood near the center of the Mission courtyard. A wall of fire raced towards the camera. The final monitor went blank.

Obermann turned away. General Barkley continued to stare at the monitor, dumbstruck at what he had just witnessed.

"How . . . how . . ." the General finally stammered.

"Remember all that stuff you learned in Sunday school?" Obermann asked rhetorically. "Your twenty-first century mind rejected it as you grew older because you looked for evidence and found none. Well, guess what General? We just got our ass kicked by evidence."

General Barkley looked at Obermann in disbelief. Obermann aware of Barkley's thoughts, shook his head, "No, General, we're on the other side."

The General fell back into a chair. "Oh my God! Oh my God!" he kept repeating.

"Get a grip, General," exclaimed Obermann. "And get the President on the phone. I want authorization to drop a nuclear weapon on the site ASAP."

"What?!" exclaimed the General. "We can't do that!"

"Sure we can!"

"No!" exclaimed Frederick, who had been listening to the conversation while in the plane that was en route to Chiapas. "Father, listen to me."

"I know what you're going to say, Frederick. It's out of the question. She's too dangerous. I want you to turn around . . . ."

"I'm not turning around!"

"Are you disobeying me?!"

"Yes, Father. It's for your own good. Incinerate her and we've lost our chance of getting a blood sample; a sample that could mean a cure for you and for everyone else infected with the blood plague."

"There's the relic," Obermann replied.

"Wherever the hell that is!"

"It will show up eventually and when . . . ."

"No, Father. You can't stop me. I can do this. She's half of what I am."

"That's what concerns me," replied Obermann. "The other half is Maria O'Conner. And I have learned not to underestimate her."

"She's dead, Father. I am stronger than Theresa. I will defeat her."

Obermann knew there was no deterring him. He was accompanied by twenty incorporeal resubstantiates. "Very well. But promise me this. Do not try to take her alive. Kill her. And I mean make damn sure she's dead. Decapitate her. Then extract a blood sample."

"I will bring her head as a trophy for you!"

"A fitting trophy," said Obermann. "I will use her head to replace Pietro's in my tabernacle."

A Brand Snatched from the Fire

And the angel of the LORD said to Satan, "May the LORD rebuke you, Satan; may the LORD who has chosen Jerusalem rebuke you! Is not this man a brand snatched from the fire?" Now Joshua was standing before the angel, clad in filthy garments. He spoke and said to those who were standing before him, "Take off his filthy garments, and clothe him in festal garments." He also said, "Put a clean miter on his head." And they put a clean miter on his head and clothed him with the garments. Then the angel of the LORD, standing, said, "See, I have taken away your guilt."

-Zechariah 3:2-5

Colin O'Conner had learned that there were few communication systems that couldn't be broken into. His staff, in the Office of Justice and Tolerance, had done this for him on numerous occasions. Many a case had been successfully prosecuted by his Office with the help of information obtained by tapping into supposedly secure lines of communication. When Colin had heard a few days ago that his daughter was alive, he had contacted those in his office who could make all the right connections for him. They had. He was now sitting in front of a computer monitor that had just gone static. He hadn't seen everything, but he had seen enough. He had just witnessed a young woman, his daughter, the daughter he had once tried to have aborted, destroy an army! She was as fierce as Elijah bringing down fire and destroying the prophets of Baal.

He sat quiet a moment, outwardly still, while within conflicting emotions buffeted him. "She's like her mother, Maria" he mused aloud. "And them some!" He felt pride as he recalled the images of his daughter's heroic efforts. But pride quickly turned to shame. "I abandoned her," he groaned. How he had wanted to reach through the computer monitor, and embrace her; tell her how sorry he was for all the misery he had caused her and the family. But, she was beyond his reach. She was not, however, beyond the reach of Obermann and his bastard son, Frederick.

"Damn him! I'll kill him," Colin growled, "I'll just kill the son-of-a-bitch!" He stood up and started pacing.

"No, Cynthia tried that . . . God! I abandoned her, too." He groaned at the memory of their last day together. "He's protected now by some invisible force. I wonder what? Maybe connected with what I overheard Frederick say . . . incorporeals. Must be demons. No, there's nothing I can do," he moaned.

He felt desperation choking him. He saw clearly how his own pathetic pride and ambition had destroyed his wife and then a girlfriend, had alienated him from his son. Now it threatened his daughter again. "There's nothing, nothing I can do," he shouted aloud, banging his fist down on his desk in furious frustration. The desk drawer rattled as if in reply. Then he remembered.

He opened his desk drawer and picked up a large bottle of pain pills. Lately, he had been popping them like candy. The damn blood plague, those tiny treacherous renegade Chimæric stem cells were eating him from the inside out. His doctor had scheduled him for multiple transplants since there were plenty of harvestable organs now available. The Office of Justice and Tolerance made sure of that. The doctor had warned him that if he didn't have the transplants soon the pain would become unbearable. The doctor certainly was right about the pain.

"But I won't go through with the transplants," he thought. "Not now. Perhaps . . . ." He held the bottle up to the light, estimating, how many pills it still contained, ". . . if I take enough I could kill myself. It would be an appropriate end for a Judas," he thought. As he lowered the bottle, his glance fell on the open drawer. Tucked in the far corner was an unexpurgated copy of Maria' Journal, confiscated from an individual convicted of Chimæric intolerance. "Yes, Judas! And why the hell did I keep a copy of that? To remind me? Poor devil that had it is probably waiting to have his organs harvested. Maybe I would have gotten them." He slammed the drawer shut with his knee. Then he popped the bottle open and poured its contents into his right hand. Approximately twenty to thirty pills filled his hand.

"More than enough to kill me." He stared down at the pills, considering the release they promised—release from the pain, release from the guilt. He had just begun to raise his hand towards his mouth when he felt a burning pain erupt in the center of his palm with the force of an electric jolt. He cried out, and instinctively grabbed his right hand with his left. The pills scattered across the floor. His knees nearly buckled from the pain. He hadn't thought it was possible to experience pain more intense than that caused by the blood plague, but this was worse, far worse. The pain went deeper than his flesh; penetrated his very essence. He fell back into his chair, staring at the palm of right hand. The dark, red mark that had been seared onto his hand by Maria's wedding ring on the night he had sent Diego away now pulsated and oozed plasma as if it he had just been burned.

"Maria! Maria," Colin cried out, still gripping his hand, "Yes! You've got my attention. Now, what am I supposed to do?" The Journal. The answer came as a feeling rather than as sound. Painfully he maneuvered it out of the drawer with his left hand, set it on the desk and began to thumb through it. The word 'betrayer' caught his eye, and he started to read.

> *But, perhaps more interesting than the act of betrayal is the betrayer's recognition of the line that he has crossed. What will he do next? One way leads to repentance and restoration, as with Peter after the cock crowed. The other leads to destruction, either of the object of*

one's former loyalty or perhaps even of the self. Such was true of the most famous of all betrayers—Judas.

Colin closed his eyes. "She was writing about me," he thought. "Even then she knew I would betray her." The pain in his palm continued to throb. He turned back to the Journal

> *Those of us who feel that we have been betrayed must never become bitter. Did our Lord, when he was betrayed by those he came to save? Certainly not! We must never stop praying for them whether we are on this side of the veil or the other, for the path of restoration is a difficult one. It is often only through suffering that the betrayer can be restored to the Kingdom of God. We must never lose faith for our betrayers. We must never cease praying . . .*

"Maria, are you still praying for me?" asked Colin. He closed the book, and put it back in the drawer, aware that the pain in his hand was subsiding to a gentle warmth. Yes! Somehow he knew she was praying for him. He felt an inexplicable and undeserved hope rising in him like a wave of new strength. Hope. He had forgotten what it was. Perhaps he had never truly known. Sure, he had known it was one of the theological virtues. But now he knew it keenly, deep in his heart, as if for the first time, because he had known hopelessness with a dark, despairing intimacy. Hope! Why did he now feel that all was not lost? Circumstances had not changed. There was still nothing he could do for his daughter. And what of his son? Might he still betray Diego and make him submit to Chimæric conversion?

"No! Now I have hope," he said aloud. Hope to resist. In hope, the strength to submit, submit to suffering, the unremitting suffering of the blood plague. "I will refuse the transplants," he said firmly, standing up as if to emphasize his resolve. If he could submit to the suffering, he knew he could then resist the imposition of Obermann's will over his own.

"Help me, Maria,' he prayed.

Instantly, pain shot through his back. His legs buckled under him. He caught himself on the chair and collapsed, kneeling with his head on the seat. "Another plague episode," he gasped. "Worse than ever. The worst yet."

Offer it up! said a still, small voice within him.

Tears welled up in his eyes. "Maria, you used to exhort me to 'offer up' my little pains and disappointments as 'intentions' for someone," he remembered. "I will. I will offer it up," he whispered. "This is for you, Theresa."

Principalities and Powers

For our struggle is not with flesh and blood but with the principalities, with the powers, with the world rulers of this present darkness, with the evil spirits in the heavens. Therefore, put on the armor of God, that you may be able to resist on the evil day and, having done everything, to hold your ground. So stand fast with your loins girded in truth, clothed with righteousness as a breastplate, and your feet shod in readiness for the gospel of peace. In all circumstances, hold faith as a shield, to quench all the flaming arrows of the evil one. And take the helmet of salvation and the sword of the Spirit, which is the word of God.
-Ephesians 6:12-17

"We should be arriving in the Gulf of Honduras within a few hours," said the Captain to Goricsan. "It will be early morning when we arrive."

There was a knock on the door of the Captain's Stateroom where he was meeting with Goricsan, Abdullah and Father Nikitas. The Captain looked over to Goricsan, deferring to the Czar.

"You're the Captain," said Goricsan.

The Captain smiled and nodded. "Enter," he said.

Artem Sagalovich timidly opened the door and stuck his head in. Goricsan waved him in and instructed him to have a seat.

"I trust everything is arranged with the government in Guatemala?" asked Goricsan.

"Well, I can tell you this," began Sagalovich. "It took some doing. First, I was connected with some assistant to the undersecretary of such and such department . . . ."

Goricsan leaned over and whispered in Abdullah's ear, "Ask Sagalovich what time it is and he'll tell you how to make a watch!"

Abdullah let out a muffled laugh. Sagalovich had overhead the Czar's comment, but was undaunted. The story had to be told in its entirety if his true diplomatic skills were to be appreciated. Goricsan looked at his watch. They had some time to kill anyway.

"As I was saying," continued Sagalovich, somewhat irritated by the interruption. "No, I said. I must speak with the President himself. That is impossible, was the reply. Do you know whom you are talking to, I said in my most imposing tone. Now, I realize that I may not look very imposing, but over the phone I am quite imposing, or so I have been told."

"Would you get on with it!" demanded Father Nikitas irritably.

Sagalovich was stunned by Nikitas' remark. Goricsan, Abdullah and the Captain started laughing.

"Excuse me!" said Sagalovich in a tone which betrayed an injured ego.

"The submarine," said Goricsan. "It will be able to surface in the Gulf of Honduras without interference, correct?"

"Yes," replied Sagalovich, disappointed that he would not be able to explain the complex and subtle negotiations, which had made that possible.

"And you arranged for transport?"

"Yes, but that was the most difficult to arrange. As you know . . . ."

Goricsan noted that Nikitas was about to protest again. He shook his head very slightly, indicating that he wanted to give Sagalovich at least some opportunity to boast about his accomplishment. Nikitas frowned but relented.

". . . Guatemala has taken a neutral position in the conflict between the West and the Alliance. The President was concerned that the presence of the Alliance's military personnel within their borders might appear provocative and threaten their neutrality. I assured them that the entire operation would only last a few hours; that we're on a rescue mission to extricate one of our operatives who was being held by rebels in Chiapas. Finally, after considerable and delicate negotiations, the President agreed. Their military will provide us with a helicopter and a pilot."

"So how many O-rings do I buy this time?" asked Goricsan.

Sagalovich took a deep breath. "The government doesn't have to buy anything," Sagalovich said.

"Excellent," exclaimed Goricsan. "Well done! Perhaps . . . ."

"We have to sell some thing to the Guatemalan government," said Sagalovich timidly.

"What?" said Goricsan, wondering what Sagalovich had gotten them into this time.

"Oil."

"Okay. We have plenty of oil. And we are always looking to expand our markets."

"At five dollars a barrel," continued Sagalovich, bracing himself for the inevitable explosion.

"Five dollars a barrel!" exclaimed Goricsan. "Why didn't you just give it to them! That's one-tenth of the going price for crude. Are you mad! For Christ's sake, how many barrels did you promise we'd sell to them?"

"10 million barrels."

"10 million barrels! Why that's a . . . $450,000,000 loss! I suspect the President will be making a tidy profit!"

"I suspect," said Sagalovich.

"You cost me a lot of money, Sagalovich!"

Sagalovich was now cowering. He was expecting to hear that he would be catching the first flight back to Siberia upon their return to the motherland. Then to his surprise, Abdullah began to laugh.

"I fail to see what's funny!" exclaimed Goricsan.

"It is a small price to pay for a Czarina, is it not?!" replied Abdullah. "The King is right," said Nikitas, admonishing Goricsan. "The mission we are on has cosmic significance. Money is nothing. Sagalovich recognized this truth even without knowing it. You, on the other hand, should know better."

Goricsan bit his lip. He had been corrected by Nikitas on numerous occasions, but always in private. But Abdullah and Nikitas were right. In comparison to rescuing Ludmelia, his Czarina, what was money? What was a fortune? Goricsan took a deep breath.

"You are right," said Goricsan. "You did a fine job, Artem. I am in your debt."

"For 450,000,00 dollars, it would seem," offered Sagalovich timidly.

Everyone in the room laughed except Sagalovich. Nikitas slapped him on the back.

"I think we have all underestimated Mr. Sagalovich," said Nikitas.

Sagalovich straightened up in his chair. He tried to prevent a broad smile from overtaking his face. He was unsuccessful.

"Goricsan, I believe we should have Sagalovich accompany us on our mission to Chiapas," said Nikitas.

Goricsan nodded. "I think that's a terrific idea."

Sagalovich's mouth fell. "No, no! I don't do missions. I'm not really good with danger and all that kind of stuff. I . . . I . . . ."

"Nonsense," said Goricsan. "You underestimate your abilities. We could use someone as versatile as you in the field of battle."

"Field of battle? But, I don't even know how to use a gun!"

"That's all right," said Nikitas. "Guns won't do you any good anyway."

"They won't?" said Goricsan, Abdullah and Sagalovich simultaneously.

Nikitas shook his head. "You brought the swords and spears I requested?"

"Yes," replied Goricsan.

"Good. Those are what we need to kill nephilim."

"Nephilim?" asked Goricsan.

"Swords and spears!" said Sagalovich. He could envision hacking and piercing, that is, not his hacking and piercing, rather being hacked and pierced.

"I will explain everything," said Nikitas.

* * *

Ch'ucha' reached the entrance of the Temple of the Ancestors. The jaguar entered before her. She carefully maneuvered Nizhniya's body so that it now hung over her shoulder. Then she got down on her knees and crawled into the narrow entrance. It was night, so even the entrance of the Temple was dark, and as *Ch'ucha'* looked down the narrow stairway she could not see anything. Getting through the Temple was difficult enough in the pitch-blackness; the physical and emotional burden she carried made it nearly impossible. Two ghostly green eyes glowed immediately in front of her. Her soul-companion had turned around. *Ch'ucha'* blinked several times. She then opened her eyes wide; now, inexplicably, she could make out the steps in front of her and the walls on either side.

When she got to the base of the stairs she stood up and readjusted Ludmelia's body so that she carried it in both arms again. She squeezed her way through the labyrinth of corridors. She could remember the way to the heart of the Temple. When she reached the great chamber, she walked immediately to the stone altar where the statue of Saint Miguel the Archangel still stood. She laid Nizhniya's body across the altar.

The jaguar leapt onto the altar and stood towards the back, its black tail wrapping itself gently around Saint Miguel. It leaned over the beaten and bloodied face, sniffed at several wounds and began to lick them. Instinctively, *Ch'ucha'* pulled back the huipil that covered Nizhniya's body and opened Nizhniya's tattered and bloodstained shirt. A gaping hole still oozed blood and fluid, but around its perimeter there were slight indications of tissue regeneration. *Ch'ucha'* bent down, sniffed the wound . . . .

* * *

"We just received word from one of our agents in Guatemala that the government has granted permission for an Alliance helicopter to fly over its airspace," said Obermann. "Apparently they are on some sort of rescue mission. We are trying to locate the position of that helicopter now. But, I think you should anticipate that you will be receiving company soon."

"Dawn is just breaking," replied Frederick, "and I can see the Mission de las Casas ahead of us. I'll be sure to arrange a welcoming committee for our friends from the Alliance."

"Excellent," replied Obermann. "Keep me posted."

"Actually, I won't," said Frederick. "It's possible that they might monitor our communication. I don't want to jeopardize our element of surprise."

"Then communicate through incorporeals."

"Ah, yes," replied Frederick with some hesitation. He had no intention of communicating. It was time, thought Frederick to demonstrate that he was his own man. He didn't want his father interfering and being over protective. Besides, Frederick had conceived a plan of his own that he was not sure his father would approve.

The helicopter began to descend into the Mission courtyard. Some of the soldiers observed women and children scurrying out of the church and into the surrounding jungle.

"Would you like us to round them up for you?" asked Frederick's commanding Resubstantiate.

"No," replied Frederick. "Let them go. We do not need to hide behind women and children like Aguilar."

The helicopter landed, and Frederick stepped out. He surveyed the devastation. "Impressive, little sister. Very impressive indeed."

"Tell your men," said Frederick, "to occupy the buildings and stay out of sight." Frederick then turned to the helicopter pilot. "I saw a small clearing just north of here. Take the helicopter there and wait until you hear from me."

Frederick and his Resubstantiate lieutenant walked away from the helicopter as it restarted its engines. "I am expecting visitors. They will likely land here. Wait for them to exit the helicopter. If you take prisoners, I will interrogate them on my return."

"Where are you going, sir?"

"To find Theresa. She is near. I sense her presence."

Frederick headed down the road away from the Mission. The Resubstantiate watched as Frederick turned from side to side as if he were searching for an invisible path. Suddenly, Frederick turned off the road and disappeared into the jungle.

*   *   *

"There!" pointed Nikitas.

The pilot banked the helicopter to the left in the direction that Nikitas had pointed. Goricsan looked out the window. He could see a clearing with several adobe buildings; one appeared to be a church. As the helicopter drew closer it was evident that most of the buildings were heavily damaged. Vehicles were turned over on their sides and were still smoldering; bodies were scattered throughout the Mission compound.

"We're too late!" exclaimed Goricsan.

Nikitas did not respond, but instructed the pilot to land in the courtyard in front of the main church building. As the helicopter descended, Nikitas gave some final instructions.

"Remember, what I have told you," said Nikitas. "Those you will encounter are not men but nephilim. Show no mercy just as Samuel showed no mercy to Agag.[82]"

Goricsan stepped out of the helicopter, he was followed closely by Sagalovich who thought it would be best to stay as close to the Czar as possible. King Abdullah jumped down and then helped Madison Ryan out.

Ryan had pleaded with Goricsan that she be allowed to accompany them. "I was there when Theresa was born. I should be there when she is rescued."

Goricsan had refused. "The danger is too great. It is likely that some of us will not return. We need soldiers, not a journalist. We will need as many soldiers as we can take with us."

"On the contrary," Nikitas had replied. Five is an appropriate number for the army of Gideon."[83]

Nikitas stepped out of the helicopter and joined the four. He carried a spear, a gift from King Abdullah Mohammed al-Sharif. The spear's shaft was of hardwood; on one end was a steel spear point, on the other, a curved, scimitar-like blade. He took his place front and middle with Goricsan at his right and Abdullah at his left. Sagalovich and Ryan stood slightly behind the trio.

Nephilim began to emerge from the church and surrounding buildings. They assembled themselves approximately thirty to forty meters in front of Nikitas and the company.

"This is not good," muttered Sagalovich. "Not good, at all."

The nephilim commander slung his assault rifle off his shoulder and cocked it. The other nephilim followed his lead. Goricsan instinctively reached for his pistol. It was not there. Nikitas had instructed them to leave their firearms behind.

"Are you mad?!" Goricsan had asked Nikitas. "What good are these against assault rifles," he had said holding up the sword that Nikitas had just given him. "This is not the middle-ages!"

"Would that is was," Nikitas had replied gravely. "That was a time of prayer and repentance. Unbelief and arrogance have unleashed a time of darkness upon us. Principalities and powers are reestablishing ancient alliances while evil spirits battle the Holy Angels for the dominion of the realm between heaven and earth. The air is their arena of battle," Nikitas said, then as he pounded the floor with his spear, "the earth is ours."[84]

The commander noted that Goricsan and his companions had a smear of blood on their foreheads. Nikitas had anointed each of them, and himself, with blood from the holy relic. The commander threw his rifle aside and snorted a command to the other nephilim. It was an ancient, harsh tongue filled with guttural clicks and clacks. Goricsan imagined that if cockroaches had a language it would sound like this. The other nephilim dropped their guns as their commander had done.

"Ak liq boc tok!" shouted the commander pulling out his sword. The nephilim behind him pulled out their swords, raised them over their heads and chanted the commander's words in a blood-curdling chorus.

Goricsan reached across and grabbed the handle of his sword. Abdullah withdrew his scimitar. A shiver went down Sagalovich's spine as he heard the scimitar being drawn from its scabbard. Ryan took a deep breath, crossed herself, and pulled out the large knife that Nikitas had given her.

"For the Lord and for the Alliance!" exclaimed Nikitas as he charged forward, holding the spear like a lance.

Goricsan pulled out his sword and holding the handle with both hands, lifted it slightly over his right shoulder, and charged forward, catching up with Nikitas.

"Allahu Akhbah!" shouted Abdullah, waving the scimitar over his head.

The nephilim surged forward, *Ak liq bock tok!*

"Ah shit!" exclaimed Sagalovich pulling his sword out. He grabbed Ryan and pulled her along. "Stay close."

Nikitas was the first to engage the enemy. He plowed the spear into the nephilim commander. The spear jetted out the back of the nephilim. The commander looked down at the shaft that extended from his abdomen. He laughed as he brought his sword down on the shaft splintering it.

Goricsan brought his sword down. A nephilim held his sword to parry but Goricsan's strength was superior and the parry failed, Goricsan's sword continued downward cleaving into the shoulder of the enemy, cutting through his clavicle and arteries. The nephilim fell, receiving what should have been a mortal wound. Goricsan was redirecting his attack when the wounded nephilim stood back up and delivered an unexpected stab into Goricsan's side.

A nephilim lunged at Abdullah with his sword. Just as the sword was about to reach him, Abdullah brought his scimitar down and lopped off the arm of a nephilim. Undaunted, the nephilim reached down, picked up his sword with his other arm and continued to attack Abdullah.

"Fools!" exclaimed the commander, reaching behind him and yanking out Nikitas' spear. "We are indestruc . . . ."

Nikitas swung what remained of his weapon. The commander's head flew off his shoulders. The head sputtered on the ground, spraying its blackish-red blood on the combatants. Ryan grimaced at the horrific sight while Sagalovich was almost sure he heard the head whistling, "Sorry master . . . sorry master."

"*Decapitate* them!" shouted Nikitas. "It is the only way to kill them."

Siblings

Like clay in the hands of a potter, to be molded according to his pleasure, So are men in the hands of their Creator, to be assigned by him their function. As evil contrasts with good, and death with life, so are sinners in contrast with the just; See now all the works of the Most High: they come in pairs, the one the opposite of the other.

~ Sirach 33:13-15

Frederick surveyed his immediate surroundings. The morning light filtered through the jungle canopy. A small hill rose above him. He knew she was near.

"*Ch'ucha*!" Frederick shouted with mock playfulness. "I know you are here. Come out, come out wherever you are!"

The jaguar's ears perked up. Nizhniya's face had been licked clean. All traces of blood had been removed, even the bruises seemed less noticeable. The jaguar jumped off the altar and started to leave the great chamber. It turned around and growled at its soul-companion.

Ch'ucha' blinked and shook herself. She was surprised to find herself straddling the body of Nizhniya. She looked down at the hole in Nizhniya's chest. It was smaller than she remembered. Time had passed. How much she did not know. As she hopped off the altar, she began to remember, but it was more like a dream. It was as if she had been dreaming someone else's dream, her soul-companion's dream. The salty taste of blood was in her mouth. She wiped her mouth and chin. They were covered with warm body fluids.

The jaguar growled again.

"What is it?" asked *Ch'ucha'*.

The jaguar turned toward the exit of the great chamber. It looked behind him. *Ch'ucha'* understood and followed. The jaguar maneuvered its way through the labyrinth of halls and rooms until it reached the stairway that led outside. It stopped and waited. Finally, *Ch'ucha'* appeared. She could see the morning light filtering through the hidden entrance of the Temple.

"*Ch'ucha'*! Don't be shy, little sister. I know you're around here somewhere!"

Ch'ucha' did not recognize the voice. How did he know, whoever he was, that she was here? She stood at the base of the stairs. Should she go up? The jaguar bent his head forward and growled. He slowly ascended the stairs as if he were stalking prey. Instinctively, *Ch'ucha'* followed; the primordial urge was again coursing through her veins. She could smell him. He was kin, and kin could not always be trusted. The male often killed a sibling to establish dominance, other times just for sport. She was not about to offer this one her jugular in submission.

Ch'ucha' stepped through the entrance. The jaguar took off, scampered up a tree, and watched. *Ch'ucha'* saw the lone figure of a man standing some fifteen meters from her. He turned around. She recognized him. It was him—the young man on the cover of the magazine, Frederick Obermann.

He slowly walked towards her. As he approached her he knew that she was like him; perhaps the only one that would ever be like him. She would understand him, perhaps as no one else ever would. In this brief moment, he felt a kinship that he had not known with another human being; not even his father. His father! He remembered his promise to bring his father her head as a trophy! He would demonstrate his manhood; prove his superiority over those who opposed them. Yet, he felt conflicted.

How beautiful she is, he thought, as he drew nearer. *Ch'ucha'* possessed a beauty altogether different from what he had known in Elaina. And she was dangerous. She had proven that at the Mission against the fool, Aguilar. A slight smile crossed Frederick's face as he considered the challenge before him. He had never known danger. It had its own attraction, especially when found in a woman.

"You can't imagine how pleased I am to see you," said Frederick.

Ch'ucha' said nothing. She knew instinctively that he was treacherous. Yet, she, too, felt inexplicably drawn to him. She took several steps towards him. Frederick sensed her confusion. He drew no closer, but began to walk slowly around her, studying her. As he encircled her he drew an invisible curtain around them so that neither corporeal nor incorporeal could intervene. This would be between him and her. She stood firm, turning to keep her eyes fixed on him. Frederick found his adversary unnerving. Was she unaware of the trap into which he was luring her or was she simply not intimidated by it?

Frederick attempted to probe her mind as his father had taught him.

He had never encountered a mind such as hers. Her consciousness was woven from threads of personal and communal identity. It was a complex tapestry; he found it nearly impossible to distinguish her memories from the experiences of the Mayan civilization into which she had been absorbed. He navigated through the complex labyrinth of thoughts, looking for that corridor that might lead to the heart of her self. Then he found it, her destiny. Frederick marvelled at the Call, ordained since the beginning, and prophesied from of old. The Enemy, in His divine arrogance, had chosen a *girl* to thwart the final plans of the Master. His father had been right. She was a far more formidable adversary then he had expected. Then, as he retreated from her mind, he found a fragment of memory that revealed to him what he needed to know.

You will be the sword in the hand of Kos; with you He will defeat the Lords of Xibalba.

No, Kos must choose another.

She *was* like him—independent, defiant. Whereas he drew his power from his Master who was Defiance, her Master was Obedience. Her power, her *Itz*, could only be wielded in submission to His will. This was her Achilles heel. She had not said *yes*. Then he sensed something deeper than consciousness—a primordial subconsciousness that his sophisticated mind could not stoop low enough to enter. One thing was apparent. It had no need to say *yes*, for it had never said *no*. Being imprudent and arrogant, he brushed aside his concern about this unfamiliar consciousness. Besides, he was confident now that he knew she was vulnerable. Perhaps, he thought, she could be persuaded to say *yes, to me!*

"I saw what happened at the Mission. Very impressive, Sister."

"Why do you call me sister?" *Ch'ucha'* said.

"You have not been told?" said Frederick. "I am your brother!"

Ch'ucha' looked curiously at Frederick. She had had that same thought when she saw his picture on the magazine cover. She had felt an inexplicable connection to him then.

"Look at me! Have we not the same eyes? We are alike in so many ways."

"But we do not have the same parents," said *Ch'ucha'*, more as a question than a statement, as if a genuine familial bond might be a possibility.

"Genes are more important than parents," replied Frederick. "Genes are more important than family. We are brother and sister genomically. Do you understand?"

"I understand," said *Ch'ucha'*, furrowing her brow, angered by his patronizing tone.

Frederick was pleased that he had angered her. It made her more dangerous and more desirable. He *wanted* her; not for his father, not for a trophy. He wanted her for *himself*. He held out his hand to her.

"Come with me, Sister."

"No!" replied *Ch'ucha'*.

"Where will you go, then?"

Ch'ucha' had no answer.

"Whatever you want to be . . . you can be that with me."

Frederick could feel her yielding. He approached her as one stealthily approaches a bird with a snare. "That's right," he continued, "No one will try to make you be something you don't want to be." Frederick continued to approach her with extended hand. "Be my sister . . . ."

Ch'ucha' reached out and took his hand. Immediately, the ground beneath them trembled, birds took flight while other animals took shelter deeper into the jungle. The grass beneath them withered, and death radiated from under their feet until it reached the trees. It traveled up their trunks like an insidious blight. Leaves yellowed and dropped; limbs cracked and fell. The sky grew dark.

". . . better still," continued Frederick, "be my queen, and the world will be our kingdom."

Ch'ucha' felt overpowered by his desire. His perverse thoughts stripped her naked and were on the verge of violating her very essence when unexpectedly Frederick's consciousness was hurled back. The primordial consciousness of *Ch'ucha'* soul-companion had not been deceived. It leapt at Frederick's consciousness driving him back and freeing *Ch'ucha'*.

"Never!" *Ch'ucha'* snarled. "I would rather die than yield to you!"

"Die?!" exclaimed Frederick, enraged by the sting of her rejection. "You would rather die than to submit?!" Frederick was infuriated. He, who could have anything or anyone, was being refused by the very one he wished to possess.

"Do you not know who I am? The world has clung tenaciously to its fragments of existence. I have come to give it life."

"You are a liar!" said *Ch'ucha'* with contempt.

"No! You're the liar. You won't die. Dying is for fools, fools like your mother. But you're not like your mother, little sister. There is more of me in you than her."

"I am my own person."

"Really? And who is that person? Is it Theresa? Is it *Ch'ucha'*?"

"Come. Find out for yourself!" snarled *Ch'ucha'*, pulling out her sword and holding it in front of her.

Frederick was enraptured by the seductive danger that challenged him.

"I shall!"

Frederick withdrew his sword and charged her. Just as he came upon her, he raised the sword over his head and brought it down towards her head. It slammed with a terrible force against *Ch'ucha's* blade, which she had raised at the last possible moment. Their swords locked with equal force. They stared into each other's faces. They could feel each other's breath.

"You see," he said, grimacing under the strain of her blade, "you are just like me!"

"No!" she growled. She pushed with all her might against her sword. Frederick fell sprawling back onto the ground.

*   *   *

Nikitas had pushed furthest into the enemy line, Goricsan was behind and to his left, Abdullah was to his right. Ryan and Sagalovich stayed close within this pocket. Sagalovich had taken on the grisly task of decapitating wounded nephilim that slipped or fell between the trio.

"Artem!"

Sagalovich turned to his left. A wounded nephilim had fallen on Ryan and had wrestled her knife away from her. The nephilim raised it above his head and was about to plunge it into her chest when Sagalovich lopped off its arm. The nephilim rolled off Ryan, howling. Artem drove his sword into its chest.

"Look out!" shouted Ryan.

Sagalovich saw that Ryan was looking behind him. He ducked down and crouched, folding his arms across and over his head. He felt resistance against his arm and a muffled groan. The nephilim that had run up behind him had impaled himself on Sagalovich's sword, which was extended behind him. Ryan crawled over to the knife that Nikitas had given her. It was still held firm by the severed nephilim hand. She cried out in terror and disgust as she pried the knife free. Artem and the nephilim where wrestling on the ground. She ran over with her knife and stabbed the nephilim repeatedly. It flung out an arm, knocking

Ryan to the ground. Artem lunged for his sword, got up on his knees, and swung the sword, decapitating the nephilim, but his sword flew out of his hand. Ryan staggered to her feet.

"Look out!" Ryan shouted again.

The nephilim with the severed arm was back on its feet. It held the sword with its other arm now. It was about to plunge the sword into Sagalovich's back when Ryan hurtled a knife at it. Sagalovich fell on his back and watched as the knife was deflected away from the nephilim. The nephilim laughed and raised his sword. Sagalovich was powerless to defend himself. Ryan watched horrified, powerless to intervene. Sagalovich closed his eyes and grimaced as he anticipated the fatal blow.

From out of nowhere a mass of insects converged on the nephilim's head; they bit and stung mercilessly. The nephilim howled, dropped his sword, and ran into the forest. Sagalovich and Ryan looked at each other bewildered.

Ryan offered Sagalovich her hand and helped him up. They found each other face-to-face. He quickly kissed her lips. Ryan's eyes opened wide with surprise. Just as quickly, he released her, startled by his action. Ryan then put her hand behind Artem's neck, and pulled his head towards her and gave him a short, passionate kiss. Now his eyes grew wide. She pulled away and smiled. Artem felt strangely emboldened. He and Ryan turned toward Nikitas and, his companions. Headless torsos and severed limbs lay strewn about. Nephilim heads spun, sputtered, and steamed in pools of blood. Nikitas, Goricsan, and King Abdullah had continued to press forward. Now they formed a tight group with nephilim surrounding them on all sides. The situation was desperate.

"Shall we?" he said to Ryan.

She nodded, and together they charged the nephilim horde.

*   *   *

Frederick jumped back to his feet. He was angry and astonished.

"You are just like me!" Frederick shouted again at her.

He ran towards her and swung his sword. She parried and riposted, lunging under his hand-guard towards his abdomen. He dropped back, bringing his own blade down to parry hers. The tip of her sword pierced his clothing and penetrated his skin. His parry pushed the blade to the side tearing a four-inch gash in his flesh. The wound was superficial, but it shocked Frederick. He took several steps back and felt his wound. He looked at his hand covered in his own blood.

"Aaaahh!" he howled in anger.

The canopy of the jungle shook. Branches and leaves fell. Dark clouds began to gather overhead. The jaguar jumped off the limb from which it had been watching. He lunged towards the enemy, but was repelled by an invisible force. The jaguar circled the combatants, seeking a way to break through to his soul-companion.

Frederick charged recklessly, but *Ch'ucha'* held her ground. He thrust his sword towards her head. She swung her sword up and across her body. It caught Frederick's blade, sweeping it up and over her head. His momentum carried him forward. *Ch'ucha'* brought her arm down, smashing Frederick's face with the sword's handguard. Blood squirted from his nose and mouth as he stumbled backwards and fell to one knee.

"Damn you!" he cursed as he wiped blood from his mouth. "Why won't you yield?"

"Yield?!" exclaimed *Ch'ucha'* ferociously. "I yield to no one. Not to you. Not to *Kos!*"

Frederick smiled. By her own words, she had delivered herself into his hands. He lunged toward her. *Ch'ucha'* brought her sword up just in time to parry it. Frederick slammed into her and both went tumbling to the ground. *Ch'ucha'* quickly crawled over to her fallen sword and picked it up.

"It is between you and me, now," said Frederick.

Ch'ucha' thrust her blade into the *en garde* position. "You speak too much," *Ch'ucha'* growled as she leapt upon Frederick. Frederick parried and swung his sword, delivering a deep gash across her upper arm.

Ch'ucha' took several steps back and grabbed her arm. Blood flowed between her fingers.

I have her! thought Frederick.

He charged her with a thrusting attack. *Ch'ucha'* dropped the blade down and across her body to parry, but at the last moment he went over the top of her handle, and jammed the tip of his saber deep into her right side. As he ran past her, he pulled the sword so that it exited by ripping her side open. *Ch'ucha'* fell to her knees.

Frederick stopped and turned slowly around to face her. He was confident now. He knew that he had inflicted a serious injury. *Ch'ucha'* struggled to her feet.

"So, you would rather die than yield?" asked Frederick sardonically. He slowly walked towards her. She was buckled over; her left arm across her abdomen, her hand attempting to hold her left side together.

"Too bad you waited so long. Everyone that has ever loved you has died. And now you have failed them!"

Ch'ucha' struggled to straighten herself and raise her sword. She fell back on her knees and dropped her sword. She teetered as if about to fall over. She was his.

"You really are like me after all," sneered Frederick. "You would rather die than be broken by another's will. But that's my strength—not yours."

Frederick plunged his sword through *Ch'ucha's* chest. He let go of the sword; the handle jutted out from between her breasts. *Ch'ucha's* eyes rolled back. She was about to topple over when he caught her hair with his hand. He straightened her up and shook her, trying to bring her back to consciousness one last time. Her eyes opened. Her pupils dilated as they futilely tried to focus. Frederick grabbed the sword and yanked it out of her chest. *Ch'ucha's* eyes rolled back.

"Pity," he said, raising the sword over his head. "What a queen you would have made."

He stood ready to complete his mission; to bring his father the trophy that he had promised him. His arm trembled. Frederick struggled to bring the sword down to decapitate his victim. He could not. Why not? She had rejected him in life. What could she still mean to him in death? Frederick shook his head and tossed the sword into the brush. The invisible curtain collapsed. Frederick released her. Her lifeless body toppled to the ground.

*　　*　　*

"Too many!" exclaimed Goricsan as he thrust his blade into the belly of a nephilim. "They keep popping back up!" he continued to bring his blade down, cleaving the head of another.

There seemed to be no end of nephilim. They had encircled the trio. Swords would slip past a parry and cut, jab or gouge flesh. Each of the trio could feel his body weakening under the physical strain and loss of blood from the many wounds each had received. Goricsan was now no longer attacking but defending. Parry after parry. There were too many swords to defend. A blade came down towards his head. There was no time to parry it. Suddenly, the head of the nephilim wielding the sword flew off his shoulders. Sagalovich's smiling face appeared over the headless torso in almost comedic fashion. Ryan stabbed another nephilim in the back, giving Goricsan enough time to finish him off. Sagalovich and Ryan joined the trio.

"Nice of you to join us," said Goricsan.

"And miss out on all the fun!" replied Sagalovich.

Sagalovich's newfound bravado was so out of character that Goricsan could not help laughing.

Abdullah heard his comrades laughing. The battle must have turned in our favor! he thought. He was inspired by a new vigor and fought with his former ferocity. He began to laugh as well.

Nikitas heard the laughter of his comrades. As he wielded his broken spear he began to shout verses from Psalm fifty-nine,

> *You, LORD, laugh at them; you deride all the nations. My strength, for you I watch; you, God, are my fortress, my loving God. May God go before me, and show me my fallen foes. Slay them, God, lest they deceive my people. Shake them by your power . . . .*

The sky grew suddenly dark. Ryan looked up. The air above them was teeming with vast numbers of birds: hawks, crows, sparrows and even the tiniest of finches. All at once, they swooped down and attacked the enemy. They pecked at their eyes while their talons tore at their flesh. Nephilim howled and cursed. They dropped their weapons, covered their heads with their arms and ran screaming into the jungle. They were met by an onslaught of the Lacandon denizens, large and small. Spiders and centipedes slipped under their body armor to deliver venomous bites and stings. Numerous little jungle rodents gnashed at them with their teeth, giant anaconda caught and crush their nephilim prey; cries and curses were quickly replaced by a silent and satiated jungle.

Goricsan dropped to one knee exhausted and injured by many wounds. Abdullah drove his sword into the ground and leaned against it. Nikitas walked over to Sagalovich.

"Here is our reluctant hero!" said Nikitas throwing his arm around Sagalovich's shoulder.

"Ow!" exclaimed the new hero, grimacing as Nikitas squeezed a deep gash he had received on his left shoulder. Sagalovich buckled over. Up until that moment he hadn't even felt the wound. He was bleeding badly.

Ryan ran over. "We need to stop this bleeding!" she exclaimed.

"There is a medical kit in the helicopter," said Goricsan. "I'll go . . . ."

"There is no time," interrupted Nikitas. Then turning to Ryan he continued, "Have the pilot help you with Sagalovich, then join us."

"Where?" asked Ryan.

"And where are Major Nizhniya and Theresa?" asked Goricsan

Nikitas looked around. He saw a helicopter begin to descend into the jungle northeast of their position.

"There!" exclaimed Nikitas.

Nikitas started running in the direction he had pointed. Goricsan and Abdullah followed.

* * *

The jaguar stealthily maneuvered through the brush attempting to avoid being noticed by the beast. It did not understand what happened to its soul-companion. He saw her body lying lifeless on the ground. She was there but not there. It was as if she were lost in the jungle when the clouds touched the earth and all was gray and formless. The jaguar relied on its keen sense of smell and hearing to find its way through the dense jungle fog. But his companion did not have such senses. She could not find her way back.

The jaguar continued to circle the beast, caught between the instinct to rip its neck open, and the desire to search for his companion. Then he smelled his companion's blood in the brush. He found it, the long, shiny claw that the beast had used to kill his companion. The jaguar licked the blade clean of blood. Then he used his nose and paws to turn the sword over. As he licked the blood off the other side of the weapon a giant hummingbird flew and hovered over the clearing. It landed just a few jumps from the beast and his companion.

Frederick ran to the helicopter that just moments before had landed not far from him and the body of *Ch'ucha'*. He threw open the door. "Keep the engine running," he shouted to the pilot. Frederick reached into the cabin and pulled out a metal box, and carried it back with him to *Ch'ucha's* body. He bent down on one knee, opened the box, and took out one of several large hypodermics, he removed the plastic guard from the needle and then laid it on *Ch'ucha's* chest. He grabbed her tattered blouse and ripped it open. He slid his left hand down her still warm abdomen and palpated her upper right groin with both his fingers and his mind.

"Here!" he exclaimed, locating one of *Ch'ucha's* ovaries. He marked the spot with his left middle finger, picked up the hypodermic with his right hand, and plunged the needle through her abdominal wall. The needle penetrated the ovary. He pulled back on the syringe. Blood and tissue filled the hypodermic.

"This is for me," he said, placing the syringe back into the refrigerated metal box. "You might not be my queen, but you may still be the mother of my prince."

He removed and readied another hypodermic. He took her left arm and laid it flat on the ground, examined her arm and found an appropriate vein, then pushed the needle into the vein and pulled back on the syringe. He had secured the blood that promised a cure for his father and all those suffering from the blood plague. He pulled the needle out of *Ch'ucha's* arm and held it up triumphantly before him.

"And this is for you, Father!"

As he stared at the hypodermic of blood his eyes refocused on the black figure in the background. Its head was slung low, its back was arched and it snarled with a ferocity that sent a shiver down Frederick's spine. He glanced about for his incorporeal protection, but they were powerless against the animal. Frederick slowly stood up. He reached down to pick up the metal box. The jaguar pounced. The hypodermic flew from Frederick's hand into the brush. Man and animal tumbled together. Frederick on his back, pushed against the jaguar's neck, trying to keep the saber sharp teeth away from his neck. Never had he encountered anything like this creature. It was pure primal fury without self-doubt or equivocation. The jaguar swung at Frederick's face with its front paws. He screamed as claws dug and tore into his forehead leaving three deep gashes. He pushed with his leg as hard as he could. As they rolled, Frederick reached down and pulled out a knife that hung from his belt. He drove it into side of the jaguar again and again. The jaguar howled and released his prey. Frederick staggered to his feet as the jaguar limped, crawled away and then collapsed across *Ch'ucha's* body.

The pilot was running towards him.

"Where the hell were you?!" shouted Frederick, feeling the slashes in his forehead.

"There are men coming," exclaimed the pilot, pointing back towards the road.

Frederick was not up for another fight. He was spent. He looked around for the hypodermic with the blood. He didn't see it.

"Hurry," shouted the pilot as he jumped into the cockpit.

Frederick grabbed the metal box and ran towards the helicopter. He saw the three men running towards them. Damn! How did they know?! Nikitas! His father had warned him about the monk. He jumped into the helicopter and immediately it lifted off the ground.

"Damn it," the pilot said, wiping blood out of his eyes.

"You're bleeding," said Frederick. There were three deep gashes across the pilot's forehead. "How did that happen?"

"I don't know."

Frederick looked at himself in the reflection of the cockpit windshield. The pilot's gashes were identical to his own.

Nikitas watched as the helicopter sped north over the treetops. He had seen Frederick running with a metal box. What was in it? thought Nikitas. What sinister scheme had he conceived?

The three ran over to the body of *Ch'ucha'* and that of the jaguar lying across her. Abdullah stood motionless, staring at the young woman's face. He was mesmerized; no amount of blood or bruises could conceal her nobility. He knew nothing of this young woman, but he felt as if his heart had been sundered in two. Inexplicably he knew he loved her; since the first man and woman had been fashioned from clay, Allah had imagined their love.

Goricsan bent down and examined the numerous wounds covering *Ch'ucha's* body. It was evident that she had fought heroically. He looked up at Nikitas who was now standing next to him.

"Is this also part of the mysterious will of God?" asked Goricsan angrily.

Nikitas was silent.

"Where is she?" demanded Goricsan. "Where is my Czarina?"

"I am not sure," replied Nikitas. "Wait." Nikitas stood motionless, staring into space as though listening to a distant voice. "The Temple of the Ancestors."

"What?!" exclaimed Goricsan.

"This way," said Nikitas, running.

"How does he know that?" wondered Abdullah.

"I don't know, but come on," said Goricsan.

Nikitas, Goricsan, and Abdullah ran beyond the small clearing and into the jungle. They split up, looking for a Mayan structure that might be the Temple of the Ancestors.

Meanwhile, the Black Shark helicopter landed near the bodies of *Ch'ucha'* and the jaguar. Ryan jumped out of the helicopter and ran over to the body of the young woman. Sagalovich stepped out of the helicopter and limped over towards Ryan.

"Who is it?" asked Sagalovich.

"Oh my God!" Ryan exclaimed. "It's Theresa!"

"How could this be Theresa?" asked Sagalovich. "This girl looks to be sixteen, perhaps seventeen."

"I don't know. Somehow I just know, it's her," said Ryan. "Wait a minute." She spied a chain around the young woman's neck. She reached underneath the tattered garment and removed a medallion. She recognized it. Maria had had one just like it. She had given it to Gabriela to give to her daughter. So it was Theresa. There was no doubt about it. Ryan fell to her knees and began to weep. Sagalovich knelt next to her and put his arm around her. He looked over at the great black cat lying next to the body of the young woman. Sagalovich marveled at how he had ended up in the middle of this incredible drama. He didn't regret being a part of it. Not now, not while Madison leaned up against him.

"Over here!" shouted Abdullah. He stood in front of what appeared to be an entrance to a cave.

"This may be it," said Nikitas

Goricsan took a small flashlight from his belt. "This way," he said, stooping down as he entered the opening. "Watch your step."

The trio descended the stairs. When they arrived at the bottom, Goricsan waved his hand. "Wait!" He bent down and examined the ground at the bottom of the stairs. "Footsteps . . . and paw prints!" He led the company through the complex of halls and rooms following the circuitous trail of foot and paw prints. They led to a cavernous room.

"Over there," said Goricsan, pointing to a flickering candle. As the trio approached the candle, they saw that it stood upon a large stone altar. Goricsan could see what appeared to be the outline of a body also lying on the altar. His heart pounded.

"Oh God," Goricsan sighed, recognizing the face of Ludmelia Nizhniya. He pounded the altar with his fist. "Four years I have waited and prayed. Four years! And this is how God answers my prayers!"

Abdullah picked up the votive candle and held it up to her face. Her cheeks were flushed. She looked as if she were asleep.

"My friend," said Abdullah. "Allah is testing you. Clearly there is more here than death."

Goricsan looked up. He saw Nizhniya's face more clearly now in the candlelight. She was even more beautiful than he remembered. He tentatively placed his hand on her cheek. She was warm! He felt for a carotid pulse. There was none. Goricsan pulled back the elaborately woven garment that covered her body. Her hands were crossed over her chest. He took one of her hands. They were warm too and the fingers flexible. There was no sign of rigor mortis. He noticed through her torn and bloodied shirt, a red, swollen mark about the size of a penny. Aside from a few bruises, he could not see any other injuries that might have been the cause of her death. Goricsan looked over at Nikitas.

"She is Chimæric," Nikitas said. "Her soul is lost in the shadow lands of the Penumbra Realm."

"What am I too do?" asked Goricsan desperately.

"Trust God," Nikitas replied. "And be Czar."

Goricsan lifted the body of Ludmelia Nizhniya off the stone altar while Nikitas picked up the statue of Saint Michael the Archangel. Abdullah led them out of the Temple.

"Here they come!" exclaimed Sagalovich.

As they approached, Abdullah stopped, and picked up something off the ground and slipped it under his belt.

Ryan looked up. "Oh no!" she sighed as he saw that Goricsan was carrying a body.

Sagalovich walked over to the trio. He recognized the young intelligence officer he had helped years earlier. Goricsan said nothing but continued towards the helicopter with the body of Ludmelia Nizhniya. Abdullah stopped and stood beside the body of the young woman. Ryan noted how anguished the King appeared. He bent down, lifted her up her body, and started to carry the body to the helicopter.

"Please, let me help," Ryan said to Abdullah.

"No," said Nikitas. "Help me with the jaguar."

"The jaguar?" inquired Ryan.

"Yes," replied Nikitas. "There is more here than even I understand."

Nikitas handed the statue of Saint Michael to Sagalovich. Ryan looked curiously at Nikitas. He did not offer an explanation. She reached under the shoulder of the sleek, black cat. Its fur was sticky with blood, but she could not tell where it had been wounded. She was surprised how heavy the jaguar was. She groaned as they lifted the animal.

"Let me help," offered Sagalovich.

"No," replied Ryan. "You're likely to open up your wound again."

The bodies were reverently laid on the floor of the helicopter. Everyone took their seats, too physically and emotionally exhausted to speak. Nikitas had taken the statue from Sagalovich and was now examining the unusual garment that was draped around it. The pilot looked back at Goricsan for directions.

"Get us the hell out of here," Goricsan finally said.

Vessel of Wrath

What then are we to say? Is there injustice on the part of God? Of course not! For he says to Moses: I will show mercy to whom I will, I will take pity on whom I will." So it depends not upon a person's will or exertion, but upon God, who shows mercy. For the scripture says to Pharaoh, "This is why I have raised you up, to show my power through you that my name may be proclaimed throughout the earth." Consequently, he has mercy upon whom he wills, and he hardens whom he wills. You will say to me then, "Why then does he still find fault? For who can oppose his will?" But who indeed are you, a human being, to talk back to God? Will what is made say to its maker, "Why have you created me so?" Or does not the potter have a right over the clay, to make out of the same lump one vessel for a noble purpose and another for an ignoble one? What if God, wishing to show his wrath and make known his power, has endured with much patience the vessels of wrath made for destruction? This was to make known the riches of his glory to the vessels of mercy, which he has prepared previously for glory.

-Romans 9:14-23

Rosario is dead . . . Mateas . . . Father Suarez . . . Santiago . . . they'll all dead . . . all because of me. Ludmelia! I couldn't save you . . . not even with *Itz* from *Xibalba*. I failed . . . all that you and Rosario tried to teach me . . . I couldn't even save myself.

A maelstrom of despair and self-recrimination sucked *Ch'ucha'* in upon herself. She could imagine her body coiled in a fetal position—if she had a body. She was dead, but her soul did not have the hope of heaven; neither did it languish in hell. Instead, her self-loathing created its own universe, separate from all others, devoid of the presence of Blessedness.

I could not even save myself . . . . No! I would not save myself. To save myself would be to acknowledge Him . . . To yield to *Kos* . . . .

Ch'ucha' was about to contract inexorably upon herself when she heard her name.

"*Ch'ucha'*!"

Ch'ucha' recognized the voice. It was Rosario! But, she could not tell from where the voice had come. It was as much inside as outside her.

"*Ch'ucha'*!"

"Where are you?" she said or thought. She was not sure how she had responded.

"I am here," the voice said. "I am within you."

Ch'ucha' looked into the deepest regions of herself.

"Take my hand."

Ch'ucha' reached in. A hand grasped hers and pulled. *Ch'ucha'* felt as though she were being pulled inside herself, like pulling on a sleeve from the inside and then finding the inside folded outward.

"What happened?" asked *Ch'ucha'*.

"You have passed through the Heart of the Temple," replied Rosario.

"I have failed," choked *Ch'ucha'*.

"No, *Ch'ucha'*. You have won."

Ch'ucha' looked up at her questioningly. "How can that be? Ludmelia is dead. Your son is dead. I could not save them."

"Do you not remember the hero twins?" asked Rosario. "They deceived the Lords of *Xibalba* by allowing themselves to be killed. In losing, they assured themselves a greater victory."

"No," exclaimed *Ch'ucha'*. "I was defeated because I refused to yield . . ."

"Even so," interrupted a woman who emerged seemingly from nowhere, "God used you to achieve His purpose."

Ch'ucha' spun around, her eyes narrowed. She recognized the voice. *Ch'ucha'* was filled with rage.

"I know you. I dreamt about you."

"Yes," replied the woman. "I am your mother."

Ch'ucha' stepped back. "You conspired with *Kos* to create a destiny that I did not choose for myself," she said accusingly. "And now I find that even when I refuse him, I am his servant."

Ch'ucha' began to dissolve into the mist of the outside. Maria reached through and took a hold of *Ch'ucha's* hand.

"I cannot hold onto you," said Maria. "You must choose not to let go."

Ch'ucha's anger urged her to let go. She could feel her mother's grip loosening. Their fingers began to slide over each other. The dark solitude of Self began to close again upon her. Now only the tips of their fingers were in contact.

"If you return to the Shadowlands," said Maria across the gray void, "you will never be able to rescue Ludmelia."

Ch'ucha' clenched her fingertips and grasped those of her mother's. It was enough. Maria pulled her back. *Ch'ucha'* fell into her mother's arm, then pushed herself away.

"What did you mean?" asked *Ch'ucha'*. "Is she not here, in heaven?"

"This is not heaven," replied Maria. "This is the outskirts of the Penumbra Realm."

"Ludmelia is where you were—the Shadowlands," continued Rosario.

"Bring her across as you did me," insisted *Ch'ucha'*.

"We cannot," answered Maria. "She has chosen to remain in the Penumbra Realm so that she might return to the Corporeal World."

"I don't understand," said *Ch'ucha'*.

"Her destiny is not yet fulfilled," said Rosario. "And she cannot return to fulfill that destiny without your help."

"What must I do?" asked *Ch'ucha'*.

"It is not for us to tell," replied Rosario. "But, we will take you to Him who will show you what you need to know."

"*Kos?*" sneered *Ch'ucha'*. "I understand now. Ludmelia is held hostage so that I must serve His will."

"Come," said Maria.

Now, for the first time, *Ch'ucha'* examined her surroundings. It was a gray, foggy, depressing place. "I have been told that my mother is a saint," she said sarcastically. "I suppose I am in heaven, then. I can see that Sister Margarita exaggerated."

"This is not heaven," replied Maria. "As I said, we are on the outskirts of the Penumbra Realm."

Maria took her daughter by the hand and began to lead her away from borders of the Penumbra Realm. As they walked, the Light on the eastern horizon began to melt the fog and warm the land and her senses filled with the presence of Life: rustling leaves, singing birds, scampering animals, the fragrance of flowers, a cool, moistness filled the air.

"Where is this place? Are we in heaven now?" It reminded *Ch'ucha'* of the beautiful jungles of the Lacandon, yet as she imagined they would have been had futility not entered the world.

"No," replied Rosario. "This is Paradise. These lands reside within Hope and are the first fruits of creation restored. They are nourished by the waters that flow from the Throne."

Ch'ucha' saw people walking in the distance.

"Where do those people live?" asked *Ch'ucha'*.

"There are many places to live here," answered Maria. "Some choose to live in gardens close to the river while others live further away. All choose to live where they are comfortable."

Ch'ucha', Maria, and Rosario walked in the gardens of Paradise for some time. Yes, time. Time and space existed in this realm although not exactly as *Ch'ucha'* had known it. Time and space had to exist here because souls were still changing.

"It takes time for us to assimilate God's love," Maria explained. "And space to respond to this love in freedom."

"Freedom?" exclaimed *Ch'ucha'*. "What freedom? I did not ask to be as I am."

"We are all made in His image," replied Maria. "We do not choose the aspect of His image which He imparts to us. But, we are free to say yes and to break our own images of ourselves. Then He will transform the image He has imparted to us into His likeness. We may be surprised, perhaps even disappointed, by what we become."

"You wished to be a sparrow," reminded Rosario. "But, *Kos* has chosen you to be the jaguar."

"We are here," said Maria, pointing ahead. They had reached the bank of the river that separated Paradise from the realm beyond. Maria pointed beyond the river.

"There is where we live. And it is there that you will find your answer. Ask Him."

No words, no thought could capture and retain what *Ch'ucha'* experienced the moment she saw the *Divine Infinitude* that lay beyond the river. It was a fearful and wonderful place. She wanted to turn away and flee from the Presence, yet she was compelled to cross the river to find out how she could rescue Ludmelia. But, the river churned and tumbled, spraying foam and mist into the air. It appeared to be an uncrossable barrier between Paradise and the Unknowable.

"Heaven is the Beloved Himself," continued Maria. "Those who choose to cross the river are invited to share in the Divine Life and to be sons of the Most High."

"Cross!" exclaimed *Ch'ucha'*, pointing to the river ahead. "How could anyone cross such a raging torrent?!"

"The river is as we need it to be," explained Rosario. "The river flows from the throne of the Lamb and is mingled with His blood. For some, it is a river of fire. For a few, it is a gentle stream. Either way, if you trust the river, it will help you cross."

"Then I will cross," exclaimed *Ch'ucha'* with determination.

Maria and Rosario began to lead *Ch'ucha'* towards the river. They entered the water together, *Ch'ucha'* between her mother and her madrina. The water flowed forcefully across *Ch'ucha's* legs. She thought it would knock her down and carry her downstream, but Maria and Rosario kept a firm grip on her. They led her deeper and deeper into the river. *Ch'ucha'* was now up to her waist. It seemed to *Ch'ucha'* that the waters no longer flowed around her, but through her.

"Yield to the waters that flow from the *Abyss of Divine Love!*"

Ch'ucha' struggled against the river that now lapped at her shoulders. As, she began to glimpse herself through the eyes of the Other she began to perceive the answer. It was Love, not an amorphous love, but the Divine Love that shares His transfiguring Spirit, and delights in the joy of those whose image has been conformed to His likeness. *Kos* loved in her the very thing she detested, and delighted in that which brought her sorrow!

"I cannot! I am drowning!"

"Yes, and when you lose yourself in Him you will find yourself anew," encouraged Maria.

"No further!" cried Ch'ucha', experiencing the panic that overtakes a person when confronted by a love that challenges autonomy. And in that timeless moment when the boundary between herself and the River dissolved, her question had been answered. She knew what she had to do and, more important, what she had to be. But, she need not yield to the love that might cause her to joyfully embrace the answer. *Ch'ucha'* reasserted herself forcing the River to recede. The waters of the River mounted up forming a wall around the three women. They now stood on dry riverbed while the River flowed around them. Maria and Rosario's garments were soaked, and their faces glowed from having bathed in the Presence. *Ch'ucha's huipel* was dry; her face set like flint.

"I will go," *Ch'ucha'* said angrily. "What other choice do I have? My love for Ludmelia determines my choice. I will be what He has chosen for me to become. My anger will be a bottomless vessel for Him to pour the wine of His wrath. My huipil will be dipped in the blood of His enemies. I will say yes to Him, but I will not break! He will find no cause to delight in me! Lead me back!"

"Please, stay a little longer," pleaded Maria. "There is so much . . . ."

"No!" exclaimed *Ch'ucha'* angrily. "Lead me back," she repeated.

"I cannot," replied Maria. "Another will guide you."

Maria then held her daughters face in her hands, lowered *Ch'ucha's* head, and kissed her forehead. Immediately, *Ch'ucha'* could feel her reality turning outside in. She began to disappear as she returned to the gray mist of the Shadowlands. Maria called out to her, "Remember, we are with you. Look for us in the Temple of the Ancestors."

The River resumed its normal course, and Maria and Rosario again stood within its gently flowing current. Rosario, understanding Maria's loss and sorrow, placed an arm around her. Maria's shoulders relaxed as she yielded to the comforting faith of her companion.

"I have heard," said Rosario, "that someday, the River will overflow its bank, even those that we have built up in fear and unbelief and then, His love and mercy will be known by all."

*   *   *

Ch'ucha' waited; waited for the guide. Who was her guide? How would she recognize him? How could she recognize him in the blinding nothingness of the Penumbra Realm. Maybe he would "call out" to her, whatever that might mean in this nowhere and notime. Would she be able to hear him? She had heard Rosario when she called out to her from beyond the void. All she could do was wait.

In this quietude of reflection she began to hear voices, not exactly voices, rather the words one used when thinking. But, they were not her words; they were those of another, in fact, several others. She recognized some of the thought words; some were in Russian like the words she had learned from Nizhniya, others were in English. They were sad, anxious words.

They are thinking about me! thought *Ch'ucha'*. They came for me, but they were too late.

There were thoughts in Russian, thoughts so strong, so passionate that her mind reeled from their intensity. *Where is she?! Where is my Czarina?!*

He is speaking of Ludmelia. He loves her. Then *Ch'ucha'* understood why Nizhniya had refused her deliverance. It was in the hope that she would return to him who loved her. So great was her love that she risked not just life, but eternal life in Paradise that she might be with him. As *Ch'ucha'* thought of Nizhniya's body lying in the Temple of the Ancestors, she knew she had made the right decision. She would unite the two whatever the cost to herself. This would be her mission, this and revenge—revenge on those who murdered her family.

Another voice formed within her consciousness, a man's voice. The words were in a language unfamiliar to her. He was young, but had already experienced more than his share of suffering—in this, she felt camaraderie with the young man. She began to perceive that there was something else they shared—a destiny.

Munthu an khulikah Alrajl wa Almura' en min tene, Allah tusowar hubarah.[85]

Ch'ucha' did not understand the words, but she felt the power and the passion of them. They were like the words thought by Czar Goricsan towards Nizhniya. But these words, these thoughts were directed towards her! She felt dizzy and confused as she had the time Rosario had made her drink *posh*.[86]

Something grabbed her hand and shook her out of her stupor. It was her soul-companion.

"Come with me," the jaguar said. "Take hold of my tail. I will lead you back."

Ch'ucha' grasped the jaguar's tail. He sniffed the thick air for the scent of organic life. He caught it and began to lead his companion towards the corporeal world, but she stopped and turned back with her mind. Something . . . she didn't understand . . . a desire to linger in the young man's thoughts . . . they were a refuge from the turmoil of her soul . . . .

The jaguar nudged her, and she snapped out of her reverie. They continued. *Ch'ucha'* rebuked herself for being so easily distracted from her mission. *There is no rest for my soul . . . not now . . . not ever!*

How far they had traveled and how long, *Ch'ucha'* did not know. The landscape looked all the same, that is to say, there was no landscape. Then suddenly, light appeared on the distant horizon. It was not like the light that shone from across the river—that was Light itself. This was reflected light; it was light though, and *Ch'ucha'* found comfort in that. *Ch'ucha'* and the jaguar continued until they came near the border of that reflected realm. A vast chasm of darkness separated them from their destination. The jaguar led them to the brink of the chasm that separated them from the corporeal world beyond. *Ch'ucha'* peered into the black void, the vast absence of light. She could see nothing, but she heard the pitiful wailing of souls trapped within its hopelessness.

"How are we to cross?" asked *Ch'ucha'*.

"We must jump!" replied her soul-companion.

"I cannot jump so great a distance!"

"Nor can I," replied the jaguar, "but together we might."

A dark form began to emerge, rising above the vast absence. There was a collective sigh from below as if those imprisoned within the void had been granted a momentary respite. *Ch'ucha'* and the jaguar watched as a horrific dragon rose and hovered over them. It carried hopelessness and despair in the shadows of its vast bat-like wings. Its seven heads spoke in a cacophony of menace.

"Daughter of Abraham, where do you think you are going?!"

"I am lost. Perhaps you could show me the way." *Ch'ucha'* knew that she was speaking with the Lords of *Xibalba*. She would have to deceive the Lords as *Hunahpu* and *Xbalanque* had done if she were to cross the Black Road and return to the corporeal world.

"Your way was to battle my children and then me. You have failed!"

She hung her head despondently. "It was a battle not of my choosing."

"Indeed!" replied the Dragon. "I am not your enemy. He is!"

"It is true, my Lords," said *Ch'ucha'* angrily. "We are all tormented by a destiny that we neither seek nor can fulfill."

The Dragon landed between *Ch'ucha'* and the Great Gulf. His multiple heads turned and tilted as he studied her. He felt the power of her rage. Surely, he thought, she had cause to be angry. And in that moment, the Dragon felt sympathy for her. The Image was too terrible a gift to give to man. Which of them could bear Its burden save the one who is the Image? He had futilely argued this very point with the *Ancient of Days*.

"If you love man," Lucifer had argued, "do not give to him that which he will long to realize but never possess in actuality. He will curse you and wish that he had never been created."

The One would not listen. The history of humanity, the Dragon was convinced, was proof that he was right. Here, before him, was just another example of His mistake. He had been pleased when Frederick killed her. How much better, he thought, if he could pervert her.

"I can show you another way. It leads back to the Corporeal World," snorted the Dragon.

"What must I do?" inquired *Ch'ucha'* continuing the deception.

Wicked smiles emerged across the seven heads. Frederick and *Ch'ucha'* will be my Adam and my Eve, thought the Dragon. Their children will be made in my image, and they will blot out the memory of those created in His.

"I will let you cross the Great Gulf," said the Dragon in a dissonant harmony of voices, "and you will be Frederick's Queen. Then, when you consummate your relationship, a new image will germinate within you, an image that you will be free to mold to your own desires unrestrained by divine expectations."

"Then, be it done unto me according to your word," replied *Ch'ucha'* bowing

The Dragon threw his head back in exaltation, "I will let you cross." He waved his arm, and a bridge appeared. It connected the Penumbra Realm with the Corporeal World beyond the Great Gulf.

"Do not disappoint me!" exclaimed the Dragon. "I will make of Frederick and you a great nation. Be fruitful and multiply."

Ch'ucha' and the jaguar were beginning to cross the bridge when the Dragon roared.

"Stop! The jaguar must remain!"

The wily Dragon knew that beasts were not so readily deceived as man. And this one had already demonstrated that he could recognize the scent of deception.

"But, he is my soul-companion!" protested *Ch'ucha'*. "He must come with me! We are one."

"Frederick will be your soul-companion," replied the Dragon.

Ch'ucha' did not know how to respond. She and the jaguar stood motionless on the bridge. The jaguar sensed that the Dragon was growing suspicious. He grabbed *Ch'ucha's* arm in his mouth and pulled her. Together, they sprinted towards the Corporeal World.

"No!" roared the Dragon, realizing that it was he who had been deceived. He waved his arm. The bridge began to crumble in front of them, hurtling bricks and stones into the black gulf below. *Ch'ucha'* and the jaguar slid to a stop just before they tumbled over the broken edge of the bridge; it was now crumbling underneath their feet. *Ch'ucha'* turned back. The Dragon waited for them, stomping and hissing on the other side. They had no choice, but to run as fast as they could back to the Penumbra Realm. *Ch'ucha'* and the jaguar leapt as the remaining segments of the bridge crumbled beneath them. The jaguar safely landed in the Penumbra Realm. *Ch'ucha'* just managed to grab the edge of the precipice. The gaping void licked at her feet. The dragon stomped towards her; the ground shook with each step it took.

"I will cast you into the pit of my dark heart where the worm dies not and the anguish never ceases!" roared the Dragon.

It raised its leg to knock her down into the chasm below, but the jaguar was too quick for the lumbering dragon. He slipped beneath it, grasped *Ch'ucha's* arm in its mouth, and pulled her up. The dragon angrily swiped at them with his arm, but they rolled away. It stalked them, its heads bent forward, cursing them. *Ch'ucha'* and the jaguar were engulfed in the foul breath that reeked of sulfur and death.

The jaguar leapt and grabbed one of the dragon's heads by the throat. The other heads squealed, mad with agony. The dragon grasped the jaguar with its arms and wrestled it loose, but in so doing it ripped out the throat of one of its heads. The head bobbed on the dragon's great shoulders while blood gurgled from its mouth. In a ferocious rage the dragon threw the jaguar to the ground. The jaguar tumbled and rolled until it finally lay motionless.

"Damn you! Damn you to hell!" shouted *Ch'ucha'*. She charged the dragon. It raised its bat wing to sweep her into the void. But, as it came down upon her a sword suddenly appeared in her hand. She sliced at the great wing severing a portion of it. She was struck a glancing blow by the wounded wing and tumbled again towards the void. She stopped just inches from the precipice. The dragon roared in pain and stomped towards her. *Ch'ucha'* shook herself trying to regain her senses. She stood and held her sword out in front of her. *Ch'ucha'* knew that she could not defeat the dragon, but she would leave her scars upon the beast. He would not soon forget his encounter with *Ch'ucha'*.

"Surely, it will be you that is damned!" roared the dragon.

Ch'ucha' stood waiting to meet her fate while the dragon displayed its awful pinions. Meanwhile, the jaguar staggered to its feet and realized the desperate situation of his soul-companion. Mustering what little strength he had remaining, the jaguar charged under the dragon's wings. He crashed headlong into *Ch'ucha'*, grasping her with his strong front legs. In a tumult, they sailed across the void and tumbled onto the other side. *Ch'ucha'* and the jaguar were now in the corporeal world. The Great Red Dragon stood on the other side of the void furiously cursing them and promising to pursue them to the end. *Ch'ucha'* and the jaguar turned away and faced the light.

He has spent most of the return voyage alone, she heard as she was reentering the Corporeal World. *Just before coming here I was topside. Czar Goricsan was standing by himself waiting for the sunrise.*

*   *   *

A cabin on board the submarine had been prepared to receive the bodies of Nizhniya and *Ch'ucha'* and the carcass of the jaguar. Ryan had washed the bodies and dressed them. Sister Margarita had provided clean clothing for the bodies before the company had left Chiapas. The jet-black jaguar lay on its own bed next to *Ch'ucha'*. As Ryan brushed the jaguar's shiny black coat, she reflected on a conversation with Father Nikitas in which he had shared his thoughts with her about the animal she was now attending.

"After the Fall, all creation was subjected to futility, but in hope. It awaits with eager expectation the revelation of the sons of God. Then creation too will be released from the slavery of corruption and share in the glorious freedom of the children of God.[87] It could be," Nikitas had continued, "that this jaguar, this son of creation, was tired of waiting. Perhaps he has joined himself with this son of God," that is Theresa, "to expedite man and creation's mutual liberation."

Ryan was not sure she understood what Nikitas meant. His theory might also explain the seemingly miraculous intervention of the jungle creatures that had helped the company defeat the nephilim in Chiapas. In any event, there was nobility about the animal that commanded her respect. Ryan gently laid his head on Theresa's leg.

There was a knock on the door.

"Come in," Ryan said.

"You are still here, Miss Ryan," said Abdullah. "Have you been up all night?"

"Yes, your highness," she said, standing as he entered.

"Please sit. We have been through too much for you to call me 'your highness.'"

Ryan sat and continued to stroke the fur of the jaguar.

"I found this on the field not far from Theresa's body," said Abdullah, holding out an old sword. "I thought it might be Theresa's. From what we heard from Sister Margarita, she was a formidable warrior."

"Yes, 'the angels fought by her side'," replied Ryan. "That's what Nikitas said."

Abdullah nodded. "I thought she might still have need of it," he said. "Do you mind?" he asked.

Ryan shook her head. She could see what was in the young king's heart. She watched as he lifted *Ch'ucha's* light brown hand and folded her fingers gently around the sword's handle. He laid them both at her side. He sighed and sat down across from Ryan.

"And what are your plans?" Ryan asked.

"I will return to Arabia. Meet with our allies. See what I can do to strengthen our alliance with the Israeli government. And you?"

"Eventually, I will head back to America. I must meet with Mrs. Lewis. She must know what a brave man her husband was."

"Ah, but you are not telling me all, are you, Miss Ryan?" said Abdullah smiling. "You must know, Sagalovich is not one to keep a secret."

Ryan blushed. "Artem, I mean, Mr. Sagalovich, promised to show me around Moscow. This time without a coup! But now, tell me about the Czar. How is he doing?"

"His heart is broken," replied Abdullah. He took a deep breath before continuing, his own heart swelling with emotion. "He has spent most of the return voyage alone. Just before coming here I was topside. Czar Goricsan was standing by himself waiting for the sunrise."

Ryan and Abdullah heard groaning from behind them. They turned around. *Ch'ucha'* was propped up on her elbows.

"Theresa!" exclaimed Ryan.

The jaguar's ears perked up. It started to raise its head. *Ch'ucha'* calmed it by stroking its neck. It did not rise but nestled closer to her.

"You . . . you're . . . alive!" continued Ryan stammering.

"Yes," replied *Ch'ucha'* in a startlingly matter-of-fact tone. "But my name is *Ch'ucha'* . . . *Ch'ucha' Bolom.*"[88]

Ch'ucha' saw the body of Ludmelia Nizhniya lying on the bed across the room. She swung her legs over the bed and attempted to stand, but her knees buckled. She caught herself as she fell back against the bed.

"Let me help you," said Abdullah who quickly appeared at her side. He took her arm and helped her back up.

"Thank you," replied *Ch'ucha'*. She haltingly took steps towards the body of Ludmelia.

"We found Ludmelia's body in the ruins of an ancient temple not far from where we found you," explained Abdullah.

Ch'ucha' looked up at the young man who appeared to be only a few years older than herself. He seemed familiar. How did she know him? Then it occurred to her. This was the young man whose thoughts she had heard in the Shadowlands. She blushed and turned away. They now stood next to the body of Nizhniya.

Abdullah stepped back and stood next to Ryan. Together they watched *Ch'ucha'* as she stooped down. It almost looked as though she was whispering something in the ear of the dead woman, but *Ch'ucha's* lips did not move.

Can you hear me? thought Ch'ucha'. She placed her hand on Ludmelia's, which were folded across her chest. *All that you and Rosario have taught me I will be.* Ch'ucha' kissed Nizhniya's cheek, straightened up and then faced Ryan and Abdullah.

"She saved my life," offered Ryan, not knowing exactly what to say. "I am Madison Ryan. I knew your mother. I was with her when you were born and when she died."

Ch'ucha' nodded but said nothing in response. She held out her arm to Abdullah who took it and led her back to her bed. She returned to the jaguar that had been watching his soul-companion. She rubbed behind the ears of the big cat. It purred so deeply that Ryan and Abdullah could feel the resonance vibrate in their chests.

"I am Abdullah Mohammed al-Sharif, your servant."

Abdullah reached out and took her other hand, raised it to his lips and kissed it. The jaguar lifted his head and studied the young human male. The jaguar then turned and looked at his soul-companion.

Ch'ucha' pulled her hand away and blushed again.

"I have no need for a servant," she replied, angered and embarrassed by the young man's boldness. Such behavior would have been scandalous in her Mayan community.

"Forgive me," replied Abdullah, startled by her rebuke.

The jaguar rested its head back down on the bed. The ritual had begun; with jaguars, the negotiations were complex and dangerous. His soul-companion now shared his instincts. The young cub did not recognize that the path his heart was leading him down was a dangerous one.

"I am sure that King al-Sharif meant no harm," interjected Ryan in Abdullah's defense.

"King?!" replied *Ch'ucha'*. "Well, if the young king is as bold with his sword as he is with his words then he is welcome to fight by my side."

Abdullah remembered the words of Father Nikitas—the Sons of Abraham would fight together in the *malahim* under the banner of his daughter.

"My sword and my armies are ready to join you in battle."

"It is well," said *Ch'ucha'*. "For there will be much bloodshed before Ludmelia is released from the Shadowlands."

"Ludmelia? . . . she'll come back . . . back to life also?" stammered Ryan.

"Yes," answered *Ch'ucha'*, with a force of determination that erased any doubt from Ryan's mind.

"You must tell Czar Goricsan," said Abdullah. "This will restore his hope."

"I will go to him. He is 'topside,' is he not?" she said, remembering the conversation she had heard when reentering the corporeal world. *Ch'ucha'* began to walk towards the cabin door.

"Yes, that is correct," said Abdullah, perplexed that she should know this. He offered her his arm again which she reluctantly took. "We are on a submarine. Do you know what a submarine is?"

"Young King," *Ch'ucha'* snorted, while pulling away her arm. "Do you think me simple because I am Mayan?"

"No . . . I . . . I . . . ." stammered Abdullah.

The jaguar leapt off the bed and pushed himself between *Ch'ucha'* and the young human male. The jaguar knew that sometimes these rituals could become violent. It would not go well for the young cub if his soul-companion became angry. Abdullah moved away.

"Is . . . is . . . your jaguar tame?" stammered Abdullah.

"No," growled *Ch'ucha'* and almost added, "and neither am I," but the presence of her soul-companion mitigated her response. Instead she asked, "Are you going to lead me to Czar Goricsan or are you too afraid of my cat?"

Abdullah decided it was best not to reply. He opened the cabin door for *Ch'ucha'*. The jaguar leapt out ahead of them. Startled submariners scampered out of the way at the sight of the ferocious looking beast. *Ch'ucha'* followed her soul-companion.

"This way," said Abdullah curtly as he stepped in front of *Ch'ucha'* and the jaguar.

Ryan followed them out of the cabin exclaiming, "I'm going to find Father Nikitas and tell him what has happened."

Abdullah was about to say something to the effect that Nikitas probably already knew, but Ryan was already running down the narrow passage that lead to his quarters.

It was not long before Abdullah, *Ch'ucha'*, and the jaguar reached the ladder that led to the top of the Conning Tower. Abdullah went up first. The jaguar scampered up next, followed by *Ch'ucha'*. Abdullah saw Goricsan, a lone figure standing on the prow of the ship, facing the horizon beyond. Dawn was breaking over the city of Saint Petersburg as they approached the harbor.

"Let me go speak with him," said Abdullah turning to *Ch'ucha'*.

Abdullah climbed down the Conning Tower and walked over to Goricsan who stood with his hands behind his back. Goricsan turned and acknowledged the king.

"Constantin, my friend, something remarkable, no, a miracle, has happened."

Goricsan looked at the Abdullah curiously.

"I have brought someone who wishes to speak with you," Abdullah continued.

Constantin nodded and turned to face the messenger. In the early morning light he could just make out the form of a young woman and a large, dark animal standing by her side. Could it be? He took several steps towards her just to make sure.

"Theresa?"

Abdullah stepped aside and watched as *Ch'ucha'* took Constantin's hands. Abdullah did not hear what she said. He did not need to. Constantin embraced *Ch'ucha'*. He then put his arm around her and led her to the prow of the submarine. The submarine was approaching the dock. As the ship grew closer, the trio could see that crowds of citizens had lined the docks and were now waving and cheering the returning Czar. Goricsan turned to Abdullah and motioned to him. The young king joined them and stood next to *Ch'ucha'*. The jaguar sat on his haunches between them. It nestled and pressed against *Ch'ucha's* leg. She reached down and rubbed behind the ears of the great cat.

"May I?" asked Abdullah.

Ch'ucha' nodded and was just a bit surprised by the young king's boldness. Abdullah tentatively stroked the top of the jaguar's head. He was relieved when it did not bite him. Instead, her soul-companion let out a deep and appreciative purr. *Ch'ucha'* turned and looked up at the young king. Their eyes met; the slightest of smiles crossed her lips.

"Look," said Goricsan pointing. "There is Eliav."

Even from a distance Abdullah could recognize Captain Eliav. He stood at the dock supported by his wife, Ruth, and his daughter, Esther. They waved as the vessel approached.

Nikitas and Ryan stood on the Conning deck just as the sun appeared over the horizon. Ryan marveled at the sight of her companions with Theresa, or rather, *Ch'ucha' Bolom*. She wondered if perhaps Maria might also be witnessing this miraculous scene.

Abdullah pointed to golden domed churches that glistened like jewels. Their bells carilloned a greeting to the morning sun. The children of Abraham and a son of creation faced East as the morning sun splashed its light over Saint Petersburg.

"Yes, Rosario," uttered Nikitas soberly, "The second woe has passed . . . ."

Ryan looked curiously at Nikitas. He glanced behind him at the darkening gloom that gathered over the West, ". . . the third woe is soon to come."[89]

EPILOGUE

The Chiapas mission had been less than a success as far as Obermann was concerned. Of course, he was pleased that his son had returned essentially unharmed. He had killed Theresa, and given what he had witnessed, she had been a formidable adversary. Still, Frederick had been unable to deliver her body or a sample of her blood. The blood plague continued unabated. Kwan, who now had access to Richardson's consciousness, assured Obermann that a cure was possible if they could be supplied with a sample of Maria's blood. In the meantime, there were plenty of harvestable criminals.

A quite inexplicable event occurred when Frederick had been "scratched" on the forehead during his encounter with the jaguar. Almost simultaneously all Chimærics, transformed as well as Resubstantiates, had also developed identical scars on their forehead. Chimærics were naturally concerned about these scars, which their stem cells could not heal. Some tried to cover them up, others resorted to plastic surgery. None of these efforts proved effective. Finally, the Reverend Muriel Hampton delivered what had become the most widely accepted explanation for the phenomenon. Frederick had been wounded in a gallant effort to preserve the rights and dignity of all Chimærics. He did not need to continue to bear the scars of this confrontation, but he chose to in order to demonstrate the sacrifice that all must be willing to make for the New Era. "The scars are a visible sign of our solidarity with Obermann and Frederick as they lead us into the New Era," exclaimed Hampton, proudly showing her own scars. In fact, she had used just a hint of rouge to highlight them for the camera. Obermann knew that this was nonsense. He knew damn well what the mark meant, and it made infiltration into nations of the Alliance far more difficult.

Frederick, on the other hand, was preoccupied with a project that he was working on with Dr. Kwan. He found them difficult to work with. Richardson, whose consciousness coexisted within the body of her colleague, resisted and interfered with Kwan's ability to concentrate on the project. Frederick had wondered if he hadn't made a mistake in placing Richardson's consciousness within Kwan's body, but at the time there had seemed very little alternative. If a cure were to be developed for the blood plague, Richardson's assistance would be needed. Frederick would have to figure out a way to control Richardson through Kwan. But, he would attend to that later. He was too involved with a project that meant more to him than a cure for the blood plague.

Kwan had successfully isolated a viable egg from the tissue that Frederick had brought back with him from Chiapas. Frederick had instructed Kwan to fertilize the egg with sperm that he had provided him. Normally, this would not have been an extraordinary procedure since this had been done countless times in fertilization clinics and labs. But, Frederick's sperm was unlike other human sperm. His had twice the normal number of chromosomes. His sperm could not fertilize human ova; rather it altered the genetic makeup of the somatic and gametic cells of the host.

Kwan was not sure why Frederick thought that the eggs he had provided might be different. Frederick would not tell him where or from whom the eggs had come. Upon inspection of the eggs, Kwan was surprised to find that they had not passed through meiosis I, the first stage of reducing the number of chromosomes from forty-six to twenty-three, the normal number of chromosomes for a gamete.

"This egg will not fertilize, it is diploid like your sperm."

"Patience," said Frederick, while watching a monitor that showed what Kwan was watching under his microscope. His sperm was relentlessly assaulting the egg. A sperm broke through!

"I'll be damned!" exclaimed Kwan.

"Probably," said Frederick delighted at the progress of his sperm.

"But this doesn't mean that the nuclei will fuse," cautioned Kwan. "And even if they do, a tetraploid zygote will not be viable."

"You don't know that for sure. Humanity has not been this way before."

What they saw next made both of them jump back in their seats. At first, the cell looked as if it had exploded. After Kwan collected his wits he examined the fertilized egg. It appeared that what they had seen was the formation of the fertilization membrane. But, then it began to change in a way that Kwan was unfamiliar with. The membrane became hard and opaque.

"It almost looks like a cyst," said Kwan.

"What's that?" asked Frederick.

"Some organisms will form a hard, protective capsule around themselves when the conditions are not right for their development. The organism enters a state of dormancy until the conditions change. Then development will continue."

X-rays, MRIs, and other imaging techniques were employed in an attempt to visually "penetrate" the cyst. They all failed. Frederick finally decided to store the fertilized egg in a vault at Chimæra Laboratories until technologies could be developed that would allow them to examine it further or coax it to shed the cyst and continue development. Frederick instructed Kwan not to discuss the project with his father. He hoped to surprise him someday with the news that he was a grandfather!

*   *   *

Synods were held to elect a new pope in opposition to Entremont who had usurped the throne of Peter. The Synod of the West was held in Washington, DC. Cardinals and bishops from all over Europe and North America assembled at the National Cathedral. The only criterion for participation was their affiliation with the Tree of Life. They unanimously elected bishops and life-partners Worthington and

Hampton to the newly formed co-papacy centered, at least temporarily, at the National Cathedral.

In Istanbul, where the Eastern Synod met, bishops primarily from the East, but a few also from the West, gathered. The vote was not unanimous, but decisive. William Cardinal McIntyre had been elected successor of Peter.

Obermann scoffed at the election of his former nemesis. The idea of electing someone who would be imprisoned for life showed how preposterous Christianity had become. No doubt, Obermann thought, they hoped to pressure the government to release McIntyre so that he could fulfill his papal duties. He would put an end to their hope. Obermann contacted the prison authorities where McIntyre was being held. The warden assured Obermann that the McIntyre problem would be taken care of—two notorious murderers had been promised their freedom if they quickly and quietly dispatched the Cardinal.

McIntyre was asleep in his bunk when the sound of his cell door opening awoke him. Immediately, a strong hand covered his mouth. It was Percy Collins. Jaime stood behind him holding a finger to his lips. McIntyre's eyes grew wide. He had anticipated that Obermann would not let the situation continue like this much longer, especially since he heard the astounding news that he had been elected as the next Pope. Percy removed his hand from McIntyre's mouth.

"I will not cry out. Do what you must quickly," said McIntyre sitting up in his bed.

Percy and Jaime smiled, and immediately their faces shown with an inner light and their clothes became brilliantly white.

"Did you not know that you were entertaining angels?" asked Jaime.

Percy took McIntyre by the hands. Immediately, the trio was standing on the outside wall of the prison. The stars twinkled, and the moon illuminated their surroundings. McIntyre was startled by the height as he looked down from the wall. He held tightly onto Percy.

"Bear but the touch of my hand and you will be upheld in more than this," quoted Percy.

"Dickens!" McIntyre laughed.

"Just so!"

*   *   *

Colin had intercepted a communication from Frederick to his father. Frederick bragged about how he drove his sword all the way to its hilt into Theresa's chest. Obermann was pleased. But, Frederick had not been able to bring back her head as he had promised, or a sample of her blood. Perhaps he was lying, thought Colin. His father was a liar, why not the son? Perhaps, Theresa is still alive. Colin would try to discover the truth about his daughter. He decided that he would leave the Office of Justice and Tolerance and flee with his son, Diego, to one of the countries of the Great Alliance. There he would plot his revenge.

Colin took a late flight, arriving in Sioux City, Iowa a little after midnight. He rented a car and drove quickly down the country roads leading to the farmhouse that he had purchased for his parents. He had wanted to buy them a beachfront estate, but they did not want any assistance from their son. They finally relented, allowing him to buy a dilapidated old farm.

"At least let me hire a crew to fix up the old place for you," Colin had offered.

His parents had refused. They had always been self-reliant. That was not about to change now. Colin knew that there was more to it than this. From the beginning they had opposed his association with Obermann and Chimæra. They were faithful Catholics who were outspoken in their criticism of the Tree of Life. More than once, Colin had had to intervene to prevent their arrest by Justice and Tolerance police. He looked at his watch as he pulled into their driveway. It was a little after one.

He knocked on the door. Colin waited. His parents would not be expecting him. He saw a light turn on and heard the shuffling of slippered feet approaching the door.

"Who is it?"

Colin recognized his father's voice. "It's me, Dad. Colin."

The door opened. His father grabbed his son by the arm and drew him inside. Colin admired his father. Though now in his mid sixties he was not afraid of aging. His lavishly wavy hair was now thinning, and his beard had become completely white. He was still robust; he could feel the strength in his arms and chest as his father embraced him.

"What's the matter, my son?" he said, releasing his son from his bear hug.

"You were right, Father. Maria was right."

"Who is it?"

Colin recognized the voice of his mother calling from the upstairs landing.

"It's Colin," said Mr. O'Conner. "He's come home!"

Mrs. O'Conner raced down the stair. She was startled to see the condition to which her son had been reduced. She knew he had the blood plague that was afflicting so many Chimærics. He hugged his mother. After about a minute, Colin finally released her.

"I cannot work for Obermann anymore. I'm going to flee the country and hopefully make my way to one of the countries of the Great Alliance. You and Diego must come with me. I will no longer be able to protect you."

"Take Diego," said his father. "We'll be fine."

"No, you won't," exclaimed Colin. "When Obermann discovers that I've betrayed him, he'll come after me and everyone that I love."

"It's all right, dear," said his mother, placing her gentle hand on his cheek. Mr. O'Conner put his arm around his wife and nodded.

"Don't you worry about us," said Mr. O'Conner. "Now you go and get your son up. We'll get his stuff ready."

"And I'll make you a little something for you to eat on the way," said his mother, as if they were heading off on a vacation.

"Please, come with us," implored Colin.

They smiled, but would not relent. "Go," Mr. O'Conner said firmly. "You are wasting time."

Colin headed up the stairs while his parents gathered what they would need for their trip. He peered into Diego's room. The night-light of the Virgin that he had had since he was a baby illuminated Diego's face. He was smiling. His hand was clutching the ring that hung around his neck. Colin knelt next to his son.

"Diego. Wake up."

Diego groaned and stretched. He rubbed his eyes.

"You need to get up now. You and daddy are going on a trip together far, far away."

"No, we can't," said Diego, pushing himself on his elbows.

Colin sat on the bed next to Diego and took his son's hand. "We have to, son. It's not safe."

"Mommy told me that you wanted to go," said Diego stretching.

"What? Mommy?" asked Colin.

"Yes," replied Diego, grabbing his mother's wedding ring. "Just now. She was just saying good-bye when you woke me."

"Are you sure it was Mommy?" asked Colin. He did not doubt that Diego had been visited by Maria in his dreams. Not after everything he had been through. But, this was too important a decision to base on a dream.

"It's true. I did see Mommy! She was as real as you are right now."

Colin stood up and walked over to the light switch. Maybe so, thought Colin, turning on the light. Then again, he hadn't seen Diego in months. It could be that Diego was dreaming about his mother because he hadn't been much of a father to him lately.

"Mommy said that you should go back."

"Back where? Back to work for Mr. Obermann? I hardly think that Mommy would want me to work for him anymore."

"She said that there would be a man waiting for you in your office when you go back," Diego continued, undaunted by his father's doubts. "She said you should listen to him."

Colin studied Diego. Go back? How could he go back? He wouldn't be able to deceive Obermann for long. The symptoms of the blood plague were too severe now. He had even been scheduled for a transplant. If he went back, some innocent victim convicted of intolerance would be harvested for his benefit. But then, Diego seemed so convinced.

"You need to get up," said Colin, opening the closet and removing some clothing that Diego would need for the trip. "We have to leave. We don't have time to waste . . . ."

"Mommy told me you probably wouldn't believe me," Diego interrupted.

"I'm sorry, son. You don't understand," replied Colin, pulling out a duffle bag and shoving several pairs of pants and a few shirts inside. "If I go back, I will have to do things that are wrong, things . . . ."

"I know, Daddy. Mommy told me. She said that sometimes God asks us to do things we don't understand."

Colin almost wanted to chuckle at Diego's last comment. It sounded very much like something Maria might say.

"I need you to get up now and . . . ."

"And it's the only way you'll be able to help my sister . . . Theresa."

"What?!" exclaimed Colin turning around and facing his son. He had never spoken of her to his son.

"Is . . . is . . . your sister with Mommy . . . now?" asked Colin trembling.

"She was."

"What do you mean?" asked Colin.

"Theresa had to come back," answered Diego. "She has to do something, something she doesn't want to do either."

Colin fell to his knees, buried his face in his hands, and started crying. Diego got out of bed and put his arm around his father to comfort him.

"It's okay, Daddy. I love you. Mommy does too."

*   *   *

"Mr. O'Conner, there is . . . ," the secretary stopped mid-sentence as she watched the Secretary of the Office of Justice and Tolerance slowly, and with great effort, walk towards his office. He grimaced in pain with each step. Why hasn't he had a transplant yet? she thought.

"A man waiting to see me?" asked Colin.

"Why, yes," replied the secretary, wondering how Mr. O'Conner knew. "He's waiting in the reception area." She peered down at the card the visitor had handed her. "A Reverend Cornelius Beaugard McGinnis."

"Have him come in, please," said Colin as he opened his office door. Once in the privacy of his office he gripped a chair for support.

He used the furniture to help maneuver around his desk. He fell into his chair and groaned. There was no way he would be able to disguise his symptoms or the fact that he had not had the transplant.

The secretary entered the office moments later. "Reverend McGinnis," she said, as she motioned with her arm for the visitor to enter.

An athletic, well-dressed black man in his late thirties or early forties entered the room. Colin struggled to stand to greet the visitor.

"That's all right," the Reverend said. Even he could see that Colin was under considerable physical stress. The Reverend sat in a burgundy leather wingback chair across from Colin.

Colin fell back into his own chair. "Thank you," he said to his secretary who left, closing the door behind her. Colin studied the Reverend McGinnis. Could this be the man his son had told him would be waiting for him at his office?

"The other night," the Reverend began, "I was reading the Scripture. Acts of the Apostles. As a matter of fact . . . ." The Reverend reached into the inside pocket of his jacket and pulled out a small New Testament. He thumbed through the pages. "Ah, here it is," he continued and then began reading the Scripture.

> *"Ananias replied, 'Lord, I have heard from many sources about this man, what evil things he has done to your holy ones in Jerusalem. And here he has authority from the chief priests to imprison all who call upon your name. But the Lord said to him, "Go, for this man is a chosen instrument . . . ."'*

The Reverend McGinnis closed his Bible leaving his index finger inside to mark the page. He then looked at Colin with keen, prophetic eyes. "You are a chosen instrument of the Lord."

"I am a Judas," replied Colin. "I have betrayed God, His Church, my wife; everyone that ever loved or had faith in me."

"Yes, but even Judas was an instrument of the Lord," the Reverend reminded Colin. "Even God may need His Judases, an ignoble calling to be sure, but does not the potter have the right to fashion his clay to make vessels for beauty and for menial use?"[90]

Colin considered the Reverend's words and then asked, "What am I to do, then? Who is there left for me to betray?"

"Obermann and his son," answered Reverend McGinnis.

"Don't think I haven't thought of it," said Colin in a tone of exasperation. "But how?"

"The Lord will show you," replied Reverend McGinnis confidently. "But you must stay where you are, keep doing what you are doing, otherwise Obermann will suspect you."

"What?" exclaimed Colin. "Continue persecuting the Church, and harvesting the organs of innocent people? How can that be God's will?"

"God allows his saints to be persecuted so that their reward in heaven will be great," replied the Reverend, paraphrasing the Beatitudes. He then added, "It is through suffering that we prove ourselves worthy of the Kingdom of God."[91]

"And what about me?" asked Colin. "Look at me! The blood plague is eating me from the inside out. How do you expect me to fool Obermann into thinking that I am loyal to him when I refuse to have a transplant?"

"You must not refuse," answered the Reverend.

"What?! You want me to have some poor Christian arrested so that I can have his pancreas?!"

"That won't be necessary."

"You don't expect someone to volunteer, do you?" scoffed Colin.

"Yes. I will."

Colin's jaw dropped in disbelief. Finally he shook his head. "You don't know what you're saying. You're not volunteering to donate a kidney, for Christ's sake. Once you're in the System they'll extract every usable organ and tissue from your body. They won't let you die until there is practically nothing left of you."

The Reverend opened his Bible to where he had left his finger and continued from the same passage he had read earlier, "'and I will show him what he will have to suffer for my name.'"

"Reverend, you have no idea what suffering is until you witness what occurs in one of our Harvesting Centers. Besides, it is me that must suffer. Suffering is the only way I can redeem myself. It's the only way I can be sure that I won't come under his power."

The Reverend reached out his hand to Colin. Colin looked at him curiously. Finally, he intuited what the Reverend wanted and extended his hand. McGinnis took Colin's hand and turned it over revealing the blistered, red mark on his palm.

"You cannot redeem yourself. Only the suffering of those who love you can redeem you. But you'll suffer," said the Reverend, his eyes piercing into Colin's very soul, "and it will be far greater than anything I will experience."

ENDNOTES

[1] United Nations resolution 07412 declared that calendar years were to no longer be based upon the birth of Christ but on the birth of Frederick Obermann, this year being declared 00 of the NewEra.

[2] "Ladino" is a term the Mayan use for non-Mayan Mexicans. It is frequently used as a pejorative.

[3] Little Frog (in the Mayan language of Tzotzil)

[4] towers from which the iman calls the Muslims to prayer.

[5] Qur'an (Q). 54:1

[6] Q. 22:7

[7] Time of Ignorance (Muslims call the time before Mohammed's revelation the "time of ignorance." It was a time of self-interest and presumption.)

[8] Q. 3.185

[9] Q. 3.145

[10] Satan

[11] Q. 8: 11,12

[12] traditional Arab head covering worn by men.

[13] Q. 4.135

[14] Community of Islamic believers.

[15] Islamic law based upon the teachings of the Qur'an and the teachings of Mohammed.

[16] A person possessed by a jinn.

[17] An unbeliever- one who is not grateful to Allah

18   Q. 7.126

19   Lord of the Sword

20   apocalyptic battle

21   Q. 11.19, 20

22   The Sword of the Prophet

23   Rev. 12:14

24   Rev. 18:4

25   Rev. 14:8

26   Damn it

27   Drop dead!

28   May you burn!

29   May you burn in a dark blue flame!

30   A stupid person who works honestly and hard but who is taken advantage of.

31   Your Mother!

32   Your mother twice over!

33   Your mother like this!

34   Your mother up, down, and all around!

35   shit heads

36   miracle (often used to refer to an economic miracle).

37   Legal reform aimed at establishing equal status of Christians and Jews in Muslim countries. Tanzimat was attempted with limited results in the Ottoman Empire during the 19th century.

38   People of the Book (ie, Jews and Christians)

39   God is great!

40   Revelation 13:3,4

41   Revelations 13:7

42   Col 1:24

43   Matt. 5:12

44   Josh. 24:15

45   Q 29:46

46   clatter

47   earthquake

48   enveloper

⁴⁹ Isaac is the son of Abraham through Sara and is the father of the Jews. Ishmael is the son of Abraham through Hagar and is the father of the Arab people.

⁵⁰ blast

⁵¹ antiChrist (Islamic apocalyptic literature, primarily Shiite, incorporate the coming of the antiChrist as one of the end-time events. Some traditions have Jesus returning and killing the antiChrist whereas other claim that it will be the Mahdi that destroys the dajjal.

⁵² apocalyptic war

⁵³ The "splitting of the sky," an event in Islamic apocalyptic tradition.

⁵⁴ Transposons are also known as "jumping genes." Such genes can jump from one chromosome to another, sometimes even between the chromosome of different individual organisms.

⁵⁵ Godmother and goddaughter

⁵⁶ Chaan-Muan was an ancient Mayan lord of Bonampak

⁵⁷ Christ

⁵⁸ True Christian

⁵⁹ Patroness of Weavers

⁶⁰ One of the five pillars of Islam is the pilgrimage (hajj) to Mecca that each faithful Muslim is encouraged to undertake at least once during his lifetime.

⁶¹ Muhammad claimed that the archangel Gabriel appeared to him in a vision. He began to preach in his native city of Mecca. Ridiculed by the Meccans, he went in 622 to Medina. It is from this event, the Hegira (q.v.) that the Islamic calendar is dated. At Medina, Muhammad soon held both temporal and spiritual authority, having been recognized as a lawgiver and prophet. War was undertaken against Mecca. Increasingly, Arab tribes declared their allegiance to him, and Mecca surrendered in 630.

⁶² A cube-shaped structure in the courtyard of al-Haram (the "inviolate place"), the great mosque of Mecca.

⁶³ The *jizya* was a tax paid by dhimmi in some Muslim countries for protection against persecution.

⁶⁴ 1Cor 6:16

⁶⁵ Matt. 18:7

⁶⁶ 1Pet. 1:23

67 Genesis 15:16,17

68 Thank you (Russian)

69 Mark 13:20 "And unless the Lord had shortened those days, no life would have been saved; but for the sake of the elect whom He chose, he shortened the days."

70 The status of "Servant of God" is the first step in the consideration of the sanctity of an individual. It precedes the status of Venerable, Blessed, and Saint.

71 The bishops outside of Rome

72 The *Processiculi diligentiarum* is the process by which the writings of a "servant of God" is evaluated for their theological orthodoxy.

73 The burial cloth or napkin, believed to have covered the face of Jesus.

74 1Cor. 4:5

75 1Cor. 2:4

76 2Chr. 20:15

77 Rev 11:14

78 Rev. 6:10

79 Rev 11: 3-5

80 fool

81 Henhen is the Tzotzil name for the toad, *Bufus marinus*. It exudes a variety of chemicals on its skin. Some of these chemicals are deadly poisons, others are powerful hallucinogens.

82 1Sam 15

83 Judg. 7:1-6

84 Dan 10, Eph. 6:12

85 Since the first man and woman were made of clay, Allah has imagined our love!

86 A liquor made from sugar cane used by Mayan shamans in religious and medicinal rituals.

87 Rom. 8:19- 21

88 Bolom is "jaguar" in Tzotzil.

89 Revelations 11:14

90 Romans 9:21

91 2Ths. 1:5

Made in the USA
Middletown, DE
14 June 2022